Praise for *The House by the Loch*

'Wark's second novel brings to life Galloway . . . This sparsely
populated but spare and beautiful landscape anchors three
generations of one family struggling to come to terms with a dark
secret. As with her debut, *The House by the Loch* draws on real
historical incident and some of her own personal history while
also being a deeply satisfying work of pure imagination . . . A
multi-generational story that is at once sweeping and intimate'
Damian Barr, author of *You Will Be Safe Here*

'Kirsty Wark has woven a brilliant tapestry, pulling together the threads
of three generations and setting their lives against the background
of one of the most beautiful and atmospheric places in Britain . . . I
loved *The House by the Loch* and couldn't wait to turn each page.'
Alistair Moffat, author of *The Hidden Ways*

'I've been enthralled by the wonderful and atmospheric world
Kirsty Wark has created – really powerful and compelling.'
Sue Lawrence, author of *The Night He Left*

Praise for *The Legacy of Elizabeth Pringle*

'Kirsty Wark's first novel gleams with beauty. Part romance, part family history, part mother-and-daughter fable and meditation on memory, *The Legacy of Elizabeth Pringle* has qualities of the heart . . . something of great worth and beauty gleams through the narrative and haunts the reader with its imaginative truth . . . Wark's presentation of a unique love unalloyed by sexuality is original and enthralling.'
Guardian

'Curl up for this big-hearted romantic debut by the *Newsnight* presenter . . . affecting and tender'
The Sunday Times

'The story is set in the beautiful Scottish island of Arran, a place Wark very obviously knows and loves . . . Wark's storytelling is direct, compelling and rewarding for the reader. She is a real writer who happens to do television.'
Daily Mail

'The narrative switches between Elizabeth and Martha . . . Martha's relationship with Anna is beautifully and touchingly written, a daughter helplessly watching her beloved, vibrant mother fade away . . . This is an appealing debut that sustains interest to the very last page. Elizabeth Pringle is a quietly heroic character and, like Arran, never fails to charm.'
Independent on Sunday

'Set on the Scottish island of Arran, Kirsty Wark's brilliantly vivid descriptions bring alive a story that reaches across the generations'
Mail on Sunday

'The book is fresh and beguiling . . . Wark has an exceptionally vivid sense of place . . . George Eliot paid homage to those "who lived faithfully a hidden life, and rest in unvisited tombs." In this novel some of those hidden stories are told and graves visited with real tenderness.'
Independent

'Wark depicts the weather, the landscape and the inhabitants of the island so vividly that all I wanted was a ferry ticket'
Woman & Home

The House by the Loch

KIRSTY WARK

www.tworoadsbooks.com

First published in Great Britain in 2019 by Two Roads
An imprint of John Murray Press
An Hachette UK company

1

A CIP catalogue record for this title is available from the British Library

Hardback ISBN 978 1 444 77764 2
Trade Paperback ISBN 978 1 529 30942 3
eBook ISBN 978 1 444 77767 3
Audio Digital Download ISBN 978 1 444 75232 8

Typeset in Janson Text by Hewer Text UK Ltd, Edinburgh
Printed and bound in Great Britain by Clays Ltd, Elcograf S.p.A.

Hodder & Stoughton policy is to use papers that are natural, renewable
and recyclable products and made from wood grown in sustainable
forests. The logging and manufacturing processes are expected to
conform to the environmental regulations of the country of origin.

Hodder & Stoughton Ltd
Carmelite House
50 Victoria Embankment
London EC4Y 0DZ

To my family, and to my friends,
who know that they are also family.

MAP TO COME

Come away, O human child!
To the waters and the wild
With a faery, hand in hand,
For the world's more full of weeping than you can understand.

W. B. Yeats, *The Stolen Child*

The House by the Loch

October 1941. Loch Doon

A lonely patch of jewel-coloured nasturtiums sheltered by the stone dyke, shivering in the autumn chill, hoping for a moment of warming sun to keep them alive just a little longer. An early morning wash hung on the line, the sheets edge to edge, shirts billowing upside down like circus artists on a high wire.

Ten-year-old Walter MacMillan sat scraping away at the loamy moss on the kitchen step, scuffing his boots, backwards and forwards, the sound filling the bare garden. Suddenly he stilled his leg, pricking up his ears, as out of the silence he heard a faint metallic thrum, like the distant rumble of his father's tractor. He jumped up, grabbing his two home-made paper flags stuck onto sticks, and charged out of the garden gate, his jacket flapping as he pounded down towards the shoreline, a notebook sticking out of his pocket. With each footfall over the rough ground the noise from above sounded louder, more urgent. He imagined that he and the plane were racing each other. He paused as he turned his face skyward to the north, above the brown and purple hills, into the glinting sunshine. His heart was thumping as he scanned the cloudless blue canopy.

Then he saw it. The Spitfire rushed into view, swooping steeply towards him. In a flash he made out the head of the pilot encased in his flying cap and goggles, and on the fuselage the Czech roundel alongside the RAF ensign. He felt the plane's thundering roar vibrating through his whole being as the plane came level with him, almost kissing the loch. He waved his flags above his head, the Czech one with its blue triangle and bands of red and white higher than the Union flag, and watched spellbound as the Spitfire banked around to rise over Mulwharcher hill and the Merrick.

But then, just when he expected the pilot to soar heavenward, he saw the slender starboard wing tip catch the water. Walter opened his mouth wide and he dropped the flags. His hands shot to his head, his fingers pressed to his face. The Spitfire cartwheeled, its wings threshing through the water, churning up white spume and then, for an instant, it seemed to stand still, balancing on one wing tip, as if it understood its terrible fate, and then it shuddered and sank down into the depths. As the engine sounded a death rattle, waves rushed towards Walter and covered his boots and legs with Loch Doon's brackish water. As he stumbled backwards he let out a long, anguished scream. All he had wanted to do was to greet the pilot, to send him on his way, imagining him, gloved hands clamped to the joystick, headed across the Channel to a dogfight with the Nazis.

Walter never forgot the pilot's face, but it was only when the war ended that he learned his name. For almost seventy years he had imagined that he had seen the boy at the edge of the loch and knew that someone had witnessed him going to his death, and even as a child Walter knew that was important. Every year Walter returned to that same spot, on 25 October, and bowed his head, remembering Flying Officer Frantisek Hekl, and the day the war came to Loch Doon.

PART ONE

The Girl with Brown Eyes

CHAPTER I

Carson and Iona MacMillan knew every inch of the twenty-mile journey south from home in Ayr to the wilderness of Loch Doon. If they closed their eyes they could track their progress by the pitches and turns of the road, the way their stomachs plummeted when the old estate car jumped over a rise in the road and then tipped forwards again. When the car veered to the right off the main road that headed south to Carsphairn and Castle Douglas, and they saw the tracing of the Galloway Hills in the distance, they knew it would be ten minutes, give or take, before they reached their destination.

The tall pines lining the single-track road to the loch stood to attention like an honour guard waiting to greet company. Carried on the breeze came the protest of the cranky old engine and the muffled sound of unruly voices belting out an approximation of the Scissor Sisters song about getting jacked up on some sweet champagne. Inside the tangerine-coloured Volvo the singing was accompanied by a timpani of wine and olive oil bottles and an old ice-cream maker clanking together as the car bumped over potholes.

Rivulets of condensation trailed down the inside of the windows and the car heater whined with the effort of combating the earthy dampness while the wipers tried to banish the misty drizzle. As the Volvo emerged from the tunnel of trees it crossed an expanse of tweedy moorland on the way to the head of the loch.

'Hey, Iona, open your window,' Patrick MacMillan called out over the music. 'Look at the rainbow over Knockower.'

His younger daughter obediently wound down the creaking window with both hands and stuck her head out. She screwed up her nose as the rain, persisting through the arriving sunshine, patterned her face with its spray. She nodded eagerly, sending the beads of water that had settled on her curly dark hair flying. 'I see it, Daddy!' she said excitedly.

Carson, at the other end of the back seat, rolled her eyes and fiddled with the friendship bracelets wound around her wrist. At fourteen, almost fifteen, she was six years the elder, and had recently emerged from childhood into a tall slender girl, her eyes a deep sea green, her face now almond-shaped like her mother's. As she sat with her denim-clad legs folded against the back of the driver's seat, she affected a casual distant look, but the truth was she had a tight knot of excitement in her stomach because she still loved coming to the loch, and especially this weekend.

'I told you the sun would break through, didn't I, girls?' Patrick gave his wife's knee a self-satisfied squeeze.

Elinor smiled indulgently as she looked down on the loch. 'Rain, hail, or shine. I love it in all weathers, you know I do,' she said.

The two identical wooden cabins that had appeared side by side on the north shore of Loch Doon a decade earlier, long gardens rolling down to the water, were a gift to Patrick and his younger sister Fiona from their father, Walter. There had been no discussion, no hint of what was to come, he had simply sent each of his two children a buff-coloured envelope containing a picture of the cabins that he had ordered from a company in the Borders, the deeds for the land, and a cheque for ten thousand pounds. 'If explanation is required,' he wrote to each, 'some family money has been sitting, untouched, in the bank, and I thought this would be a good use of it. I hope you think so too.' That was all.

The irony of the possibility that it was their late mother Jean's money anchoring them to the loch was not lost on Walter's children. 'You do know what Dad's doing, don't you?' said Fiona when she telephoned Patrick from London.

'Yes, of course I do,' he replied, 'but there's nowhere I'd rather be. It'll give the kids the same freedom that we had.'

There was silence on the line for a moment. 'I know that, Patrick.' He heard the voice as taut as a piano wire. 'And it's all very romantic, but do you ever remember Mum saying, even once, that she loved it?'

Walter's gift, though, was a godsend to Patrick and Elinor, since a teacher and a freelance illustrator's income did not run to a second home. But to Roland, Fiona's husband, the senior partner in the London architectural practice of Stratton and Miles, the simple wooden house was something of a joke, an affront even, and, by dint of distance, the Strattons' visits to Loch Doon had been few and far between, and certainly not with any of their Notting Hill friends.

Carson loved their cabin. When she was younger she imagined herself the heroine of her very own Laura Ingalls Wilder story, peering out from her window in the roof, looking over the lapping water, transported to Wisconsin. Sometimes, burrowed down in her bed in Ayr, her eyes pressed shut, she conjured up the cabin and everything in it: the high shelf that ran around the four walls of the big room downstairs, books and photographs and keepsakes jostling for position; Elinor's watercolours pinned carelessly to the front of the counter; the spiders scurrying around in the wood basket by the stove; Granny Jean's bejewelled velvet drawstring bag hanging over her bedpost; and the fairy lights that Iona had begged Patrick not to take down after Christmas one year. She even liked to picture the Moses basket in the corner of Iona's bedroom, filled with peach-coloured dolls, their arms and legs poking out of the pile of mildewed soft toys at impossible angles, as if they'd been suffocated. When Carson was six, the basket's appearance at the foot of her parents' bed and the mewling sound from within had been an unwarranted intrusion into her perfect world. 'Can't you make her stop?' Carson had wailed at Elinor when her mother was reading a story with her in the bed. 'Okay, maybe the baby would like to hear "The Worst Witch" too,' her mother had said cheerily and, to Carson's horror, lifted Iona from the basket and latched her onto her breast.

Carson thought of the two cabins as best friends, twins even, but at the beginning of that year, as soon as the unusually heavy snowfalls that had marked the start of 2005 had melted into the loch, the MacMillans had watched, amazed, as the Strattons' cabin was bulldozed into matchsticks one Saturday and dumped in a line of skips. Patrick didn't keep any wood for his log store. 'It would be too weird,' he said to Elinor, shaking himself, 'burning Fiona's house. I would feel like a grave robber.'

Almost as quickly, a beautiful two-storey larch-clad box appeared in exactly the same place, following detailed plans and strict instructions faxed by Fiona to a local builder in the nearby town of Dalmellington. Walter had been absent, but not unduly dismayed, during the demolition, and became a regular visitor as the new house took shape, asking the construction team technical questions, which they answered, sometimes testily, fretting over the installation of a burnished dark wood floor, checking more than once that the plate-glass front elevation would withstand a bird strike and that the glass balustrade on the upper balcony was firmly enough in place. Then, days before the weekend of the unveiling, he was there when the furniture van arrived from London and, with Fiona's precise diagrams in hand, he directed the placing of the pair of huge pale linen-coloured sofas, the copper arc floor light, the faintly patterned rugs imported from America that to Walter just looked washed out, and the positioning of the paintings, most precious of all the Sean Scully oil, purchased specifically and perfectly for the only windowless wall, upon which the light from the south would fall at the height of the day.

Patrick steered the car down the incline along the single-track road that hugged the loch until, almost halfway along the six miles, the MacMillan land hoved into view. 'Whoa . . . it's finally unwrapped,' exclaimed Patrick as they approached the turn-off and he swung the car through the open gates. 'What a difference a month makes. Not a bay tree out of place, and look over there' – he pointed to a plinth at the bottom of the garden at the water's edge – 'Roland's very own Barbara Hepworth!'

Carson strained her neck to see what Patrick was talking about and made out the squat, smooth bronze mother with her protective arm around her baby.

'So that's the secret he promised Fiona,' said Elinor, raising her eyebrows. 'Hmm, it's quite something.' She looked askance at Patrick. 'Maybe he'll christen it with a magnum of something expensive – or perhaps champagne's a bit common for Roland.'

'Do I hear the tiniest bat squeak of jealousy – about the house, I mean?'

Elinor shook her head. 'Not at all. I mean it. I love our rustic home.'

Patrick brought the Volvo to a halt beside the Strattons' gleaming black Range Rover. 'Well, if it means we'll get to see more of them, that's all to the good, isn't it?'

Before Elinor could reply Iona suddenly let out a wail. 'Where's our cabin?' She unbuckled her seat belt and pushed her way between the front seats. 'I can't see it any more.'

'Don't be such a baby, Iona,' Carson said mockingly, 'it's where it's always been.'

'But I can't see it,' she whined.

'That's because it's behind that bloody great box,' Elinor hissed under her breath.

'Mum! Stop it.' Carson's face was aflame.

'Come on, Eli,' said Patrick. 'You never know, maybe we'll do the same one day.'

Elinor snorted, and, waving at Fiona who was waiting for them on the newly laid turf at the side of the house, spoke through a rictus grin. 'What? When we win the lottery?'

Fiona came towards them blowing extravagant kisses and put her head through the driver's window before Patrick could get out, leaning in to hug him. 'So lovely to see you all. Roland says could you park round at yours, so he can take some photos of the house in the evening light.'

Patrick guffawed. 'Are you serious? Surely Roland's not suggesting our old banger is a blot on the landscape?'

A nervous look flickered across Fiona's eyes. 'Oh, you know how Roland is. Everything in its place.'

Carson caught the look of sympathy on her mother's face as she smiled at her sister-in-law. 'Of course, Patrick will park round the back. It's fine ... really,' she said brightly as she jumped out of the car.

Carson and Iona followed behind Elinor and stood watching the two women embrace. They looked so different to Carson, as if a bear were hugging a bird. Her mother, slightly dishevelled, the tumble of sandy red hair, an old fisherman's knitted sweater and a pair of cowboy boots peeping out from her jeans; and Fiona, engulfed by a pale blue linen shirt, her collarbone jutting where the fabric fell away at her neck. Her perfectly highlighted blonde hair was tied into a ponytail and two gold bangles jangled loosely on her arm. The two women stepped back, still holding on to each other. Carson had the odd impression that her mother was holding her aunt up.

'I can't believe it's been six months since I've seen you,' said Elinor. 'We're all excited about the house. You are so talented, Fiona.'

Carson heard the fervour in her mother's voice.

Fiona lifted her hand in protest. 'It's Roland's design.'

Elinor grimaced. 'I know better than that. It's your vision.'

Fiona flushed a little. 'Well, we're all going to celebrate. I want us all to have a great time. Especially Pete.'

'Where is my nephew?' Elinor grinned.

'He's on the jetty, helping Dad varnish the boat.'

Fiona turned to Carson and Iona. 'Let me look at you both.' She hugged her nieces to her and Carson felt her ribs, one by one, so thin and hard she was alarmed at the sudden thought that they might snap. Fiona tightened her grip as if she were unsure of her bearings, and took a deep breath, and when she finally let the girls free and flicked her hand to her brow, Carson was sure she glimpsed a tear on her eyelash, glinting like a tiny diamond. 'Go find Pete . . . and Granddad too. They're desperate to see you.'

Pete Stratton had just turned sixteen, fourteen months older than Carson. He was sallow-skinned and rangy, his mouth had

a downward tilt, and his unkempt hair flopped across his forehead like an attitude. He had an infinitesimally small skull
tattoo concealed beneath his watchstrap which he had revealed
secretly to an adoring Iona the Christmas before. Carson's
relationship with her cousin was trickier. That same holiday
he had left her smarting when he had opened the door of the
MacMillan cabin and found her wrapped in her old baby blanket on the sofa, her treasured copy of *Peter Pan* propped up on
her knees. 'Finished *War and Peace* already?' he laughed.
Carson had just glared at him, unable to find an instant retort
that was witty or cutting enough, and quickly turned back to
the lost boys, her face scarlet.

She wondered at her aunt's insistence that Pete and Walter
could not wait to see her. Pete always paid attention to Iona –
her sister would not allow it any other way – but Carson could
feel the indifference to the older of his country cousins from
two hundred paces; and as for her granddad, he and she were
forever in each other's company at the loch. She sensed a
desperation in Fiona's eagerness that the weekend should go
well.

Carson's earliest memory of the cabin almost a decade
before was the pungent smell of raw timber which made her
nose itch and the great clatter she could make with her feet
when she marched across the new boards while Walter clapped
in time. He was as constant to her as the North Star which, he
told her back then, and often since, protected them all every
night.

The MacMillans often spent weekends on the loch. In the
early days the car was always laden on the journey from Ayr: a
gate-leg table bequeathed by an elderly aunt, Turkish rugs and
kilims from a second-hand shop, cardboard boxes with lamps
and lanterns and old books about the flora and fauna of

Galloway, a CD player, fishing rods, life jackets and a beautifully framed antique map of Loch Doon which had been a wedding present from Walter. When Patrick had opened the envelope from Walter, it occurred to him that the map might have been a hint about the much greater gift that was to follow.

Carson slept under the eaves in a room at the top of a narrow set of stairs and, eventually, Iona joined her there in the identical bedroom across the landing. At night, more often than not, Iona would tunnel in like a warm mole beside her sister, and Carson never minded, not at the loch. At home in Ayr she was always prying into Carson's stuff, taking her jewellery and digging her finger into her lip balms, messing up her CDs and parading around in her shoes, but at Loch Doon she seemed less irritating, as if she had turned into an entertaining little pixie. Perhaps it was because the girls were less confined at the cabin. The air was soft and clear, the skies big and, surrounded by the Galloway Hills, the loch seemed to be in its own benign world. When Carson and Iona were younger Elinor kept them both in her sights, sitting them down with paints and paper, or dragooning them into hoeing weeds in her vegetable garden, but gradually she let them wander beyond the garden, and Carson surrendered herself to the task of being Iona's keeper.

'Come *on*, Car, I want to see Pete,' shouted Iona as she tore off to the jetty, racing past Roland who was making his way in the other direction. Neither uncle nor his younger niece paid each other any attention but he stopped when Carson came level with him.

'Hello there, Car,' he said fondly, his tall frame looming over her. He gave her an expensively scented hug, his blue linen jacket falling open to reveal a paisley-patterned silk lining. He nodded up in the direction of the new house. 'Ready for tomorrow's celebrations? How do you like it?' Carson reddened, trying to think up something sophisticated to say, but Roland went on, almost to himself, as if listing the house for a catalogue entry, 'You know, I might just win a prize or two with this one, low energy costs, sedum roof, larch cladding . . . It's a small pavilion in the park, really.'

Carson was not quite sure what he was talking about, but she turned around and looked intently at the house, and thought how settled it looked among the trees, its strong outline softened by the pattern of the branches, the glass wall sparkling at them. 'I like it,' she replied finally. 'I watched the men working on it even at the weekends. It happened so quickly. It's handsome.'

Roland looked pleased. 'Why thank you. I must admit I left all the hard work to your aunt' – he winked at her – 'but I drew up the plans, of course,' he added with a wave of his hand as he strode on up to the house.

'He's so damned pompous.' Elinor's words rang in Carson's ears as she walked on, but she found her uncle more interesting than most people she knew. She liked his conversation.

It wasn't so long ago that she had crept to the door of her cabin bedroom the better to catch her parents' murmured voices.

'She wants to make it work, Eli. I think that's what the house is all about.'

'She shouldn't have married him in the first place. And she should have left him when she miscarried. She's so talented and he has just undermined her every step of the way.'

'For God's sake, you can't say that. Then there would have been no Pete.'

'I'm sorry, I don't mean that; but Patrick, he's pathologically incapable of being faithful. It's destroying her.'

'What can I do if Fiona won't do anything – except drink more?' said Patrick. 'He thinks it's all part of being a player, I imagine.'

As Carson reached the jetty, a pair of mallards executed a perfect flypast as if for her, dipping and rising gracefully over the ripples in the midday sunshine. In the distance the ridges of the Merrick shimmered softly. She felt a flutter of anticipation as she looked for the others.

Walter's wooden rowing boat, which had been his father's before him, was raised on blocks on the shingle and as Carson approached she heard her grandfather's steady clear voice, with its trace of Galloway burr, before she saw him, half hidden by the hull. 'Now, Pete, the wood below the waterline won't rot. Why not?'

She looked down and saw Iona squatting by her cousin, her hands pressed on her knees, gazing at him eagerly. Pete stared at his grandfather blankly.

'Because it's cut off from the air,' Walter said, 'but you mustn't let water lie in the bilge. If you do it will eventually get underneath the varnish.' He handed Pete a brush. 'Right, lad, it's dry now, so get the final coat on while the sun is shining.' Just then Carson blocked Walter's light and he looked up, blinking. 'Well, my chickadee. How are you this fine Galloway day?'

'I'm good, Granddad,' she replied distractedly, her eyes flitting towards her cousin, his mouth pressed shut and his sharp cheeks flushed as he painstakingly swept the brush backwards and forwards with long even strokes.

'Good lad,' said Walter, looking thoughtfully at his grandson. 'Feel the weight of the brush; not too much varnish.'

Carson bridled a little. She knew that voice, the fondness in the words as they rolled around Pete. As she furrowed her brows she observed her cousin, the bend of the neck, the way he jutted out his chin as he concentrated, and wondered with a pang of jealousy if the traces of her grandfather in her were as evident as they were in Pete.

'If you're going to go fishing on Sunday, we'll need to get a crack on,' said Walter as he picked up another brush and dipped it into the varnish. 'Now the Lord says that on the Sabbath you can only fish for brown trout, so I'm going to have to give you some of my best flies. I don't want you coming back empty-handed.' He turned to Carson. 'You're going too, aren't you, m'girl?'

Her eyes flicked to Pete as she nodded. 'I think that's the plan.'

Walter had dreamed up the idea of a fishing trip and mentioned it in passing some weeks earlier. 'You'd enjoy that, wouldn't you, Car?' he had said in a way that allowed for only one reply.

'I'm coming, amn't I, Pete?' wheedled Iona, ignoring her sister. 'I can fish.'

'Waving a toy net around on the beach is *not* fishing,' Carson snorted.

'Carson!' Walter said sharply.

Carson felt the rebuke like a slap and saw the hurt on her sister's face. 'I'm sorry, Iona, it's just that you've never fished from a boat,' Carson said in quiet voice.

'I'll take you both,' said Pete, his eyes meeting Carson's for a moment before he looked back at his brush. 'I can handle the boat. I've been out with Granddad before, and anyway I often go fishing on the lakes in the Cotswolds.'

Walter pressed his lips together, trying to hold in a smile. 'Well, it's a bit different here. The wind can get up before you know it. But if you stay in sight, and if you're careful, no reason why not.' He flicked Iona's chin. 'And I've got just the thing for you: Granny Jean's old dapping rod – not that she ever used it, but it's a good one. Shorter than usual and you won't have to cast. We'll put a big juicy fly on it and you can dance it about in the water. You'll have a trout after it in no time.'

Iona gave Carson a hard stare. 'Thank you, Granddad.' Her hands were thrust into the pockets of her denim dungarees, mimicking Walter in his overalls, cementing her alliance. 'I can share it with you, Carson, if you like,' she said sweetly.

'No, Iona,' Walter said firmly. 'There's a couple of junior Hardy rods in the garden shed.'

'That's okay, Granddad,' said Pete, 'I've got a new fibreglass one.'

'You have, have you?' Walter stroked his tidy grey moustache. 'Well, I've got some swanky new flies to use with it. The trout up here are a bit different – they're wild for a start.' He chuckled, and then winked at Carson, and immediately her world seemed sunnier again.

Carson knew that now that she was almost fifteen some of her friends, who congregated conspiratorially in cafés, and smoked and drank in the corners of shaded parks, and lately believed that make-up heavily applied added to their allure, thought it odd that she spent so much time with Walter. They assessed her slyly, with pity even, but were secretly relieved that she was out of the competition on some faraway loch, because Carson had an effortless beauty, luminous skin, long dark eyelashes that needed no help from mascara and unruly auburn hair that she often scraped behind one ear.

She had always cleaved to Walter's quiet solidity, his benign gaze, and never minded that his stories were oft repeated. Sometimes they just sat together on the jetty in old canvas camping chairs and listened and watched: the whoosh of water when ducks made a landing, the plop of oars when a fisherman rowed past, momentarily pausing to doff his cap to Walter, a swift darting onto a soft wave for a drink.

When she was eight he told her that the night sky over Galloway was very special because it was darker than anywhere else in Europe. They stood outside the cabin, the air so cold and sharp on her face it stung her skin, and he mapped out the coal-black sky for her, holding on to her shoulder, directing her gaze to a shimmering band of light. The Milky Way was the first galaxy he showed her, and then the Andromeda. 'Come on, Car,' he whispered, 'let's take a run down the loch. I'll show you my special observatory.' She had no idea what he meant, but they drove two miles to the old red sandstone house where he had lived long ago and walked a hundred yards onto the moor by the light of the moon, to a great slab of rock. 'I used to climb out of my bedroom window and drop down onto the woodstore as quietly as a cat and come here. Climb up and I'll show you.' They both lay on the rough granite, looking heavenward at the sea of quivering lights, Walter's tweed cap beneath his granddaughter's head. 'It looks like magic, doesn't it, Car? I was your age when I first lay here, and it feels just the same as when I was a wee boy.' Carson blinked as the stars started to dance on her eyes. 'And do you know that sometimes when I can't sleep I come and lie here for a while.' He sat up and patted the rock. 'See, there's the dent my head has made I've been here so often.'

Carson looked around at the spot and frowned. 'Granddad, that's not true. The rock's too hard.' She thought for a moment. 'You could have frozen to death in the winter.'

'Don't you worry about me. Just look at the stars.'

'I think the spirals look like the sequins on Granny Jean's black velvet bag.'

Walter looked at her in surprise. 'Well, well. I didn't know you had that bag.'

'Aunt Fiona gave it to me, but don't worry,' Carson said solemnly, 'I'm keeping it safe.'

Walter could conjure up facts and stories like a magician pulling an endless string of knotted handkerchiefs from his top pocket. The Sunday before the Strattons' arrival, after the removal van had disappeared back to London, Carson and her grandfather spent the afternoon on the moorland above the loch, by Whitespout Lane, near the high streak of water that fell one hundred feet and splashed onto the rocks, sending a fine mist shimmering in the air.

They moved over the soft ground like the search party they were, scanning it for a strange little bog plant, the round-leaved sundew that Walter had described to Elinor and she, immediately excited at the prospect of it, had printed out a picture for Carson. She and Walter traversed the moor for more than an hour, a few feet apart, faces to the floor, before he called out, 'Found the little blighter!' He knelt down gingerly and pulled back the peaty moss to reveal a little ball-like flower with red-tinged leaves surrounding its spiky yellow centre. 'Look, Carson,' he said to her, 'it's caught a spider.'

Carson dropped to her knees and watched, horrified, as a tiny spider, trapped in the sticky residue on the tip of the flower's tendril, tried desperately to free itself. 'Is the flower really going to eat it?' she asked in a plaintive voice.

Walter nodded his head. 'The leaves will close over the spider eventually so that the sundew can digest it. Not much of a meal, I admit.'

'Oh, that's gross!' she said.

'It's not all bad. Sundews love midges, and God knows we don't need so many of them.' He laughed as he cut a tiny circle of moss around the flower and eased it into a box he had fished out of his pocket.

'What about ladybirds?'

'Good point. Life's not always fair, is it?' He sighed and put his hand on Carson's shoulder to hoist himself back up. 'My, look at that.' Walter nodded into the distance where a curtain of rain was drawing along Cairnsmore of Carsphairn. 'We had better be getting back.'

Carson pulled herself up straight and cleared her throat.

> There's Cairnsmore of Fleet,
> And there's Cairnsmore of Dee,
> But Cairnsmore of Carsphairn
> Is the highest of all three.

'Good girl,' Walter said fondly.

'You used to give us a twenty pence piece out of your waist-coat pocket when we recited that properly.'

'Well now, it obviously worked, didn't it?' he said with a chuckle.

CHAPTER 2

Walter was born in the red sandstone house by the loch near Craigmalloch that had been built by his own grandfather fifty years before. The window frames and the fretwork above the upstairs dormers and the wooden porch were painted dark green, and beyond the garden wall there had once been a long meadow, patterned yellow with dandelions and buttercups in the spring, that ran down to the water. It was where his own father Alistair had grazed his flock of Cheviots when he brought them off the moor at lambing. But when Walter was not yet five he watched Loch Doon rise and cover the meadow until the loch was little more than a hundred yards from the house.

Alistair MacMillan worked on the hydro scheme when it was begun in 1931, and he made more money from the sale of his meadow to expand the loch than he had made in the ten years before that as an engineer, and much more than his cousins who farmed the hard, inhospitable land further up the moor would ever see.

When he was a boy Walter used to imagine all the fences beneath the loch sagging under the weight of the water, the unsuspecting fieldmice flooded out of their homes, the drowned flowers and abandoned birds' nests. And he would repeat the epic story of the original hydro scheme to his

grandchildren, the herculean effort of the thousands of workers, who dug and drilled and blasted through the rocks with
gelignite, deepening and widening ancient pools of water all
over the Galloway Hills, fashioning tunnels and gigantic
cement dams and, best of all, five gleaming white power
stations, one marker after the next, all the way to the Solway
Firth. 'Great modernist cathedrals in praise of electricity,'
Walter called them.

He asked ten-year-old Pete to pull out the old wooden chest
from the cupboard under the stairs and put it on the garden
table. The initials A. MacM were burned into the lid and he
would sit his two older grandchildren down and explain the
diagrams of turbines and barrages, aqueducts and fish ladders.
'Look at it all,' Walter said expansively, throwing his arms out
over all the unrolled papers on the table. 'It was all planned
perfectly. Imagine these hills teeming with engineers and
welders and navvies. It started the year I was born and finished
when I was five. Explosions echoed around the hills from
morning to night and when they finished there was a beautiful
chain of water that sparkled like a diamond necklace when you
looked down on it from the air.'

'When did you see it from the air?' asked Pete, wide-eyed.

Walter looked startled for a moment, as if he had not
expected the question. 'I didn't, but a pilot who did told me
about it.'

Walter grew up feeling gravity was holding him fast, keeping him anchored to Loch Doon. His recurring dream of
finishing school and travelling, even for a short while, perhaps
to America to see the Brooklyn Bridge and the mighty Boulder
Dam which, he read, was begun the same year as the hydro
project, were just fanciful longings. He would never leave. He
joked that his family had been there so long they must have

been amphibians. And so, he became an engineering apprentice on the hydro scheme and put away his imaginings. He felt that the lonely waters of Loch Doon ran through his veins as surely as they flowed through the sluices and pounded through the dams when the water was let down, brackish water full of brown trout and Arctic char.

Sometimes he thought of the fish swimming through the Spitfire, flashes of silvery brown, nibbling on the leather flying helmet resting in the fuselage. Perhaps they darted away from it when they came upon it, sensing it was a grave.

Sometimes he sat on the smooth concrete beside the fish pass watching as a trout strained against the fuming water before falling back, over and over again. He willed it on, in awe of its primeval determination to create life.

'Why don't they just lay their eggs in the loch, Daddy?' Fiona asked with the simple logic of a seven-year-old.

'Because it's not safe and the shallow waters upstream are more sheltered.'

'But what if the trout can't get there?'

'She will eventually. She'll just keep trying. It's the most important thing in the world for her.'

She frowned. 'Is that the same for all mummies?'

Walter was so startled his breath caught in his throat. 'Yes, darling, and for daddies too.'

He looked intently at his daughter, and realised that it was true: the most important thing to him in the world was to keep her and Patrick safe.

Fiona nodded, deep in thought, and Walter caught the look of infinite trust in her eyes. What if that trust turned out to be misplaced? He had anchored his family in the house in which he was raised, in the sheltering embrace of the hills, but what if that was not enough?

CHAPTER 3

The first time Walter brought Jean Thompson to Loch Doon he could not have orchestrated a better day. He felt the autumn sunshine on his face when he awoke, and it tingled with jittery excitement. He heard the morning sound of the swifts scraping their beaks inside the gutter, scavenging for food, while a pair of crows flapped across the window, caw-cawing him out of bed.

He had planned the day like a military operation. He shaved carefully, staring at his clear blue-grey eyes in the mirror, casting a look over his freshly shorn sunburned face and wondering if his eagerness shone through too clearly. He dressed in a new checked shirt, freshly pressed moleskin trousers and polished tan brogues, and picked up his brown fedora, which he'd brushed specially. He packed a picnic of ham and tomato sandwiches, his mother's fruit loaf and a flask of tea. He had cleaned out his father's Land Rover and wiped the scratched old leather seats, and on the back he had strapped two bicycles which he deposited at the dam at the top of the loch before driving to Ayr to collect Jean.

He had first glimpsed her a month before at the Pavilion, her face in profile, a profusion of dark chestnut hair curled around her strong cheekbones. Her head was tilted back a little as she exhaled her cigarette smoke, sending it swirling up through the beam of the dance floor light, and then she whispered conspiratorially with her friend as they assessed the couples revolving in front of them, and uttered a deep velvety laugh. Every so often his view of her was obscured by the dancers, and each time he felt a little more panicked by the thought that when the couples sashayed away she might have disappeared off on some young man's arm, or been an illusion all along. Walter and his friend Drew, another young hydro engineer, had driven to Ayr that afternoon in time to collect Walter's first bespoke suit from Orr, the tailor in the Sandgate. It was a heathery grey three-piece tweed, with turn-ups and bone buttons. He put it on there and then and wrapped his everyday clothes in a brown paper parcel. It was fate, he later thought, that that night he looked his best. The Pavilion was famous as the best dance hall in the whole country on account of its sprung floor, its sweeping balcony and the wonderful acoustics. The top bands flocked to play in the white stucco Edwardian building on the corner of Wellington Square where it met the promenade, but Walter could only afford an occasional visit, and never before had he seen anyone there like Jean.

Walter nudged Drew and nodded over to the table where she sat with her friend. 'Isn't she something?' said Walter, his voice quavering a little.

'Which one?' enquired Drew. 'They're both lookers.'

'The one with the long curls and the lovely smile.'

'Well, luckily for you I like the blonde one.' Drew laughed.

They edged their way along the side of the dance floor until they were level with the table, but with the band playing 'Now Is the Hour' it was impossible for Walter and Drew to do anything until the music ended except feign interest in the throng. When Jean turned from her friend Joy to see who was blocking her light she looked up at Walter's back and narrowed her eyes. She noted his square shoulders and his hair, neatly trimmed on the back of his neck, the cut of his jacket and the very shape of him, and she smiled to herself.

As the final chord sounded and the applause died away he turned to look at her, and the force of her gaze rooted him to the spot. It was an effort to put his hand out to introduce himself. She took it firmly in her own cool one and started to rise from her seat, looking at him all the while. He found himself gently pulling her up towards him until she was so close he could feel the quickness of her breathing. Just as they each began to speak the band struck up another Bing Crosby number and she laughed and put her hand on his shoulder, fitting her body to his. He pressed his hand lightly into the curve of her back, just above her hip, feeling her body against his hand, and as the 'Shadow Waltz' played the room fell away and they moved as though they had been dancing together their whole lives. He opened his mouth to ask her name, but she pressed her forefinger against it and laughed once more. Soft creases appeared around the edge of her dark brown eyes. 'There will be plenty of time for talking,' she said, her lips brushing his ear. He grinned at her shyly and tightened his hold, sweeping her around the floor until the room spun.

When the music ended, Walter brought Jean to a stop and they stayed put, her fingers resting on his collar bone, his hand on the small of her back, and as they held each other's gaze they laughed stupidly as if sharing a secret. He wondered if she knew she was unlike any girl he had met before, and she thought he must be able to feel the magnetic pull deep inside her. Finally, Walter took her elbow and guided her back to her table. He pulled the chair out for her and then sat down at her side, hoping that she would not hear his heart thudding against his ribs as he glanced over at the dewy perspiration above the sweetheart neckline of her dress. Drew and Joy were nowhere to be seen.

'Would you like a drink?' asked Jean.

Walter quickly pushed his chair back. 'Please let me get you one.'

She put her hand on his arm. 'No need.' She winked at him slyly as she took a silver hip flask from her beaded drawstring bag. 'It's not whisky I'm afraid. Will you settle for a gin martini?'

He nodded, entranced by her boldness, and she handed him the flask. He surreptitiously took a swig, the powerful flavour of the cocktail filling his mouth, and returned the flask to her.

Without wiping the neck she took a long draught. 'Well' – she laughed as she put it away – 'now we've practically kissed we should introduce ourselves. You go first.'

Walter drew a rough sketch of his life which, even as he spoke, seemed to him embarrassingly dull. Jean gave him her full, eager attention, but when it was her turn she delivered but a few bald facts, nothing else. 'Well, my name is Jean Kennedy Thompson – Kennedy, my middle name, is my mother's maiden name, and apparently I look just like her. I'm twenty-one and I live a stone's throw from here on Racecourse Road. I cycle to work each day practically in a straight line through the Sandgate, across the River Ayr to the Carnegie Library, where I am a junior – but hopefully soon, not so junior – librarian.' She finished with a smile that seemed to Walter like a full stop, which brooked no further enquiry.

Over the next hour, at Jean's instigation, there was much more dancing than conversation. Walter was only too happy to be both in her beautiful gaze, and never more than an arm's length from her. As they twirled she suddenly looked up beyond him, above the lights, into the dark, without blinking, and he had the strange sensation that she was somewhere else. He stared at her, hoping to engage her attention, but it was only when they bumped into another couple that she turned back to him with a broad smile. Walter felt a flood of relief and as the last dance ended he asked if could see her again, perhaps the next Saturday, and a look crossed her face as though something intriguing had struck her.

'Would you like a ticket to see me on stage?' she said, in a voice designed to be doubtful.

Walter was taken aback. 'Well, of course, but where?'

'Here. In Ayr. At the new Civic Theatre in the old church near the station. It was the Robertson Memorial Church?' She paused. 'I'm in the first production there. I'm Lady Windermere.'

She registered the lost look on Walter's face and laughed. 'It's a play by Oscar Wilde.'

Walter relaxed, and nodded at the name, relieved to have passed a test.

'I'm in the Ayr Fort Players,' she said, her eyes twinkling, 'the amateur dramatic society.'

'Well, isn't that something!' Walter said in admiration.

'Do come! There's a two o'clock matinee on Saturday. We can meet at the stage door afterwards.'

Walter, completely smitten, studied her expectant face. 'I'll be there, don't you worry.' He drew himself up. 'Maybe we could go to Mancini's afterwards?'

Jean clapped her hands and laughed. 'How perfect. I'll leave a ticket for you at the box office.' She hesitated, and her eyes flickered. 'Daddy will be at the performance. But I don't think he'll come to the stage door afterwards,' she added quickly. 'Shall I meet you there?'

Walter nodded, and Jean turned to go. 'See you then.' She smiled under her eyelashes and put a soft kiss on his cheek.

'Can't I walk you home?' asked Walter, desperate for the evening not to end.

'No, really,' she replied with an airy wave of her hand, 'you better get back to that loch of yours.'

And with that Jean Kennedy Thompson was gone.

The following Saturday Walter arrived at the theatre half an hour before the performance. As he approached the building he thought how odd it looked, a new white front tacked onto the old sandstone church, but mostly he was drawn to the poster on a stand, a line drawing of a young woman in a large hat, unmistakably Jean. He collected his ticket and as he stood at the side of the newly finished foyer where the audience was gathering, he became aware of a tall portly man in a loud checked suit holding court on the other side of the room. He appeared to be greeting people, guffawing every so often as he spoke, and Walter thought he must be the theatre manager.

He took his seat as soon as the doors opened and sat studying the programme, fixed on Jean's name, marvelling that she had invited him. Suddenly the house went dark and once the curtain rose, he saw her on stage in an ankle-length brown taffeta dress, a tight belt at her waist and her hair piled in a loose bun on her head, arranging flowers in a blue bowl. Walter hardly registered what she was saying; she seemed to be in sharp relief compared to the other characters, as if she were in a different dimension, but when he finally tuned in he was captivated by her clear voice. 'I did not spy on you. I never knew of this woman's existence till half an hour ago. Someone who pitied me was kind enough to tell me what everyone in London knows already – your daily visits to Curzon Street, your mad infatuation, the monstrous sums of money you squander on this infamous woman!'

It took Walter all his self-control not to clap there and then and by the time Lady Windermere uttered the play's final line, 'Ah, you're marrying a very good woman!', he was completely entranced. Nobody applauded more enthusiastically than he did when the curtain rose for the first bow. Jean looked radiant as she took in the audience's appreciation, and on the second bow a stage hand appeared on stage with a bouquet, to her obvious surprise.

Walter, as Jean had instructed, walked round the gravel path to the old entrance to the vestry, now hung with a sign saying 'Stage Door', and just as she emerged the imposing figure from before brushed past him.

Jean looked startled. 'Daddy, I didn't expect you to come to the stage door,' she said, glancing at Walter who hung back, taking in the encounter.

'Where's your bouquet?' asked Mr Thompson.

'I . . . I left it in my dressing room. Thank you, but it's not really the custom to—'

'Oh, to hell with custom, Jean, you're my daughter.'

She smiled uncertainly at her father. 'Did you enjoy the performance?'

'Yes . . . yes.' He waved his hand in front of her. 'But it was a silly sort of story, wasn't it?'

Jean ignored him and turned to Walter. 'Daddy, this is Walter.'

Billy Thompson looked bemused. 'Do I know you?' he asked in a not unfriendly voice.

Walter put out his hand. 'No, sir. I'm Walter MacMillan, pleased to meet you.'

He felt the crushing grasp of Jean's father's thick hand but just as he was about to say how much *he* had enjoyed the play, Jean slotted her arm through his and propelled him away.

'We're off for an ice cream, Daddy, toodle-pip!'

They left Billy Thompson standing open-mouthed, and as they walked towards the town centre Walter wondered if his eyes were narrowed, following them. Had Jean's father thought he had been impudent and rude, turning his back on him? He had a slight fear that he had perhaps stored up trouble for the future. Worries pinged around his head and it was only when Walter knew they were out of sight that he stopped and whirled Jean round to face him. 'You were terrific, Jean, a natural. You commanded the stage!'

Jean blushed and smiled broadly. 'You really think so? Well, I'll tell you a secret: I forget everything when I'm on the stage. I'm a different person, really. I don't mean the character I'm playing, I mean I feel . . . free.' She stood back from him and he admired the way she looked: her primrose-patterned three-quarter-sleeved dress, its full skirt billowing gently, her orange-painted toenails peeping out like a row of petals from her brown sandals.

'You look lovely,' he said, 'like a perfect summer's day.'

'How did you know?' she said as he handed her an ice-cream cone outside Mancini's.

'Know what?' he asked.

'That Mancini's is my favourite.' She leaned in to him and gave him a lingering ice-cream-tipped kiss.

Walter felt dizzy with desire. 'I just knew,' he said, his face burning.

They headed for the beach and she kicked off her sandals and ran to the water's edge. Walter took off his shoes and socks and rolled up his trouser legs so he could follow her along the frills of briny foam. 'Typical of my father to be splashy at the theatre,' said Jean suddenly, kicking a wave viciously. 'He's so embarrassing.' Walter, momentarily shocked by her candour, had no co-ordinates with which to form a reply. As he was scrambling for something to say Jean released her hair from its bun, shook her head and laughed mirthlessly. 'My parents are like chalk and cheese.'

'How so?' ventured Walter carefully.

They strolled on as she told him that she was Billy Thompson's only daughter. His family had fished out of Dunure harbour for generations, but he was ambitious. When the war ended he realised that if he moved his two trawlers five miles up the coast to Ayr, where there were fish merchants and an ice house and the railway, there was a fortune to be made out of herring, cod and hake. They were half a mile along the beach when Jean stopped and pointed inland.

'Do you see the rooftop with the widow's walk beyond the high stone wall?'

Walter turned and scanned the row of mansions well back from the sea until he found the one with the tall platform and railings around a small tower. 'That's our house. My father bought it with borrowed cash the year he moved the boats, and he paid it all back within the year.' She shook her head. 'Racecourse Road, the best address in Ayr, so they say. My father thought he had finally arrived.' She looked further on towards the far end of the beach. 'And do you see those grey granite turrets? That was my private school. I went there because my father wanted me to be a young lady, and it was a school for young ladies. My brother Tommy got to go to Ayr Academy, but I was Billy Thompson's status symbol. The uniform was meant to mark us out but not the way we were. Nouveau riche. At least my father was.'

Walter took it all in. He had the sense that she had never spoken to anyone before in this confessional way, but maybe, he thought, he was flattering himself.

'What about your mother? Did she want you to be a lady too?'

Jean was silent. He glanced at her face, set now, her jaw tight, and then she stopped and looked out into the waves. 'My mother didn't want any of it, the grand house, the social niceties and my father expecting her to ingratiate herself in Ayr society among the doctors and lawyers.' Jean turned back to Walter. 'She was mortified by it all. She didn't want to move to a new church and wait to be invited into the coffee morning sets, and she certainly didn't want the grocer to call on her every week to take her order.' She breathed deeply and Walter, without thinking, took her hand.

'Are you all right?' he asked gently.

'Yes ... yes,' she replied, surprised by his concern. 'I just want to tell you all this ... now, I mean.' She pulled herself up and raised her chin. 'The irony is that Mother is a Kennedy from a much older and better family than my father, and she just wanted to stay in Dunure.' She paused. 'She has never got used to it.'

'Do you mean socially?'

'I mean any of it – all of it.'

She shivered and settled herself on Walter's shoulder as a rain cloud covered the sun. He felt the weight of her body moulding into his, as if she were making herself solid. 'I'm sorry, I've prattled on and you've told me next to nothing about your family.'

Walter laughed. 'I think I pretty much covered it last week. I suppose my parents have always just stayed put, much of the time in each other's company on Loch Doon; there's not much society down there. Neither of them is very talkative, but that's not to say they're dour. My father can still make my mother laugh. She has a lovely laugh. Sometimes it crosses the loch and comes back again, ten times as pretty.'

She looked at him squarely. 'You love it there, don't you?'

Walter thought for a moment. 'I can't imagine being anywhere else, if that's what you mean.'

Jean cupped his face in her hands. 'I'm looking forward to seeing it. It sounds very romantic living in a house by a loch.'

With each Saturday rendezvous Walter became more besotted. He loved her vivacity, the languorous way she smoked, the clothes that looked like they had been made with only her in mind, her chiselled shoulders and neat waist, the way she sauntered along the street attracting admiring glances from the prosperous men and women in the Sandgate, some of whom knew her from the library, others as Billy Thompson's daughter. When she had told Walter she worked at the Carnegie Library over the New Brig he was taken aback. He told her he could not imagine anyone who looked less like a librarian. 'Well,' she had replied, in mock indignation, 'I think you'll find there are some bonny *and* brainy girls in the Carnegie.'

He met her outside the library at lunchtime one Saturday after she finished work. They were going to the pictures. 'Do you know, my father has never been inside this library,' she said as she took his arm. 'He couldn't believe I wanted to work here. I told him it was the profession of an educated and refined young woman, and that's what he wanted, wasn't it? It was my way of outwitting him.'

'What did he want you to do?'

'He said he didn't want me to be in trade but then he opened a car dealership and expected me to help my brother to run it.

Of course, I refused, and my mother took my side. So that was the end of it.'

They went to see *High Noon*, the film her colleagues were all talking about on account of their pash on Gary Cooper. They sat in the back of the packed art deco cinema in Burns Statue Square, cocooned in plush velvet seats, and watched the action through a haze of blue cigarette smoke which hung in the air like a special effect. 'You're much more handsome than Gary Cooper,' Jean murmured in Walter's ear.

He coloured in the dark and squeezed her hand. 'And Grace Kelly's got nothing on you.' He put his arm around her shoulder and she placed a soft kiss on his neck like a promise.

When he dropped Jean off and pulled away in the throaty old Land Rover he did not see her wave into a window as she approached the door. She entered the room where her mother was embroidering a piece of plum velvet. 'Hello, Mama, how was your day? Did you get out to the garden?'

Edith Thompson looked up and smiled at her daughter. 'I did! Of course!' she exclaimed. Her gentian-blue eyes twinkled, and she nodded towards the posy vase. 'I picked the ranunculus. Do you like the clashing colours?'

Jean nodded enthusiastically. '*Very* modern, Mama.' She sat down across from her mother. 'Let me tell you about *High Noon*. The song that opens it is marvellous.' She sang the first two lines. 'Do not forsake me, oh my darling, on this our wedding day . . .'

Edith gave her daughter a lingering look.

'Walter was very complimentary. He said Grace Kelly had nothing on me. Not true, I know, but it was a lovely thing to say, wasn't it, Mama?'

Edith put down her needlework. 'Have you set your cap at him?'

Jean blushed. 'He makes me smile.' She searched her mother's face. 'He's steady as a rock and very respectful. He's . . . what is it? . . . courtly.'

'Is he up to you?'

'What do you mean?' asked Jean, pressing her nails into her palms.

'You know what I mean, darling,' Edith said softly. 'Is he strong enough for you?'

'Was Daddy strong enough for you?'

'Jean, please,' Edith said sharply, but then almost immediately a cloud flitted across her fine features and she sighed. 'We make choices. I made the choice to marry your father, and I have you and your brother, and that's enough for me. But you, you have so much to look forward to.'

'Maybe I'm looking forward to being a wife. Maybe I'm not like you.'

'I couldn't be the wife your father wanted.'

'Or wouldn't be, rather.'

Edith took the blow. She looked at her daughter, her hands shaking. 'You've achieved so much in a short time at the library. No one had thought of a section devoted to female writers before, but you did, and so young.' Edith paused, picking her words. She pressed Jean again. 'All I'm saying is would you and Walter have a conversation about the books you love? Would that be something you could share?'

'There's no reason to think not. Just because he's an engineer doesn't mean he doesn't appreciate good books,' replied Jean, looking a little dejected now, but she had one last salvo. She looked at her mother. 'I'm sure of one thing, Mama, we'd certainly enjoy each other's company.'

As soon as she had spoken she wished she could swallow back her words and took Edith's hand. 'I'm sorry, Mama, I shouldn't have said that.'

On the Saturday of Jean's planned visit to Loch Doon Walter crossed the threshold of Stoneleigh for the first time. He clicked open one side of the wrought-iron gates and the crunch of the gravel under his feet announced him loudly. As he looked at the house, he thought he caught a flicker of movement beyond the window on one side of the pillared front entrance. Adjusting his eyes, but careful not to stare, he fleetingly saw the outline of a woman before she stepped backwards into the dark of the room. He walked up the wide stone steps to the stained-glass front door and pulled a little too hard on the brass bell ringer. A series of clangs resounded around the hall for what seemed to Walter an eternity.

Eventually he heard footsteps clattering across the tiled hall and Jean flung open the door, pulling on her jacket at the same time. She threw her arms around Walter's neck and kissed him full on the lips. Alarmed, he quickly scanned the expanse behind her for any sign of the shadowy figure. 'Let's go,' she said excitedly, as she lifted a bag from the side of the door and held it high. 'I've got a bottle of champagne. Daddy ordered a shipment from France.' She took his arm and as they started down the drive she suddenly stopped. 'There's something I want you to see.' She wheeled him round and guided him towards a wooden panelled door set into a high stone wall attached to the house. She turned the handle and stood aside to let him pass. He had to duck down to avoid the low lintel and once he was inside and had pulled himself to his full height he was met by a scene of exquisite beauty.

Before him was a huge square walled garden. It was as if he had entered a living kaleidoscope, even in autumn, designed by someone with a heightened sense of colour and shape. Espaliered apple and pear trees stood with their backs to the side walls like lines of sinuous dancers, and a profusion of old roses, holding on to summer, patterned flower-beds bordered with low boxwood. Rosemary bushes lined the path between the two rectangles of lawn on which was a scattering of russet leaves, and the scent of jasmine mingled with the salt sea air. As Walter walked forward he noticed that even the vegetable garden had been arranged to create alternating light and dark green rows. In the near distance there were rows of soft-fruit bushes and, beyond that, a long glasshouse, built along the back wall that abutted the Low Green on the seafront, glinted in the sunshine. He made a quick calculation and decided that the garden was at least an acre.

'I've never seen anything like it! Culzean's gardens are not a patch on this. It's magnificent.'

Jean smiled with pleasure. 'I'll tell my mother,' she said softly, glancing round to the big bow windows that overlooked the garden. In the middle was a French window and steps lined with pots of blue hydrangeas.

'It's all Mama's work. It was bare and unloved when we arrived.'

'It looks like the work of ten gardeners,' Walter said admiringly.

'No, it was just Mother alone. It was eight years in the making.' Jean's face clouded. 'And few people have ever seen it. Isn't that sad – that something so beautiful is almost a secret?'

'But why?' Walter looked baffled.

'Instead of going out into the world she has made her own one. She lives out here every single day, rain or shine. If she wasn't digging or hoeing or pruning I would be worried.' Jean paused and looked directly at Walter. 'She's a recluse,' she said, enunciating the word as if she were uttering it for the first time.

At that moment Jean turned away, lost in thought, her hand on her cheek. It was the year they arrived at Stoneleigh. She was due to begin her new school and she remembered she was dressed in her new grey uniform waiting at the front door. Edith came towards her and gave her a kiss. 'I'm sure you'll have a lovely day, darling,' she said.

'What, are you not coming?' Jean was puzzled. 'Daddy's in the car. Why aren't you ready?'

'I'll stay here.'

'But you must come, Mummy. I don't want to go just with Daddy. He says we have to drive but I want to walk with you. Please, Mummy, come with us.' Jean pulled on her mother's hand. 'I need you to come.'

'Don't be silly, Jean. I'll be here when you get back,' Edith said briskly, almost pushing her out of the house.

When Jean walked home from school that day she opened the lock with the key hanging behind the storm door, carried on through the house to the garden, picked up a hammer from the shed and started to smash the windows of the new glass-house, one by one.

'Jean, what are you doing? Stop it,' shouted Edith as she ran towards her, but Jean kept on swinging her hammer.

Her mother grabbed it from her and Jean, her eyes wild, screamed in her face, 'You care more about this glasshouse than you do about me.'

Walter thought he heard Jean mutter, '. . . glasshouse . . . than you do . . .'

He stayed still, not sure whether to disturb her. Then he cleared his throat, and Jean blinked at him and smiled.

'Will she mind my being here?' asked Walter. 'Won't it upset her?'

Jean shook her head slowly. 'I'm sending her a sign,' she said softly.

Walter stared at the house, his brow furrowed. 'I'm sorry to be so dim, but what do you mean?'

Jean moved towards him until she was so close that they were almost touching. 'I wouldn't have brought you here unless I liked you.' He was hypnotised by her deep brown eyes, so dark that they appeared to be flecked with glittering jet. 'Very much.'

Walter felt dizzy, his face on fire. Eventually he focused on the smile playing on Jean's mouth, and noticed the dewdrops just above her top lip. He thrust his hands in his pockets to steady himself and eventually he laughed ruefully. 'Well, isn't that something,' he heard himself say.

When they arrived at the dam at the loch, Walter jumped out of the Land Rover and sprinted round to the passenger door to lift Jean down. It amazed him that his hands could encircle her waist, and as she stepped off the running board he swung her around as lightly as a ballet dancer and set her down on the track. Then he retrieved the bicycles and put the picnic in one front basket and a rug and the champagne in the other.

'What a sight!' she called out as they pedalled along the loch together. 'It's as if the hills have come rolling down to meet us.' She sounded her bicycle bell and shouted out, 'Hello, hello. Is there anyone here?' A startled heron lifted off from a dead tree at the side of the track, as if a branch had suddenly come to life, and flapped across to the loch fifty yards away.

'There's your answer,' Walter said with a laugh, 'and if any of its feathers land on you it will bring you luck, so pedal fast!'

They kept pace with each other along the track, and every so often Jean let out a shriek as she bumped over a rut on the rough ground, and then she laughed at Walter as he copied her with an exaggerated yell; they could feel each other's exhilaration and skittishness as keenly as if they were cycling through solid air. Five miles along the shore they came to the ruins of a thirteenth-century castle sitting in a clearing.

'We're here!' Walter called out as he braked. 'Your castle awaits, m'lady.' He shook out the rug and opened the picnic basket.

Jean dropped to her knees, her legs suddenly shaky from the ride, and held out the tin cups while Walter uncorked the champagne with an echoing pop. She took a sip. '*Dejeuner sur l'herbe*,' she said as she offered her mouth for a kiss.

'How delicious,' murmured Walter. 'I've never tasted champagne before, and in a kiss too.'

They sat against the warm stone, looking at the loch, their shoulders touching, shy suddenly. He told her that for eight hundred years the castle at their back had stood on a rocky outcrop in the middle of the loch. 'Imagine. On mornings when the mist was on the water the castle must have looked as if it was levitating. What I remember is when it really did start to disappear, just before I started at school.'

Walter told Jean that he sat day after day watching as more than a hundred stonemasons and labourers, laughing and joking in an Irish brogue that he could hardly understand, took the castle down stone by stone, and marked each one with a number. They loaded the huge blocks onto a barge that went back across the hundred yards to the shore to be unloaded onto barrows on a makeshift jetty. The men on the island and the men on the jetty used to shout insults at each other through loudhailers. 'C'mon, you shitehawks. You're slower than a wet weekend in Bantry!' The ashlar blocks were laid out on the ground like a jigsaw and then hoisted up by a giant crane and inched into position by men whose strong hands, as big as shovels, had never before been put to such a strange task, and never would again. 'Get away, Padraig, you can't count, you eejit, you'll be putting five next to eight – it'll be like the leaning tower of Pisa.'

Walter was captivated by the weather-beaten army who lived in a canvas encampment, dressed in their uniform of flat caps and collarless shirts and who could always find a boiling sweetie for him in their waistcoat pockets when they put their hand in to search for their tobacco.

'Maybe that's why I'm good at numbers. Maybe that's why I like the precision of engineering,' he mused. 'It was like an initiation.' He turned to see Jean staring out at the loch. He reddened. 'I'm sorry. I'm boring you.'

'No, you're not,' Jean said quickly and squeezed his arm. 'Go on, please.'

He told her that the castle would have been lost for ever if they hadn't moved it for the hydro project. 'Sometimes at low water you can see the outcrop in the middle of the loch. The castle was held by supporters of the Bruce and the story goes that the portcullis gates were wrenched off by James V's men when they attacked. Now they're buried deep in the loch in a cat's cradle of weeds.

'How romantic it all is,' Jean said dreamily. Then she raised her hand and pointed at the hills. 'The Merrick and the Range of the Awful Hand, Mulwharcher, Corserine, Cairnsmore of Carsphairn: it sounds like a spell, doesn't it?'

Walter opened his eyes wide and stared at her in amazement.

She smiled at him, pleased. 'I studied the Ordnance Survey map in the library. The names are beautiful aren't they?'

Walter put his hand on her cheek and kissed her. It was enough. He had planned to tell her more. He wanted her to know that when he was ten he had built a cairn on the moor in memory of a man called Frantisek Hekl and visited it still, but now she was enchanted, he did not want her to think of the loch as a place of death. A curlew trilled overhead as she lay back on the rug, drowsy with champagne, and closed her eyes. He looked down at her and stroked her cheek, and then he laid his fedora over her face to keep her from the low autumn sun.

CHAPTER 4

Carson walked back up to the cabin feeling unwanted, redundant, Iona's stream of adoring words designed, she was sure, to needle her. 'Ooh, that looks good, Pete, doesn't it, Granddad?' 'Pete, will you play Monopoly with me like you always do?' 'I want to fish the way you do, Pete. Will you teach me?' On and on until Carson thought she might burst. She rolled her eyes at no one in particular and turned on her heel.

Carson had arrived speedily the year after Elinor and Patrick were married, but Iona was, her parents told her, a miracle. Her birth, soon after Carson's sixth birthday, was long and difficult, and followed two miscarriages. The fact that she was 'a miracle', it seemed to Carson, accorded her special status. But recently, when she had railed against her little sister for some misdemeanour or other, Elinor, reproving her, had blurted out that, had she not lost two babies, Carson would have had a brother, not a sister, and would she have liked that better? Stunned, Carson thought about that with eventual relief, because a boy right there in the middle of the MacMillan family, not like Pete in London, might have stolen Walter away.

As she walked towards the cabin she saw her mother leading her aunt towards the door. Fiona seemed uncertain on her feet, like a new-born lamb, Carson thought, and Elinor had her arm around her waist as if she were supporting her. Carson hung back until the door closed behind them, and then she dawdled to the vegetable plot at the side of the house, troubled by what she had just witnessed but also resentful at this second rebuff, as she saw it, in a matter of minutes. She began to hoe some weeds, and as she savaged some unfortunate dandelions she heard the murmured voices within and reluctantly stepped further away, anxious not to be thought to be eavesdropping.

As Elinor clicked the cabin door shut, Fiona slumped down at the table. 'Cup of tea – or coffee?' she asked hopefully.

Fiona put her head in her hands. 'Have you got any wine open?'

Elinor hesitated for a moment and then pulled a bottle from the fridge.

'Is it okay if I smoke?'

'Of course,' replied Elinor, putting a saucer down in front of her.

Fiona lit her cigarette and took a long drag. 'It's bad this time.'

'God, Fiona,' she said gently, 'why is this time any worse than the rest?'

'She's twenty-six, top of her year at MIT and then mentored by Frank Gehry. He gave her a letter of recommendation – the golden ticket, and bingo, Roland gave her a job.' Fiona took a swig of wine and laughed bitterly. 'Saffron, she's called fucking Saffron, had dinner at our house; you know, far from home, finding her feet. Then bingo again, she's in Roland's bed. It's so humiliating.'

'Leave him.'

'I can't. I'm so worried about Pete. He's struggling at school.'

Elinor banged her fist on the table. 'He's such an old goat; how dare he behave like this. You gave him everything. You handed him your talent.' She grabbed her sister-in-law's hand. 'Do you want me to speak to him? Though frankly I'd actually prefer to cut his balls off.'

'Please don't say anything, not this weekend; maybe this will change things – the house, you know.'

Elinor studied her teacup as if she were looking for a sign. 'Look, Fiona, just remember we're here this weekend for you. Not for Roland. For you. Because we love you – and Pete. This is your place, your work.'

'I just want it to go well. That's what I want.' She looked imploringly at Elinor. 'More than anything.'

Fiona drained her glass and as she stood up from the table she ground her cigarette butt into the saucer. 'Unpacking to do,' she said in a bright, brittle voice. 'Thank you, Eli.' She straightened up and redid her ponytail, wiped her hands over her face as if she were putting on a new mask, and in an instant she was gone.

When Carson heard the click of the cabin door she put down her hoe and cast a glance at the small pile of cats' ear and dandelion. Elinor would be pleased. As she rounded the corner she met Patrick arriving at the cabin, carrying a jute bag. He swung open the door in front of her. 'May I?' he said, standing aside theatrically to let her pass. He followed behind and held the bag up in front of Elinor.

'Ta-da!' he said. 'A gift from Roland. Some very expensive Barolo to go with the humble but artisanal lasagne.'

Elinor put her hands on her hips. 'Why do I think that present just might be a little self-serving?'

'C'mon, Elinor. Can we just enjoy it?' said Patrick, giving her a quick peck on the cheek.

Carson had become used to the undertow of hostility towards Roland, the tremor in the air when he was mentioned. Over the years she had gleaned small pieces of information about its origins. She knew how proud Walter had been when his daughter had won the much coveted position at Stratton and Miles, even though it meant she would be far away. Patrick had his solidity, but there was no mistaking that Fiona had her mother's creativity. When she was in her final year at university Walter had insisted that she enter a competition for a new bandstand in the Pleasure Gardens in Ayr. Her roof design, a circle of overlapping glass sails and the supports (the old wooden posts of a disused quay) was the unanimous winner. When Carson hung around the bandstand swinging her legs against the sandstone plinth with her friends after school, she would tell them proudly that her aunt designed it when she was just twenty-three.

'My mum said she always carried around books about buildings when she was at school,' said Carson's friend Flora one day as they shared a cigarette on the sandstone steps. 'Everybody thought she was amazing . . . and beautiful. I bet you look like her, Car.' Flora leaned and nudged Carson.

The bandstand had certainly impressed Roland Stratton at Fiona's interview at Stratton and Miles. But he was bowled over as much by Fiona as by her design. Even now he would praise her aunt extravagantly, but always for her help with one of his projects, and it perplexed Carson that she never seemed to talk about any designs of her own.

Sometimes late at night in her bedroom in Ayr, when the dark sharpened her hearing, Carson would hear Elinor and Patrick in the next room, at the kitchen table, going over the same conversation again and again.

'He took advantage of her, Patrick, right from the beginning.'

'But she wasn't stupid, Eli. She knew fine well he'd already had one wife and God knows how many affairs.'

Carson heard a glass bang on the table. 'It's as if she's got lost in Roland's slipstream. She's just fading away. Why doesn't she leave him?' Elinor wailed.

'You know why, Eli.'

'But what'll happen to her when Pete goes? What if she starts to drink more?'

Carson was startled from her daydream by Elinor standing over her as she lay on the sofa. 'Thank you for weeding for me.' She handed her daughter a tray of home-made hummus and carrot sticks. 'Here, just for you – and I promise no more lasagne after tonight, even though it's Iona's favourite.' She bent down and kissed the top of Carson's head. 'Love you.'

Carson glanced up and thought how lovely her mother looked in her favourite floral shirt, big gold hoops glinting in her ears, tendrils from her soft red hair escaping from the clasp at the nape of her neck. Elinor was gazing at her older daughter as if she were her whole universe, and Carson felt a sudden start in her chest. 'I love you too, Mum.'

That night the MacMillans and Strattons sat squashed together around the gate-leg table. Roland, making his reluctance obvious, had, with Pete and Walter, carried four of the Strattons' new Wishbone dining chairs across to the cabin to be mixed unceremoniously with the MacMillans' rickety selection. Tall candles stuck in a variety of holders and bottles cast a festive glow around the room and mismatched plates and glasses, with embroidered napkins Elinor found in a charity shop, made a colourful pattern on the oak table. Elinor stretched forward and deposited a huge dish in the middle of it all, giving Carson a conspiratorial wink.

A spoon tinkling sharply on a glass brought the room to quiet. Patrick stood up and pushed his curly salt and pepper hair back from his forehead and then scratched his short beard. Elinor waved her hand at him impatiently. 'Patrick! The food will get cold.'

'We are gathered here,' he said with mock solemnity, 'in front of Eli's wonderful lasagne, to celebrate the coming together of the family on the eve of the great unveiling.' Carson darted a look at Roland and noticed his jaw tightening just above the edge of his black polo neck sweater. 'Tomorrow night we'll christen Fiona and Roland and Pete's handsome new home, but tonight I'd like to thank Dad again for our cabins on the loch, the place that is our spiritual home. To Walter!'

'To Walter' everyone repeated. Carson watched her mother give Roland a friendly smile as they clinked glasses and wondered if adult life was full of lies.

'Is it really over a year since we were all together?' Elinor said gaily.

'Culzean Castle,' Patrick said with a nod. 'Patti Smith singing Burns' songs.'

'That curtain of hair and her long black coat. I remember,' said Fiona a little too loudly. 'She looked like a white witch. I thought she might fly off.' She raised her arms, sending her gold bracelets concertinaing together noisily like a hail of coins.

Carson looked anxiously at Elinor, wondering if she'd registered Fiona's strange reedy voice, but her mother seemed oblivious.

'You kids loved it, didn't you, Petey?'

Pete glared at his mother and Carson saw him gripping his fork, his eyes glittering. 'Mum, just stop speaking . . . and drinking. Could you?' he said coldly.

'Oh Petey, darling,' Fiona sailed on, 'you had a great time. I seem to remember you dancing with Iona.'

Pete flushed. 'Don't call me Petey. You're only doing it because you're drunk.'

An uncomfortable silence descended on the table. Carson's heart whooshed loudly in her ears as she waited for Roland to say something to his son, but he appeared to be engrossed in cutting the end of a large cigar that he had taken from a box he'd carried in under his arm.

Walter sat with his hand cupped over his mouth, his thoughts focused somewhere else until suddenly he turned to his grandson. 'Wheesht, Pete. Don't talk to your mother like that,' he said in a quiet voice.

Pete's tall body seemed to collapse into itself on the chair and Carson saw Iona lean in towards her cousin and put her hand on his beneath the table as he dropped his head and stared into nothing.

Fiona took a long sip from her glass, ignoring Patrick's imploring gaze.

Walter kept his eyes on his grandson, his consternation evident, and then he cleared his throat and put his hands squarely on the table. 'I had a surprise visitor last week,' he said slowly, 'a young man who had hitched all the way here from Prague.' He looked around the group. 'Any idea who that might be?'

Nobody spoke. Patrick sighed inwardly and Roland fiddled with his cigar. Carson wondered if this would be one of her grandfather's long stories.

'Well,' Walter went on, 'you'll know the name when I say it. Frantisek Hekl. Isn't that something?'

Something stirred in Carson's memory and Patrick leaned in to the table, furrowing his brows. 'But that was the name of the pilot, Dad. He's long dead.'

Walter nodded vigorously. 'It was his great-nephew. I saw the resemblance to the picture in the Aviation Museum straight away. The same thin face. The sharp features. It was uncanny.'

'What pilot?' asked Iona impatiently. 'What are you talking about?'

'When Granddad was young, just a little bit older than you, we were at war with Germany. Pilots from a country called Czechoslovakia came here to train to help us fight the Germans.'

Iona looked quizzical. 'But who was Francis Heck?'

'He was one of the pilots,' replied Patrick, throwing a warning look at his father. 'One day when he was training he swooped down in his Spitfire plane and one of the wings caught the water and the plane sank. Granddad raised the alarm.'

Iona's eyes widened. 'Did he die, Granddad?'

Walter nodded. 'He died straight away.'

'Is he still in the loch?' she asked in a small voice.

Elinor set her glass down hard on the table. 'Yes, but it was a very long time ago, darling.'

Iona turned to Pete, a look of dread on her face. 'Will we see him when we are fishing?'

Pete's head was still down, as if he were paying no heed to the conversation, but he immediately turned to Iona. 'We'll be nowhere near, I promise,' he said in a voice so gentle it took Carson aback.

'He went to the Aviation Museum to see the fuselage,' Walter went on, 'then he came to find me.'

'Did you take him to the cairn?' asked Carson.

'I did. I did.' Walter looked around the table, about to continue, but stopped himself. 'But that's for another time. I'll be getting home now. It's a big day tomorrow, eh.'

As he pushed his chair back a little voice piped up. 'Are you bringing Marie to the party?' asked Iona. 'You should be able to bring a friend, Granddad,' she added, gazing at him eagerly.

The room quieted. Walter sighed as he pushed himself up. 'Not tomorrow night, Iona. Sometime soon, maybe. Goodnight to you all,' he said quickly to forestall further enquiry from his youngest grandchild. The question of Marie Doherty's presence at the celebration had gnawed at him for days. She was a part of his life, had been for years, but Marie was reluctant to, as she put it, 'inveigle herself again in his family', and he acquiesced, perhaps too easily, in the face of his children's apparent unease.

'Marie, what about tomorrow night?' he had ventured at breakfast that morning.

'Walter, you know my thoughts on this. I've known Patrick and Fiona since they were knee high. We have perfectly cordial relations. I like them both very, very much, but it seems it will always be awkward and I don't want to cause any distress.' She put her slender hand over his broad weather-beaten one. 'I have my own family, plenty of them, and grandchildren of my own. It's fine, Walter, please don't fuss.' Her bright eyes twinkled at him and she broke into a reassuring smile. 'Look at us, we are happy with each other, and that's pretty good at our age. That will always be enough for me.'

CHAPTER 5

The million silver pinpricks in the indigo sky could not ease Walter's heart as he drove home to Carsphairn. Looking out of the windscreen he saw, not the road, but Fiona's tight, unhappy face before him, just as she was at the dinner table. Then it merged into Jean's, their features so similar, the look in his daughter's eye so unmistakably her mother's, and his breath caught in his throat.

Then as he clicked on the wipers to clear a misty squall that smeared the darkness in front of him, he saw instead the face of the pilot. He had wanted to tell young Frantisek that he'd always hoped this day of pilgrimage would come, but the teenager spoke little English. He took him to the spot on the shore where he saw the Spitfire hit the water, and the boy bowed his head. Walter wanted to tell him that, when he was ten, he looked out every day for the Spitfires that were stationed nearby at Heathfield in Ayr and kept a note of the dates and times he saw the Czech pilots swoop the length of the loch and the numbers on the fuselages. Nor could he tell him that when the plane crashed into the water he had pedalled furiously more than six miles to the main Ayr road and flagged down a car to take him to Dalmellington to raise the alarm. But what young Frantisek already knew was that although pieces of metal were eventually recovered some forty years later, his great-uncle's body was never found.

After the plane crashed Walter was told to say nothing except to his parents. In the weeks that followed he watched intently, sometimes through his father's binoculars, as RAF recovery teams scoured the water in their motor launches, but after a month they gave up. It was as if the tragedy had never happened.

But secretly, Walter started to build a cairn high up on the hill, his own memorial to the unknown pilot. He collected stones from the moor in his small hands, sometimes hacking them out of the ground with a claw hammer, and carried them to his site in a sling. After the war, when the RAF returned to make a cursory search, he asked the pilot's name. Then he found a large flat stone, and on it he chiselled 'Flying Officer Frantisek Hekl, RAF 312 (Czech) Squadron. Died Loch Doon 25.10.1941', and set it into the peaty ground in front of the cairn. The memorial had stood there for more than sixty years, defying all weathers. It was all but destroyed once, but Walter rebuilt it, every stone in its original place.

Walter guided young Frantisek up to the cairn, and when he realised what he was looking at he fell on his knees and began to weep. He put the palm of his hand on the plaque, pressing down hard as if he were trying to make an imprint of the words in his skin. Walter stood back, twisting his cap in his hands, listening to the boy's sobs rise into the air. Then he spoke a little in Czech and, raising himself up, his face streaked with tears, he put his hand on his heart and stepped towards Walter and shook his hand. He took a small camera from his bag and indicated to Walter to take a picture of him. Frantisek wiped away his tears, and stood erect, arms by his sides, and when Walter clicked the shutter he had the overwhelming dizzying sensation that it was the pilot himself who was standing there looking directly at him. Then the boy signalled to Walter to change places. As he waited for the young Czech to take the photo, he felt a weight lift from him as he handed the memory on. Now others would come and bow their heads and place their hands on the plaque.

He thought about Jean then and felt ashamed that, out of cowardice, out of fear that she might have taken against the loch, he never told her about the pilot. In 1953, exactly a year after Walter had first caught sight of Jean across the dance floor, Billy Thompson invited him to join his party in the Members' Enclosure at Ayr Racecourse. It was the Saturday of the Ayr Gold Cup, the richest sprint handicap in Europe, and the town was bursting with excitement. Cars and buses and horseboxes navigated Burns Statue Square with much shouting and honking at the fruit lorries and bakery vans, and the odd tractor, which saw no need for the hurry. Racegoers and day-trippers alike crowded the pavements. Gaily striped canopies hung over every shop, creating the impression of oversized strings of bunting all along the street, and shoppers milled around, calling out greetings to each other, weighed down with bags from Hourstons Department Store or from Picken's, the best butcher in town. And in among it all, children were heading to the ice rink, the lucky ones with their own skates hung in a bag over their shoulder.

Jean had risen early, elated at the prospect of the day ahead, her mind on the anniversary of their meeting, and wondering how things would go between Walter and her father, and had run down to the beach to catch the horses exercising along the shore. She loved to watch them prancing and cantering through the shallows, sending up sea spray over their flanks, sensing the occasion to come. She was awestruck by their beauty and their strength, their muscles rippling below their silken coats. She imagined them galloping unencumbered, free of jockeys and saddles and harnesses, their manes and tails flying.

When she returned for breakfast, her hair and face salty, high colour on her cheeks, Edith was waiting for her, pancakes freshly made, a pot of coffee on the stove. 'You look radiant today, darling. Are you expecting some excitement?'

'You know I love race day, Mama. I suppose it's something that Daddy and I can share.'

'Is there something else?'

'What do you mean?'

Edith set down a plate of pancakes, lemon and sugar in front of her. 'Jean, you know what I mean. Have you decided?'

Her daughter's eyes burned bright as she looked away to the window. 'I want you to meet him. It's been a year.' She looked up at her mother. 'You'll approve. I know it.'

'I'm sure I'll like him very much from all that you have said. But will he make you happy? That's what I care about. And I'm asking you again, is he up to you? Is he ready for the ups and downs?'

'Mama! Of course he makes me happy.'

'But there are times when you are not so happy.'

'What do you mean? Like you, is that it? But I'm not like you. I go out and greet the world.'

'I'm only asking you to think about it.'

Jean laughed. 'Walter's strong and good and he loves me. What more could I need?'

Edith put her hand on her daughter's cheek. 'Just be sure, that's all.'

When Walter arrived at the racecourse he plunged into the tweedy chaos. It was a new world to him. The smell of cigarettes and pipes and perfume mingled with the pungent scent of horses, and he was assailed by the same strong Irish brogue that he remembered from his childhood. The tic-tac men in their slouch hats and braces stood on wooden boxes calling the odds in what might as well have been a foreign language and signalling with their white-gloved hands for all the world like the clowns he had seen once at the circus when he was a child.

At the door of the members' restaurant he paused to brush himself down and straighten his new silk tie. He felt for his father's handsome gold fob watch on his waistcoat and held on to it for a moment before he removed his brown fedora and the maître d' showed him to the Thompson table, the best in the room. Jean was first to spot him and she jumped up and threw her arms around his neck, to his slight embarrassment, and as her lips brushed his cheek he breathed in the familiar musky scent of her perfume. She looked dazzling in an emerald-green short silk dress with a full skirt and a bolero to match, and even if he had just stood there and looked at her the day would have been complete, but Billy Thompson's florid face suddenly loomed in front of him sullying his view.

He felt a meaty hand pumping his and was aware of a brightly flecked tweed suit and a waistcoat stretched almost to bursting. His son Tommy, at his shoulder, looked like he belonged to a quite different family. A grey sharkskin suit hung loosely on his rail-thin frame and his jaundiced complexion looked ghostly against his slicked-back hair. Beside him sat Joy, a fur stole about her shoulders, the pretty fair hair that he remembered from the Pavilion now dyed platinum blonde. She had a cigarette in a long silver holder in one hand and a saucer coupe of champagne in the other which she raised to him in greeting. 'Lovely to see you again after all this time.

Who would have thought that night would have been the night?' she said with a sly wink. Walter coloured, irritated by her crassness, but flattered too, and without replying took the empty seat between Jean and her father.

Billy Thompson had arranged smoked salmon and steaks and ordered the finest red wine, and as he sent the waiter away with a wave of his napkin, he puffed out his cheeks and exhaled a plume of cigar smoke. He then turned and fixed his eyes on Walter. 'We've never had a proper conversation, have we? You've always been picking up Jean or dropping her off in that old Land Rover of yours. How's life at the Hydro Electric?'

Walter was not really sure what was being asked of him, but he replied that most of his time was spent at either Tongland or Glenlee power stations, checking the machinery and calibrating the water levels daily depending on the demand for electricity.

Billy Thompson sucked on his cigar and narrowed his eyes. 'Scottish engineers are at a premium all over the world these days. Have you a notion to travel?' Walter, disconcerted, tried to work out where Billy Thompson was going with his interrogation. 'There's plenty of money to be made, Walter, mark my words.'

Walter spoke carefully. 'I like the challenge I have now, Mr Thompson. We're getting better at harnessing the power of the hydro all the time. It's all about precision.' His heart sank at how feeble and unworldly he sounded.

'Aye, well, you're young yet, but you can't be too ambitious,' Billy Thompson said, waggling his cigar in front of Walter.

'Have you always loved racing?' Walter said quickly.

Billy Thompson guffawed. 'I don't much care for the horses, but yes, I love racing. It's exciting – as long as I win, and hopefully win big.' He looked across the table at his son. 'Tommy knows how I feel about winning, don't you?' He went on before Tommy could answer. 'The dealership has hardly been going a year and we've wiped out the competition from here to Glasgow.' He looked across Walter to Jean. 'I keep telling that girl it's a goldmine. She should join us.'

Jean squeezed Walter's knee under the table. 'I've told you, Daddy. I'm happy at the library. They're letting me build up the section on fiction by women. I've ordered in all the new editions of Daphne du Maurier.' She turned to Walter. 'It all started when Mother read aloud to me; even though *Rebecca* was terrifying it was wonderful. She used to sit on my bed with her arm around me tightly as she read, as if she were keeping me safe from Mrs Danvers.'

'I've no time for all that. The only books for me are the accounts.'

'Philistine.'

Billy Thompson looked confused by the reference. 'Pah,' he said, flustered.

Jean tapped her nail on the table. 'If you read anything other than car magazines and the pink paper you'd understand.'

Billy Thompson tsked and snapped his fingers at the waiter. 'We'll have brandies with dessert. But bring them sharpish. We have to get down to the paddock.'

They stood at the rail admiring the horses, some of them stamping skittishly, raring to be at the off. Billy Thompson ducked under the bar and strolled over proprietorially to have a word with his jockey and trainer. High Born Lady, her ears pricked in excitement, whinnied and pranced beside her owner who, to Walter's dismay, ignored her. He wished he could go to her and reassure her, whisper in her ear that she was a beauty. He looked about him, entranced by the ritual of the

day, the craic between the well-heeled and the punters, respectful of each other's intimate knowledge of the form. It was
thrilling. He took Jean's arm excitedly and she gave him a look
from under her long lashes that almost knocked him sideways,
as if she knew that he would do anything she asked of him.

When Billy Thompson returned to the group he put his
hand inside his wallet pocket and pulled out an envelope
containing a thick wad of cash. He handed them fifty pounds.
When he told Jean's father he could not accept such a sum, he
waved away his protestations almost angrily. 'Get to the tic-tac
boys now, all of you, before the odds shorten. I reckon she's
fifteen to one right now and she's going to win, so move fast,'
he barked.

'But Mr Thompson, if she wins, the money's yours, surely?'

'What? Can I not make you a gift?'

'It's too much . . .' stammered Walter, as he looked down at
the note.

'Is my money not good enough for you?' Walter heard the
menace in Billy Thompson's voice.

'No . . . not at all, thank you,' he said, defeated, and looked
askance at Jean.

Within minutes the horses were cantering out onto the oval
course, jockeys standing in their stirrups, the banter over. All
around Walter people pressed binoculars against their eyes as
a loudhailer announced that the race was under starter's orders.
The pistol cracked and the crowd erupted as one. 'Come on,
Jinky Joe!' 'Push on, Creetown Lad,' they screamed and yelled,
waving their programmes. The horses pounded the six-furlong
course, bunched together tightly. 'Yes, High Born Lady! She's
neck and neck,' roared Billy Thompson and then suddenly
Jean was grabbing Walter's arm and jumping up and down.
'She's done it! She's done it!' Walter was thunderstruck. He

was almost seven hundred and fifty pounds richer than he had been three minutes earlier. He tried to return his stake but Billy Thompson, who was so puce he looked ready to explode into tiny pieces, just slapped him on the back. 'Don't be daft, boy. What's fifty pounds to me when I've just won three thousand!'

The heady excitement of it all fortified Walter. When Jean was out of earshot he stepped towards Billy Thompson and cleared his throat. 'I was wondering, Mr Thompson, if there was a convenient time when I could speak to you in private. I could come to your office if that was suitable.'

Billy Thompson put his thumbs in his waistcoat pockets and scrutinised Walter's face. 'Well, well, Walter. Here is as good a place as any.'

Walter suddenly felt a claw gripping his chest. 'If you're sure?'

'Where could be better? It's a pretty good day so far, eh? Let's walk.'

They strolled away from the melee onto an empty stretch of grass. Walter suddenly felt very exposed and the speech he'd prepared came out in a headlong rush. 'I would like to ask for your permission to ask Jean if she will do me the honour of marrying me.' Billy Thompson did not miss a step and kept on walking. 'I hope I would make her happy. My parents are resolved to move to a house they've inherited in Carsphairn, and give me the house on Loch Doon and a large piece of land to go with it.'

Finally, Billy Thompson stopped and put his hands on the railings. He turned his head to look at Walter. 'And do you intend that my daughter should work if you were married?'

Walter was taken aback by the question. 'Well, that would be up to Jean, Mr Thompson,' he stammered. 'Naturally we would talk that over. But if she did, it's not a long journey to Ayr on the bus.'

'On the bus. Is that so?' Billy Thompson slowly relit his cigar and sent up a swirl of smoke like a warning signal. 'Well, we better wait to see what she says then, hadn't we?'

Walter excused himself and made a quick call from the telephone box at the back of the stand. Then he searched out Jean and Tommy and Joy who were gaily reliving the race. Suddenly nervous he encircled Jean's waist with his arm. 'I was looking for you,' she said, laughing, leaning into him. 'I thought you'd taken your winnings and deserted me!'

'You know I would never do that,' he replied, clasping her a little more tightly and burying a kiss in her hair. Jean gave him a quizzical look, bemused by such unaccustomed abandon. 'Let's go for a walk on the Low Green after the last race, and maybe a bite to eat,' he whispered to her, 'just the two of us.'

As they walked along the cobbled Sandgate, weary shopkeepers were winding in awnings and dropping their window blinds, and bidding farewell to straggling customers. The elegant steeple of Sandgate Church stood in silhouette, like a way marker to the candlelit restaurant that Walter and Jean thought of as their own. When they reached the Magic Lantern Jean made to go in, but Walter walked her on diagonally across Wellington Square, holding her arm in his, past the blank stares of the statues of long dead local worthies. 'Let's go and see the sea before we eat,' he said casually.

Jean squeezed his hand. 'Yes, let's get away from this dull lot. They make you look even more dashing, if that's possible.'

He laughed delightedly as he moved his hand to the curve of her lower back and guided her towards the Pavilion. 'We're going to the Piv?' she asked, perplexed. 'But nothing's on here tonight.' Walter made no answer and walked on towards the closest Italianate corner towers. He stopped suddenly, swivelled Jean towards him, and dropped down on one knee. As soon as he opened his mouth to speak, she bent over him, cupped his face in her hands, and stopped him with a long deep kiss. 'The answer is yes,' she said with a laugh. 'Yes, yes, yes!'

They sat at their favourite table at the rear of the Magic Lantern, exotic for the fact that it was the only French restaurant beyond Edinburgh, and because the clientele liberally smoked the Gauloises sold behind the bar. Atop the red-and-white checked tablecloth there was a small posy of flowers and a candelabra. '*L'hymne à l'amour*' played on the gramophone. 'You thought of everything, darling,' murmured Jean as she sipped her red wine, 'even my favourite Piaf.'

Walter laughed and blew a ring of toasted smoke so that it made a halo above her head. 'Engineers love plans. But I can't claim that was my doing. And I certainly didn't know that a win on a horse would give me the chance to buy you a bigger sparkler.'

'Well then,' said Jean, clapping her hands, 'it's all a sign that we were meant to be, but I don't need a sparkler; you're my sparkler.'

She took a fresh pack of cigarettes from the green silk clutch embellished with a jockey on a racehorse, embroidered in her father's colours. Walter had not noticed it until it glinted in the candlelight.

'This expresses the difference between us perfectly,' he said, lifting the bag. 'I am methodical and plodding, but you are an artistic talent.' He examined it closely. 'This is quite something.'

She drew hard on her cigarette and waved her hand. 'It's just something frivolous I do when I'm sitting with Mother. Some of her creativity has rubbed off on me, I hope.'

Walter opened his mouth to say he was looking forward to meeting her when the owner of the restaurant arrived with a bottle of champagne and tapped a spoon on a glass. Immediately the room fell quiet as if the other diners were primed for the moment. 'Congratulations to two of my favourite customers on their engagement. I am honoured you chose to celebrate in the Magic Lantern.' Immediately there were whoops and whistles and a chant of 'Kiss. Kiss. Kiss.'

Walter smiled ruefully, and Jean leaned forward to accept her beau's embrace. 'I know what you were about to say.' She nodded, her eyes shining. 'I want you to meet her too. It's time.'

Walter arrived back in Ayr the next afternoon, almost undone with nerves. He checked his collar and tie in the rear-view mirror, smoothed his wayward hair and, before he got out of the Land Rover, took a rag across his perfectly polished brogues.

'Don't look so worried,' said Jean as she shooed him into the garden, 'I've already told her you're perfect.'

'But that's not true, Jean!'

'Oh, I'm sure she'll know that too,' she replied coquettishly, birouetting away, holding the skirt of her halter-neck sundress, before giving him a little push.

Walter had the feeling this would be one of the most important meetings of his life. He was aware of every step he took the length of the garden, to where Edith Thompson was working in the glasshouse, painstakingly sorting out bulbs into different trays. He tapped gently on the glass pane of the door and entered just as she turned to look at him. He was startled by the softer, more delicate version of Jean. Her azure eyes were made more brilliant by her tanned face, and her greying hair was fashioned into a French roll, while her ears were adorned with pearl studs. A large cameo brooch held her white cotton blouse closed at the neck and a camel-coloured cardigan was draped over her shoulders. Walter had never set eyes on such an elegant woman. She turned towards him and gave an almost imperceptible smile. 'Good afternoon, Mrs Thompson,' he said courteously. 'I have admired your garden often. It's a privilege to meet its creator.'

She took off one of her suede gardening gloves and put her small firm hand in his. 'Isn't God its creator?' she replied, her eyes twinkling.

Walter was enchanted. 'In this case I think God had very little to do with it,' he said, almost flirtatiously.

Edith smiled and the creases around her eyes deepened. 'That is the correct answer.' She laughed.

Edith asked after Walter's mother and father and said how kind it was of them to give Walter and Jean their house, especially as Jean had told her that Mrs MacMillan was very fond of her garden.

'Yes,' he said, 'but it's a wilder sort of place. The flowers have to be hardy. My mother is looking forward to the more sheltered one at Carsphairn.'

'I imagine I would like the wilder one.' Edith Thompson carried on with her work. 'My garden at Dunure was hewn out of a rocky field and the wind from the sea was far from kind. When I lived there I sometimes visited the walled garden at Culzean. The flowers did so well there.' She looked directly up at him. 'And now, here I am in my own walled garden.' Her words hung in the humid air of the glasshouse, waiting, but Walter felt ill-equipped to reply to them.

'I gather from Jean that you miss Dunure a lot,' he said instead.

'I am a Kennedy. We have farmed land there for more than three hundred years. I'm not one for the town – unlike the rest of my family.' A steeliness had entered her voice which disconcerted Walter. She dropped a bulb into a pot and tamped down the earth around it. 'I know I am a great inconvenience to them, but I'm afraid I can't step out into the hustle and bustle.' She pulled her cardigan around her shoulders. 'Ayr is booming more than ever, don't you think? At least it is for my husband.' Walter heard the faintly sardonic tone and wondered if Edith Thompson was picking out her words with the same precision she accorded her garden during her solitary hours. 'Shall we?' She took his arm and they stepped outside and strolled between the rose beds. 'At least out here I can close my eyes and when I breathe in the salt-blown air I can imagine I am back at Dunure.'

'I worry that Jean will find the loch too quiet,' ventured Walter tentatively, searching Edith's composed profile. 'I'm keen that she carry on with her amateur dramatics, she has such a talent, but she told me she might put an end to it. Wouldn't that be a shame?'

Edith took his hand and patted it. 'Let's wait and see. I'm sure you will entertain her, and besides, she might change her mind; you know, she can be very headstrong.' She stopped on the path and fixed him with her bright eyes. 'But you, Walter, you will be her anchor. That matters to her a great deal.'

'She's going to carry on at the library, she says, and so she should if she wants to. But I want you to know that I can provide for her, Mrs Thompson, though we'll never be rich.'

Edith Thompson tightened her grip on his hand. 'Maybe not, but you have the chance to make someone happy. Money can't buy that, believe me.' She paused. 'Though my husband seems to think so.'

The next morning, Monday, Walter arrived at work at eight o'clock sharp, his speech for the senior engineer rehearsed. He knocked on the mottled glass of his office door at five past eight. 'Come in.' Mr Reid's tone was always clipped, but not unfriendly. He took in Walter's freshly laundered shirt and neat tie beneath his clean, and newly pressed, overalls.

'Well, good morning, Walter. You look ready for a good week's work.'

'I am, Mr Reid.' Walter hesitated, looking down at the older man at his desk in his tweed waistcoat, glasses low over his nose, revealing his rheumy eyes.

'I became engaged to be married at the weekend.'

'Is that so, Walter? My congratulations.' Mr Reid smiled warmly and stood up briefly to shake Walter's hand across the desk.

'I was wondering, sir, if there would be any chance of promotion? I'm happy to undertake more studies. There are courses at the Royal Technical College in Glasgow. Perhaps I could go on day release?'

Mr Reid signalled for Walter to sit down at the table. 'I know you're even more eager now, and engineering runs in your blood, but you have to be patient. Look at me. I only got this job when your father retired.'

'But I'm qualified now.'

'Aye and you should be proud of that so young.' A thought came to the senior man. He rocked back on his chair and pulled a sheet of paper from his drawer. 'This arrived last week,' he said, passing it to Walter. 'There's a huge push coming in the north, dams and power stations galore. What

about going to Loch Tummel? And there's talk of one at
Cruachan.' Mr Reid tapped the page Walter was holding.
'These jobs are two grades higher than your salary here.'

'But Ben Cruachan must be two hundred miles from here.'
Walter could not hide his dismay.

Mr Reid shook his head. 'I know. I know, but that's where
the big expansion's going to be. And the promotion. You're
clever enough to go far, Walter.'

Walter tried to marshal his thoughts, but he felt as if his
brain was exploding. Argyll might as well be on the moon. And
just as remote as Galloway. What would Jean say to that?

He heard Mr Reid indistinctly. 'Look, lad, I don't want to
lose you, but I know you'll be thinking of married life.' He
studied Walter's stricken face. 'I tell you what, I'll look into
the technical college anyway. It won't do any harm.'

Walter felt unsteady on his feet, his head pounding. All day,
as he worked on his own stripping down one of the turbines,
he wondered what to say to Jean. He dreaded the idea of working away from home, most likely staying in a camp, like the
Irish navvies who built the whole damned hydro, and only
coming home at weekends. But then a thought lodged itself
like a small nut in his chest. What if, against all expectation,
Jean, with her sometimes capricious nature, thought it would
be a great adventure? Walter would go ahead, and she would
follow after they were wed. In that case, if he baulked at the
opportunity, she would think him weak and unambitious.

All that week he wrestled with what to say. They had planned
to drive to Culzean the next Saturday and picnic on the beach
at the bottom of the castle's huge escarpment. It was a glorious
Indian summer's day, and as soon as they arrived on the empty
stretch of sand Jean stripped off her dress to reveal a yellow
halter-necked swimsuit that hugged her figure like a second

skin. 'Come on, Walter,' she called over her shoulder as she ran to the water, 'don't be such a slowcoach.' She looked to him like a nymph, so beautiful and lithe, her long hair flying down her shoulders, her arms open to welcome the waves. He had the sudden strange thought that she was not real and if she walked out into the sea she would disappear below the waves. He jumped up and followed her into the chilly water so as not to lose her. He dipped his toe into the foamy tide and when she laughed and kicked water at him it felt like needles piercing his skin. 'Splash me back,' she commanded. 'Doesn't it make you feel so alive?' They began to pound water at each other and Walter made a grab for Jean's legs, upending them both under the waves. Jean screamed with the shock of it as she surfaced again, spluttering her protest.

'That'll teach you to call me a slowcoach,' he called to her as they charged out of the sea and back to their towels. Walter stuck the striped canvas windbreaker into the sand, encircling them in a private shelter, and they wrapped themselves up in the travelling rug, laughing at each other's goose pimples. 'We'll bring our children here,' Jean said as she kissed his icy lips.

Walter felt his throat tightening. 'But what if we didn't live here? What if I got the chance of promotion somewhere else?'

Jean pulled the blanket up to their necks. 'That's a crazy thing to say, darling. You'll get promotion here. I know you will. This is where we want to live. Don't we?'

Walter felt all his anxiety ebb away, and all he could think of was the warmth of Jean's body. 'I'm just teasing. I'd never spirit you away from here.'

'I wouldn't let you.' She laughed.

They were married the following May, not in church as the MacMillans would have preferred, as Alistair MacMillan was an

elder at Carsphairn Parish Church and Anne was in the choir, nor
with the lavish display that Billy Thompson had imagined for his
only daughter. Instead there was a simple civil service in the
rather severe red sandstone Ayr County Building at the sea end of
Wellington Square. Jean wore an oyster-coloured silk off-the-
shoulder dress cinched tightly at the waist and a matching short
jacket. Her hair was curled and held back on both sides by silk-
covered clasps sewn, by Edith, with seed pearls, and she carried a
posy of peonies fresh from the garden. To Walter she looked like
a goddess. For his part he had ordered a dark grey worsted suit
from Orr's, and Edith had also made a peony corsage for his lapel.
Tommy and Joy were the only witnesses at the Register Office,
and Tommy's new Box Brownie captured the first image of the
newly-weds. Jean had returned her engagement ring to her finger
and the large solitaire sparkled on her hand. It was the photograph that Walter kept by his bed, and he always thought he saw
the flash of the ring, even when times were darker.

The celebrations were to take place at Stoneleigh. Jean
would not have it any other way. She said that she would not
feel married until her mother had seen her, and so the wedding
went to her.

The wedding breakfast was set out in the garden under a
canvas canopy, its edges laced with ivy, and small vases of
peonies studded the white linen tablecloth on the rectangular
table. Alistair and Anne MacMillan had travelled from their
new home in Carsphairn in their Sunday best. They carried a
basket of preserves and a brace of pheasants as a present for the
Thompsons, and had sent the wedding cake ahead with the
carrier. The home-made cake, which took pride of place at the
top of the table, was a single square, iced simply with pink-
tinged fondant roses at the centre, and when Anne MacMillan
arrived she added a sprig of fresh rosemary.

'A love charm.' Edith smiled. 'How thoughtful you are, Mrs MacMillan.' In her own domain Edith proved to be an attentive host. She and Anne toured the garden slowly, stopping every so often so she could take cuttings for Walter's mother to nurture in her new flower-beds.

'It's very generous of you to give Walter and Jean your home,' said Edith.

'We're very glad to do so. It would have been rightfully Walter's one day anyway, and I'm afraid we could not give him money.'

'You've given them more than enough, Mrs MacMillan.'

'Well, it has room enough for when they start a family. Walter was a happy child there.'

Edith took Anne MacMillan's hand. 'And I'm sure when they have children they will be happy there too.'

Walter's father was not one for conversation and Billy Thompson filled in all the spaces with stories that always seemed to come back to some triumph or other. Now Walter had the measure of him, he attempted interventions. First, the news that Frank Sinatra was to perform at the Playhouse in Ayr in two months' time. Walter announced that he had just bought tickets to surprise his new wife. 'Too late, Walter,' boomed Billy Thompson, 'I've bought up the first row of the dress circle so we can all go together.'

Walter was silent for a moment, then he gave his new father-in-law a broad smile. 'Jean and I will be in the front row of the stalls. We'll wave up to you,' he said lightly.

Billy Thompson frowned, but said nothing, and walked away towards to his son, a bottle of champagne in his hand.

'Not someone who likes to be crossed,' said Alistair MacMillan quietly. 'You are going to have to stand your ground.' Walter turned to his father, a gentle-looking big

man, grey at the temples, his old black worsted suit emphasis-
ing his broad shoulders. He was wearing round steel-rimmed
glasses which he took off to wipe with his white handkerchief.
'Now I know why his nickname is Billy Blowhard.'

'You never told me that, Dad,' Walter said, surprised.

A smile played on his father's lips. 'How could I? I've just
made it up.'

'Well,' Walter said, shocked, 'you're a man of few words,
but that certainly makes up for it!'

Alistair MacMillan grinned with quiet pleasure. 'No point
in speaking just for the sake of it, is there?'

Just then they heard a burst of girlish laughter and they
looked over to where Jean and Joy were huddled conspiratorially, champagne in hand. 'I can't quite believe she's my wife,
Dad, she's so beautiful and clever.'

Alistair MacMillan put his solid weather-beaten hand on his
son's shoulder. 'She's the lucky one, Walter, and don't you
forget it.'

Walter thought he heard his father's voice catch. He felt the
weight of his hand, and in it the affirmation of his love.

Tommy arrived beside the two women and took Joy off to
talk to his father, and Walter followed Jean's gaze to her mother
at the other side of the garden. Then he looked back at his new
wife and watched a veil come down over her beautiful face. He
couldn't fathom her look. In that moment, everything he knew
about her vanished. She was somewhere unknown to him,
somewhere he could not reach. She was composed, trance-like
even, her eyes unblinking. The thought came to him that she
could withdraw from him, as her mother had done from the
world, and a small shard of fear pierced his chest.

Despite the intimate nature of the wedding lunch and the
fact that Walter did not have a best man to make a speech,

Billy Thompson insisted on addressing the gathering. As he stood up and tinkled his glass, Walter noticed Edith lowering her head to examine her hands. Billy Thompson cleared his throat and took out his heavily engraved gold fob watch from his waistcoat. It was twice the size of Walter's father's.

'It's three o'clock on my daughter's wedding day, and with a bit of luck High Born Lady will win the Irish 2,000 Guineas at the Curragh shortly and make this an extra special day,' he said with a chortle.

Tommy raised his glass. 'Amen to that,' he slurred, and Walter and his father exchanged a glance.

Billy Thompson went on. 'Edith and I are delighted to welcome Walter into our family. I know that my wife is especially happy that Jean is going to begin married life, just as she did, in the countryside. It is most generous of you, Mr and Mrs MacMillan, to give your home to the newly-weds. We all do what we can for our children, don't we?'

Walter tried hard to concentrate, but he was distracted by Edith. Her face was set, staring ahead to the garden, seemingly unaware of her husband's speech. Eventually he heard his father-in-law's booming voice. 'To the bride and groom!' Edith, blinking suddenly, began to clap and everybody joined in. Then everyone stood and walked to the little table where Jean and Walter cut the cake, to more applause. Jean took a piece to her father and as she handed him the plate Billy Thompson studied his daughter, his eyes unusually melancholic. 'You look just like your mother the day I married her. I hope Walter makes you happier than I've made her.'

Jean spoke to him in a whisper. 'You wanted to give her everything the only way you knew how. It's not your fault that she didn't want it, Daddy, not really.'

Billy Thompson turned away quickly and called out to his son to bring over his cigar cutter.

Walter and Jean were spending two nights at the grand Edwardian railway hotel at Turnberry further down the coast near Girvan. Walter had secretly arranged with Tommy to rent an Austin Healey Sprite convertible from the dealership for the trip, but as they were saying their farewells in the garden, Billy Thompson pulled out a set of keys on a white ribbon from his trouser pocket and flourished them at his daughter. 'If you're going to be living at the ends of the earth, I don't want you relying on the bus,' he said as he pulled open the garden door.

Walter stiffened and looked at his father who opened his eyes wide and raised the palm of his hand almost impercept-ibly, as if to say, stay calm. When they stepped through the door out to the gravel drive, before them was a brand-new cream-coloured Morris Oxford Traveller with an exposed wooden frame at the back and hanging from the rear bumper were old tin cans attached by string.

Jean shrieked with delight. 'Daddy, how wonderful!' She turned to Walter, her eyes glassy and her face flushed with champagne. 'Isn't it marvellous, darling?'

Walter turned around to Billy Thompson and straightened himself up. He extended his hand. 'Thank you very much, Mr Thompson. It really is far too generous.'

Billy Thompson pumped his hand. 'As I said at lunch, I want my daughter to have the best.' He turned and beamed at Jean. 'And would you know it, High Born Lady has just paid for it! That's horsepower for you!' Billy Thompson laughed uproari-ously at his own joke as the others stood around the car, uncer-tain of what to say. Billy Thompson thrust the keys into Walter's hand. 'You should drive the wedding carriage,

Walter. Carry your bride off. I've put another bottle of champagne in the glove compartment.'

As Walter walked obediently round to the driver's seat, discomfited by his new father-in-law's largesse, he glanced back through the open door. Edith was standing framed as if in a portrait, looking at him steadily, a faint smile on her face. He stepped back into the garden swiftly, drawn to the liminal figure, to repeat his farewell. As he shook her hand he thought he saw her turquoise eyes glistening as the sunshine flared for a moment through the trees.

Then she put her hand on his arm and pulled him forward a little, and as he inclined his head she whispered, '*Courage, mon brave*,' in his ear.

PART TWO

The Weight of Water

CHAPTER 6

The day of the Stratton house celebration began unpromisingly with a squall that came in from the Solway Firth and drew a curtain of gauze across the gentle peak of Cairnsmore of Fleet. Carson stood on her bed to open the skylight and craned her neck to see the old Volvo grumbling its way down the track. Then she lifted the window high above her head, and looked up to the sky, allowing the soft smirr to wash her face before she padded downstairs.

'Morning, darling,' said Elinor brightly as she laid out her painting materials on a large tray, each thing exactly in its place: two jars of water, a Daler watercolour palette, a bundle of brushes and sheets of special Fabiano 5 paper and some clean rags. Carson found it funny that her mother was so meticulous about her work when she was so casual about the house, and often careless about her clothes, certainly compared to her aunt. 'Hippy couture' was how Patrick described his wife's style. As Carson grew older it dawned on her that her mother's art was more important to her than almost everything except her daughters and, sometimes, her husband.

'Are you sure you don't mind being on your own? There's plenty of room in the Range Rover,' Carson asked, the answer never in doubt. She watched Elinor shake her head a bit too vigorously.

'No, no, it's fine. I think your aunt wants to take you three on a jaunt.'

Right on cue Fiona opened the door, startling them both. Carson looked at her mother fleetingly to gauge if she too was taking in her aunt's pallor, her sunken eyes and the downward droop of her mouth. When Fiona spotted Carson lounging on the sofa her face brightened suddenly as if a metal shutter had been sprung from its lock. 'Hello, Car, you look so lovely, even in your pyjamas. How did you get to be so grown up?' She enveloped Carson in a hug, just as tightly as when the Strattons had arrived. Carson felt the urgency in the crush of her aunt's arms as if she were trying to hold on to something that would help her feel alive. Carson detected a mix of stale alcohol and mint on her breath. 'We're off to see the sea,' Fiona said as she held Carson in her grasp.

Carson gently extricated herself to get dressed, and Elinor put a mug of black coffee in her sister-in-law's hands and wrapped her own ones around them. 'Here,' she said gently, 'have some of your brother's extra-special brew to kick-start the day.'

By the time Pete had helped Iona up into the back seat of the Range Rover next to Carson the mist had lifted and the sun's rays spilled over the loch. Carson looked back towards the house and watched as her mother carried her precious painting tools to her table in the garden, already too absorbed to say goodbye.

Elinor sat down in her painting chair and sighed as she heard the purr of the engine fade to nothing. She closed her eyes and listened to the gentle swish of the water washing across the stones at the loch's edge, and the short gossipy honks of the mallards racing low along the water. Now she was ready to paint. Nobody was calling on her time, no meals to be made, homework to help with, no child in need of reassurance, no husband asking for a last-minute errand as if she could pick up and drop her paintbrush and it would make no difference. Worst of all were the requests for a free illustration for one good cause after another. 'Could you dash something off?' asked one mother airily at the school gates, as if Elinor were engaged in a hobby. 'People wouldn't ask a doctor for an operation to raffle, would they?' she railed at Patrick. But at the loch, solitary and focused, she was an artist, and even just a single morning of drawing and painting was enough to keep her resentment at bay.

There had been times, especially when Iona was little and fractious, when Elinor would tiptoe down the stairs of the flat soon after dawn and close the front door behind her with practised stealth, when, finally, her baby had given up on battling sleep. She would walk across the square along Pavilion Road and onto the Low Green, speeding up as she neared the beach, and when she reached the deserted expanse of sand she would let out a ragged howl of protest that nobody heard except the seagulls, who rose unusually silent from the sand as if shocked that their thunder had been stolen so spectacularly.

Maybe it was a curse to be an illustrator when so many of her contemporaries were exhibiting in galleries in Berlin, or Boston, or winning commissions for public art that made a 'statement', or triumphing in portraiture awards or Turner prizes. And yet deep inside she knew that she loved what she did: every stroke, every hair on a stem, each tiny knot on a branch, the translucent beauty of a petal, the veining she achieved with a brush the width of the point of a pin. It amounted to more than the anatomy of a plant or a flower. Her passion was in capturing the infinite wonder of botany. She often went through these same thoughts as she walked alone along the shore, her hands deep in her pockets, her woollen scarf wound round and round her neck, and then she would turn for home, reinvigorated, her mood reset, her hair whipping across her raw face and her boots covered in sand, a bag of still warm morning rolls in her hand, calmly ready to prepare for the day.

Fiona sped through Dalmellington and swung the four-wheel drive onto the high road to Girvan, up the steep hill past Grimmet Farm onto the moor and over the cattle grid. The rumble and clank of the metal bars beneath the wheels was Pete's cue. 'Okay, Mum. There's no traffic up here. Let me have a shot.'

Carson noticed her aunt's knuckles turn white and sharp as she gripped the steering wheel. 'No, Petey,' she said emphatically. 'Apart from anything else – like you're only sixteen . . . And just . . . – your cousins are in the back, or hadn't you noticed?'

He banged his hand on the armrest. 'For God's sake. Dad would let me drive.'

'Taking the old Saab along the loch at ten miles an hour is completely different.'

Peter turned slowly and deliberately towards Fiona, and Carson saw a snarl form on his mouth. 'I'm as safe a driver as you. At least I don't drink and drive.' His voice rose. 'You're still pissed!' he spat out.

Suddenly Carson and Iona were thrown forward against their seat belts as Fiona slammed on the brakes and cut the engine.

'Get the fuck out!' Fiona screamed as she pushed her hand against Pete's shoulder. 'Don't you dare talk to me like that.' She shoved him again. 'Get out *now*! You can walk home.'

Carson felt Iona's hand find hers across the back seat.

Carson squeezed it and motioned to her to close her lips tightly.

'What are you waiting for, Pete?' their aunt barked.

Pete pressed his back against the seat and stared straight ahead. Carson could see a crimson flush spreading over his cheek and travelling down his neck.

'Well, aren't you getting out?'

Carson's eyes smarted as she heard the mixture of hurt and dismay in her aunt's voice.

A motorbike roared past with an exaggerated swerve and the pillion passenger turned and gave them a prolonged V-sign. They sat in silence listening as the throaty sound of the bike spilled over the moor.

Still Pete did not move and then a small hiccupping sound erupted and Iona, unable to control herself any longer, burst into tears.

Fiona swivelled round and put her hand on Iona's leg. 'It's okay, sweetheart.'

'Okay, I'm sorry,' Pete broke in, his voice strained and hoarse.

'Are you, Pete? Are you really?' Fiona's voice was trembling.

Pete nodded and glanced at his mother and in that fleeting look Carson saw nothing but unhappiness.

Fiona started up the engine and the car moved forward tentatively as though like the passengers it was slowly recovering from the shock of the outburst. As they drove through the village of Straiton and on to the verdant stretch to the coast, Iona spotted the great granite cone of Ailsa Craig on the horizon almost hovering above the water. 'Look, Paddy's Milestone!' she yelled.

Fiona nodded and glanced at her niece in her rear-view mirror. 'Granddad's taught you well, Iona.' She laughed, and with that the air had cleared.

Ten minutes later the cousins walked together from the car park at the harbour to the Gelateria Italiana, while Fiona headed for the butcher and then to collect prawns straight from one of the fishing boats.

Iona slipped her hand into Pete's and gave him a worried look. 'Are you better now, Pete?'

Her cousin shrugged. 'She drinks too much. It's embarrassing. I don't really care about the driving thing. I can always drive with Dad.' Carson heard the sad bravado in his voice.

'But Aunt Fiona's not drunk now. Is she?' Iona persisted.

Pete laughed bitterly. 'No, but she will be topping up tonight.' He gave Carson a look as if to say, you understand this, don't you? 'And then that will give Dad the opportunity to weigh in.' Pete pushed his hair back from his forehead and sighed. 'Anyway, who cares, Iona? It's ice-cream time.'

They stood at the glass ice-cream counter studying the array of tubs of every colour in front of them. 'You choose,' he said, nudging Iona, his mood lighter now, the weight shared among the three of them, even his younger cousin. Iona put her hands on her hips and bit her lip.

'Granddad likes toffee fudge,' said Carson.

'No, Car,' said her sister emphatically, 'he likes mint and chocolate chip.'

'For Chrissakes, don't you two start,' Pete teased.

'Here you,' said the matronly Italian owner, slapping her spatula down on the counter, 'less of the bad language.'

Iona giggled, and Maria gave her a hard stare.

'I'm having quite a day, aren't I?' Pete said to Carson out of the side of his mouth and she burst out laughing.

'I know what,' he said to Iona, flourishing two twenty-pound notes, 'let's go crazy and get a tub of every flavour.'

'Really, Pete?' Iona said, wide-eyed.

'Why not? It's a party.'

Fiona was waiting for them by the car, beside two orange lifeboats tied together against the harbour wall. Three men in yellow waterproofs were scrubbing the decks and their raucous laughter echoed around the lagoon.

'Look, aren't the new lifeboats snazzy? What would your great-great-great-grandfather have made of them?'

'They look like giant plastic bath toys,' said Iona.

'Shh, Iona,' whispered Carson, 'that's rude.' She glanced at the men. 'They don't get paid for it.'

'What do they do – for work, I mean?' asked Pete.

'Everything,' said Fiona. 'Years ago there was even smuggling.'

'Granddad took me to the smugglers' caves at Culzean,' said Carson.

'Did you dress up?' sniggered Pete.

Carson stuck up her middle finger in his face.

'Nice,' he said, raising his eyebrows.

Soon after they left Girvan, Fiona swung the car onto a broken-down track, straight past a tattered wooden sign with 'Private' scrawled across it in flaking paint.

'Oh no,' groaned Pete. 'Really? Again?'

Carson realised this was what her mother had meant when she said her aunt had planned 'a jaunt'.

'We're here because Robert Adam was a genius and it's a masterpiece. Who knows when it will fall down completely?'

'You said that before,' said Pete sarcastically, 'and it didn't.'

Carson looked out at the towering castellated building. It was strangely familiar, like a negative image of Culzean Castle, its roof gone and its windows like rows of empty hollowed-out eyes. It had a ghostly look as if it were yearning for all the people to return. Frenzied swifts, startled by the intruders, looped through the huge rectangular voids.

'It's very beautiful, Aunt Fiona,' Carson said, anxious to show her appreciation.

'Welcome to the Addams family home,' Pete muttered.

'I don't like this place,' Iona whispered, tugging at her sister, her eyes pleading. 'I don't want to go inside. It's scary.'

'Don't be such a baby,' said Carson scornfully. 'Do you want to be left behind?'

Iona shook her head, her eyes welling up. 'No, Car. Please don't.'

As they made their way gingerly on their hands and knees through some torn chicken wire, hundreds of crows screeched out of the bastion tower and swooped in front of them, turning the air black. Iona screamed as she felt the wind from their wings flapping over her head. 'Car, please,' she cried out as she fell to the rubble, 'get them away from me!'

Carson quickly helped her up and put her arm round her. 'You're safe with me,' she said guiltily, 'hold my hand.'

'You won't leave me behind?'

'Iona! I'd never do that!' Carson grasped her sister's hand as they walked on through a doorway into the hollow heart of the grand house.

They were surrounded by a swirling cantilevered staircase that wound round and round up to a perfect circle open to the sky where once, Fiona said, there had been an ornate cupola. 'It looks as if it might rise all the way to the clouds, doesn't it?' said Fiona, looking heavenward. Pieces of plaster still clung to cornices as if to keep alive the memory of salons and grand parties. There were yawning mouths where fires had once blazed and, beneath their feet, fallen rafters and broken flagstones where ferns of cow parsley created patterns in the cracks.

'Everything has gone,' said Pete, his tone awed now. He looked at a bell-pull hanging off a piece of lathe as if still waiting to be rung to summon a maid or a butler. 'Where have all the mantelpieces gone?' he asked.

'You'd be surprised. Some of them aren't so very far away,' Fiona replied.

'What do you mean?'

'There are farmhouses all around here with Adam fireplaces.'

'They won't have a clue,' he said scornfully.

'You're wrong,' replied Fiona, smiling fondly at her son, 'people know exactly what they've got – and there are a few Kennedys among them. Anyway, better that than they lie smashed up in here.'

As they turned to go Fiona stopped and put her hand flat on a wall and held it there for a moment. They all looked at her silently. 'We're good to go,' she said brightly and hooked her arm through Carson's.

As they returned to the car, Pete loped ahead with Iona on his shoulders, her hands clamped to his shock of dark brown hair, his hands holding her ankles safely against his chest. Fiona walked in step with her older niece. 'The last time I was here, at Dalqhuarran, I mean, I was with Meg. It seems ages since I've seen her. I missed her the last few times I was in New York. How is she?'

Carson was startled by the unexpected mention of her mother's sister. 'I don't really know,' she replied. 'I don't think Mum hears from her very often; or maybe it's the other way around. She's so far away.'

'It's such a shame,' mused Fiona, 'when there're just the two of them.'

Carson had a hazy memory of sitting squeezed between Elinor and Meg on a bench on the esplanade at Ayr, when she was three or four, feeling safe in the soft warmth of their bodies, each of them holding one of Carson's small hands in theirs. But she had no recollection of any words spoken. But there was another more vivid image.

Carson had woken early on her tenth birthday.

'Rise and shine,' she heard Elinor calling as she pulled back the curtains, 'it's your one-oh day. You're my double-digit birthday girl.'

Carson rubbed her eyes and looked up to see Elinor by the bed, a breakfast tray in her hands.

'It's your favourite: Nutella and banana sandwiches and a raspberry milkshake.'

She pushed herself up against the pillow and looked at the tray. There were colourful squiggles on a white paper napkin and a pink rose in a teacup in a tiny puddle of water.

'Iona has done the decorations with her own fair hand,' said Elinor, smiling.

At that moment Patrick appeared with a bunch of balloons tied together and at his side Iona was holding a box which she had wrapped herself and covered with bits of Sellotape. She thrust it at Carson. 'Open it now, please, Car.' Inside some loose Maltesers rolled around an old plastic watch of Iona's and one of her favourite books, *Messy Baby*.

Carson tried not to laugh. 'Thank you, Iona. It's all lovely.'

Patrick looked at his older daughter fondly and pulled a present from behind his back. It was the Walkman that Carson had coveted. She was the last girl in the class without one, but not now.

She hugged her parents excitedly. 'This is the best present I have ever had.'

Then Elinor quietly produced another package festooned with American postage stamps. Inside was a hand-drawn three-dimensional card with a picture of the Empire State Building. Carson's name was emblazoned in neon pink on the parapet and round it ten glittering candles. Also inside was a special lavishly illustrated hardback edition of *Little House on the Prairie* inscribed with the words, 'To dear Carson, from your fairy godmother on your tenth birthday. Love and kisses, Aunt Meg.'

As she read the message out loud, Elinor smiled sadly. 'That's lovely, Car; something to treasure.'

'Will we see Aunt Meg soon?' Carson had asked.

Elinor shook her head slowly. 'One day. Your aunt has few holidays and not much money; and we don't have the money either. I should write more often though,' she added wistfully.

'I'll write her a thank-you letter.' And that was the pattern on subsequent birthdays. Beautiful packages arrived on cue and Carson stored their treasures, wondering if Aunt Meg would ever come back.

Fiona reached the car, still waiting for Carson to divulge a detail or two, but none was forthcoming. She had been in New York often enough when she and Roland had some client meeting or other in the city, but in the endless go-round of gallery openings, dinners and weekend heli-copter trips for brunch in the Hamptons there had never seemed to be the right moment to call Meg. When, she wondered, had she become the person who fitted into Roland's life, attached to his arm so carelessly that he hardly remembered she was there? When did she settle for Roland sleeping beside her in bed, when she could have had Robert Adam in her head? What would Meg make of her now, Meg with her caustic wit and her conversation that fizzed with a New York energy?

As soon as the car came to a halt outside the Stratton house, Carson jumped out and headed through the garden gate between the two houses to her mother's painting spot. Elinor was sitting with her eyes closed and her face up to the sun. She crushed her cheek against her mother's soft warm one. 'I missed you, Mum.'

'Whoa – what's brought this on?'

'Nothing.'

Elinor squinted up at her daughter. 'Come on, spill.'

'Pete and Aunt Fiona had a fight about driving. But it was really about her drinking.'

Elinor puckered her lips. 'Hmm. You okay? How's Iona?'

Carson shrugged. 'She's fine. As long as she's glued to Pete nothing can go wrong.'

'Good,' replied her mother distractedly, turning to the illustration on the table. 'What do you make of my sundew? Or, to give it its Sunday name, my *Drosera rotundifolia*?'

Carson peered down at the watercolour secured to the table with a pebble at each corner. 'It's beautiful – for a killer.'

Elinor laughed. 'Okay, find me purple saxifrage next. It's harmless.'

Carson studied the illustration. 'I like the way you've drawn those spiky pink hairs, and the bright yellow you've used for the centre.' Tiny brushstrokes created the effect of shimmering sticky resin on the reddish-pink fronds. Carson's eye travelled to a sheet of paper covered with individual watercolour drawings of all the elements of the bog plant. 'I always like your workings just as much,' she said as she lifted the page to look more closely. 'Can I keep it?'

Elinor nodded. Carson had always treasured her drawings, and it made Elinor happy to have something so special between them. 'Of course. You are my specimen hunter after all.'

Carson put the watercolour away carefully in the pink pais-ley-patterned cardboard box that she kept on a shelf in the cabin. It was the repository of myriad keepsakes: a letter from Santa apologising for not giving her the puppy she had asked for, a matchbox containing her first tooth, and a photograph of her holding Iona when she was new born, smiling with all her might for the camera. As she closed the box she heard the unmistakable braying and boasting noises that emitted from Patrick and Roland when they returned from their occasional games of golf.

'I haven't seen you putt better on the eighth, Roland. That green's a real bastard,' she heard her father say.

Carson grimaced to herself and when she went outside saw the two men were sitting side by side at the water's edge, coffee in hand. She tried to slip behind them unnoticed but Patrick caught sight of her.

'Hey, Car, not so fast. Come and give us the benefit of your conversation.'

Carson pulled a horrified face for her father to see. 'Thanks, but no thanks. I'm going to help Aunt Fiona.'

'Ah, what a perfect child,' Patrick called after her.

Ignoring him, she walked up the grass towards the Stratton house but when she glanced up at the balcony she saw Fiona standing motionless behind the glass, looking out at the water. The way the light hit the window it was as if she were trapped inside the glass itself, a beautiful ghost. All at once, Carson's excitement about the evening ahead evaporated, and in its place she only felt dread. Unseen by her aunt, she quickly skirted round the back of both houses to avoid Patrick and Roland and then made her way down to the jetty.

She found Walter sitting on an old camping stool on the wooden pier, his capacious fishing bag at his feet, peering into a battered tobacco tin lined with foam and thick with his favourite fishing flies stuck by their hooks. Carson had often sat with her grandfather at his kitchen table as he bent over his fly vice, surrounded by bundles of feathers: starling, mallard, golden pheasant and sometimes hare's ear. She knew all their names before she was ten. His instruments were set out on a white cloth: gold-tipped scissors, hackle pliers, a bobbin holder, tweezers, clear nail varnish. He moved his mottled calloused hands with the precision of a surgeon, delicately winding black silk thread around a hook shank, over and over, moving the thread up the metal almost imperceptibly. 'A fly has got to be a thing of beauty,' he would say to her as he deftly created a flash of iridescent green, or a sparkle of gold, or a pinprick of yellow. Other anglers came to him for advice about rods and reels, or the best fly for the day. Sometimes they wheedled one or two from him, but he never minded, not at all. Often, he would find a brown trout or a lovely rainbow in a bag hanging from the knob on his back door. He fished all over Galloway, from the west bank of Carsfad, or the tree-fringed Drumlanford Loch where he had reeled in a three-pound rainbow trout with a Silver Butcher that spring. Some evenings he would head to the narrow sliver of water at Loch Kendoon to send a shimmering Teal and Black dancing coquettishly through the air and land it gracefully on the water.

Carson skiffed her feet along the jetty, sending the newly varnished boat bobbing up and down on its mooring as if in a frenzy of excitement.

'What a racket, Carson. And how can I put flies on your line for tomorrow when the jetty is jumping up and down?'

'Sorry,' she said sheepishly. 'Where are the others?'

'They'll be back any time now. Pete's gone to get his new rod, and Iona's gone too – of course.' He chuckled. 'You don't mind sharing the dapping rod with your sister, do you? I've decided two rods will be enough, less chance of getting fankled up.' He looked up at her from under the brim of his fore and aft, waiting for the correct answer.

Carson shrugged. 'Okay,' she said with the trace of a pout.

'Good girl. We'll have a day on the loch soon. The two of us.'

Just then Carson heard the sound of shrieking and giggling from afar and felt a stab of irritation when she saw Iona clinging to Pete's back as he zigzagged across the grass, pretending to try to dislodge her, his new rod quivering in the air like a spear. He let her down gently and presented the rod to Walter for inspection.

'Well, son, it's a fine one. A Hardy too.'

'It's a graphite deluxe.'

'Is it now!' His grandfather smiled. 'Well, I better give you two of my best flies then.' He handed Pete a pretty Teal and Yellow for the dropper, and for the point fly, a Black Pennell. 'If they don't dazzle a trout, I don't know what will,' he said, looking approvingly at his grandson as Pete knotted them perfectly to his cast.

Carson stashed a fishing net beneath the stern along with a zinc bucket for the catch, and Pete fitted the oars into the rowlocks. Then Walter helped them fasten both rods into the clips along the sides of the boat.

'Have you checked tomorrow's forecast, Pete?'

'Yup, just like you asked me to,' replied Pete eagerly. 'It's going to be a fine day. Not too sunny and not too much of a breeze. Just enough to create a bit of movement on the water.'

'Good stuff. Now remember, don't go far from shore and favour the west bank. Stay in sight of the jetty, and drift down towards the castle. That's your best bet. Got that now?' Pete nodded. 'And put Iona on a bench at the bow. You row.'

'Can't Carson row?' Pete glanced at his cousin.

'Hmm. Only in the shallows. Remember, you're in charge of the boat. I'm trusting you.'

Pete squared his shoulders, pushed his hair back from his brow and gave Walter the thumbs up.

The afternoon in the Stratton house passed in a flurry of preparation designed, Carson sensed, to keep tensions, and even conversations, at bay. Fiona cooked and iced the prawns. Elinor, one eye on her sister-in-law and the wine glass by her elbow, tied the racks of lamb in two circles and made an apricot and couscous stuffing for their centres. Then she and Iona cut up white paper to fashion little crowns to decorate their tops.

Carson helped her aunt unpack a crate of china she had ordered from Denmark specially for the occasion. She noticed Fiona's trembling hands, and listened anxiously as she clattered the plates together, as if oblivious to the danger. 'I'll finish emptying the box, Aunt Fiona,' she said lightly, catching her mother's worried frown.

'Thanks, sweetheart, but I'm fine.' Fiona drew her lips back into a grimace of a smile. 'Really, I'm fine.' A few minutes later when the final plate had been stacked on the counter, Fiona rummaged around a big shopping bag and produced a box of gaudy glass lanterns and some candles. 'I got these in the Pound Shop,' she whispered to Carson, a smirk on her face. 'Be a darling and set them out on the balcony. Roland will have a seizure, but he won't say anything to you.'

Roland was too busy constructing a long ash dining room table to notice. He had insisted that he and Patrick wear gloves, but that was making it hard for Patrick to screw on the legs. 'Steady, old man, it's not from Ikea you know,' Roland said testily.

'Roland, if it was from that well-known Swedish store, it would be a lot easier, believe me,' Patrick retorted.

Finally, they flipped the table over and Roland spent what seemed to his brother-in-law like an eternity positioning it and then inching chairs this way and that around it. Next he set down a modern expensive decanter at each end of the table filled, he announced with great fanfare, with Château Lafite Rothschild. 'They rather set off the pale ash, don't they?' he said to Patrick, hands on his hips.

'Hark at Martha Stewart,' Fiona said to Elinor out of the side of her mouth. 'Next thing you know he'll be collecting jelly moulds and taking up quilting.' She turned to look at her husband at the other side of the huge room. 'Well done, Roland, I really don't think I could have done it better myself. Perfectly executed as usual.'

Carson caught her aunt's razor-edged tone as she walked in from the balcony. Fiona looked from Elinor to her niece and smiled sweetly. 'You'd never know I chose that bloody table.'

Three hours later as the family assembled for the party, the late May evening air was soft and patterned with insects as if they too were congregating for the celebration. A pair of kites swooped in front of the house, shards of red and chestnut, their forked tails sharp against the lilac sky. Fiona and Patrick watched their display from the balcony. 'I do love this place; there's a different show every day!'

Fiona smiled. 'London feels a million miles away.'

Patrick took the cigarette proffered by his sister from a soft turquoise packet and inclined towards her as she flicked on her lighter. 'To keep the midges at bay. Just to be clear.' He inhaled the toasted smoke deeply. 'Ah, American Spirit. If you're going to smoke, this is the cigarette for me.' He sighed as he sent smoke rings spinning over the newly planted garden below. They clinked glasses of large vodka tonics and leaned over the edge of the balcony. Patrick gave his sister an affectionate nudge. 'Dad's very excited about the house. It's like it's the start of something new.'

Fiona took a long drag of her cigarette. 'He's right. It is. I don't really care what Roland does. I'm going to come here as much as I can. Pete too, I hope. Dad's a good influence.'

Patrick scrutinised his sister for a moment. Sometimes the way she jutted her chin, the arch of her eyebrows, brought a long-ago memory of their mother flooding into his heart. 'Are you okay? Is there something going on? I mean between you and Roland, something different?'

Fiona screwed her mouth into a mordant smile. 'Well, there's something going on between Roland and someone just young enough to be my daughter.' She drained her glass and gave her brother a swift peck on the cheek. 'Don't worry, big brother. I'll handle it.'

'Okay' – he tapped her glass – 'but go easy.' He took her lighter and bent down to light the lanterns, sending a series of jewel-coloured motes dancing along the balcony as the sky turned a rich purple.

The sound of a cork popping was the cue for the party to begin. Everybody had dressed up for the occasion. Iona's hair was newly washed and two sparkly pink clasps held her dark curls back from her face. She wore a blue and white stripy top and a denim skirt and a chunky necklace that she had eyed up in Elinor's jewellery box. Carson had chosen a short floral drop-waisted dress which accentuated her slender frame and new black patent chunky sandals. She had applied mascara carefully at the bathroom mirror, fending off her sister's repeated demand for some, finally pushing her protesting out of the door; she finished with some lip gloss. Elinor was dressed in a new red corduroy shift with embroidery on the collar and on the patch pockets, along with new felt clogs that she had ordered from a Swedish catalogue especially for the party.

'Well, will you look at my girls,' Patrick exclaimed, draining his glass, and bowing extravagantly in front of them in his new blue linen shirt.

'And my handsome boy!' Fiona grabbed Pete by the arm as he walked past her chair and, pulling him down, buried her nose in his unruly thatch of hair. 'Like warm toast,' she said effusively.

Pete frowned and disentangled himself hastily. He smoothed down his T-shirt then thrust his hands into his drainpipe jeans. 'Do we get champagne too?' he asked gruffly.

'Of course,' said Roland, 'and once you've charged your glasses I'll say a few words.'

Pete let out a groan, and Walter immediately put his hand on his grandson's shoulder and gave it a warning squeeze. Roland poured two glasses, put a splash in a third for Iona and finally topped up everyone's glasses except Walter's who was driving home later. Then he stood with his back to the vivid Sean Scully canvas, its luminous red and black and orange rectangles juxtaposed to create a spectacular backdrop, just as he had planned.

'I don't think I have ever thanked you properly, Walter, for giving Fiona the gift of the cabin and the land.' Walter gave his son-in-law a short nod and raised his glass in his direction. 'It has given me, or I should say us, the opportunity to design something on quite a different scale to the buildings for which I am best known.'

Carson thought there was something strange about her uncle's gaze and realised he was addressing an invisible audience above her head, as if he had just accepted an award.

'Though I feel an undeniable connection with Thoreau's Cabin on the Lake in principle, in practice, well . . . this is a much more pleasing structure, and of course environmentally advanced, which, naturally, Thoreau would have thoroughly approved of.' Elinor gave Patrick a look from their private lexicon of expressions. She banged her wine glass down on the table noisily while Roland removed a piece of fluff from the sleeve of his black velvet jacket that was offending his eye and sailed on. 'I imagine there might be quite a few people who will come to see it' – he paused, and his mouth twitched in a smile – 'because I can reveal it has already been shortlisted for the Saltire Society's Best New Home award.' Walter and Patrick started clapping but Roland waved them away. 'But enough of that now. Please raise a glass to our new house on the loch. Formally known as the Stratton House.'

'House not home, you'll notice,' Elinor whispered to Patrick a few minutes later as she put a plate of prawns encircled in smoked salmon in front of her husband.

Walter sat at one end of the long table opposite his son-in-law, sipping his water, quieter than usual, his eyes straying to Fiona's eternally half-full wine glass every so often, a tight feeling in the back of his neck as if someone were crushing his vertebrae into pieces. He was suddenly aware of Roland's voice.

'One day you'll design something like this, Pete. Pete? Are you listening?'

'It's not going to happen,' Pete said firmly. 'I'm crap at maths. You know that, or do you and Mum never actually listen to me?'

Carson looked at her cousin's anguished face and thought she could see a little lost boy, his misery plain to see.

'Petey, darling, this is not the night,' said Fiona plaintively as she scraped back her chair and clattered unsteadily across the floor to retrieve another bottle of wine from the fridge.

Eventually Walter, who was looking pensively at his grandson, put his hand on his neck and rubbed it hard and shifted in his chair. 'It's not the end of the world, Pete. If you really want to be an architect, we'll get you there with your maths. But if you don't, there will be something else for you.'

'Now now, Walter, please don't discourage him,' Roland admonished his father-in-law as he strolled the length of the table, decanter in hand. 'He just needs to put in some more bloody effort.'

Carson watched as the muscles in Pete's jaw tensed, his eyes glittering. He caught her stare and glowered at her. She stood up hastily and, to Iona's annoyance, started helping her settle the paper crowns on the roast lamb. When Iona shoved her away she picked up the potato gratin and carried it to the table, avoiding looking in her cousin's direction.

Just as Patrick rose to toast the chefs, Fiona cut across her brother, oblivious. 'I'm so happy when I go to Dalqhuarran,' she slurred. 'I'd like to sleep in the drawing room under the stars.'

'Maybe you should lie down now,' Roland broke in coolly.

Fiona waved her fork at him. 'Don't be so patronising, darling, not in company, pretty please; save it for when we're alone.' She stretched out for the decanter and filled her glass sitting alongside her glass of white wine.

The only break in the silence was the soft knocking of the new bird box Walter had brought and hung against the corner of the balcony as it shuddered in the evening breeze. Finally,

Walter could stand the sound no longer as it clattered through his skull. He cleared his throat and tapped the table. 'Iona, I was over by Knockower the other evening and do you know what I saw?'

Iona shook her head. 'No, Granddad,' she replied in a small voice, her eyes darting around the table, sensing she was a decoy. 'What was it?'

'It was a mountain hare. She had lovely tawny ears that stood up straight and I could see tufts of her white winter coat.' He smiled at his granddaughter. 'She was a real beauty.'

'Wasn't she scared? Didn't she run away?'

'Not at all,' replied Walter, warming to his story. 'She was watching me watching her. She had bright orangey-brown eyes, and she was as close as Uncle Roland is to me. It was as if she knew me.'

Iona's eyes were wide. 'Really, she knew you? Was she like the hare in the story? The one you used to read to me?' She knitted her brows. 'I know. It was called "Guess How Much I Love You".'

'The very one!' exclaimed Walter.

The whole house seemed to relax. The glass became less sharp, the wooden floor softer and the candlelight warmer.

'Of course, she might have been a white witch,' Walter started again.

A look of panic crossed Iona's face.

'Dad, please,' Patrick pleaded, rolling his eyes at Elinor.

'I'm only kidding, Iona.' Walter chuckled. 'It's just a fairy tale. Long ago, people in these parts used to think hares were witches.'

'Tell me about it, Granddad,' ordered Iona.

'It's too late tonight,' Elinor interjected, her voice slurring a little. 'Maybe tomorrow. And when you're older I'll read you my favourite story about a girl called Prue Sarn who is born with a hare-lip after a hare crosses her mother's path.'

'You read it to me,' Carson said quickly. She turned to her sister. 'I'll read it to you if you like.'

Iona shook her head firmly. 'I want Mum to do it.'

Walter looked at his children and wondered if they remembered that it was he, and not Jean, who read bedtime stories. He recited them like an incantation. He thought a story could soothe away pain, and sometimes he would carry on reading aloud long after they had fallen asleep in the twin beds. Then he would sometimes carry Fiona back through to her own little bedroom. Suddenly a memory crowded in and the party receded to a quiet buzz in his head. He had laid Fiona down gently on her own bed. Her head was on the pillow, her fair hair tousled, long pale lashes sweeping her cheeks, but as he stood up to go she mewled like a lamb, and he sat back down and read some more. He knew she was listening to his lilting voice, fighting sleep, but when, at last, she had given in, he could not release his hand from hers. Even in sleep she held fast to his fingers as if she thought he might get up and leave her that night and never come back.

'Are you okay, Granddad?' He heard Carson at his shoulder.

'Of course, Car,' he replied, forcing himself back to the present. 'I was just daydreaming.'

She set down a three-tiered chocolate cake with flowers made from candied peel which sat on a tray surrounded by small circular tubs of ice cream. 'Mum and Aunt Fiona made Granny Jean's cake, especially for you.'

He looked up at his granddaughter, and Carson saw a flicker of sadness behind his eyes. 'Goodness, isn't that a cake! And do you know it was Great-Grandma Edith's recipe. She made it

for special occasions.' Walter's voice wavered. 'She made it
when Patrick was born, and Fiona too.'

'Well,' said Roland, opening a bottle of vintage Armagnac
and pouring some into balloon glasses on a tray, 'I think this
certainly qualifies as a special occasion. It's not often I get to
have dinner in one of my buildings.'

Fiona suddenly snorted with laughter and banged her hands
on the table. 'For God's sake, Roland, give it a rest.' Her words
all slid together. 'You're not fucking Frank Lloyd Wright.'

Carson held her breath and looked at the mixture of shock
and fascination on Iona's face. Elinor, trying desperately to
keep a straight face, put a slice of cake down in front of her
younger daughter.

'Your Aunt Fiona bakes like a goddess, Iona, like a goddess.'

Roland gave his wife a mirthless smile. 'It's a pity you don't
behave like one, darling, isn't it,' he said, and swallowed a long
draught of brandy.

'Steady the buffs, Roland!' Patrick said woozily.

Roland put his palms up in front of him. 'Just my little joke.
Fiona is truly an angel.'

At that moment Walter rose from the table. 'Time for me
to go if I am going to get to my bed before the witching
hour.' He gave Iona a reassuring smile. 'Sorry, Iona, I mean
midnight.'

Carson saw a look pass between her mother and father.
Elinor's eyebrows seemed to have risen permanently over the
course of the night, she thought.

Walter put his hand on Pete's shoulder. 'If you're on the
loch around nine tomorrow morning there should be plenty of
rises.'

Pete felt his grandfather's hand drawing out the rancour
coursing through him, and he felt steadier, calmer, ready to

slough off the discordant air of the evening for the pure excitement of the morning ahead.

The older two cousins took their cue to leave from Walter, sensing he was a restraining influence on their parents, still seated at the table groaning with wine and brandy. Carson tempted Iona away with the promise that she could share her bed. Sometimes Carson felt the gap between them was far greater than six years, but at others it was a relief to feel Iona's foot against her stomach or hear her soft breaths escaping through her puckered lips and listen to muttered fragments of her unfathomable dreams.

It was decided there and then that Pete, Carson and Iona would wake at eight, the parents would wave them off at nine, and watch from the shore and the balcony. Patrick was charged with making ready the primus stove, frying pan, butter and oatmeal and setting it all on the shingle beside the jetty so that they could eat their catch straight away. The fact of which was in no doubt to the young anglers.

Before they went to bed the three were called upon to make the rounds of the table. Iona announced that she wanted to kiss Patrick's eyelids. 'Hurry up,' said Patrick, waiting for the second kiss, 'for some reason the room is a bit off kilter.'

Carson shook her head in scorn, and just then, to her wincing embarrassment, Roland aimed a kiss at her cheek that landed somewhere in her hair. She quickly ducked away from him, calling out her goodnights, and she took Iona's hand as they walked across the grass and through the gate to their cabin, their path illuminated by the thin sliver of a silver moon.

As they entered the cabin Iona kicked off her shoes. She looked at Carson earnestly. 'Do you like the new house, Car?' She looked around the cabin. 'It makes ours look very messy and' – she searched for the word – 'old.'

'I like all our old stuff,' Carson replied emphatically. 'It's just the way we are. We're different.'

Iona thought about that for a minute. 'And Mummy and Daddy don't fight,' she ventured, searching her sister's face for reassurance. Carson smiled at her fondly. 'Well, not like Uncle Roland and Aunt Fiona anyway.'

Upstairs, Iona unplugged her nightlight and took it into Carson's room. 'You don't mind the light, do you, Car? It used to be yours anyway.'

Carson shook her head. Iona still had two bedtime rituals. She tucked her teddy bear in beside her very tightly and she switched on her merry-go-round nightlight, sending silent shadow dancers pirouetting around the walls. Routine completed, she was asleep within seconds, one arm thrown towards her sister as if she were trying to reach her. Carson studied her face in repose, patterned by the moving light. Her skin was sallow and as smooth as a peach, the faint freckles on her cheeks accentuating her childlike appearance. Her chin was almost pointed and she reminded Carson of Tinkerbell in *Peter Pan*. Carson stretched over her and put out the light and, in the dark, her hearing tuned to a different frequency.

At first she heard the scraitching ee-ee-ee of a barn owl and imagined its slow-blinking yellow eyes trained on a darting shrew as it sped through the bracken to the safety of its nest under a rock. Then she picked up the distant static sound of a familiar voice, and she realised it was Bob Dylan, sounding as if he were playing a concert far out on the loch. Carson knew every word of *Blood on the Tracks*, and as she listened out for each song she became more aware of the laughter and the bellowed drunken conversation that accompanied it. Then, as if she'd flicked on to a different radio station, she suddenly heard Fiona's voice begin to crescendo and, at its screeching climax, a glass shattering on the floor. Carson raised herself on her elbows, her heart knocking against her ribs, and strained to hear what was being said. She made out Roland commanding Fiona to calm down, but the next sentence was drowned out by Patrick singing along to 'Jack of Hearts'.

Carson slept fitfully until she was woken abruptly by two voices coming closer. Irritated now, she put a pillow over her head to blot out the cacophony of incoherent chatter and uncertain footsteps as Patrick and Elinor shuffled and stumbled around the cabin for a few minutes. They kicked off their shoes as if they were firing them at the walls, and sent water gushing out of the tap into glasses that they would never drink, before there was a sudden, utter silence. By then night had given way to pale dawn light that crept in around the sides of the blind, and as Carson finally drifted into a dreamless sleep she heard a sweet clicking sound as a nightjar called to her mate.

CHAPTER 7

When Walter left the party, he started towards his car but then stopped, turned and, thrusting his hands in his pockets against the midnight chill, walked to the edge of the loch. Standing on the shingle, he stared back up at the house and thought how strange it looked, like a box of flickering light under a dark blue dome. The coloured lanterns on the balcony lent an air of magic, and all the people he loved most were safely inside. Yet he could not help but think of his daughter's self-loathing that curdled the air in the room, and the darkness that clouded Pete's eyes.

He turned and stared at the deep black loch, illuminated now and again by the sparks of the stars that seemed to be falling onto the surface of the water, and tried to banish the unease that spread through his chest. He breathed deeply and pulled the collar of his jacket shut, and remembered a day not long after he and Jean were married.

They were on the boat, drifting by Grapple Bay where the Carrick Water meets the loch. The day was overcast but warm, close even, as if thunder were lurking in wait behind the hills. Walter pulled back his rod smoothly and let the fly line travel between the thumb and forefinger of his right hand. Then, with a languid flick of his wrist he cast the line out to land as lightly as a feather on the water.

'You do that so beautifully, Walter. I swear that rod is part of your arm.' He half turned towards Jean, shy suddenly that she had been studying him. She stretched out and rested the palm of her hand on the back of his neck, holding him until he secured his rod and moved to face her. 'That's better, now I can look at you properly.' She smiled. Her wavy hair hung loose around her shoulders, one side caught in a slide, and her cotton skirt creased around her bare brown legs. She leaned in to him. 'You always look so serious when you are fishing, Walter. You never take your eyes off the cast, and I can't get a word out of you.' She pulled the lapels of his jacket towards her and he caught the scent of her perfume on the breeze. She gave him a kiss and then threw her head back and let out a throaty laugh as her skirt slipped up to her thigh. 'Sometimes I think you'd sooner talk to the fish than to me.' She cupped her hand in the water and began to drench Walter. 'Isn't this meant to be fun?' she said, her voice rising nervily.

'Jean! You're soaking me. Stop it, please.'

Walter's face was splattered with water and his shirt sodden but still Jean kept on flying water at him, until, finally, he caught her wrist. 'Darling, maybe if you fished a little you'd feel the same. You might enjoy it.' He looked at her pleadingly, but she pursed her lips and shook her head vigorously.

'Trying to prise a hook out of a poor fish's mouth is my idea of hell. I'll just try to pretend I'm on a gondola in Venice, imagining the beautiful buildings and bridges and the gondoliers serenading us as we float along the canals.' She looked at him querulously. 'Will we ever go there, Walter?'

'One day, if you want to, darling. We can save for it.'

Suddenly she sat up straight. 'But what if I want to go now? Would you take me?' She threw out the words like a challenge.

Walter was perplexed. 'Well, I could maybe use some savings . . .'

She clapped her hands quickly. 'Don't be silly, Walter. I was only teasing!' Her voice was light again. She opened her bag and took out her monogrammed silver hip flask and poured each of them a gin martini in thimble cups whether Walter wanted one or not. He felt the alcohol hit his throat just as she took his free hand and placed it between her legs.

It was always at this point in the daydream, when he wanted desperately to hold on to the pictures he held of her as gay and playful, that he heard the momentary menace in her voice, and then his mind would slip a gear and other memories would arrive like storm clouds gathering, when she was harder, furtive, closed against the world, and most of all closed against him.

Walter released a long sigh, as though sending his anguish out on a breath across the loch. Then he retrieved his car keys from his pocket. When he reached Carsphairn and turned into the drive he saw that the bedroom curtains were closed and a lamp was lit. He switched off the engine and allowed relief to wash over him that tonight he would not be sleeping alone. He would listen to Marie's slow breathing, the kind that comes with peaceful sleep, and try to synchronise it with his own ragged breath. Despite what she always said, she should have been by his side at the celebration. It had been long enough. She had done more for his family than anyone. As he put his key in the door he resolved that, in the morning, he would finally speak to Patrick and Fiona.

CHAPTER 8

'Wake up, Car, *wake up*,' Iona hissed loudly into her sister's ear.

Carson, startled from her disturbed sleep, flailed at Iona. 'Get out of my face, Iona. Piss off!'

Iona hissed again. 'Pete's here. It's time to get up.'

Carson heaved herself into a sitting position and as Iona released the blind on the Velux, Pete was suddenly visible at the end of the bed. She blinked at him, too surprised to be embarrassed. He raised his hand in shy greeting and she smiled groggily.

'I've got everything ready.' He grinned. 'Even Irn-Bru and Jaffa Cakes and a priest to knock the fish dead.'

'I know what a priest is, for fuck's sake,' she replied, suddenly rankled by his assumption of command.

Pete shrugged and followed Iona out of the bedroom.

When Carson descended the stairs, she was surprised to see everything laid out for breakfast: cereal, milk in a jug, even kitchen roll folded for napkins. She could not recall a time when Iona had ever helped without prompting. She was thinking about this when her sister appeared out of her parents' room.

'Since when have you been so eager to set the breakfast table?'

'I'm good at helping.'

'Are you, hell,' replied Carson, a disdainful look on her face.

'You got out of bed on the wrong side, Car,' she said, parroting a phrase Elinor used often. She pointed at the bedroom door. 'I've tried to wake them but even when I gave them a shake they didn't open their eyes. You try.'

'It's a waste of time,' Pete said in a flat voice. 'My parents are dead to the world. I counted the bottles. They're not going to wake up any time soon. Mum didn't even take her clothes off; pathetic,' he added and then his face reddened and he looked away. He was embarrassed by the fact of it, but more by his betrayal.

'They promised to be there to see us off. And watch us fishing,' Carson said emphatically.

'Look,' Pete said, irritated now, 'they're hardly going to miss us, are they? They'll probably still be asleep when we get back.'

'Come on, Car. Listen to Pete,' Iona said, looking slyly at her cousin for his approval.

Carson glared at Iona. 'I'm going to try to wake them anyway.'

When Carson pushed open Elinor and Patrick's bedroom door she was hit by air as solid as smoke, a rancid mix of exhaled alcohol and cigarette breath. She almost retched but, taking short shallow breaths, she knelt down beside her mother and shook her shoulder. 'Mum, it's almost nine. We're going fishing now. You need to get up.'

At first there was no response. Carson put her hand on her mother's clammy brow and finally she opened her eyes just enough to see her daughter.

'That's good, Car ... great,' she muttered and burrowed further into her duvet.

Carson sat back on her heels and studied her mother's slack face, rendered a dull yellow by the curtains, mascara flecks on her cheeks, and wondered whether to persevere. She looked over at her father, sprawled on his back, completely inert, his dark hair matted and his mouth open, and wondered if he might actually be dead. She could not hear him breathing and just as she began to panic, he gasped, emitted a loud rattle, and jolted back to life as though someone had attached jump leads to his body. Then he turned over and started to snore gently. 'Dad,' Carson called out urgently, 'wake up! You are meant to be on the jetty. Please!' she said imploringly. But Patrick simply snuffled and nestled into Elinor's back. Carson blanched, a reluctant witness to such unconscious intimacy, and gave her now entangled parents an exasperated last look and banged the door behind her.

The others were already standing impatiently at the boat when Carson marched down to the jetty carrying two life jackets. She handed Iona the smaller one and narrowed her eyes at Pete who was wearing a hoodie, jeans and wellington boots. 'Where's your life jacket?' she asked him.

'It's okay. The weather's fine. Just like Granddad said. Look at the loch.' He jerked his thumb behind him. 'There's hardly a ripple on the water. My life jacket's got too tight since last summer.' He flexed his shoulders. 'I don't want to be uncomfortable. How would I cast?'

'But you have to wear one, Pete,' Carson said, her voice severe and chiding.

'Hey. You don't get to tell me what to do. You are not my parent,' he threw back at her.

Carson felt Pete's rebuke like a slap.

He turned and smiled conspiratorially at Iona and put his hands on the boat to steady it. 'Right, Iona, just step in carefully and sit at the bow.'

Carson seethed at his deliberately genial tone. Then Pete pointed at the stern and, curt again, told Carson to perch there and hold on to the wooden post of the jetty while he untied the fore and aft ropes. She moved into position, her face clouded, and he stepped swiftly into the boat and nodded to her to let go. Straight away the boat started to rock from side to side and Iona let out a shriek, nervous and excited in equal measure. Carson opened her mouth to tell her sister to calm down, and then clamped it shut again. The two of them ganging up on her would be too much to bear.

Pete settled himself on the centre bench with his back to her and from their position below the Wee Hill of Craigmalloch began to row steadily south.

Carson felt the warmth of the morning sun softening her body, the heat moving through her, relaxing her vertebrae one by one. Her head felt lighter, her neck more mobile. It was easier not to have Pete looking in her direction. She put her splayed fingers into the water and felt its coolness eddy through them and slowly she became aware of Pete's even strokes as he dipped the blades into the loch with hardly a sound and drew them back expertly, his shoulders squaring and then rounding again. She found the steady rhythm soothing, and it seemed only moments later, when Carson looked at the shoreline, that she realised they would soon be in sight of the castle and out of sight of the jetty. 'I thought Granddad said we were to fish where they could see us from the jetty?' she ventured in as light a voice as she could muster.

'We're going to fish Starr Bay,' Pete replied emphatically. 'Granddad said that was his favourite place to fish.'

'But it's away down the loch,' she replied, her voice now freighted with worry.

'Jesus, Carson, are you always like this?' Pete called over his shoulder. He looked ahead at his younger cousin. 'Is she, Iona?'

Iona clamped her lips together, caught between the two of them.

'Anyway, we're almost there.'

'Can I have the rod first?' wheedled Iona, now she had picked sides and was alert to her sister's discomfort.

Carson shrugged, resigned to defeat. 'I don't care. Do what you want.'

They all sat for a moment, suddenly dismayed by their disharmony, bobbing silently on the water, their boat as tiny as a marker buoy on the vast deserted loch. The only other movement was a scattering of sanderlings racing hither and thither, sending high-pitched chirrups across the water as if they were sounding an alert. And in the distance a circle of Scots pines listed to one side, worn down by the wind, the deserted steading within no longer in need of their protection. All this was familiar to Carson and yet she felt as though they were floating on a distant sea.

Pete shipped the oars and eased the dapping rod out of the clips. It vibrated in the air as he raised it upright and then released the big feathery fly that Walter had stuck into the cork grip. He threw the cast onto the water and passed the rod to Iona, instructing her to waft it gently from side to side. 'Hold the rod firmly, but not too tightly, and make the fly dance, like it's showing off to the trout.'

Carson heard Pete's fond encouraging tone again and it struck her that Iona was possibly the only child he knew, and in that moment she felt differently towards her cousin. Pete unclipped his own rod. 'Do you want to swap seats?' she said. 'If I sit in the middle, you can cast more easily.'

Pete looked surprised. 'Thanks,' was his only reply, but as they began to manoeuvre into each other's seats and the boat wavered on the water he caught her eye and smiled apologetically. 'Sorry. I've been a bit of a dick.'

'What's wrong?' Carson looked at him sympathetically.

'Couldn't you tell last night?' he replied flatly. 'Mum is behaving like an out-of-control teenager.' He lowered his voice. 'Ironic, eh, when I'm supposedly the truculent one. It wouldn't even surprise me if she was on something.' He laughed grimly. 'And Dad doesn't really give a shit about anyone but himself. That's pretty obvious.' Pete sent his first cast out so fast it cracked like a whip.

Just as it sheared the water Iona, who had been diligently waving her rod to and fro like a dowsing stick, let out a squeal. The rod was pulled taut and jerked forward. 'Pete ... Pete, I've caught a fish. I'm scared.'

'Wow, that was quick,' he called encouragingly. 'Now hold your rod firmly and keep it up a little. Don't move it too much or you might lose your trout. Can you reel in a little?'

'I can't do both things,' Iona wailed.

Carson leaned over to steady her so she could wind in her line. Suddenly the shimmering fish broke the water, arched in protest, and flipped over trying to get free of the hook. 'It won't stop!' Iona shouted.

'Raise your rod until it's standing straight. It's a lovely brownie. Good for you!'

Gritting her teeth in concentration, her face flushed scarlet, Iona held the handle of the rod against her stomach and tried to keep it upright until Pete edged his way past Carson and grabbed the line. Then he grasped hold of the trout and deftly released the hook from its gaping mouth and gave the fish a quick tap against the side of the boat. 'No need for a priest.' He grinned at Carson who laughed good-naturedly. He laid the brownie on the palm of his hand and its burnished scales glittered in the sunshine. 'The first fish of the day!' he said triumphantly. 'Want to hold it?' Iona grimaced and shook her head. Pete smiled. 'Okay, get that fly back in the water.'

Pete sat back on his bench and cast his line and this time Carson heard a sound going by her like the stealthy swish of an arrow released from a bow. She watched, mesmerised, as he laid the line on the water and then moved the Black Pennell across the pellucid surface.

'You're lucky you can come here whenever you want,' he said, keeping his eyes on the fly.

'Don't you like living in London then?'

Pete shrugged. 'Right now, I like it a lot better here.'

Carson studied her cousin's profile, the unmistakable trace of their grandfather; the slope of his shoulders, the head forward a little as if always looking for something beyond, and then the imprint of Fiona came into focus: the strong cheekbone and the vertical ridge above the upper lip. She wondered if Roland saw himself in his son, or if he thought Pete was altogether too much of a MacMillan.

'Aunt Fiona says she wants to spend more time here. You can come with her,' Carson said in a hopeful voice.

'Yeah, well, she says that,' he said despondently, 'but it'll never happen.' Pete's eye was caught by a movement above the water. 'Look at that,' he said, pointing with his free hand, and they all watched a heron in the distance moving over the shallows with a slow flap of his elongated primeval wings.

Carson thought he was hardly travelling fast enough to stay in the air but then the bird gained speed over the reed beds and as she followed his wingbeat she realised that not only were they in line with the castle, they were almost halfway across the loch. She heard Walter's voice in her head: 'There's no need to go far from the shore. There are no trees on the bank to snag your cast, and there are brownies everywhere. They don't congregate to have a chat. They don't say, "Let's all sashay down to Starr Bay today."'

A leaden cloud suddenly blotted out the sun, and a sharp gust of wind whipped Carson's hair across her face. 'I think we should row closer to the shore,' she said as casually as she could.

Pete frowned a little. 'What's wrong? The weather's fine.' He squinted up at the sky. 'A bit of cloud is better for fishing. We're drifting very slowly.'

Carson dug her teeth into her bottom lip.

'Oh no,' called Iona in an irritated tone. 'Help me, please, Pete,' she said imperiously. 'My line's stuck under the boat. It doesn't feel like a fish,' she added with all the certainty of an experienced angler.

Carson was startled to see Iona get to her knees on her bench. Then she leaned over the hull still holding on tightly to her rod. 'Iona, don't do that,' she shouted. 'Sit back down. Now!'

'Stay still, Iona,' Pete commanded. 'Don't move!'

Iona's arm was now in the water, tugging the line. 'I can get it. Don't worry.'

'Hang *on*!' Pete called urgently. 'The line can't be snagged. We're too deep. It must be caught on the underside of the hull.'

Iona bent over a little more to have a look. 'I'm pulling it, but it won't move.'

'Stop! Sit back down, Iona!' Pete barked, panicked now. 'I'll sort it.'

At that moment, from the distance, came the whine of an engine, straining to pick up speed. Within seconds a grinding sound screeched around the loch, ever closer and louder, until it filled the air and a flash of silver and blue and white roared past them and disappeared out of sight in seconds. For an infinitesimal, eerie moment there was calm before the first wave hit. Then, wave after wave of the speedboat's wake rushed at the boat, pounding it and punching it relentlessly, sending it jerking violently from side to side. Iona started screaming and Carson, gripping the bench, howled at her sister to hold on to the boat tightly and push herself back down.

But Iona was staring down at the water, rigid, one hand still trying to grip the dapping rod, sobbing in terror, unable to get her balance. Pete tried to manoeuvre himself past Carson to get a hand to her, but just as he almost reached her, Iona suddenly tipped over the side, silently, as if she were sacrificing herself freely to the churning black water. Carson screamed in horror as her sister started twisting and tumbling through the spume. She thrashed at the water, gasping and choking as her head appeared for a moment and then sank below again, each time further from the boat. 'Car, Car—' she gurgled desperately, and then a shock ripped through Carson's body like a bolt of electricity. Iona's life jacket was wide open.

'I'm coming in for you, Iona!' Carson screamed, but just then Pete bellowed at her to stay put as he crashed over the side, almost capsizing the boat immediately.

He struck out frantically towards his cousin, but even as he put his arm in an arc over his head and tried to repeat the movement with his other arm he could not seem to make any headway. His wellington boots were as solid as concrete. He let out a great bellow of fear. 'Get the oars, Carson! Row towards us!' he yelled as the boat bobbed away from the maelstrom created by Pete and Iona as they flailed in the water, as if an unseen force were toying with them, tossing them this way and that, dragging them each further apart.

Carson caught a glimpse of Iona's contorted face as she tried to breathe. 'Turn onto your back, Iona, please . . . please!' she pleaded, but her cries were lost in the air. She grabbed an oar and tried to wield it, but it slipped from the rowlock and became twice as heavy and she could not slot it back in. 'I'm coming in,' she shouted again.

'No, Carson,' Pete shouted through mouthfuls of water, 'you have to get the oars!' He was desperately trying to kick off his boots but they would not budge and, as he yelled the same words again, his voice was catching, fainter now, as if he already knew it was hopeless.

Carson yanked at the oar again, as heavy as a tree trunk now, but she could not fix it in position. 'I can't do it, Pete. I can't do it!' she screamed, and let out an anguished howl.

Then his exhausted words came to her, no louder than a whisper, but they obliterated everything else. 'I can't reach her, Car. I can't move. I'm so sorry. I'm so sorry.'

Carson looked at the water roiling around her sister and saw that in the whirlpool of hands and hair and the cherry-red life jacket there was no face, and only silence.

'Iona, Iona, turn over! Swim to me! Please, please!' Carson thought she could hear the words bursting from her chest and hurtling around the loch, booming from hill to hill, and soaring up into the sky, but as she listened in the stilled boat, all she could hear was the screaming in her head. For a moment she watched Iona's body swaying on the surface in the distance, as gently as a mooring buoy, before she sank down into darkness.

CHAPTER 9

Walter drove along the lochside, flexing his fingers on the steering wheel to ease the stiffness that arrived as surely as each dawn. Eager to join the excitement of the fishing expedition, he scanned the water, blinking hard, cursing his rheumy, morning eyes. He peered at his watch. It was almost ten. Whichever way he looked, the loch was undisturbed. He shook his head, disappointed after all the preparations, but as he turned the Land Rover off the track and onto the newly gravelled drive at the side of the Stratton House he frowned, perplexed by the empty jetty. He walked down the grass onto the shingle, more in hope than expectation, to see if his son, as he had said he would, had set up the primus stove and the frying pan, but there was nothing there. He could make no sense of it. He turned on his heel and walked back up to the two houses and stood looking for a sign of life. They stared back at him at him blankly. 'Patrick, Fiona. Are you there?' he hollered. There was a great commotion in the trees as squawking crows burst out of the branches and flew around the compound in a frenzy. He shouted again above the cacophony and banged on Patrick's door, his clenched fist pounding faster and faster.

Eventually he heard feet shuffling across the wooden floor. Patrick opened the door, hunched up and shivering, his bleary eyes narrow against the light. 'Hey Dad, good morning to you too. What is it?'

Walter stared at his son in disbelief, his temples throbbing. He tried to keep himself in check. 'In the name of God, Patrick. Where are the children? The boat's not at the jetty and I can't see it on the loch. You were meant to be up at nine to keep an eye on them. You all were and it's now ten o'clock!'

The words pinballed around Patrick's head. As he started to order them he felt an iron claw grip his stomach; he almost lost his balance and put his hand on the doorframe to steady himself. 'Oh my God, Dad.' He felt hot bile rising in his throat and he swallowed it down hard. 'We were up so late last night.'

'Get the others up. I'll drive down the loch.'

'Wait. I'm coming too.' He pushed past Elinor as she appeared at the door, still drowsy, an Indian shawl pulled round her shoulders.

'What's hap . . .' Her voice trailed away as soon as she looked at Walter's ashen face and realised what was wrong. 'Where are the girls?' she shouted. 'Oh my God, we didn't wake up. *We didn't wake up!*' She grabbed hold of Patrick as he pushed past her, pulling on his jacket. 'How could we have done that, Patrick? How could we?'

Patrick put his arm around her shoulders and propelled her to the garden gate between the houses. 'Go and wake Fiona and Roland. I'm going with Dad. Don't worry, Pete knows how to handle the boat.'

Walter threw the old Land Rover into gear before Patrick had the chance to close the passenger door, and they swerved onto the track, kicking up a storm of dust behind them on the gravel. He pressed his foot to the floor, pushing the vehicle to its limits, and sent sheep that were meandering down the track scattering in panic with loud staccato blasts of the horn.

'I should have been here,' Walter shouted above the engine as he scanned the loch. 'I should have been here.' He gripped the steering wheel, almost light-headed, his heart beating far too fast.

Patrick put his hand across his mouth to stop himself throwing up, and then, suddenly, he saw a small flat shape on the water in the distance. 'Stop, Dad,' he yelled. 'There they are.'

Walter braked hard.

On the eastern side of the loch opposite Portmark they saw the boat floating on the breeze in the dappled sunshine. Patrick put up his father's binoculars but all he could make out was the contours of the boat, and a family of coots zigzagging past it, the hen at the head of her brood. 'I can't see any of them, Dad,' he shouted frantically as he jumped out of the Land Rover and began to strip off.

'Stop it, Patrick. It's too far. Think straight!' Walter thought he might pass out and put a hand on the bonnet to steady himself. He gulped in some air and bent forward with his hands on his knees. Just then the Range Rover screeched to a stop behind them. Roland and Fiona and Elinor jumped out and followed Patrick's gaze to the little boat.

'Are they in it? I can't see anyone,' Fiona wailed, and began to retch until she was sick at the side of the track.

'Have you got your mobile phone, Roland?' Patrick shouted. 'Dial 999, now!' Roland started at him for a moment, uncomprehending. 'Come on, man, do it,' barked Patrick, but before Roland could punch in the numbers Patrick leapt over to his brother-in-law and grabbed the phone from him.

The Royal Navy helicopter swooped over Loch Doon Castle like a huge moth, its bulbous nose tilted towards the water and its rotor blades sending blasts of air shuddering along the shore. Elinor felt the vibration of the engine in every one of her nerve ends and thought it might shatter her into tiny pieces. She strained to see the little boat and locked onto it as it dipped jauntily through the soft waves, willing the three to sit up and show themselves, and shout 'surprise', comeuppance for their parents' late-night excesses. Suddenly a motor boat entered her view speeding across the water, Patrick at the helm, and just then she looked up as two orange-suited figures, in helmets and harnesses, leaned out of the helicopter's yawning side as it moved low across the loch. She squeezed her eyes shut and prayed that they would make everything all right.

A moment later two police officers drew up beside Walter. The older one put his hand on Walter's arm and the three stood, their heads close together. Then Walter pressed his fingers into his eyelids and the older officer, Sergeant Sturrock, handed him a small bottle of water but Walter was shaking so much he almost dropped it. The officer took it back from him gently and unscrewed it.

As soon as Patrick had made the emergency call he had taken off without a word in the Land Rover and hurtled further down the loch to the Outward Bound Centre. He unhitched the instructors' motor boat from the jetty and turned the key hanging from the starter. He gunned the cruiser across the loch and reached Walter's boat just as the helicopter started to hover overhead. The crew watched from above as Patrick grabbed hold of the other boat. It was then that they radioed to Sergeant Sturrock.

Carson lay motionless on the bottom of the boat, on her side, curled up into a ball, her hands over her head as if to protect herself from an expected blow. 'Carson, darling, Carson, it's me, Dad. It's okay. It's me. Please wake up.' Patrick repeated his words over and over, battling the whoosh and grind of the rotor's blades, until he saw a shiver, a tiny ripple, and he let out an involuntary cry of relief, but in that instant he felt a pain as acute as a stab from a knife. Carson was alone. He opened his mouth wide, in an expression of utter agony, and started to yell up to the crew, but the words were obliterated by the helicopter engine.

Just then a voice cracked through a loudhailer. 'Mr MacMillan, please don't try to move her. She may be injured. Stay still, please.'

But Patrick was already on the move. He tethered the boats together and climbed over beside his daughter. He bent over her and stroked her hair as gently as he could, tears streaming down his face. It took him all his strength not to ask what had happened to Iona. 'Darling. You're alive. I'm here. You're safe.' It sounded like a nursery rhyme. At first she remained still as Patrick's tears fell on her hair but then, slowly, she moved one arm from in front of her face and tried to focus on her father. She began to shake and a strange high-pitched keening sound came from deep within her and she clamped her hands over her ears as if she could not bear to hear her own agonised cry.

Sergeant Sturrock walked heavily from Walter to where Elinor was standing, her fingers intertwined so tightly at the back of her neck she fantasised she could snap a vertebra. Roland stepped forward from where he was bent over Fiona's slumped body. As the officer relayed the news that, so far, only Carson had been found, the elation with which she had tricked herself like an anaesthetic when she saw the orange-suited rescuers turned to cold dread and she clutched her head. Roland fell to his knees beside Fiona and held her tightly, his eyes swimming and his mouth slack in disbelief. 'I have an officer on her way who will be dedicated to you,' Jock Sturrock said kindly. 'She will make sure you know everything we do.' Just then another police car pulled up and the four officers went into a huddle.

Elinor charged over to the group. 'You *have* to find the others,' she screamed into the face of the youngest officer, Constable Amy Ramsay. 'Why are you just standing talking?' She balled her hands into fists and beat them against her temples.

Before the constable had a chance to reply, Walter took hold of his daughter-in-law and gathered her to him as if he were trying to draw her pain to himself. Just then Elinor's legs gave way and the policewoman rushed to break her fall as Walter tried to hold the weight of her. Between them the officer and Walter lowered her onto the grass, comforting her all the while.

'Mrs MacMillan, look at me now. Your daughter will soon be safely on the shore and the ambulance will be here any minute now, and you can go with her to hospital. Come with your father-in-law to the Outward Bound Centre in the police car.'

Suddenly Fiona got up from the ground, her eyes wild, and lunged at the policewoman. 'But where are Pete and Iona? *Where are they?*'

Roland gripped Fiona's arm. 'Darling, they're doing their best,' he said, his voice hoarse.

Walter could not look at his daughter's face. He would have ended his life right there if it would have saved his grandchildren.

A walkie-talkie kicked into life and Roland, alerted by its urgent tone, followed Sergeant Sturrock out of earshot of the group. He strained to decipher the clipped, tinny conversation between the helicopter pilot and the officer and then his hands flew to his mouth. This was all their doing. It was the end of everything. Walter stared at Roland, his eyes haunted, ringed with tears. They heard the helicopter, out of sight now, but he knew by the timbre of the engine that it was standing still above the loch.

At Starr Bay, where the loch narrowed to its head and the land beyond rose a little, sheltering the shore, out of sight of the family, the winchman descended from the helicopter like an angel, a sling attached to his winchline. Below him a bright red life jacket floated on the dark water. Iona lay face down as if she were looking for something beneath the ripples, her arms and legs spread in the shape of a star. The pilot held his position precisely as the winchman dipped into the water and gently raised Iona into the sling, folding in her arms and legs, cradling her carefully. Then they rose as one into the sky and into the outstretched arms of the crew who settled her down in the cavernous dark of the helicopter's belly.

It flew fast above them, a harbinger like no other. Elinor stared up at its underside and clasped her hands. 'I'm begging you,' she said to Constable Ramsay, 'tell me what's happening. You promised you would. Why is it going away?'

The police officer took her arm gently at the jetty of the Outward Bound Centre and directed her gaze to the water where Patrick was sitting in the little wooden boat, roped to the other and pulled by another launch from the Outward Bound Centre. 'Look, Mrs MacMillan, your husband has Carson safe.'

Walter was pacing on the shingle when the flotilla came into the jetty. Before Sergeant Sturrock could stop him, he waded into the water and caught hold of the hull of his boat to ease its arrival. 'Oh dear God,' he said under his breath as he looked down on his granddaughter. Carson lay motionless, Patrick's jacket under her head and a blanket around her. Her skin was so pale it was almost translucent, her eyelids were veined with blue, and her lips were parted a little as if she were thinking carefully about every breath. Patrick did not take his eyes off her, but he reached out and found his father's hand and held on to it so hard Walter thought he might crush his fingers.

Walter leaned forward. 'It's Granddad, Car.' He tried to steady his voice. 'You're safe now.'

Carson's eyelids began to flutter. 'Granddad . . . I couldn't . . . Iona . . .' Walter tried to make out the fragments falling from her lips. 'The noise of the boat . . . so fast . . . and then the waves . . .' But then she thrashed her arms in the air and shouted out 'Iona!'

Patrick shushed her gently and stood back to let the ambulance crew lift her onto a stretcher, swaddle her gently in tinfoil, then drape a huge blanket over her.

Walter stood at the back doors of the ambulance looking in. Patrick and Elinor sat on either side of the gurney, staring at their daughter, each in a deep well of their own suffering, unable to speak about what they now knew to be true. They had both seen the speeding helicopter, its thundering complaint an intimation of death.

Then, very quietly, Elinor started singing, a sound so fragile, so lamenting, that it seemed to be coming from a place far away on the loch. 'You are my sunshine, my only sunshine . . .'

Walter remembered Carson rocking Iona in her arms, earnestly trying to teach her the words, and he wanted to shout at his daughter-in-law to stop. He looked at Patrick as his son put his head in his hands, and then slid his hands over his ears.

The paramedics closed the doors as softly as they could, and Walter followed the ambulance back along the loch in the Land Rover, watching the driver taking infinite care to avoid every bump and crack on the track to the main road north. There was no siren, no blue flashing light, not now. As he stopped at Portmark, and let it carry on to the hospital in Ayr, he slumped against the wheel, staring at his daughter sitting on the grass, bent over like a rag doll, almost catatonic, smoking mechanically, cigarette stubs all around her like spoiled confetti. Then she began scratching at the earth as if she were trying to dig her own grave. For a split second he thought she was Jean, lost in despair, and his whole body shook uncontrollably. He wished that he could hold his daughter tightly and draw all her pain and guilt to himself and add it to his own.

As he got out of the car to go to her, there was a great roar overhead and he felt the powerful draught as another rescue helicopter crossed the loch. He saw Roland freeze where he had been pacing on the shingle and felt a wave of compassion for his terrified son-in-law, now so devastatingly and bewilderingly powerless.

The helicopter began to hover over the far side of the loch and suddenly they heard the rapid rat-a-tat of words from the police radio. Walter trained his binoculars on the distant shore, trying to keep his hands steady. He picked up a police Land Rover travelling fast. It lurched over the rough terrain, past Blackcraig Hill, almost leaving the ground at times, and then it careened to a stop near the water's edge.

'What's going on, Walter?' yelled Roland as he helped Fiona to her feet and put his arm around her waist to support her, but she broke away from him and ran at Sergeant Sturrock, almost knocking him over.

'Please, please,' she begged, 'is it Pete?'

The officer put his hand over hers. 'Mrs Stratton . . .' – he nodded over to Roland – 'Mr Stratton, I'll be able to tell you something in a moment. I promise you.'

Fiona turned to Roland and buried her face in his chest.

Walter raised his binoculars again and followed a member of the RAF rescue crew as he was being lowered to the ground just as two police officers beneath him knelt down on the shingle. He held his breath. It was as if everything was waiting: the castle walls, the heron, the sundew, the soft-edged hills, even the Czech pilot, and then, finally, time started again and over the radio they heard the words: 'He's alive. The boy is alive.'

Fiona started sobbing hysterically and Walter took hold of her and handed Roland the binoculars. In the distance they could just make out a small bundle, attached to a winchman, rising into the air, and as they swung to and fro, Roland, with the better view, let out a gasp. 'Hold on to him, dammit!' he shouted involuntarily into the open sky. Soon they were level with the gaping side of the helicopter and guided into the dark. Roland started to shake, oblivious to Sergeant Sturrock's arrival at his side to lead him to the police car. He was consumed by the realisation that he had almost lost the thing most precious to him in all world, more precious than his wife, his buildings, his prizes. He had almost lost his beautiful, stubborn, unhappy boy.

CHAPTER 10

Elinor and Patrick stood, two hollowed-out figures, utterly bereft, unable to find a language sufficient for their conflicting emotions: their terrible unspeakable grief, and the exhausted relief of watching the gurney carrying Carson disappear to safety, down the bare, neon-lit hospital corridor. When the sound of the trolley faded to nothing, Constable Ramsay moved forward unobtrusively and guided them both into an empty room, a drab peach-coloured space with a window high up on one wall. She showed them to the plastic chairs and made them a cup of tea from the machine and then left the room, closing the door behind her.

Patrick took Elinor's hand. 'We haven't had any confirmation yet, Eli.'

Her hand flew to his mouth, grabbing it roughly. 'Stop it, Patrick. Stop it!' she screamed into his face. 'Stop pretending. I *know* she's dead.' She looked around and took hold of a chair and flung it to the floor. 'Why are we being kept in this horrible place? This prison. Why, Patrick? They're shutting us in because we know!'

There was a soft knock at the door and Constable Ramsay stood back to let Walter pass. He looked smaller. His worn misshapen tweed jacket and muddy, still wet trousers engulfed him and the lines on his ashen face seemed deeper than before.

There was no need for him to say anything. Elinor let out a great howl that filled the room and exploded its way into the corridor, and then she collapsed on the floor.

Patrick looked at his father, stunned, and began to shake his head. 'No, no . . . no, Dad. Please. No.'

'They said it would have happened very quickly.'

'They don't know that. How can they? They weren't there!' Elinor raged, her fists against her forehead, and her body contorted in a paroxysm of grief. All the questions and accusations and recriminations arrived in droves and settled in silently among them.

Walter took a long intake of breath, trying to summon some strength. 'I know this is a terrible thing to have to do.' He swallowed hard and swayed a little. 'A member of the family will have to identify Iona's body.' As he said his granddaughter's name his voice collapsed.

Suddenly there was a dull, hard thud and Walter and Patrick looked in horror as Elinor began to jerk her head backwards against the wall, and the sickening sound cracked around the room as she hurt herself over and over again, her eyes wild and staring.

Patrick rushed over and put his hand between the wall and his wife's head. 'Eli, darling. Please don't . . . you must stop doing that.'

'I don't care,' she threw out, sending flecks of spittle at Patrick's face. She pressed her head against his hand. 'I can't see her. I can't. I can't bear to see her.'

'It's all right . . . shh. I'll do it.' His voice faltered. 'I want to see her one last time.' He started to weep and slumped to the floor at his wife's feet.

Elinor felt a searing pain rip through her head, like sparks exploding in her brain. Then the room receded until it was a dark hole and she saw her dressing table in her bedroom at Wellington Square. She opened the drawer and looked at two little wooden boxes, each bearing a painted initial. She watched herself take out the one marked 'I' and open it. Inside were a pair of scuffed tan-coloured shoes with a yellow chick embroidered on the front, tiny Fair Isle mittens that Fiona had knitted, and a matchbox containing a lock of hair.

She suddenly let out a piercing scream and with that she was back in the thin grey light of the hospital waiting room, curled up with Patrick on the linoleum floor. Walter sat, shrunken into the plastic seat, nothing he could do, no salve that he could apply, no story he could tell that could cauterise their deep dark wounds.

And so it was Patrick who saw Iona for the last time. He walked uncertainly towards the mortuary with Constable Ramsay and a nurse by his side. The nurse opened the door quietly and motioned for him to enter. As the door closed behind him he found himself alone with his daughter, lying covered over on a little table for all the world as if she were sleeping. She looked so small and perfect, and he struggled to control the desire to pick her up and carry her home. He knelt on the floor, so his face was level with hers and stroked her unblemished pale skin and felt the beautiful dark curls around her face and never wanted to leave her. He had failed his child. He had abandoned her and he was alive and she was not and now she was dead for ever. Time lost any meaning, and it was more than an hour later that Constable Ramsay, who had been observing through the glass pane in the door, approached Patrick silently, helped him to his feet, and led him gently out of the mortuary.

CHAPTER 11

'You should go home for a few hours, Mr MacMillan. I can get someone to drive you.'

It took Walter a moment to register Amy Ramsay's kindly face. 'Home?' he replied uncomprehendingly.

The police officer nodded. 'Just for a while. I'm sure your grandchildren will want to see you as soon as the doctor gives the okay, but that won't be for a few hours.'

He saw the concern in her eyes, and felt as if his heart was being rent from his chest.

'They'll all need you, Mr MacMillan. You must rest when you can.'

He wiped his eyes clear with his hands. 'I'll drive myself.' He looked at her anxiously. 'I don't have a mobile.'

She touched his arm. 'Don't worry. I'll call the house if we need you. I promise.'

When Walter reached Carsphairn he took off his shoes and sank down on his bed in his shirt and trousers and immediately fell into a deep anaesthetic sleep. Had anyone seen him they would have thought he had collapsed and died. When he came to five hours later he could not make sense of where he was. At first he thought he was on his back on the single bed tucked above the turbines at Tongland. As a young man he had never minded the night shift. In fact he volunteered for more than his fair share. It was the only time that he slept away from his parents, strangely comforted at being alone in the huge power station, attending to the pressure gauges by the light of the moon rather than switching on the lamp, and alert, even in slumber, for the sound of the alarm. Now, lying on his back on his bed in Carsphairn, he strained to hear the comforting thrumming of the turbines, and was confused by the eerie silence.

It was then that he gasped out loud, like a man coming up for air. Images of the winchman swinging in the sky and his daughter retching on the ground, and Patrick bringing Carson to shore flickered in front of his eyes and he sat bolt upright, fighting to catch a deeper breath.

The crescent moon sent a watery grey light into the bedroom, cold and unforgiving. He turned his back on it and changed into old winter trousers and a thick Guernsey and struggled into his mackintosh and did what he had done so many nights before: he headed for the dam on Loch Doon. Twenty minutes later he sat studying the huge weight of water, wondering whether his abiding love for the place had blinded him to a malevolence lurking under the surface, and in that moment of utter confusion he hated it.

Rain started to fall like tears, drenching the hills, smearing their edges. As the morning broke, Walter searched through the haze for the outline of the old MacMillan house in the distance. He could just make out its tall gable end, the wooden fretwork of the porch and the two dormer windows.

When he and Jean were first married she had been quite taken with it. She called it her Gingerbread House. 'We'll make it ours. You'll see what I can do with this old place,' she said, clapping her hands excitedly. She would often come home from the library, the car laden with her latest purchases. She bought brightly patterned ceramic lamps, and geometric design rugs, and expensive Susie Cooper china from Hourstons Department Store in Ayr where the Thompsons had an account. When twenty-three-year-old Walter stood in front of her and told her solemnly that they could not afford it all, Jean just laughed. 'Think of it as my dowry,' she said and kissed him quiet. She had a joiner from Dalmellington flush the wood-panelled doors with plywood and close in the spindles on the stairs with panels and install a fitted kitchen complete with Formica countertops and a new Frigidaire. Then she brought home a catalogue for furniture in the modern style that he had never seen before, anywhere.

It was Jean's idea to celebrate the arrival of their new dining room table and matching chairs by dressing up in their finery and holding a cocktail party for two with drinks mixed at their new glass-fronted cocktail cabinet. When Walter suggested that she might like company, Tommy and Joy perhaps, she would not hear of it. 'It's just going to be me and you and that great big loch out there – at least for now,' she added, glancing at him coquettishly. That evening she came downstairs in a new red organza dress shaped to her silhouette, a pretty sweetheart neckline showing off a single tear-drop pearl on a long chain, and black high heels. Walter was speechless with desire. He encircled her waist, but she pushed him back gently. 'Wait,' she said with a tinkling laugh as she pulled a cocktail book from behind her back. 'I'm going to make us gimlets and grasshoppers and sidecars. It will be just like *All About Eve*.'

Later they lay together is a soft stupor in front of the roaring fire, Jean's red dress abandoned on the sofa, its job done, her shoes and stockings strewn on the floor beside Walter's crumpled wedding suit. He kissed the downy peach skin between her shoulder blades and she shivered and turned from staring into the fire, her eyes shining, and put her tongue around her top lip. 'I'd like you to pour a vodka martini straight into my throat before you kiss me,' she murmured. Walter, hypnotised, took a sip from his glass, pursed his lips and slowly released a stream of liquid into her upturned open mouth. She swallowed and then enveloped him in a martini-scented kiss. 'We're celebrating,' she said languorously.

'I know!' Walter exclaimed. 'But we've drunk the new cocktail cabinet dry.'

'No-oo.' She giggled, lifting herself onto her elbow. 'Not that. We're *really* celebrating.'

She took his hand, kissed the palm, and then put it on the soft mound of her stomach.

Walter felt his heart might explode with happiness. Woozy with drink, he stared at his wife and thought she was aglow, pulsating. 'I worship you,' he blurted out suddenly.

Jean smiled contentedly and curled up like a cat in front of her husband.

The next morning Walter rose early, his head a little thick, and excitedly prepared the boat with cushions and a travelling rug, a parasol and a flask of tea. When Jean awoke and called down to him, he wrapped her in an eiderdown over her silk pyjamas, put a pair of fishing socks on her feet and carried her, giggling in protest, to the jetty. There was a ripple on the loch, and a flock of Canada geese flew in a perfect V-formation overhead, honking loudly as if in greeting. 'They're offering their congratulations,' grinned Walter as he began to row. When they reached the middle of the empty loch he shipped the oars and poured them both a cup of hot sweet tea. Jean lay back contentedly, the parasol shielding her face and Walter began to sing: 'Oh what a beautiful morning, Oh, what a beautiful day, I've got a wonderful feeling . . .' His serenade eddied out over the water and came back from the hills, as Jean laughed delightedly at her husband and trailed her hand lazily through the cool water.

Jean thrilled in her pregnancy and, unencumbered by any morning sickness, eagerly advanced her plans to celebrate women's writing at the library. She and Walter went to see a performance of *Men Should Weep*, staged by Ayr Fort Players, and she immediately wrote to the author.

Dear Mrs Lamont Stewart,

I hope you don't mind my writing to you but as a librarian at the Carnegie Library in Ayr I try to see productions of Scottish plays and *Men Should Weep* has packed out the theatre here for a whole week. I am sure if you would do us the honour of coming to the library to speak about this play and other aspects of your work it would be equally packed out. We would, of course, pay your travel expenses and a, sadly small, honorarium.

Yours sincerely,

Jean MacMillan

The playwright had responded straight away.

Dear Mrs MacMillan,

Thank you for your letter which I received this morning. I am flattered. I rather fear my play has gone out of fashion and try as I might I cannot get the great James Bridie at the Citizens Theatre to countenance any of my new plays. So I should be delighted to come to the Carnegie Library and discuss *Men Should Weep*, if for nothing else than to visit Ayrshire with which I have a strong connection.

Yours sincerely,

Ena Lamont Stewart

Jean excitedly showed the reply to Miss McPherson, the chief librarian. 'Well, young lady, you've shown great initiative, now get on and organise the event. I'm leaving it up to you.'

When Jean announced the playwright's visit there was a great rush for tickets. Then, six weeks later, on the eve of the event, Walter, who had risen early, heard Jean cry out for him from upstairs, and he found her, kneeling on the floor, leaning her head over the bath, being violently sick. He knelt beside her and gently wiped her clean and helped her back to bed where she remained for a week, only narrowly avoiding a stay in hospital when she finally began to eat again. Walter, in rare accord with his father-in-law, agreed that the library, with all the lifting and sorting of books, some of them quite possibly germ-laden, Billy Thompson said, and climbing ladders to precariously high storage shelves, was not really a suitable workplace, and Jean, too weak to protest, gave way. Not only did she miss the author's talk, she only managed to say farewell to her colleagues a fortnight later when she had recovered her strength.

'Of course you must do what's best for your baby,' said Miss McPherson, as she pushed her round metal spectacles on top of her head, the better to focus on Jean, 'but you are a clever girl and, as I know, full of ideas for the library. I doubt many of our readers would have come across Edith Wharton before you introduced her to them.'

Jean smiled to herself as she remembered the day, not long after she started at the Carnegie. She was just eighteen.

She tapped on Miss McPherson's door. 'Jean, come in, my dear. How are you settling in?'

'Well, I'm very happy here already, Miss McPherson . . . and I was wondering,' she rushed on, 'could I perhaps put up a display of an author to encourage people – well, women – to read more of her work?'

Margaret McPherson sat forward. 'Who did you have in mind?'

'Edith Wharton. I've found a good many of her books here, and most of them have hardly ever been read.'

'You know about her?' Margaret McPherson could not hide her surprise.

Jean nodded. 'My mother has her books. She particularly likes *The Age of Innocence*. It speaks to her, she says, and she likes gardening, just like Edith Wharton. And she likes the fact they have the same name.'

'Well, well; these are all good reasons.' The chief librarian smiled indulgently. 'I wonder if the women of Ayr would recognise Mrs Wharton's observations?' She put her hands squarely on the table in front of her. 'Go ahead, Jean, and let's see what you can do.'

'Thank you! Thank you!' Jean turned to go.

'Oh, and Jean, imagine – Andrew Carnegie and Edith Wharton might have met in New York, and he would certainly approve of your idea.'

Jean raced home and told her mother excitedly that she would begin straight away. She gathered together what memorabilia she could find for a display, beginning with a photograph of the author sitting looking into the distance, in a delicate white lace blouse under a black bodice, a pearl choker at her neck and her curly hair piled up into a bun. She asked her mother if she could borrow her first edition of *The Age of Innocence*, which she had bought from a dealer in America, its cover plain but for the title and a watercolour of a young woman in a pink dress. She sent away for a picture of The Mount, the house and gardens that Wharton designed on Rhode Island, and other photographs of the author in Paris during the First World War. In the library she searched out some beautiful book jackets of her novels, including one illustrated by a beautiful painting by Whistler, and she also made a selection of her writings on architecture. Then her mother suggested Jean cut some purple phlox from her garden and set it beside her display. 'Phlox were Edith Wharton's favourite flowers. They will look lovely.'

'Jean . . . Jean, a penny for them?' said Miss McPherson.

'I was just remembering the quote I wrote out for the display: "No children of my own age . . . were as close to me as the great voices that spoke to me from books."'

Miss McPherson nodded. 'Yes, a lot of us can identify with that.' She sighed. 'You bring such energy and passion to your work, Jean. You know, it would not be impossible to return once your child is older.'

Jean laughed. 'I don't know about that. I do love it here, but I imagine I'll have my hands full.'

Margaret McPherson smiled and her whole face suddenly radiated warmth, her eyes conveying more than her carefully chosen words. 'I'm sure you will have your hands full, but you will need to keep that brain of yours full as well, my dear.'

Jean looked at her wistfully for a moment and then suddenly leaned forward and kissed the chief librarian on the cheek and was gone.

After that there was less of a reason to journey to Ayr, and so the regular lunches with her mother at Stoneleigh became less frequent. There were no more sociable walks arm in arm with her colleagues to buy ice-cream cones from the Wellington Café at lunchtime. Nor could she make the short detour to Tommy and Joy's brand-new ranch-style house in Alloway to have a drink on the way home.

With only the wireless for company, she would sit, surrounded by velvet fabric and boxes of glass, jet and pearl beads, constructing evening bags of all shapes and colours, intricately decorated with designs of birds and butterflies and constellations, a sherry at her elbow. She made them to give them away, taking pleasure in compliments about her creativity and exclamations of thanks from former library colleagues. There were days when she saw no one from morning to night.

'It can be lonely, Mama,' she said quietly to Edith one day as they sat sewing together in the warmth of the glasshouse at Stoneleigh.

'Well, dear, for once your father's extravagance will pay off. After all, you are able to drive here whenever you want.'

A heavy brooding silence filled the space between mother and daughter. A bee that had inveigled its way in through a crack in the window started to buzz indignantly, throwing itself against the pane. Jean dug her needle into a piece of velvet. 'Do you realise how much it hurts me that you will never see where I live with Walter? It hurts me to know that. I want to show you my new furniture, the adorable wallpaper Walter has put up in the little bedroom.' Her voice rose as she rushed on. 'I want you to walk in *my* garden. I'm only twenty-three, Mama. This is hard for me!' Jean's eyes welled up.

'We've been through this, Jean,' Edith said in a resigned voice, her eyes on her needlework.

'But are you actually ill? Haven't you just set your face against the world? That's it, isn't it? You have decided that *this* is your world. What I want, what I *need* doesn't matter.'

Edith put her sewing down in her lap and Jean noticed that her mother's hands were shaking. She squeezed them together so tightly that her knuckles turned a milky white, and summoned up a deep breath. 'I'll tell you how I feel. Even the thought of stepping across the threshold of the front door, or through the garden gate makes me feel as if I might collapse.

My throat closes. My legs seize up. You have to believe that. Please, Jean.' She stretched out for her daughter's hand, but Jean put it quickly in her pocket.

'I don't have to believe it, Mother, but I have to live with it. Do you know what I think?' Jean hesitated as if wrestling with her own question. 'I think you didn't want to leave Dunure, and this is about punishing Daddy for dragging you here. But all you're doing is punishing me and Tommy. Daddy doesn't care. That's the joke of it.' Her voice was hard now. 'He doesn't care.'

Edith looked squarely at her daughter, her turquoise eyes pools of sadness. 'It's true that I didn't want to leave Dunure, but I'm not like this out of spite.'

'Daddy said he would pay for anything that would help. Anything. But you refused, remember?'

'It wouldn't help.'

'No, Mama.' Jean put her hands to her face. 'I don't think you want to be helped. It breaks my heart because you know how much I love you.'

Jean looked down to the cream velvet on Edith's lap. On it were scattered spots of blood from the finger where Edith had just pricked herself with her needle.

'Mama, you're bleeding,' Jean said, her voice wavering.

'Am I?' replied Edith distractedly. 'I didn't notice.'

In her second trimester Jean's mood lifted as she felt a burst of energy flood through her body. It was as if she had had a jolt of power. She walked, loose-limbed now, her stomach beauti-fully rounded, her breasts heavier. People remarked on the bloom on her cheeks. Most days she ventured to Carsphairn for provisions, racing along the lochside in her car, windows down and hair flying. Standing in line at the grocer's, checking her shopping list, she heard the shop girl call out, 'Mrs MacMillan, what can I get for you today?'

She looked up, her mouth open to reply, when the woman in front of her spoke. 'A half-pound of Ayrshire back, and slice it thinly please.'

'How funny!' exclaimed Jean, and the woman turned around, a slightly querulous look on her face. She was of similar age to Jean, her mousy shoulder-length hair held back from her pale freckled face at one side with a clasp, and her dowdy tweed coat too large for her thin frame. 'I'm Mrs MacMillan too – Jean MacMillan.' She put out her hand. 'Pleased to meet you.'

A flicker crossed the other woman's eyes as she took in Jean's green-and-black checked smock beneath her mackintosh. She extended her hand slowly. 'I am Peggy MacMillan, I'm married to Kenneth MacMillan, your husband's cousin.'

Jean opened her eyes wide in surprise. 'Walter has never said. How strange.' Her gaze dropped a little. 'What a coincidence. I'm pregnant too' – she laughed excitedly – 'but not quite so pregnant!'

Peggy's hand automatically smoothed down the bump distending the front of her coat. 'I'm due in six weeks,' she said stiffly.

'Well, we should get together before then,' Jean said effusively. 'I don't really know anyone of my own age here. We're so far along the loch. Where do you live, Peggy?'

Peggy looked at her disbelievingly. 'You don't know?'

Jean shook her head vigorously.

'We live on the farm on top of the moor. You turn off the road to Loch Doon as soon as you reach Craigenellen Estate and travel three miles to nowhere. There's just my husband and me and hundreds of sheep.'

Jean sailed on, deaf to Peggy's deflated tone. 'Well, come for lunch on Saturday. We can talk about babies ... And about being country wives – young, country wives,' she added, smiling.

'That's kind of you, I'm sure,' replied Peggy, softening. Then she hesitated. 'I'll have to see what Kenneth says.'

Jean thought for a moment. 'I know what we'll do. Let's say one o'clock. I'll cook a chicken, and if you don't come, we'll just eat it twice.'

Peggy smiled thinly and turned to pay for her bacon. 'Well, I'm making no promises, but thank you.'

As soon as Walter walked through the door that evening, Jean handed him a gin and tonic, clinked his glass against hers and excitedly blurted out the story of her encounter, eagerly anticipating his reaction. 'Imagine,' she said, 'they must live less than three miles away as the crow flies.' A look of consternation crossed Walter's face and Jean pouted at him. 'You don't seem very happy to hear all this. You didn't even tell me you had a cousin nearby. I had to find out for myself.'

Walter put his arms around her. 'I'm sorry.' He kissed her on the forehead. 'I should have told you. But there's bad blood. We don't really talk.'

Jean looked perplexed. 'Why ever not?'

'It was a falling out over land – and money. When the Hydro was buying up land to be able to flood the loch, Dad's brother, Kenneth's father, got nothing, not a penny.'

Walter explained that long before the hydro scheme was dreamed up, their grandfather, just before he died, divided up the land. Ironically, he had thought it would be fairer. 'Kenneth's father was the farmer in the family. He had left school to work on the family hill farm, so he got that. My father was the engineer, so he just got the house and a good stretch of land along the loch, and a bit behind. Of course, it was all worth nothing until the hydro scheme came along.'

'Shouldn't your father have given his brother some of the compensation money?'

'Maybe. But it wasn't his way.' Walter sighed and shook his head. 'God knows. It's a hard life, hill farming.'

'But this is all in the past. It wasn't your doing,' Jean said firmly.

Walter drained his glass. 'No, it wasn't, but it's a wound that won't be healed.'

Jean looked crestfallen.

'You weren't to know, darling.' He looked out of the back window up at the moor. 'But they won't come. I'm sure of it.'

When Saturday came Jean prepared the meal just in case, taking great pleasure in doing so, her first lunch party. She smoked some fresh trout, roasted the chicken and potatoes and baked an apple tart. She laid the table with a blue linen tablecloth and contrasting green napkins, the new Suzy Cooper china, silver cutlery and crystal stemware. She finished it off with a centrepiece of fresh flowers from the garden and stood back to admire the table; then she changed into a bright pink seersucker dress and applied even brighter pink lipstick.

Walter was in the garden in his overalls and work boots soldering the old swing when, dead on one o'clock, he heard the distant rumble of a car engine. He could hardly believe it. He dashed into the house and yanked off his work clothes just as an old Austin pulled up at the gate. Kenneth MacMillan, looking stiff in an old-fashioned, ill-fitting suit, helped Peggy out of the passenger seat just as Walter and Jean stepped outside to greet them. The cousins shook hands awkwardly while Jean ushered Peggy inside.

She took in her old tweed coat and admired her thin floral maternity smock. 'It's very pretty,' Jean said, 'and so are you; you have beautiful skin.'

Peggy blushed and lowered her head.

'Walter will get us drinks. The cocktail cabinet is full, so what would you like?'

'Water is fine, thank you.'

'Oh,' said Jean, 'I thought you might like to join me in a martini?'

'I don't really drink, thank you – and I wouldn't right now.' Peggy put her hand above her stomach. 'I don't think it would agree with me.'

Jean looked quizzical for a moment. 'What? Because you're expecting? It doesn't seem to affect me.'

'It's not me I'm concerned about,' Peggy replied, looking Jean directly in the eye.

'A cigarette then?' Jean said brightly.

Peggy shook her head.

Jean turned to Kenneth. 'It's so nice to have you for lunch. Were you ever here before?'

Kenneth bristled, taken aback by the question. 'Not that I can remember,' he said gruffly.

Jean persisted. 'Not even when you and Walter were wee?'

Kenneth shook his head. There were only two years between the cousins but he appeared much older, as if he had been battered by the elements. He put his huge weather-beaten hands on the table on either side of his cutlery. 'We were always busy on the hill,' he said from under the shock of dark brown hair that fell across his forehead. 'There's not much time for socialising when you are a farmer – or a farmer's son.'

Jean served the plates of smoked trout with a garnish of lettuce and sat down and unfolded her napkin before quickly finishing her martini.

As Peggy lifted her fork, she noticed Jean move almost imperceptibly in her seat and, glancing down, realised she should be using the fish cutlery. She reddened and looked at her husband who glared as he lifted his fish knife and stabbed at the trout.

'May I have some wine, darling?' Jean asked lightly. When he poured her a glass of Hock it sounded like a thundering waterfall. As she took a deep sip of the fragrant wine and felt the alcohol spread through her chest, she began to feel irked by Kenneth's truculence.

'Maybe this could be a new start,' she said suddenly. 'After all there is about to be a new generation in the family – two babies. Peggy and I will have a lot in common.'

'I very much doubt that,' Kenneth replied in a low voice, his belligerence unmistakable. 'I don't think she'll be traipsing along in your wake, cycling behind your fancy car. I don't want Peggy sitting drinking in this gin palace while the babies are asleep or, for that matter, awake, hearing all about your daddy's latest racehorse.'

'Kenneth, that's enough. Stop it.' Peggy and Walter chimed as one, but Kenneth was already on his feet.

'It is enough, Peggy. I won't be patronised, and neither will you. We're going home.'

Peggy's eyes filled with hot tears of embarrassment. She stood up and leaned on the table a moment. 'Thank you for inviting us to lunch,' she said, her voice quavering.

'This is ridiculous,' said Jean, squeezing Peggy's hand, her own voice shaking now as she watched Kenneth stride out to his car, leaving Walter to help Peggy on with her coat.

Jean and Walter stood in the garden watching the little black Austin buzzing along the loch like an angry bluebottle. 'I feel such a fool, Walter.' She laid her head on his shoulder. 'I'm sorry this was embarrassing for you. I didn't mean to be patronising.'

Walter shook his head. 'You made a lovely gesture.'

'Should I just have put some soup and bread and cheese out on the bare kitchen table? Wouldn't *that* have been patronising?'

Walter listened patiently as she went back through the truncated lunch, one twist and turn after another, even adding an extra one – 'Might he do something awful?' – until Walter said finally, 'Please stop it, Jean. It's not your fault. It's a MacMillan problem. It's our embarrassment.'

The next day they awoke to a blowsy mixture of sunshine and showers which patterned the windows like tiny diamonds. 'Come for a walk, darling,' Walter cajoled his despondent wife. 'Fresh air will blow all your bad thoughts away.'

But Jean said she wanted to sit by the fire and sew. 'Maybe if I listen to *Bandstand*, that will cheer me up,' she said as she lifted her face for a kiss.

Walter set off up the moor, swiping at tussocks of grass with his shepherd's crook, consumed with the idea that the lunch episode would weigh heavily with his wife. Before he realised it, he had covered the mile that led to the boundary between his land and his cousin's farm. He checked his bearings: a hundred yards from the misshapen Scots pine standing like a proud old warrior to his left and to his right a strange outcrop, a fusion of granite and sandstone resembling a craggy face, and yet there was no sign of the pilot's cairn directly ahead. He stopped dead. It was impossible. He walked forward a few paces and his heart lurched. Jagged rocks and smooth stones lay scattered as if felled in battle. Only the biggest boulders that formed the base of the cairn were still tucked together safely. At first he was bewildered, but then he walked a few feet across the border, onto Kenneth's land, and saw the freshly churned-up tracks on the moor, and knew immediately that they were made by the wheels of a car Kenneth had transformed into a bogey to carry sickly lambs and venerable sheepdogs. It was as if they were there for him to find. He bent over and put his hands on his knees and tried to suppress the bile rising in his chest at such a desperate act. Then as he straightened up he felt an overwhelming sadness as he imagined his cousin desecrating the memorial, one vicious blow after another in his blind fury and frustration, not towards Jean or Walter, but at his circumscribed life. He decided never to speak of it, not to Kenneth, not to anyone else. He would not shame him. Nor would he tell Jean, not least because that would have led to a story of a death on the loch that he did not want to tell.

He set to work, a dull ache in his heart. He had a picture of the cairn in his head and he worked steadily, gathering the stones slowly and methodically. He felt the shape and the weight of each piece, adding and taking away and adding again, until he had rebuilt the monument exactly and the sky had turned an iridescent violet grey. Finally, he sank the piece of slate, chiselled long ago in a boyish hand, into the peaty earth in front of the cairn. Then he took a step back and bowed his head. He walked down the hill, heavily at first, but then as he neared home his mood lifted and his step became lighter and faster at the thought of Jean's welcome.

The disastrous lunch put an end to Jean's short-lived interest in finding local friends. She began to travel to Ayr again more days than not. She and Walter had decided that they would make do with the carriage pram and cot that were stored in the cupboard under the eaves at Loch Doon, but Jean went to Hourstons and ordered the latest Silver Cross pram and cot and instructed that they be delivered to Stoneleigh as soon as the baby was born. 'I want you to be able to push the baby around the garden, Mama, and sing to him, and look after him, because I'm sure it will be a him, when he sleeps.' She ventured just once more: 'I'd so love it if we could take the pram to the beach and play in the sand, the way you played with me at Dunure.' She spoke as if she were delivering lines she had rehearsed over and over on the journey from the loch.

'Well, I will prepare a lovely sandpit here, I've chosen a spot already, and we'll get a paddling pool too,' said Edith evenly. 'This place is made for children, isn't it? It will be Grandma's secret garden.'

Jean heard the familiar finality in her mother's voice and had no appetite to fight on. Instead she smiled at Edith's delicate profile, the pearl studs shining in her ears, the hair that she cut herself caught in an elegant French roll. 'My children will worship you. I know they will.' They retreated to the kitchen where, every time Jean visited, they cooked ever more adventurous dishes to take to Loch Doon, with ingredients ordered from and delivered twice weekly by the grocer and left at the door for one of the family to bring inside for Edith.

Jean rarely stopped at Tommy and Joy's on the way home now, preferring to reach the loch before Walter, pour herself a glass of sherry and listen out for the Land Rover. Then she would greet him on the doorstep with a passionate kiss. 'What is it tonight?' he would murmur in her ear, and she would laugh at the routine.

'Elizabeth David's boeuf bourguignon.'

He, in turn, was captivated by her voluptuous figure, the heaviness of her breasts and the beauty of her rounded stomach, and there, on their own, under the lintel, in the pale glow of the evening light, he would lift up her dress and put a hand on each side of her belly, hoping for a tremor, or even a little kick.

Three weeks before the baby was due, Jean went to Ayr to help her mother in the garden. The further her pregnancy progressed, the stronger and more invincible she felt, and no matter how much her mother urged her to take care she insisted on getting down on her knees to weed the flower-beds, and stretching up to prune the espaliered fruit trees. 'I feel that everything I touch is growing, Mama,' she said as she worked alongside Edith in the glasshouse, luxuriating in the feeling of the rich loamy soil falling between her fingers as she potted up geraniums. 'I don't think I have ever felt alive like this. It's as if I've somehow grown out of the earth. Is that silly?'

Edith put out her hand and gently pushed her daughter's hair back into the scarf she had knotted at the top of her head. 'Not at all,' she said as she wound the last wave into the scarf, 'it's rather lovely.'

Jean looked at her mother sideways. 'What if I'm not a good mother?'

Edith started. 'Why ever would you say that? Of course you'll be a good mother.'

'What if I'm not?' she said imploringly. 'You once called me capricious. What if I'm bored? I might miss the library and amateur dramatics.'

'But you can do these things too, in time, Jean.'

But her daughter wasn't listening. She clutched her potting spade. 'Walter will be good enough for the two of us.' She looked at Edith, her eyes shining. 'I know I am lucky, Mama. I am, amn't I?'

'Well, you will make your luck, darling.'

Jean pressed the earth firmly around the roots of the geraniums and then lifted the urn to carry it to the wooden table in the centre of the lawn. She was halfway along the gravel path when she felt a fierce pain travel through her like forked lightning. She gasped and dropped the pot to the ground, sending earth and pieces of clay spilling all around her. She clutched her stomach as the fluid from her waters soaked her and fell on the geraniums scattered at her feet. 'Mama!' she screamed. 'It's happening. It's too soon. It's too early!' Edith came racing from the greenhouse. 'We have to go to the hospital. Call Walter. Call Daddy.' Edith ran to the house but by the time she returned, Jean's contractions had begun, slowly at first, but faster and harder, taking Jean's breath away. She staggered towards the door to the front garden. 'We have to go now,' she shouted, pressing the car keys into Edith's hands.

Edith looked down at them, her lips together in a thin line, and took a few steps forward, but then she stopped, her face ghostly white. 'I can't, Jean, I can't,' she said in a strangled voice.

'Mother!' Jean screamed. 'You have to!'

But Edith stood as if rooted into the ground. 'Daddy will be here very soon. He said no more than half an hour. He'll take you, darling.'

Jean looked at her mother with a mixture of terror and disbelief. 'But there's no time to wait,' she panted, 'the contractions are coming too quickly.'

'I'm so sorry, Jean. I'm so sorry. He'll be here soon.' Edith's anguish was etched on every line of her face. She tried to put her arm around Jean but her daughter let out an animal howl of pain, grabbed the keys from Edith and pushed past her.

'Call the hospital!' she shouted, tears streaming down her cheeks. 'I'm going now. I'll drive myself.'

By the time Walter arrived at the hospital less than two hours later, Patrick had been born by emergency caesarean section. 'Your wife did well to get here as quickly as she did,' the matron said as Walter set a fast pace along the corridor. 'Another hour and it might have been too late. It wasn't just that the baby had turned breech, the cord was around his neck.' Walter faltered for a minute. 'Don't worry, Mr MacMillan, they're both fine.' She patted him on the arm. 'They are both more than fine.'

Walter sat down at Jean's bedside, light-headed with happiness and relief. He watched the rise and fall of her chest as she slept, a little cage over her wound to hold the weight of the bedclothes. Her skin was paler than he had ever seen, and her hair was loose about her shoulders. As he studied his wife, he smiled to himself as it occurred to him that the plain white hospital gown, drawn closely at the neck, and her arms laid out on the hospital blanket, palms facing upwards, gave Jean the air of a nun, like Deborah Kerr in *The Black Narcissus*. He was making a mental note to tell her when a nurse silently wheeled in the cot and stopped beside him. Walter pressed his hands together, trying to keep control as he looked down at his tightly swaddled son, his smooth unblemished face and the mass of dark wispy hair, his eyes shut to the world as if to say, 'Not yet. Not yet!'

Jean stirred, opening her eyes briefly and murmured Walter's name with drowsy relief. He looked at her shyly, in awe at her for enduring such an ordeal. 'Look at you,' he whispered, 'how brave and beautiful you are and now we have a perfect son.' He took her hand and raised it to his mouth. 'Thank you,' he said, tears blinding him, and kissed her hand softly.

She moved to the nearby maternity home for two weeks

until she had healed and the baby was finally feeding satisfac-
torily. It was a fretful time. Jean could not produce enough
milk and Patrick began to lose weight and gurn with hunger.
The nurses mixed in goat's milk and even a little cow's milk to
the little Jean managed to express, but it was a relief for her,
and Walter, when, eventually, the baby sucked hard on a bottle
of powdered baby milk and Jean let what little she had dry up.
Now she could go home. 'As soon as we get back to Loch
Doon,' she said conspiratorially to Walter, 'we're going to
celebrate with a bottle of Daddy's best champagne, now there's
not a chance in hell that Patrick will get tipsy.'

Each day for those two weeks a letter from her mother was
delivered by one of Billy Thompson's workers to the maternity
home, which itself was only two streets away from Stoneleigh,
and on each page, in elegant script, she poured out her love and
her regret, and all her hopes for her first grandchild.

> You have given me the gift of a grandson, a gift that my
> darkest thoughts tell me I do not deserve, but I promise
> that I will cherish Patrick and make my garden his
> enchanted world. I will keep him safe there. I have marked
> out the sandpit and ordered a new red swing. I miss you,
> my dear daughter, with all my heart.

At the end of each note she drew a flower from her garden in
cobalt or viridian or canary-yellow Indian ink. Jean imagined
her sitting in the silence, alone, pouring everything into that
one flower. She put the single pages to her nose and kept them
all in the leather box in which had arrived a pear-shaped
diamond on a platinum chain from her father, and when
Walter hugged her and repeatedly told her how brave she had
been on that day, Jean just laughed. 'You know how much I

love to drive myself,' she said, with a wave of her hand. 'It's always faster that way.'

When the matron handed the baby over to her on the front steps of the maternity home, Walter drove his newly made family straight to Stoneleigh, and only when she put Patrick in her mother's arms did Jean tell Edith that she and Walter had chosen Kennedy, for their first-born's middle name, not Thompson, which was the usual old Scots way. Edith looked from her daughter to Walter in bewildered gratitude. 'I don't deserve this; you both know I don't.'

'It's in the past, Mama,' Jean said with sudden force. Walter heard the undercurrent in his wife's tone, as if she were desperately trying to make it so. Edith began to rock her grandson gently, staring at him with a burning intensity until Jean eventually touched her arm. 'It's all right, Mama,' she said, 'you're going to be seeing a lot of Patrick. I promise.'

True to her word, Jean drove to Ayr with the baby, first in his Moses basket, sometimes twice a week, and then sitting up, secured by a blanket on the back seat, entertained by books and toys, assiduously cultivating the bond between her mother and her son. Sometimes she would withdraw, offering the excuse that she needed a nap, and spy on them from an upstairs bedroom window as Edith read to the toddler on the travelling rug, or held the pail steady while he shovelled in sand. She waited for the moments of affection, willing them excitedly, when Patrick put his chubby sandy hand up to his grandmother's mouth, or when Edith patiently received and returned the same flower over and over again.

Edith almost always fed and bathed Patrick, and Jean would lift him out of the car at Loch Doon and put him straight to bed. Walter joked that Edith saw more of his son than he did, especially on the days when he left not long after dawn for the technical college in Glasgow and returned home late. On those days particularly, as Jean drove along the empty ribbon of road beside the loch to the blank-faced house, sometimes she fantasised that it was never-ending, and that she would hurtle on, bumping across the moorland, careering over the bogs, up over the Merrick, into the incandescent sky and oblivion. Then the house loomed into view, like a crusty old termite hill, and she wondered if she, not yet thirty, would live and die there.

On other days Jean would slip away to Joy's house to gossip over a large vodka tonic, or share a bottle of wine with her at the new Trattoria Il Forno in the Sandgate. Secretly, Jean thought Joy, who had given up her job in the accounts department at Hourstons as soon as she and Tommy were married, supposedly to help him in the car dealership, was a bit of a gold-digger, full of new-minted airs and graces, but she provided Jean with harmless company.

'Don't you miss the town?' asked Joy as she gestured to the waiter to refill their wine glasses. 'I mean, I'm sure Walter is a darling, but you can't even go to the pictures, and I bet there isn't a coffee shop in Carsphairn?'

With that Jean bristled. 'Of course there is,' she said tetchily. 'It's more of a tea shop, but Patrick and I like it.'

Joy lit a cigarette with a new monogrammed gold lighter. 'And is there sawdust on the floor?' She laughed, putting her hand up to her platinum-blonde fringe and pushing it away coquettishly.

'It's funny to see you doing the washing-up wearing your diamond pendant,' whispered Walter in Jean's ear one evening as he came up behind her at the kitchen sink.

She turned to him with a flicker of a smile. 'Where else do I have to wear it? It makes me feel like the Lady of the Lake. Maybe I've cast a spell on you!'

'There's no doubt about that.' He laughed, but the pear-shaped diamond glinted mockingly at him. He wanted to be the one to shower her with gifts, to be the one to adorn her. He had smarted when his father-in-law produced the jewel.

Then one evening, after a long hard shift, during which he had spotted a weakness in the dam wall at Carsfad and had to write an immediate detailed report, he came home to find a suit bag hanging at the side of Jean's wardrobe, a note pinned to it in crude capital letters.

Dear Jean,

Something to keep you warm when the wind blows in from the hills. It might not be what your neighbours are wearing, but no need to care about that,
Your loving Daddy.

He unzipped the bag and inside was a mink jacket with a high mandarin collar. He wanted to grab it with both hands and rip the fur apart and fling the pelts in the loch. When, that night, he told her that he wanted to be the one to provide for her she put her arms around his neck. 'You provide the most important thing, darling. My happiness. What could be more important than that?'

But even as she made light of his fears, Walter saw something at the back of her eyes, coal black, that he could not fathom. Over her shoulder, on the side table, next to her cock-tail glass, he noticed a sheaf of fine parchment and her fountain pen beside her bead box and the blue linen evening bag she was stitching with crystal buttons and seed pearls. Walter looked at it enquiringly: 'Writing to someone?'

'Oh no,' she replied breezily, her arms still around him, 'I'm just making a to-do list.'

CHAPTER 12

Carson opened her eyes slowly and saw the blurred outline of a figure slumped in the chair beside her bed.

'Granddad?' she said in a thin, hesitant voice.

Walter snapped awake and started forward. 'I'm here, Car, I'm here,' he said gently as he put his hand over hers on the bed.

Carson flinched and pulled her hand away and a high-pitched scream burst from her lips. 'Iona's dead, isn't she? I saw her in the water . . . I didn't . . . oh no . . . I didn't.' She reared up from her pillow. 'I didn't fix her life jacket properly.'

'Shush shush, you'll make yourself sick, Car.'

'I let Iona drown!' she howled. 'I couldn't get the oars to work. Where are Mum and Dad? They'll hate me now. They won't want to see me again.'

Walter held his granddaughter's shoulder to steady her. 'Mum and Dad will be here soon. It's early. It's not even six o'clock. You have to rest.'

Carson threw her head from side to side. 'No, no . . .' A flash of terror crossed her eyes. 'Is Pete dead?'

'No, Car. He's safe. He's going to be fine. He's in a room down the corridor.'

It was as if Carson was unmoored, unable to comprehend anything. She started to vomit and Walter put a cardboard bowl in front of her as her body convulsed in shock. Walter poured water on a handful of tissues and gently patted her tear-streaked face but Carson jerked her head away. 'There was a huge roar,' she stammered, 'it was white and silver and blue . . . it was a boat. It went past us so fast . . .'

'What?' Walter was taken aback. 'Are you sure?'

Carson nodded her head wildly. 'You have to talk to Pete . . . Pete knows . . . the boat rocked so hard . . . and Iona fell into the water . . . Pete will tell you . . .!' Her voice was hysterical now.

At that moment there was a soft knock. A nurse opened the door and Elinor and Patrick both barrelled towards the bed, and enveloped their daughter in their arms, but Carson, who had covered her face with her hands as if trying to shield herself from a blow, fought her way out. 'Stop it . . . stop it . . . I let Iona die . . . I should have saved her. It's my fault!'

Walter stood back, twisting his cap in his hands, unable to bear to hear his granddaughter's torment, worried that he might not be able to hold himself together. 'I'm going outside,' he said in a whisper.

'Don't go, Granddad,' Carson implored him, looking at her parents, panic-stricken. 'I need you to stay.'

'I'm not going far. I promise, Car. I promise.'

As Walter emerged into the unforgiving yellow light of the strip-lit corridor, he was startled to find Constable Ramsay waiting. 'Can I talk to you for a minute, Mr MacMillan?' she said in a kindly voice. 'I have told your son and daughter, but Sergeant Sturrock wanted me to tell you too. The procurator fiscal has instructed that the post-mortem will be carried out in a matter of days.' He looked at her blankly. 'Then your granddaughter's funeral can take place as soon as the family wishes.'

When he heard the word 'funeral' Walter felt his heart beat faster, and, dizzy, he struggled for words. 'Thank you for telling me,' he said eventually, his voice barely there.

Constable Ramsay touched his arm. 'And there is no question of any interviews until the doctors say that Carson and Pete are ready. There will be no pressure from us, I can assure you.'

He let out a gasp, imagining his grandchildren's anguish, hearing the guilt-laden answers. 'It will be awful for them . . . whenever it happens.' He breathed in deeply to try to slow his heart. 'Carson is adamant that she heard an engine roaring right beside the boat. She's very distressed about it. I don't know if Pete heard it too.'

'I promise you, we'll check everything.' The sympathy in Amy Ramsay's voice was too much for Walter.

'Excuse me,' he said quietly, 'I think I will go and see if my grandson has woken.' As he walked away he paused and turned around. 'Constable Ramsay, you've been so kind and thoughtful. We are very grateful.' He hesitated and his voice cracked. 'All of us.'

The echoing, antiseptic, hospital corridor seemed never-ending, as if it had been designed for dark thoughts. His eye registered the cheap prints on the walls: the gleaming lighthouse, brilliant white against clear blue sky, puffins congregating on the rocks below; the next, girls in Edwardian dresses, parasols high, walking through a field of waist-high bright red poppies; and the farmyard with a plump hen clucking contentedly over her fluffy brood. He wanted to pull every picture from the wall and smash them to smithereens.

He stopped under a fluorescent light to collect himself. He wiped some moisture from his eyes and looked down at his trembling hands criss-crossed with purple veins that stood out through the dry weather-beaten skin. Had he become even older overnight? He tried to bring them under control but finally he gave up and stuffed them into his pockets.

He inched forward, craning his neck to see through the small glass square in the door to the room unobserved. Pete lay on his back, his unruly dark hair falling across his brow, his arms by his sides on top of the hospital sheet as if he were trying to keep it shipshape. To the left of the bed Roland was slumped in a chair with his elbow on the armrest and his hand supporting his head. His eyes were shut and his unshaven crumpled face seemed that of a stranger who had somehow slipped unnoticed into the room, not the urbane dandy whom Walter had once reluctantly accepted as his son-in-law. Catastrophe had crushed him.

Fiona sat on the other side, stooped over a little. Walter could see her shoulder blades standing out through her thin cream shirt like the folded wings of an emaciated bird. He knew by the angle of her head that she was staring intently at her son, willing him to wake, for her face to be the first thing he would see.

Such was the almost religious stillness of the scene that Walter jumped when Fiona put her hand on Pete's and began to stroke it over and over. He watched, mesmerised, until after some minutes there was a tiny flicker of movement in Pete's fingers, and Fiona instantly moved towards him. Faintly, through the glass, Walter heard his daughter say Pete's name and Roland jerked awake at the sound of it. Then, with great effort, Pete opened his eyelids. He looked uncomprehendingly at Fiona and then when Roland took his other hand he turned his head slowly towards his father and let out a long, terrible moan as if he had just surfaced the water and understood that he was alive.

Fiona leapt up to stroke his head, and as Walter shrank back from the door he felt the floor slipping away and he had nothing, and no one, to hold on to. He put his back hard against the wall and closed his eyes to stop his head spinning and there in front of him in the distance, on the shingle, was Jean, her summer dress billowing around her bare legs and her hand holding her hair back in the wind. He tried to move towards her but no matter how much he willed himself forward he could not get any closer and when he waved to her and tried to call to her no sound would come out of his mouth. Eventually he gave up and dropped his hand to his side heavily, and when he opened his eyes in the draining light of the corridor it was as if he had lost her all over again.

CHAPTER 13

Carson and Pete sat at Walter's kitchen table, both of them mute and dead-eyed, as their grandfather busied himself polishing his old brogues to a perfect shine. It had been just five days since the drowning and the fact that neither had sustained any injuries and had been discharged from hospital only added to the morass of guilt that was so acute Walter could almost feel it emanating from their bodies. It had been agreed that while the others went to the County Buildings in Ayr to hear the procurator fiscal's response to the post-mortem and the initial police report, Pete and Carson would remain at Carsphairn.

Back and forth, back and forth went Walter's brush long after the leather was as burnished as it could be, and the only other sound was the mantelpiece clock marking time with his rhythmic strokes. His grandchildren sat like automatons, eyes unfocused, each one slumped under the weight of it all, until suddenly Carson broke in. 'I don't deserve to be alive,' she cried, gripping her head so tightly her knuckles turned white. 'I should have wakened Mum and Dad. I should have closed Iona's life jacket properly.'

Pete stared at her, round-eyed, and banged his fists on the table. 'Stop it! Stop it! It's my fault, my fault.' His haunted eyes bored into Walter. 'I didn't even *try* to wake Mum and

Dad. I didn't keep the boat in sight of the jetty. I wore fucking wellington boots.' He emitted a howl of animal pain. 'I should go to prison. You all know I should.'

Walter stretched his hand towards Pete who flinched away, and at that moment Walter realised that his grandson was expecting his world to end. He put down his brush and took a hand of each firmly in his. 'Both of you. Look at me,' he ordered. 'We all feel that it was our fault. I should have come along in time to see you off. I was the one who suggested you go fishing. Remember?' He tightened his grasp. 'We could all have done things differently, but I know one thing, you two are not to blame.'

His words hung over the table for a moment and then the high-pitched ring of the telephone cut through the air like a drill. Walter stumbled a little as he stood up to reach it. He clutched the receiver to his ear and listened hard and then he pushed out a long breath and said goodbye.

'Now pay attention to me,' he said firmly, surveying his grandchildren's fearful faces. 'That was Patrick. The procurator fiscal has decided not to take matters further. There won't be an inquest. Iona died by drowning. The fiscal read the police report and she is clear that it was a dreadful accident.'

Carson and Pete did not move. Walter put his hand on Pete's shoulder. 'You were never going to prison, Pete. It was an accident. You were not to blame.'

'But what about the speedboat? I'm sure it was a speedboat. Did they say anything about that? I *heard* it and Pete did too.' Every syllable was shot through with agitation. 'We both told Constable Ramsay. Why can't they find it?'

'I did hear something. Car is right, and it almost capsized us.' Pete looked beseechingly at Walter. 'I'm not making it up to get out of the blame, Granddad.'

'It's not that I don't believe you both, but right now there's no proof. A boat travelling through water leaves no trace. The wake falls away. The petrol disappears. I've looked for trailer tyre marks on our side of the loch *and* the Eriff side. The police have too, but there's nothing. I'm sure they'll keep looking. Just because it has been ruled an accident doesn't mean they won't keep looking. I promise.'

PART THREE

The Striding Arch

CHAPTER 14

The small wickerwork coffin lay on the oak communion table in the nave and jewelled light from three stained-glass windows in the apse of the church patterned the white walls and spilled onto the wooden floor like confetti.

Elinor and Patrick sat on each side of their daughter, two sentinels, their shoulders pressing into hers. Carson stared ahead at the central window, the words in stained glass, 'Our Lord the Good Shepherd', shining out at her. She had been in Carsphairn Parish Church before, not to a church service, but on the occasional Saturday with Walter when he put his engineering skills to work on the antiquated heating system, like his father before him. Carson had laughed when he repeated his father's words: 'I'm no yin of the Unco Guid but I reckon I'm more use to God as one of the Unco Handy.' She'd liked the church then because Walter liked it, its airy plainness, its simple pews, the warm polished wood. It felt sturdy and safe. She only ever imagined fairy-tale weddings there, nothing like this, never her sister's funeral.

She made herself look at the coffin and followed the trail of pale pink dog roses woven into the wicker. 'I will not have any lilies in the church,' she had overheard Elinor say to Patrick, 'no rancid smell of death around Iona.'

For a moment Carson fantasised that the roses were growing out of the wickerwork, the branches bindings to keep Iona trapped inside. She dug her nails into her palms and looked past her mother through the old wavy glass window in the side of the church. She could just make out the sheep on the hill above the cottages on the far side of the road, and as they moved over the grass looking for fresh grazing, unperturbed by the goings-on in the kirk, she suddenly realised that there was a world outside the church where Iona's death meant nothing. She glanced back at Elinor and watched as narrow streams of tears fell from her cheeks unchecked, painting black stripes on her bright blue shirt. Then she felt her father's strong hand seek hers and when he finally succeeded in prising open her fingers, he squeezed it so hard it was as if he were trying to fuse the two together.

Carson heard the minister speaking from a long way away, words that Patrick and Elinor had crafted but could not trust themselves to say out loud. Patrick had read them to her before the funeral so she would not get a shock. 'Maybe there's something you would like to add?' Carson looked mystified. What? That she was sorry, sorry, sorry, that she missed her so much her body hurt, that she was so ashamed of the way she treated her, as if Iona were an annoying fly buzzing around her that she would sometimes bat away.

'What do you mean, Dad?' she had asked in a small voice.

'Well, sweetie, if you can think of a funny moment.'

For the next two hours she had sat staring at a picture of Iona draped round her neck, both of them wearing Elinor's lipstick and her dangly wooden earrings under floppy sun hats. Finally, she went to find Patrick and found him lying on the sofa clutching an old soft toy, his eyes brimming.

'I'm sorry, darling. I shouldn't have asked you. It's too hard.'

Carson perched on the edge of the sofa. 'Do you remember the time Iona moved the tadpole bowl into the airing cupboard without telling us because she thought they'd get a better sleep in the dark and she forgot all about them for three whole days?'

'Elinor and Patrick and Carson heard Iona shrieking at the top of her voice and when they found her at the open door of the airing cupboard there were hundreds of tiny frogs jumping over the sheets and towels and cascading onto the wooden floor. Iona tried to catch them with her fishing net but they disappeared all over the house,' said the minister, and laughter sounded in the kirk, like the release of a pent-up burst of rain on a hot thundery day.

As the congregation sighed back against the pews again Carson heard a stifled sob and looked past Patrick towards her Aunt Meg. Her hair was cut stylishly short, and an emerald-green-and-cream checked scarf was tied neatly at her neck over her khaki trench coat. Carson saw the same deep-set eyes as her mother's, the slightly protruding upper lip, the neat small ears, except that Elinor was less angular, softer, shabbier. Meg had arrived on the overnight flight from New York and there had hardly been time for more than a Chanel-scented hug for Carson before the funeral and a hurried word with her twin sister who was too distraught to pay attention. Distracted now from the service, Carson wondered how long she would stay. When she had returned to Wellington Square after she was discharged from hospital Iona was everywhere. She was on every drawing taped to the fridge, in the scribbled-on books spilling out of the book box, the scent of her on her bedclothes and, worst of all, on the frayed pink comfort blanket that Elinor had brought home from the cabin and laid on Iona's pillow. Overwhelmed, Carson laid her head on the kitchen table and Elinor had gathered her up and nudged her towards the bathroom. 'Take a shower, darling, and let's get rid of that clingy carbolic smell of the hospital.'

Carson closed the door behind her and undressed mechanically. She turned the dial on the shower and waited until she saw steam rising from the cubicle. She stepped inside but as soon as the water hit her she cried out in panic, gasping as it hit her skin like a hail of arrows. She fumbled for the dial but as she did she felt the slimy spray on her face and backed away, sliding down the wall, screaming as she tried to protect herself from the relentless torrent. It was as if she were dissolving into the wetness, losing her shape. Between jagged howls she plaintively called out Iona's name and banged her fists against her head. Elinor burst into the bathroom and thrust her arm into the stall to turn off the water. Then she stretched in and put her arms around Carson and gently manoeuvred her onto the floor and swaddled her in towels. When Patrick reached the door, Elinor was rocking her daughter to and fro, her face buried in Carson's neck and he got down on his knees and gathered them both in.

Every pew in the church was taken up by family friends, Patrick's colleagues, the parents of Iona's classmates, locals from Carsphairn and Sergeant Sturrock and Constable Ramsay. The minister ended the eulogy and as the first notes of 'Morning Has Broken' sounded there was a commotion towards the back of the kirk. Walter turned around and saw Kenneth MacMillan's two sons, Robert and his younger brother Graeme, trying to edge in at the end of a pew. As people bunched up to let them sit down Graeme waited until his brother was seated and then dragged his lower leg in and hooked his walking stick over the end of the seat. Walter turned back to face the nave and closed his eyes as memories from another time crowded in.

Pete too was flanked by his parents, his eyes fixed on the coffin as if to do anything else would bring God's wrath down upon him and haunt him for ever. He tried to concentrate on the minister's words but all he could think of was Iona's stricken face as it rose up from beneath the waves, her eyes burning and her mouth wide open as she desperately tried to get a breath, and then her body sheathed in the useless life jacket turning over again and the churning water closed over her dark brown curls. He squeezed his eyes shut and imagined himself sliding from the hard pew onto the ground and slipping between the gap in the floorboards, down into the damp dank earth where no one could see him.

Iona's death had brought about an immediate alteration in Pete that no one, least of all Fiona and Roland, had expected. The day before the funeral he asked them both to sit down with him in the lochside house where, in the aftermath of the accident, Roland had taken charge of his wife and son, and had demonstrated an uncharacteristic tenderness. And so it was Roland who spent hours listening to the unaccustomed river of words from Pete, each one freighted with shame and self-reproach over not only Iona's death but the devastation he had caused everybody. Roland kept his own heavy weight of regret locked inside even when in one outburst Pete had railed against his preternatural calm.

Roland steadied Fiona's thin hand and held the lighter to her cigarette. Then he made them all coffee, frothing the milk and swirling it into the cups in a pattern before setting the tray down on the table. Fiona glanced at her husband and thanked him absently and as Pete thought how fragile and lost she looked, a powerful jolt of love spread through his chest.

'Well, Petey,' Roland said softly as he studied his son over his half-moon glasses, 'we're here to listen.'

Pete took a deep breath. 'I don't want to go back to London. I want to stay here. I don't want to go back to that school,' he rushed on, 'and I never want to see those people again.'

Roland and Fiona exchanged shocked looks. 'Petey darling, it's because of the trauma. It's too soon to make decisions,' Fiona said, stretching across the table to take his hand.

He grasped hold of it. 'No, I mean it, Mum. I'm not going back.'

'But where would you live? Where would you go to school?'

'Fiona, please . . . Pete, go on.'

'I've got two years to go at school, maybe even one. I could go to Ayr Academy. I could stay here . . . or with Granddad.' He looked at Roland. 'You're pretty much always away, and Mum, you say you want to spend more time here anyway.' He paused. 'And you've *both* always said Glasgow's one of the best places in the world to study architecture.'

Roland opened his eyes wide and rocked back in his chair. 'Seriously, Pete. You mean this?'

'I've been pissing away everything at school. Maybe if I work hard here my life won't be all bad.'

Fiona pressed her fingers to her forehead as if trying to steady all the thoughts fighting for attention. Then she took a long drag on her cigarette. 'There's something else, Petey, darling, something you're not saying.'

Pete raised his ashen face towards her, his eyes great pools of sorrow. 'I want to be near Iona. I . . . I don't want her to think I just abandoned her and carried on the same way.'

'By cool Siloam's shady rill,' sang the mourners at the end of the service, tentatively at first, but then the congregation found a collective strength and sent their voices soaring to the roof and into every corner of the kirk, touching every particle in the atmosphere, filtering through the coruscating light that fell from the windows, reaching the spiders in their gossamer webs and the fieldmice in their nests behind the lathe and plaster walls. The heartfelt singing oscillated among the roses in the simple pewter vase beside the coffin until a single petal fell gently onto the oak table.

As the last note faded the minister walked to the communion table. He put one hand on the coffin and the other on a simple wooden cross that hung on a cord around his neck.

'God bless and keep Iona. She will live on in our hearts for ever. Amen.' The organist started up a plaintive staccato rendition of 'Amazing Grace' and the congregation stood, their eyes lowered, as the family walked back up the aisle. Walter looked over to the final pew searching for the only person who had been able to understand the depths of his grief. There stood Marie Doherty, her short grey hair soft around her face, a paisley-print scarf tied at the neck of her blue tweed coat, and as their eyes met she gave him the saddest of smiles.

CHAPTER 15

Elinor existed in two separate worlds. In one, she got
dressed, she washed, she talked to Patrick about arrangements and tried not to cry at his bewildered bereft face. She
tended to Carson and kept her close, threaded dog roses
through the coffin, thanked the minister for the service and
smiled at a neighbour from Ayr as she left the church. In the
other world there was no one but herself and Iona, Iona holding her hand, asking for her favourite cake, Iona buttoning her
pyjamas and waiting patiently for a bedtime story, singing
together, helping her paint, hugging her, closing her life
jacket. There was never a moment when they were apart, when
Iona did not feel her protective arm.

Patrick and Walter spent a good part of the day before the
funeral digging the grave in the small abandoned sheepfold, a
short walk from the cabin, around whose walls were sheltering
silver birches and pretty alders and long-limbed sycamores.
Elinor said she would not go to the burial. She could not bear to
see the coffin lowered into the darkness, she said. She would wait
until the next evening when she had planned for the family to
plant a mountain ash by the grave. So, in the old Scots way, only
the men accompanied Iona's coffin onto the hill.

But the truth was different. Elinor absented herself from the
grave because she was too afraid that when she stood looking

down on her daughter, she would not be able to stop herself from climbing down to be beside her and waiting for the earth to bury them both.

There was to be no gathering after the church service and so the congregation stood among the headstones in the church-yard and watched in silence as Pete, Roland, Patrick and Walter carried the wicker coffin to the hearse, and as the small cortège made its way through Carsphairn people came out of their houses and lined the pavements, their heads bowed.

As it disappeared along the Main Street, back towards Loch Doon, Meg took Elinor's arm. 'Let's walk a little way up the Moniaive Road. We could do with some fresh air, and I'm here for such a short time.'

'But I have to be with Car,' Elinor said, 'I can't leave her.'

Carson looked from one to the other, unsure as to what to say.

'Car and I will walk back to Dad's and have a cup of tea,' Fiona said quickly.

'It's okay, Car,' said Meg gently, 'we won't be gone for long. Will we, Eli?'

Elinor shook her head absently but said nothing, and they walked off in step, Meg's arm hooked firmly through that of her younger twin.

'It's important for the two of them to have a little time with each other. Sisters should talk.' Fiona stopped abruptly. 'I'm sorry, Car . . . That was thoughtless.' She rummaged furiously for her cigarettes and lighter, cupping her shaking hands around the flame. She inhaled fiercely and as her head started spinning she held on to Carson. 'God, I'm not much good at getting things right.'

'It's okay,' Carson replied in a thin voice, 'nothing's right any more.'

Elinor and Meg walked on to the crossroads, past the war memorial and onto the narrow road that wound its way past Loch Kendoon, and on up the hill to Moniaive. The midday sun illuminated creamy frills of cow parsley and the crisp green verges. When the twins were children their father used to take them for picnics to Loch Kendoon, a narrow stretch of water where Walter also fished sometimes and the girls would count out the shimmering rings on the surface when a trout came up to catch a fly.

Elinor put her face up to the sky and closed her eyes. 'How do we ever recover? I go over it all again and again. We're all to blame – the adults, I mean. When I do sleep I wake up in the night . . . always. And for an instant, one wonderful moment, I think the house is peaceful, everyone is safely in bed, and then it comes crashing down on me. Sometimes I just throw up.' Elinor stopped on the road and turned to her twin, trying to hold back her tears. 'And I'm so worried about Car. I don't know how we will ever heal.'

A tractor rumbled up the road behind them. They stood back to let it pass and when the driver doffed his cap and smiled they automatically smiled back and gave him a wave. They watched as it heaved its way up the hill and a pheasant, startled by the engine's grinding gears, took flight and flew low across their path towards Bardennoch Hill in a flash of red and gold. Elinor put her hands up to her head. 'I just can't get used to the idea that life goes on as normal. The farmer toots his horn, we wave. He has no idea what happened to Iona or even who she is. I look at a beautiful pheasant and it is still beautiful. How can that be?' She searched her sister's face. 'Because the truth is everything is dark and horrible and I will always know that I let my daughter die.' Elinor stumbled through the rosehip bushes at the side of the road and sank down on the dyke, gripping hold of the old stones. 'How could I be so careless?'

'Why are you taking all this on yourself? When Patrick called me he was obviously very upset. He didn't say much but, Eli, for God's sake, Pete's practically an adult—'

'Don't say that, Meg,' Elinor broke in, suddenly wild. 'You know nothing about what happened, nothing.'

Meg recoiled. 'I'm sorry, I was only—'

'Don't you dare blame Pete, blame me,' Elinor hissed, 'the good mother. We drank far too much at dinner. Car tried to wake me but I was comatose. We all were . . .' Her voice trailed away and her head fell on her chest.

Meg sat beside her on the stone wall. 'I'm so sorry, Eli. I should never have said that, but you cannot take the weight of it all. You can't be the lightning rod for everyone's guilt.' Meg took her handkerchief out of her pocket and wiped Elinor's face very gently.

They sat in silence for a moment, oblivious to the honey bees around them hovering over the dog roses.

'We haven't seen each other for three years. And now the only time I see you is when my daughter has died. How can that be?'

'I'm sorry about it, Eli, really I am. Americans get so few holidays and it's only now that I'm getting well paid; and you couldn't afford to come to me.'

Elinor started to cry. 'I miss you, Meg. Why did you have to go? You left me. We had hardly graduated and you were gone.'

'You know I had to go. Ayr was no place for me, not even Glasgow then, not really. Remember it was 1988. All those sly glances: oh, here's the lesbian twin, the weird one. Oooh, how does that happen with twins? Dyke, lezzie– it was relentless. From the girls too.'

'I didn't protect you from it; I was pathetic. I'm so sorry.'

'Eli, we were just young. It wasn't to do with you, but I'd had enough. It was good for me to go. You had Patrick. I knew you'd be okay.'

'But New York, it was so far . . .' Elinor trailed off.

'It doesn't need to be far, especially now,' Meg said gently.

'Are you happy there?'

'I am now, yes, and life is good.'

'Are you in a relationship?'

Meg shook her head. 'Not just now. There have been lovers, but no one special.'

'I need you, Meg.' Elinor could hardly get the words out for her sudden tears.

'I'm here, for you all, Patrick and Carson too. I'll do anything for you that I can.'

That evening the family sat round Walter's kitchen table, the room a labyrinth of loss. Photographs of his grandchildren, their first day at school, uniforms pristine, hair perfect, wide smiles; the wedding days, his own and his children's, were all displayed on the wall above the old range, as though Walter had curated an exhibition especially for this evening, but the sight of it was both so familiar and so distressing that no one looked at it. A huge cottage pie sat in the middle of the table, as if by magic, and an apple crumble and custard waited on the sideboard. Patrick put his hand on Walter's arm. 'Thank Marie from all of us, Dad. It's very kind of her to make us dinner.'

Walter smiled. 'I will, but she won't want any thanks. She's happy to help.'

Patrick looked at his father intently. 'We should be telling her ourselves. Marie should be here. I saw her at the funeral.'

Walter nodded, and Patrick went on. 'I did see someone unexpected in church, in fact two people. Your cousin

Kenneth's sons. One had a walking stick, and the other one's a bit older, my age I think.'

A shadow crossed Walter's face. 'Yes, I was surprised to see them too.'

'We never saw them when we were growing up,' added Fiona. 'Wasn't there some falling out?'

Walter gripped the table involuntarily. 'There was no love lost between my father and their grandfather. They fell out over a land deal and the rift was never healed.' He hesitated for a moment. 'I don't suppose it will ever be now.'

'Maybe not,' replied Patrick, 'but the minister said they'd given him a cheque towards the restoration of the playpark in the village. They said the donation was in Iona's memory.' He took Elinor's hand. 'Would you like something in the park to remember Iona by?'

Elinor looked lost. 'I . . . I don't really know. Car, what do you think?'

Carson thought for a moment. 'Maybe a new roundabout. The old one's broken. Iona used to put her dolls on it and order them to hold on tight. Then when she pushed hard and they all fell off she would give them a row for not listening to her.' Her voice shook as the scene flashed before her. 'Do you remember, Mum?'

But Elinor was thinking about her own commemoration. She began to put words together to shape a bright monologue. 'Patrick and I are going to Threave Castle in the morning to choose a mountain ash to plant by Iona's grave. I've called ahead to make sure it's the yellow berry variety. When it fruits in the autumn it will contrast beautifully with the slender red leaves.' Elinor talked on, her soliloquy filling the empty air in the room. 'I saw a cloud of goldfinches twittering around one and it would be lovely if they made their home in the old sheepfold. And then I'll plant a carpet of wood anemone. The deciduous trees will be perfect for them.'

'That will be such a beautiful display, Eli,' Meg broke in, as if to staunch her sister's sadness. 'I hope I'll be here to see them bloom in springtime.' She turned to Carson. 'It's my last day tomorrow. I'd like to see Andy Goldsworthy's new sculpture at Moniaive. Do you want to come with me, Car?' Carson hesitated, and before she had a chance to answer Meg had already asked Walter if she could borrow his car for a couple of hours.

'Of course,' he replied, with one eye on his granddaughter. 'You know, Car, you could also walk up the hill to the covenanter James Renwick's monument on your way. When he was captured he refused to swear fealty to James VII, so after they hanged him they fixed his head and hands to the gates of Edinburgh.'

'Right, Dad,' said Patrick sharply, 'not a history lecture, please.'

'But Renwick was from Moniaive.'

'And Car will appreciate it another time – just not now.'

A faint apologetic look crossed Carson's eyes. 'We'll go together, Granddad.'

It had always been the same, Patrick thought. He remembered that when he and Fiona were young, an anxious question ventured as to why Mummy was in bed and Daddy making dinner, and supervising their homework, was always met with a story or a scattering of random facts, because a story could open a door when another one was firmly shut.

The next morning Elinor and Patrick set out for Threave in exhausted silence. Elinor laid her head on the headrest and closed her eyes. Her nightmares came in battalions and she knew it was the same for Patrick. She had heard him stumble from their bed in the dark, calling out for Iona, his voice ragged with grief. Her heart had raced then as she strained to hear something about their daughter, jealous even of a memory from which she was shut out. But as he drove she could not bear to ask him if he remembered what it was that made him shout out, and she wondered if they would be forever locked inside their own wretchedness.

Even the car reproached them. There was no gleeful giggling as Iona repeatedly pressed her feet into the back of Patrick's seat, no squealing as he put his hands round to grab her ankles when she was least expecting it, and music, once as certain as turning on the ignition, was out of the question.

Alone together, properly, for the first time, and without the business of the funeral to occupy them, Elinor's pent-up fury exploded. 'That fucking pompous self-indulgent dinner! If we really wanted to support Fiona we should have helped her dry out and told Roland to go to hell.'

'But Eli, that's not fair on Roland. It was Fiona who was desperate for the party.'

Elinor stared out of the window, ignoring his response. 'And Walter . . . Why did he put it into Pete's head that he had something to prove? If he was so bloody keen he should have stayed at the loch to see them off. But no, he had to get back home. Maybe Marie was there. She should have been at the party watching over us. She would never have let this happen.'

Patrick sighed.

'Don't sigh at me, don't you dare. Fiona's always had this ridiculous idea that Marie somehow spirited Walter away from your mother. It's ridiculous. If you and Fiona had accepted Marie like grown-up civilised people none of this would have happened.'

'Eli, you can't possibly know that. Please, we're hurting and we need to be good to each other.'

Elinor pressed her hands to her mouth. When she stopped speaking, stopped shouting, she felt ill and empty, ashamed of lacerating Patrick when she blamed herself most of all. She studied his profile, the contours of a face she had kissed a thousand times and saw that it had changed. It seemed to have collapsed in on itself. The corner of his eye drooped, and the lid sagged over it. His cheek was hollow and ravaged and his beard was unkempt and suddenly completely grey. His lips were pulled tightly as if they had been sewn together.

'What shall we do?' he whispered.

'I don't know what to do, Patrick. We killed her, as surely as if we had held her head under the water.' She gasped as the image caught up with her tumbling words.

Patrick pulled the car onto the verge and laid his head on the steering wheel.

Alarmed, Elinor leaned over and held him tightly. 'We can't bring Iona back, Patrick, but we have to put Carson back together again, otherwise we will have lost both our daughters.'

They sat clinging together at the side of the road, oblivious to the rain that first pattered spots on the roof and then sent rivulets trailing crazily down the windscreen. Cars swished backwards and forwards untroubled by the misted-up tangerine Volvo, splashing it carelessly with their spray until finally Patrick started the engine and put his hand across the fogged-up windscreen and slowly pulled back onto the road.

CHAPTER 16

For the first time since Iona's death nobody needed Walter. He wandered around the garden aimlessly, picking early spinach and retying raspberry canes. He half-heartedly hoed the lettuce patch and dug out some weeds from the path, but he saw only futility in the garden. Even the friendly linnet whose high trill always greeted Walter when he stepped out of the door, seemingly to lift his spirits, irritated him. He thought to visit the cairn but then he remembered that Meg and Carson had taken the Land Rover to the Striding Arch. He went inside to the dark of the kitchen where the sun had yet to reach into the corners and made a cup of tea, but the quavering tick-tock of the old clock reminded him of his uselessness second by second.

Even his single Indian Tree china cup, one of the few surviving pieces of their wedding service, was a reminder of his enforced solitude. He took his tea through to the living room and looked at the bookcase. There where it had always sat, between *Old Mortality* and *The Riddle of the Sands*, was *Sunset Song*. It was a first edition, still with the dust jacket intact, a black and white photograph of a little girl with short square-cut hair atop a horse-drawn plough alongside her father. Walter remembered how excited he was when he had found it in a second-hand bookshop in the Sandgate when he and Jean were courting. She had laughed in surprise when she had opened the brown paper package and exclaimed that no one else could have bought her such a perfect present. Walter took the book from the shelf and put it to his nose and could still detect the faint scent of Chanel No. 5. As he opened it to find his inscription, a brochure fluttered to the ground. It gave him such a start he felt light-headed, and sat down heavily and closed his eyes.

'It's a fairy castle! It's a fairy castle!' Fiona exclaimed, bouncing up and down on the back seat as Walter turned the Morris Traveller through the gates and up the long wide drive to the hotel. Ahead of them, set among tall fir trees, was a handsome cream Edwardian building with a red tiled roof. An ornate garden ran down to the River Tweed.

'Where are we, Dad?' asked Patrick, awestruck. 'There must be a hundred windows on the front of that big house.'

'More, I think, Patrick. Look at the two rows set into the roof,' replied Walter, revelling in their excitement.

'What a wonderful surprise, darling!' Jean leaned over and kissed him on the neck. 'For all of us.'

A few days earlier Walter had learned he was to be awarded a bonus and a pay rise for a piece of machinery he had devised at Tongland. No longer would an engineer have to stay at the power station overnight. The chief engineer had clapped him on the back. 'Well, Walter, that course at the technical college paid off. It's all about automation– though we don't want to take that too far, do we.' Mr Reid laughed. 'Then we'd all be out of a job! But you'll be in charge of all this one day, Walter, mark my words.' On his way home that day he stopped at the telephone box in Carsphairn and called Peebles Hydro Hotel, seventy miles away. When he reached home he informed the family that they were to pack their good clothes and swimsuits. 'We're going somewhere very special this weekend,' he said with a sly smile and a wink.

'Not even me?' Jean asked coquettishly that night as they undressed for bed. 'Don't I get to know? How will I know what to pack?'

Walter shook his head. 'You could wear sackcloth and you would still be the most beautiful woman in the room.'

Nonetheless the next day Jean took the children to Hourstons in Ayr and bought Fiona a red and black drop-waisted dress. 'You will be the belle of the ball in that dress, Fiona darling,' Jean exclaimed, to her daughter's delight. For Patrick, there were brown corduroy trousers and an Aertex shirt. She picked a blue-checked shirt for Walter and for herself a long bell-sleeved Dior dress with a high neck and a new pair of hooped earrings. 'Right, you two,' Jean said gaily as they left the shop, 'we'll show Grandma your new clothes.'

'Why couldn't she have come with us shopping, Mummy?' enquired Fiona.

'You've asked me this before, darling, and you know the answer. She likes to stay at home.'

'But how does *she* get new clothes?' Fiona persisted.

'Grandma has a wardrobe full of clothes. She doesn't need any more.'

'But so have you and you buy things; you've got lots of dresses.'

Jean stiffened. 'Fiona, that is very cheeky for a little girl. Shall we take your dress back right now? Your pink one will do.'

A look of panic crossed Fiona's face. 'No, Mummy. Please don't. I'm sorry.'

They arrived at Stoneleigh for a sandwich lunch and as Fiona twirled in her new dress for Edith, Jean slipped through to the dining room and poured herself a large glass of sherry from the decanter.

When she returned with the glass in her hand Edith raised her eyebrows. 'What is it, Mama?' asked Jean testily. 'I just need a pick-me-up after shopping with the children. It's sometimes a struggle on my own.'

Walter stopped the car in front of the hotel and a uniformed porter ran down the steps to greet them and take their luggage while another stepped into the driver's seat and whisked the car away. Fiona and Patrick were saucer-eyed. 'Where's the swimming pool, Daddy?' Fiona asked, looking around at the gardens.

'It's inside.' Jean laughed.

'What do you mean, Mummy? Inside the hotel?'

Jean nodded. 'Go and have a look. I bet it's lovely and warm.'

The children charged up the steps and as the doorman held the door open to let them pass he slipped them both a sweetie. When they stepped onto the plush carpet they stopped in their tracks, agog at the vast mirrored reception hall and the hubbub as families moved to and fro, greeting others or sitting among pots of ferns playing card games while maids in starched black and white uniforms delivered silver pots of tea and cake stands laden with scones, empire biscuits and chocolate fondants. In the corner a man in bow tie and tails played show tunes on an ebony piano. Walter had requested a suite at the front of the hotel and the family was shown to the first floor where a sumptuous master bedroom with a balcony adjoined a twin-bedded room.

There was a bottle of champagne on ice on a table beside matching chintz sofas. 'Watch out, you two!' called Walter as he popped the cork and it bounced off the ceiling. Fiona squealed and watched as her father poured two glasses, handed one to Jean, and pulled a long box from inside his jacket pocket.

'What it is?' demanded Fiona as she jumped up and down.

Patrick was preoccupied with the huge marble bathroom. 'Look,' he shouted, 'there's a bath *and* a shower and dressing gowns!'

Walter called to him to come back to the bedroom. 'This is a special present for Mummy' – he smiled – 'for giving me you two scamps.'

Jean gasped as she opened the lid. 'Walter, this is far too much. They must have cost a fortune.' She lifted out the heavy double string of pearls and held it up. The necklace had a luminous glow in the late afternoon light.

'You deserve them, and anyway' – he lowered his voice and whispered in her ear – 'you're not the only one with money.' They clinked glasses and Jean kicked off her shoes and sat back on the bed languorously. Walter looked at her adoringly. 'I'll take the children for a swim. You relax.'

Patrick raced to the pool and executed a perfect dive, surfacing to catch the admiring looks from the other children who were playing a game of water polo. Minutes later he was in the midst of it.

Fiona, more tentative, hung her arms around Walter's neck as he swam on his back until she spied a little girl playing with two dolls on the pool steps and finally released her grip. The children settled, Walter headed off for the swimming lanes and began to power up and down, his limbs strong and supple, his strokes even, enjoying the unaccustomed luxury of it all, luxury that he had provided.

When he returned to the suite Jean was lying reading *Sunset Song*, her silk kimono draped about her, the pearls loose around her neck, glistening against her sallow skin, and a full glass of champagne beside her. 'Where are the children?' she said, startled. 'You didn't leave them in the pool, did you, darling?'

'Of course not.' He laughed as he threw himself onto the bed beside her, invigorated by his swim. 'They're both happy as clams with their new friends, and for the next hour they're being supervised at high tea.' He deftly lifted himself up and hovered over her, balancing on his hands and feet. 'It's truly amazing what money can buy,' he murmured as he lifted her hair and kissed her slowly where the pearls draped down from her throat.

By the time the children were delivered back to the room by a waitress, the bottle of champagne was upside down in the bucket and Jean had poured herself a generous gin and tonic from the covered wicker basket she had brought with her. 'I hope you'll still enjoy the Riesling I'm planning for dinner tonight,' Walter said lightly.

Jean lit two cigarettes and handed him one. 'Now, Walter, are you giving me a ticking off? When have I not been able to enjoy fine wine? One G and T before dinner? It's hardly anything.' She waved her hand, sending a trail of smoke around her head.

'Mummy, you look like you're on fire,' Patrick said with a giggle.

'If you give me a kiss, I'll blow you some smoke rings.' Jean put her cheek out for her son.

'Jean,' Walter said, half laughing, 'that's not very ladylike.'

She gave Walter an irritated look. 'Oh well, Patrick, Daddy doesn't approve. I'll do it another time.'

She sat down a little heavily at the dressing table and began to apply her make-up. Fiona sat down beside her on the stool and studied her intently in the mirror. 'Can I have some eyeshadow too?'

'No, darling, but here's a little powder for your beautiful button nose.' She opened her compact and dabbed powder liberally over Fiona's face. Then she lifted her can of Elnett hairspray and wafted it around her head.

Suddenly Fiona started coughing. 'You've sprayed me, Mummy. It's stingy in my eyes, like you've stuck pins in,' she whined.

'Oh, for goodness sake,' Jean snapped suddenly, 'stop making such a fuss. It's just a little hairspray.' Fiona's face turned red, and she began to cry.

Walter swept her into his arms and carried her through to her bedroom, shushing her with a kiss on her crumpled face. Patrick was lying on his bed engrossed in his Superman comic. 'Patrick, play with your sister.' Patrick looked up, about to protest when he saw his father's warning look. 'The baby-sitter will be here any moment now. I'll tell her you can watch television until nine o'clock. Maybe *Adam Adamant* will be on. And if you are asleep when Mummy and I get back you can both go riding tomorrow. That's a promise.'

Jean arrived behind him and bent over her daughter as if nothing untoward had happened. 'Night-night, darling girl.' Her drawstring bag hung from her arm.

'You made that bag, Mummy. It's very pretty – just like you.'

Walter heard the nervousness in Fiona's voice and thought his heart might break in two.

The maître d' showed Jean and Walter to their table in the grand dining room. Walter was aware of admiring glances as his wife, elegant in her floor-length gown, preceded him to one of four semi-circular banquettes. 'One of our best tables, sir.' Two huge chandeliers cast a sparkling light over the diners, and candles flickered on every table. The pianist played jazz and the air buzzed with flirtatious conversation and laughter, and the odd plume of cigar smoke spiralled its pungent way up to the cupola in the centre of the ceiling. On their table a thick cream card announcing Mr and Mrs W. MacMillan was written in a beautiful hand.

They ordered vichyssoise soup and then lemon sole followed by rack of lamb. The sommelier suggested a wine for each course, including, to Walter's shy satisfaction, a Riesling, and began by bringing them each a glass of champagne. Walter had never been in such opulent surroundings and wondered what conversation they might have in such a room rather than their commonplace exchanges about the children.

'I find this all quite dazzling,' he said in a confiding tone, 'but lovely. Your father would approve, I think,' he added.

'But you think Daddy's crass, don't you? I see it on your face when he says something a little too loudly, or when he buys me something. Or when he flashes the cash – even that day at Ayr Races when he was really only trying to be friendly, and you won. Remember?'

Walter was taken aback that she'd remembered his look to her that day and disconcerted at the sudden belligerence in her voice and quickly calibrated his reply. 'He's a businessman, and a very successful one at that. That's an admirable trait, and yes he was kind to me that day at the races.'

But Jean would not be deflected. 'But I can tell you like my mother more.' She signalled to the waiter for more wine.

Walter held his breath for a moment and then spoke with care. 'It's true that I feel easier in her company. Yes, I do like her. I find her very interesting. She's put her heart and soul into creating something of great beauty.' Met with silence he ploughed on. 'I think she is very refined.'

Jean drained her glass, her face clouded now. 'But you really don't have a clue what it's like to live with someone who won't leave the house.'

'Can't,' he corrected.

'Is it "can't"? I hope you're right. Have you forgotten our son could have died?'

'Of course not, but let's not talk about that again tonight of all nights. How often do we have time together, just us?'

Jean took a cigarette from the enamel case in her velvet bag, and Walter lit it for her. She inhaled hard. 'Who knows why they married. I suppose he was once a handsome young fisherman on the make and she was unattainable.' She laughed mirthlessly. 'It was the chase. A beautiful Kennedy girl; or maybe she wanted a bit of rough.'

'Jean!' Walter reddened and put his hand on hers as if to steady her. 'Can't you just be thankful she's so good with the children? That's something, isn't it?'

Jean grimaced and gazed into her glass. Walter tried again. 'You know the children should stay with her sometimes. They would love that. We could go dancing with Tommy and Joy and stay the night somewhere with them. What do you think?'

It was as if he had pulled a switch. Jean immediately perked up, all annoyance forgotten, and moved closer to him, affectionately pushing a strand of hair from his brow. 'Now that's a wonderful idea,' she purred, 'we should do it soon.'

Walter couldn't get the imprint of her sudden smile out of his mind. Was it really for him? He had the nagging thought that she was only imagining another weekend away from the loch.

By the time they had ordered baked Alaska, for which the sommelier suggested a glass of Sauternes, Jean was glassy-eyed and expansive, laughing a little too loudly as she recalled that first night at the Pavilion. 'You were standing over me like Humphrey Bogart in *The African Queen*. It was a little scary how fast I fell for you – but quite thrilling all the same.' The other diners eyed her once again but this time differently, their judgement evident in sly sidelong glances and the suggestion of a smirk on their bright lipsticked mouths.

Walter looked around the tables angrily, caressing Jean's hand at the same time. 'Darling, I think it's time to go upstairs,' he whispered.

Jean pulled her hand away. 'But there will be dancing soon,' she said petulantly.

'There will be dancing tomorrow night, I promise.' Walter paused, and then calculated it was better to play his ace now, rather than keep it another surprise. 'Joy and Tommy are joining us.'

Jean's face lit up. 'Really?' Walter nodded and she clapped loudly. 'That's wonderful,' she slurred.

Walter seized the moment. He quickly stood up and manoeuvred her from the table as elegantly as he could and, holding her arm tightly, propelled her from the dining room.

In the morning Walter awoke to find Fiona looking down at him with all the seriousness she could muster. Patrick hung behind her, a worried, confounded look on his face. 'Mummy is asleep with her dress on,' said Fiona, her eyes searching for an explanation.

He turned to look at Jean, mascara clinging to her cheeks like iron filings, her half-open mouth ringed with faded chalky lipstick, her gold hoop earrings sticking up like a pair of gymnasts' rings. He put his finger to his lips. 'Shh, Mummy was very tired. I said to her not to take it off.' Walter ignored Patrick's look of disbelief. 'Now, let's leave her to have a long lie.'

Walter leaned on the paddock fence watching as the instructor and the stable-hand guided the children's ponies around the oval on lead reins. He was amazed at how absorbed they both were, sitting naturally and moving effortlessly with the rhythm of the horse's gait, attentive to the instructor's words. 'Now give your ponies a pat. Remember, Patrick, you are on Jasper and Fiona, you are on Stella. Say their names softly as you ask them to walk on. Squeeze your legs a little. Good boy, Patrick.' Patrick smoothed his hand over Jasper's mane and glanced over at his father, a self-conscious smile on his face. Walter gave him a wave. As he studied his son he wondered if he had stored away the image of his mother, dead to the world, her still stocking-clad feet over the eiderdown and her pearls caught up around her neck like a noose. He tried to banish the final memory of the night before when she had collapsed on the bed, smashing a final glass of wine against the bedside table as she fell. He had spent the next hour searching for every shard, every last splinter, on the carpet, his head throbbing.

Just then Jean's familiar perfume arrived on the breeze and he turned to find her at his side, a scarf tied stylishly at the back of her neck and dark glasses obscuring much of her face. She put her arm through his. 'I woke up and you were all gone. Thanks for leaving the note, although I did remember the children were having a riding lesson,' she added casually. 'Gosh, they both look good, don't they?'

Fiona rode along the fence and as she passed she gave Jean a look out of the corner of her eye. 'Mummy, take your glasses off. It's not sunny,' she said in an imploring voice, but Jean merely blew her a kiss.

'How are you feeling?' asked Walter quietly, looking straight ahead, concentrating on the paddock.

'Oh, I'm fine.' She looked at him sideways. 'Sorry about the broken glass. I noticed it in the bin. It was very careless of me.' She reached up and gave him a peck on the cheek. 'It was a lovely night, wasn't it?'

Walter looked round at her, bemused. 'Yes. But do you remember it, Jean? Really?'

'Walter, for goodness sake. Don't be so silly, darling, of course I remember it.' She laughed breezily and walked to where the children were dismounting.

Patrick and Fiona talked about their riding lesson and little else for the rest of the day, bickering gently about whose pony was best, Fiona's Connemara or Patrick's Paint which he said was just like Tonto's one in the *Lone Ranger*. Jean smiled dreamily at the children but suddenly Patrick's Lego stable toppled over and Jean jumped up from the seat in the hotel lounge as if she'd heard a pistol crack. 'Come on, you two. I'm taking you for high tea. Let's give Daddy some time to himself to have a swim. He's been on duty all day, hasn't he?' She gave Walter an affectionate smile and he allowed himself to believe that this was exactly the family day he had planned.

By the time Walter and Jean joined Joy and Tommy for cocktails, the vodka tonic that Jean had ordered along with the children's macaroni cheese and choc ices had kicked in, and she sashayed gaily to the bar in a slash-necked ankle-length black velvet gown which showed off her pearls perfectly.

Joy was wearing a dress of emerald-green satin with a full skirt and her blonde hair was styled in a French roll, the better to show off long sapphire and diamond earrings and pendant to match. 'Aren't they just divine?' she gushed when Jean admired them.

Walter suppressed a laugh, wondering if she'd learned the line from a film, something starring Marilyn Monroe perhaps.

'It was the most wonderful surprise. Imagine, one moment we're boarding a plane for Paris at Prestwick, supposedly to do business with the car dealer Tommy met in Monte Carlo, the next I'm sitting in a Citroën convertible he's dropped off for us at the Crillon. It was like a dream.'

Walter tried to arrange his face into an expression of sufficient awe but he saw that Jean was quite entranced.

'Tommy's such a darling,' Joy babbled on. 'We zoomed straight to Chopard in the Place Vendôme and he bought me my jewels.' She threw her head back to set them sparkling and Walter saw a trace of smugness playing on his brother-in-law's lips as he pushed his fingers through his hair, leaving long oily furrows.

'Good for you, big brother,' said Jean, supping her third vodka martini. Walter waited for her to mention his own surprise gift but she merely played with the strands and as he looked at them he imagined that the pearls were little plastic balls threaded together with string.

Tommy ordered vintage champagne throughout the dinner and by the time the band had struck up all of them but Walter were tight. He held Jean firmly for the first waltz, and longed for her to tell him that he was a good husband, and that she loved the children to distraction and that she would not swap any of it for sapphires and diamonds because they both knew that Joy would have thrown all her jewels out of that damned convertible if she could have had children instead. But Jean just looked up at him hazily from under her dark eyelashes and pursed her lips at him. 'The room's spinning a little, Walter. Hold me more tightly, please.' She put her lips softly on his neck and in that moment he melted all over again.

On the journey home the next morning, as Jean dozed in the front of the car, Walter asked the children what they had liked best about the weekend.

'Now, was it the lovely bedroom?' he teased.

'No,' they both chorused.

And so the conversation went, was it the swimming pool, the choc ices, the games room?

'You *know*, Daddy!' Fiona wagged her finger at him from the back of the car.

Walter scratched his head. 'I don't know. I can't think.'

'Yes, you can, Dad,' chimed Patrick, going along with the game.

'It was the riding lesson, silly billy,' squealed Fiona.

'Ah,' said Walter, tapping Jean's leg gently to rouse her as he turned off the main road towards the loch. 'Did you hear that, Jean? Their favourite part of the weekend was the riding lesson.' He winked at his wife. 'Now, we're going to make a short detour.'

Jean, a little foggy, straightened up in her seat, trying to work out what was happening. Half a mile along the single-track road Walter swung the car right at the signpost marked 'Craigenellen Estate' and bumped down a steep road. He stopped the car just outside a courtyard that had a clock tower on the opposite facade.

Patrick leaned through from the back seat. 'We're at the stables, Dad, aren't we?'

'It's a weekend of surprises, isn't it?' Walter turned and ruffled his son's hair. 'Mummy and I have decided that you are both going to have riding lessons once a week.' He caught the puzzled look on Jean's face, but he carried on: 'And in the holidays you can perhaps spend the day and help muck out the stables. What do you think about that?'

'Really, Dad?' Patrick grinned.

'Can I stay for the day too?' clamoured Fiona.

'When you're a bit older.'

Patrick and Fiona both let out whoops of excitement.

Walter took Jean's arm as they walked into the tidy, well-swept stable yard. 'It'll be good for them,' he said firmly, 'and you too. You will have some time away from the children – for yourself.'

They stood still to let a trek go past, and as the last pony cleared the yard they saw a slight neat woman in a hacking jacket, jodhpurs and polished brown boots watching the riders depart. She smiled as she walked towards the MacMillans and put her hand out to Jean. 'Hello. I'm Marie Doherty. Haven't I seen you all going past the road-end in your car? I can't believe we have never met.'

Walter drew his hand over the cover of *Sunset Song*. He remembered everything about that meeting at Craigenellen, the terracotta-red stable doors, the half whisky barrels filled with wallflowers, the smell of warm manure in the courtyard, but most of all he remembered the look the two women gave each other that day, as if they already knew what lay ahead, as if this were the moment they had both been expecting.

CHAPTER 17

When Carson and Meg reached Moniaive they turned onto a narrow road that passed a line of low white-washed cottages and opened out into a long verdant glen shaped like a bowl and edged with whitebeam and Sitka spruce. The signpost at the start of the track read 'Craighead' but there was no clue as to what lay along the deserted road. Carson was content to sit with her head against the cool glass of the side window, quietly incurious, praying that her aunt would not so much as utter Iona's name. Meg concentrated on the rough road, navigating the Land Rover cautiously, bumping over potholes and taking care to keep the wheels away from the verge on the passenger side which dropped away steeply to the Dalwhat Water, a shallow brackish burn that tumbled and twisted over rocks and tufts of grass for more than three miles. Finally, the road petered out and Meg parked. 'We're here,' she said brightly, but Carson could see nothing but two abandoned stone cottages and a small byre in a clearing behind a low stone wall. She stared at the scene, her face blank.

'I know what you're thinking, Car, but I promise, you'll get a lovely surprise.' They walked alongside a stone wall, past its sandstone insert chiselled with the inscription of long gone settlement 'Conraight 1547', through a gap where the rusting iron hinges were all that was left of a gate, and into a lush meadow studded with brilliant yellow dandelions. They walked towards the byre and attached to the gable end of the building was one half of a magnificent sandstone arch two metres high, which gave the startling impression of having sprung out of the building and then buried itself in the grassy ground.

Carson frowned, intrigued in spite of herself. 'But what is it?'

Meg took her arm and guided her towards the window. As they peered into the dark shadows they could make out the other side of the arch, completing the arc. 'Can you see now why it is called the Striding Arch?' said Meg. 'It sort of leaps out of the building. There are more on the hills.'

'But what do they mean?'

'They signify people leaving and most times never coming back.' Meg's voice tripped up a little. 'They connect the ones who stay and the ones who have left. Andy Goldsworthy has also set them in the places where the Scots emigrated to – like America.'

Carson ran her hand over the warm solid stone. 'Maybe you and Mum should have your own striding arch.'

Meg gasped and fought back tears. 'That's a lovely thought, Car. And you know, I'll always come back.'

Suddenly Car found a stronger voice. 'Iona would have thought it was funny. She would have thought it was a stone rainbow.'

Meg let the thought settle and took a flask from her bag, poured tea into two elderly mugs and then rummaged for a couple of caramel wafers. She sat with her back to the byre and Carson sank down opposite her inside the arch, her vertebrae pressed one by one against the rough stone as if she were trying to fuse her back to the curve, to find some solidity. She sipped the hot sweet tea, avoiding Meg's questioning eyes, and they listened to the rustle of the trees and the loud ta-ta-ta of the red grouse in the ferns beyond the settlement.

'How will you feel about going back to school, Car?'

Carson started. 'I don't know.' She searched Meg's face. 'How should I feel?'

Meg stretched across and took her hand. 'It might help you to be in a routine; and to be back with your friends. Pete might be there too. Nothing will seem normal, Car, but that's okay.'

Carson held herself tightly. One word, one unbidden memory and a dam might burst.

'Sweetheart, this must be so overwhelming. Can I help?'

Her niece blinked.

'I'm not asking you to tell me anything you wouldn't discuss with Mum, Car, truly.'

Carson turned scarlet, but slowly her shoulders dropped, and the nagging pain in her temples faded.

'I don't feel that this is the real world any more,' she blurted out. 'The grass is too green and the sky is too blue. The birds are too loud. It should be grey and grainy and unhappy-looking because that's how I see it.' She started to weep quietly.

She put her head on her knees and stayed that way until she had cried herself out. A cool breeze moved through the arch. Meg silently offered Carson her hankie but she had already pulled up her T-shirt to wipe her face. 'I'm sorry.'

'What for? Tears are good.'

They stood up and Car pressed her hand over the rough stones of the arch. 'I think I'll come back here with Mum.'

Meg smiled. 'I think she would like it. When she's ready.'

They fell into step naturally as they walked back to the Land Rover. 'Maybe you could come to New York sometime and stay. Any time you want. I've got a fancy schmancy new salary to go with my new job at the Morgan Library, so I would happily pay for your flights.' She stopped on the path. 'And you know, Car, when you're thinking about university . . .' Carson looked round in shocked surprise. 'I know it's a long way off, but New York is a great place to study.'

Carson imagined Elinor's appalled expression. 'Please don't mention anything about this to Mum,' she implored Meg, panic in her voice.

'Of course not, Car. But I *am* your other godmother. You'd be safe with me, I promise. And, I know it doesn't seem like it right this moment but there is a future.'

Carson, suddenly all at sea, unsure what to make of the conversation, bit hard into her lip and said nothing.

On the road back to Moniaive Meg chattered on about a new project in New York that she was helping with, to turn a disused railway freight line into an urban garden. 'People will be able to walk high above the Hudson River, right along the route that brought cotton and tobacco and meat into the city for almost a hundred years. I reckon a lot of these rich Upper East Siders I'm meeting in my new job will be happy to write some pretty big cheques.'

Carson half listened to Meg's monologue, unable to make sense of what she was talking about, but relieved not to have to respond. When they reached Moniaive Meg swung the car onto the ground at the side of a small petrol station and the two of them walked the short distance along the narrow street to the Tartan Chocolatier, a pretty shop selling decorated chocolate discs. To Carson's amazement her aunt bought a box of fifty, each with a different plaid painted across the surface.

'Are you here for long?' asked the shopkeeper as Meg handed over thirty pounds.

Meg looked puzzled. 'I'm from here – well, from Ayr.'

'Oh really? It's just that you sound like an American.'

'Well, I assure you, I am not.' Meg spoke as if it were no business of the shopkeeper. 'I live in New York, but this is my home.'

'Well,' chuckled the woman, persisting, 'I hope my chocolates are better than – what are they called? – Hershey Bars.'

Meg turned on her heel. 'We'll soon find out, won't we?'

Carson was embarrassed by her aunt's tone and gave the shopkeeper an apologetic smile as they left and walked back to the car.

'Were you just using my forecourt as your personal parking place, or were you mulling over plans to actually buy some diesel?'

Meg and Carson were startled by a portly older man in overalls who was walking towards the Land Rover.

'Oh, I'm sorry,' said Meg breezily, 'the street is too narrow to park on. Shouldn't we have stopped here?'

'The big red sign over there says "Dalwhat Garage".'

'We were just at the chocolate shop,' said Meg by way of explanation.

'I can see that. Did you think to pay for the chocolates or did you just assume they were free, like the parking?' he said gruffly.

Carson's heart began to race. 'Aunt Meg, maybe we should buy Granddad some diesel.'

Meg opened her mouth to reply but the garage owner's eyes had flickered from Meg to Carson and then to the car, and he quickly broke in. 'You're Walter MacMillan's granddaughter, aren't you?' The man's voice was now regretful. Carson felt her colour rising.

'I'm sorry for your loss, lass. To all of you,' he added, look-ing at Meg. 'It was a very sad business. Please tell Walter that Jimmy from Dalwhat was asking for him. No need to buy diesel.' He touched the brim of his tweed cap and turned and walked slowly back to the garage office.

As Carson hauled herself up into the Land Rover hot tears started to pour down her cheeks. 'You're Walter MacMillan's granddaughter, aren't you?' had brought her face to face with the truth. Everyone knew. He should have added, 'You let your sister drown, didn't you?'

Meg said nothing until they had left Moniaive well behind and the empty moor stretched in front of them under a huge azure dome.

'It's going to be very hard to bear when people mention Iona's death. They'll want to say how sorry they are and they're not blaming you. Really, they are not.' Meg looked across at her niece's tear-streaked face.

'You don't know that.' Carson let out a long sigh that oscil-lated with anguish. 'They'll know I didn't fasten Iona's life jacket.'

'Carson, many things went wrong, but it was an accident.'

Carson looked down at her palms, the red weals made by her nails at the funeral still visible. Then she clenched her fists so tightly she wondered if, this time, she might have pierced the skin and moments later, when she looked again, there were tiny trickles of blood smeared across the cushions of pale skin.

CHAPTER 18

That evening Elinor carried the tall sapling in its pot towards the sheepfold, the almond-shaped serrated leaves fluttering on their slender branches. At the garden centre at Threave she had been adamant to the point of rudeness, Patrick thought.

'I must have the *Sorbus aucuparia* with yellow berries, not red ones,' she insisted when Sally, the senior horticulturalist, showed her a selection. 'I'm well aware that red is the most common colour for a rowan, or mountain ash, whichever you call it.' She looked at the tag on the tree trunk. 'Can you guarantee that the Joseph Rock variety has yellow fruit?' Her voice was like a violin string, stretched so tightly it was on the point of suddenly and violently snapping.

Sally's patient expression suggested to Patrick that she was aware this was no ordinary request. She smiled at Elinor. 'I'm sure it—'

'And can you guarantee it will fruit this autumn?' Elinor broke in. 'If I buy this tree and you are wrong about the colour, *or* it doesn't fruit I will dig it up and bring it straight back.'

'I promise this sapling is the Joseph Rock,' Sally said gently. 'It's one of my favourite trees. It should fruit this autumn, but that's the only thing I can't guarantee. I'm sorry.'

'I'll just have to pray it does then,' replied Elinor, more subdued now. 'Thank you for your help' – she looked at the horticulturalist's badge – 'Sally.'

Elinor watched as Patrick manoeuvred the young tree carefully into the boot of the Volvo. 'You thought I was stroppy, didn't you, that I was out of order? You're not saying anything but that's what you're thinking, isn't it?'

'Elinor, stop. I know it was important to get the right one.'

'But you thought I was rude. I can tell.'

'No, darling, but I think she knew what you wanted straight away. She knows her job.'

Elinor pressed her hands together in front of her mouth. 'I couldn't say I don't want a red rowan because there will be no need to ward off evil, could I? No need to stop Iona leaving her grave.' She put her face up to the sky and let out a long keening sound.

The terrible cry rent Patrick in two. 'Please, Eli. I think we should get back home.'

Elinor shrank into herself on the journey back to the loch. She had thought she might find beauty in the sapling, and comfort in the thought of it growing strong and true, close to Iona, protecting her, but she was tricking her heart. How would she ever take pleasure in spring flowers or even a wisp of cloud in an ice-blue sky, or the song of a nightingale at daybreak? Now she would think of it as a song of death, not love.

As the evening light fell over the loch and the moorland above it, the world turned a soft greeny grey. The family followed Elinor into the sheepfold, through the opening in the stone wall, and she and Patrick worked in silence, carefully setting the rowan tree into the hole that Walter had dug beside the simple sandstone headstone that read: 'Iona Edith

MacMillan, born 1 November 1996, died 28 May 2005'. As Patrick prepared to tamp over the roots with earth, Elinor asked him to stop. She took a little velvet-covered wooden box from her pocket and opened it. Resting on a lace handkerchief was a lock of baby hair and on the linen square was embroidered the initial I, intertwined with it the letters P, E and C, all enclosed in a circle of daisies.

'It's very beautiful, Eli,' Patrick said as he fought back tears and hugged Carson close. Elinor knelt down and placed the box close to the roots of the tree and, as Patrick sprinkled in a spadeful of earth, she kept her eyes on the keepsake.

In the weeks that followed, Carson was convinced that the whole family might explode into tiny fragments at any moment. When she was alone with Patrick and Elinor they were incomplete, like a house with three walls. And sometimes when she looked in through a doorway she glimpsed Iona crayoning at the kitchen table, biting her lip in concentration, or crouched over her doll's house in her bedroom. It was like an afterimage she sometimes saw when she closed her eyes in bright sunlight and when her eyes settled Iona had faded to nothing.

But she felt most alone when Elinor withdrew into herself. She sat at her work table at the rear of the flat, by the window that overlooked the top of the trees. Carson observed her staring out, motionless, and wondered where she was. She knew that she was somewhere with Iona and she longed to ask her, but her throat seized, her heart thumping. She could not find the words. In front of Elinor was an exact replica of the materials she kept at Loch Doon, and beside them a clay flowerpot filled with a profusion of purple sage. A well-meaning friend had given her a commission for the artwork for her new restaurant of that name in the town, but the page in front of her was blank. Carson slipped away and curled up on her bed, watching her digital clock, counting out the minutes. Fifteen minutes passed before she quietly returned and stood at Elinor's shoulder. The Mason jars were still crystal clear. 'Mum,' she said softly, 'you haven't painted anything. Are you okay?'

Elinor looked at the page, startled. 'Oh, have I not?' She sighed. She took Carson's hand. 'Do you remember when you and Iona cut potato pieces and dipped them into paint to make patterns? You were so patient with her when she stamped her shapes all over your page. I was the one who got mad. I . . . I ripped it up.' She shook her head. 'I don't know what got into me. Now I wouldn't care if she made a mess of every single thing I've ever painted.'

Carson put her arms round her mother, and they clung together. A pain surged through Carson's body as if she had been stung by thousands of nettles. 'Please, Mum,' she whispered, 'don't stop painting. Everything can't stop. What would happen to us then?'

Patrick had taken on, as he called it, 'an avalanche' of work, setting history papers, an endeavour that seemed to fill every evening. After dinner, at seven o'clock, on cue, he would hug Carson and tell her he loved her and then excuse himself. 'I'm in the middle of the Third Reich,' he said, shaking his head, 'before the world woke up to the danger of Hitler.' Carson thought he was there because he felt it was the safest place to be.

CHAPTER 19

Pete was due to arrive in the middle of August ready to start the term at Ayr Academy, just as it would be Carson's first day back at school since Iona's death. Knowing that he would be there gave her unexpected solace; even the silent sharing of grief was a kind of comfort. When Pete had telephoned his grandfather to ask if he could stay with him he had hardly got the words out before Walter replied. 'You don't even have to ask, Pete,' he said, smiling into the telephone receiver. 'I'm ready – chief cook, bottle washer and maths tutor.'

Walter threw himself into the preparations for Pete's arrival. He bought a new freezer and filled it with trout and venison and Marie's home-made soup and apple pies and ice cream. Carson dragged him to Ayr and finally made him buy a mobile phone which she patiently helped him to figure out. He marked the bus timetable from Dalmellington to Ayr and calculated exactly how long it would take to drive Pete the ten miles from Carsphairn to Dalmellington each morning. 'I can't have Pete being late for school, can I?'

Carson rolled her eyes at him. 'You've been driving that road for almost sixty years, Granddad.'

'Ah, but now I'm on a schedule,' he replied. 'I've got new responsibilities.'

Pete was to have the bedroom that had belonged to Patrick when the family moved from Loch Doon soon after Jean's death. The wallpaper was patterned with spaceships and astronauts, and the threadbare curtains with moons and stars, while posters of David Bowie and the Doors were still taped to the door. Walter slid open the built-in wardrobe to empty it and pulled out a couple of sleeping bags and an old rucksack. Below was a huge box of Scalextric, the biggest set ever made. It had lain forgotten about for more than thirty years. He sat down heavily on the bed, assailed by a vivid memory.

On the Sunday afternoon of Patrick's ninth birthday they had driven to Stoneleigh to have cake and presents. Just as Patrick blew out the candles Billy Thompson appeared home unexpectedly, carrying a big box. 'I wanted to celebrate my only grandson's birthday too,' he said, ignoring Edith's quizzical expression, before turning to Jean and nodding at the glass by her side, 'and with something other than gin and tonic.'

Patrick ripped off the wrapping paper and stared slack-jawed at the picture of an enormous racetrack and cars and a spectator stand on the chequered-board front. 'Thank you, Granddad. Is it really for me?'

Billy Thompson nodded. 'Yessirree, it's the best one. I'll get you the Le Mans edition next. Maybe you'll be a racing driver, one day.'

Patrick blushed and kept staring at the box in disbelief.

Billy Thompson lit a cigar, his florid cheeks inflating and deflating like bellows until it caught, and then he asked Walter if he could have a word. Before his son-in-law had a chance to reply, he walked out of the room, leaving behind a pungent wall of smoke for Walter to walk through.

'I'll cut to the chase, Walter,' he said as they sat down, face to face, at the dining room table. 'The car business is making more money than I could have dreamed of, but I need someone to run it with Tommy. I'm offering you a job and, eventually, if you work out, shares in the business.'

Walter, incredulous, managed to frown and smile at the same time. 'It's very kind of you, Mr Thompson, but I'm an engineer.'

'And I'm a fisherman. So what?'

'But I'm not interested in cars. I like the job I've got. It's what I trained to do.'

Billy Thompson puffed hard on his cigar and narrowed his eyes. 'But you'll never make any money. Don't you think Jean might like you to be successful?' He tapped his cigar ash over the edge of the table onto the rug. 'And don't you think, given her fondness for the drink, it might be better if she was in Ayr, where we can keep an eye on her?' Billy Thompson saw him recoil. 'You're a good man, Walter, but you've got a lot on your plate; too much.'

'We're doing fine, really, but I thank you for your generous offer.'

'Aren't you going to think about it, talk it over with your wife?'

'I will, of course, but I think Jean will feel the same way as me.'

'Dammit, Walter, I'm doing this for the good of your family.'

Walter felt his colour rising, the uncomfortable feeling that for the first time in his life he was being bullied. 'We'll talk it over.'

Later that night when they were home sitting by the fire, the children asleep, Walter relayed the encounter to Jean. She looked at him, bemused. 'What? Go into business with Tommy?' She laughed coldly. 'He just takes orders from Daddy and you would have to too. You'd hate it.'

'But there would be more money, and maybe you would rather live in Ayr?'

Jean shook her head furiously. 'He would interfere in our lives. I wouldn't be able to breathe.'

Walter put his hand over hers and spoke as carefully as he could. 'He suggested you might be able to temper your drinking better there.'

'How dare he? What did you say? I hope you told him that I was fine.'

'But you're not fine, darling.'

Jean snatched her hand away. 'I am. Don't be such a puritan, Walter.'

Maybe if he had accepted the offer, if they had moved to Ayr, everything would have been different. Ten years later the car dealership had been sold to a man with an even more voracious appetite for business than Billy Thompson, and Tommy and Joy were living in Franco's Spain on Tommy's share of the proceeds. Ten years later everything had changed.

He sighed and with a huge effort pushed himself up from the bed and got back to work.

After Walter had emptied the room, Carson helped him paint over the astronauts and their rockets. They scrubbed the furniture with vinegar and water, and once a new carpet was laid they moved Walter's old desk to the bedroom window and added the Anglepoise light he depended on when he tied the most finicky of his flies. Then Walter unwrapped a brown paper package. Inside was a pair of blue gingham curtains.

'These are lovely! Did Mrs Doherty make them?' she added casually.

Walter smiled. 'She did indeed. Now let's put them up, shall we, if we want to get up the hill.'

An hour later they were striding up Craiglee Hill which rose behind the two lochside houses like a protective shield. An old khaki knapsack, filled with a flask of tea and Marie's buttered scones, hung over Walter's back. In his hand was his walnut shepherd's crook, as much to test the boggy ground as to steady his step. Walter looked at his watch. 'Right, m'girl, two hours, Car, just me and thee,' he said as he pushed aside spiky clumps of yolk-yellow gorse and tramped down rust-coloured bracken.

Carson had some questions planned, but before she could begin three ravens came racing towards them, flying low like fighter jets, screaming their rasping caw-caw-caw cries as they mobbed a kestrel that had strayed into their territory. 'That poor bird,' called out Carson, 'stop them, Granddad!'

Walter waved his stick in the air but by then they had flown on, pursuing their enemy over the gleaming loch. 'It's just nature, Car, and sometimes it is brutal, you know that.' He paused. 'You've got things to teach your cousin. He's not used to all this.'

They walked on in silence, navigating their way around boulders and black, peaty pools.

'It'll be good to have Pete here, won't it?' she asked tentatively.

'Yes, it certainly will.' He put a hand on her shoulder. 'But there will always be time for just the two of us, especially if you have worries. I know it's hard for you to speak about Iona.'

'I cry when I hear her voice in my head, and I have to look away when I see girls just like her. It hurts me everywhere.' She looked at Walter's familiar profile as they walked side by side. 'I don't want to talk to Mum and Dad about it. Is that okay?'

Walter nodded. 'You can talk to me. Always.'

They walked on, easier now, the blowsy clouds chasing the sun and dappling the ground in front of them.

'Can I ask *you* something – something personal?'

'Ask away.' Walter felt a claw grip hold of his stomach.

'Will Mrs Doherty mind that Pete will be staying?'

Walter relaxed. 'Call her Marie, please. Why would she mind? She's got grandchildren too. She doesn't spend all her time with me you know.'

She searched his face. 'Yes, but I'd like her to come to dinner sometime.'

They both automatically stood still, silently, suddenly intent on a pair of greenfinches on a bare patch of moor a little way ahead, flitting together then separating in an elaborate court-ship dance before skittering off over the heather.

Walter sat down on an outcrop. 'I've got a terrible drouth all of a sudden.' He poured them both some tea and rummaged for the scones. He felt the comforting burn of the hot liquid hit his throat. 'It is complicated, Car. Your dad and Aunt Fiona have ideas about Marie that I've never entirely been able to change.'

Carson stared into her teacup, alarmed now that she'd over-stepped the mark.

'When they were young and Grandma Jean wasn't well, Marie was a great help. She was very kind and they liked her.'

Carson waited. She had no idea what to say next.

Walter shifted in his rocky seat, his legs stiff now. 'When Patrick and Fiona were older they got it into their heads that I ... well, that there was more to it than that. Marie was divorced and they put two and two together and got ten.' He cleared his throat. 'But they were wrong.' He felt oddly peaceful, now the words were out, even though he was talking to his fifteen-year-old granddaughter.

'But they know that now?'

Walter nodded and poured out the dregs of his tea. 'It was a long time after Jean died that we became . . . close.'

'I'm sure I'd like her if I knew her better. We only really say hello.'

'I'm certain you would. She's a fine person. I'm very fond of her.'

Walter spoke the words like an affirmation, and in that moment Carson felt something had changed between herself and her grandfather, like a precious gift.

They made their way back to the cabin and as they entered they were taken aback by the sight of two cardboard boxes in the middle of the floor.

In their absence Patrick and Elinor had begun to sort through Iona's things, a box for keeping and a box for the charity shop, but only her spotty raincoat and frog-faced wellies were in one along with some baby jigsaws, and in the other her dog-eared copy of *Goodnight Moon*, a necklace of brightly coloured beads and a Fair Isle cardigan that Elinor had knitted when she was a baby.

Elinor sat on the sofa, tears dried on her face, staring into space, and Patrick was on his knees by the bookcase, a photograph album open at his feet at a picture of Carson and Iona in identical striped Breton sweaters, delight on their faces.

'Mum, Dad, are you okay? What's going on?' Carson's voice was edged with panic.

Elinor shook her head slowly. 'We started to sort through Iona's things' – she looked up at Carson and stretched out her hand – 'but it's too hard.'

Carson sank down beside her mother and they folded in to

each other, burying their faces in each other's necks. She could not bear to look at the boxes. The glimpse of the toy cooking set brought a rush of memory that floored her, the day that three-year-old Iona tried to force-feed her cold baked beans and she had batted the spoon away, splattering the congealed beans all over the rug. Iona had started to wail. 'Shut up, shut up, you cry baby,' Carson had shouted in her face.

'Hello, Dad,' said Patrick flatly, looking up at Walter with haunted eyes. 'It was too soon.'

Walter felt a rush of love for his son. 'Let me help, please.'

Carson could feel Elinor shaking, and stroked her hair softly. 'Mum, please, don't cry. We'll do it together, but not now, please. We're just not strong enough yet.'

CHAPTER 20

'It's weird to think I have four places to stay now. Granddad's, the loch house, your flat in Ayr *and* London.'

'Won't you miss London?' asked Carson as they walked together to Ayr Academy on the first day of term.

'Nope,' said Pete emphatically, 'not a bit.'

The new term had loomed over the MacMillans like the charge in the air before a thunderstorm. The night before, Carson sat with Elinor at the kitchen table, her stomach twisted like a skein of rope, her throat dry. 'What Meg said was right,' said Elinor. 'Some people might say how sorry they are and others will be tongue-tied. I'm sure your friends will help you. Flora for sure.' She pressed her hands together as if in prayer and put them on the table. 'But if it's too hard for you or you get upset, just excuse yourself from the class. I can be there in minutes.'

Carson looked at her mother, horrified. 'But you can't just show up at school. I'm in fourth year. I'll have to cope.' She put her palm up to Elinor. 'And before you say anything, I'm not going to run to Dad either.'

She walked into the classroom with Flora, a look of calm on her face that she had practised in front of the mirror. Some of her classmates smiled shyly and a couple of girls, tears in their eyes, gave her a hug, which she accepted with determinedly dry eyes.

When Mr Wallace, a gangly, dishevelled thirty-year-old, wandered in with a sheaf of papers in his hand he barely greeted the class, opting instead for a brisk reminder that this was a make or break year, the year that hopes and dreams would be realised or dashed against the rocks of indolence. Thirty teenagers looked at him unperturbed. Then he jutted his neck forward, a self-satisfied look on his face. 'However, you do have an opportunity for some light relief. We've been allocated some places on an Outward Bound programme near Helensburgh which is designed to promote' – he looked down at his papers – 'health and well-being.' He started to stroll around the class, distributing forms. 'There's kayaking. You can master a surfboard. You can learn to sail. You'll be real water babies before you know it.' A gasp went round the room, and someone stifled a nervous cry. Carson felt everyone's eyes on her and she froze, her face scarlet. Mr Wallace was suddenly at her side, his mouth gawping, alarm in his eyes. 'I am . . . so . . . so sorry,' he stammered. 'I can't believe I was so thoughtless.'

'Shut up. Shut up. Shut up!' she said in her head. She felt Flora reach for her hand and hold it tightly as if she could hear her staccato commands, but the only sound in the room was the crazed buzzing of a bee as it tried to fight its way out of a strip light. Carson looked neither left not right. She heard nothing of what passed in the lesson and avoided the maths teacher's abject gaze. She concentrated on not throwing up and tried to steady herself by conjuring up her grandfather's kindly weather-beaten face; when the school bell rang, Flora hooked her arm through hers and guided her out into the corridor. As she pulled back one of the doors to the school yard a tall dark figure filled the other.

'Car, are you okay?' Carson narrowed her eyes against the light and Pete came into focus.

Flora realised by his accent that this was Carson's cousin. She looked up at him. 'The teacher was a bit of a dick. He said something really, really stupid. Car was so brave to stay in her seat.'

'Come outside, Car,' he said gently and smiled at Flora as she handed over her friend for safe keeping. They walked to the perimeter wall and leaned against the railings.

'I don't want Dad to know. He'll have a fit and I don't want him to be upset. It was no one's fault.'

'Except that thoughtless idiot.'

'It's going to happen. Please don't say anything,' she begged him.

Pete frowned and cracked his finger joints nervously.

'What about your morning?' she went on.

'They seem friendly enough. A bit wary. They'll all know ...' Pete pushed his hair back. 'I suppose they just think I'm a posh boy from London, but I've signed up for football trials, so that might break the ice.' He paused. 'I feel good about the school already; it's a lot better than my old one where they don't give a fuck about anything except how much money Daddy's got.'

Carson scraped away at the wall with her finger. What would it be like to be somewhere where people knew nothing about her story; would it be better, or worse? She interrogated that thought for a minute, at the back of her mind Meg's invitation, and although she made a half-hearted attempt to banish it, ashamed by it, it persisted in her imagination, the desire to escape from the weight of her sister's death.

Pete settled into his new life, living companionably with his grandfather, staying with the others in Wellington Square the odd night. Everyone thought that as he made friends he would gravitate to Ayr at weekends too but, even when Fiona was in

London, he preferred Walter to drop him at the loch to be by himself at the house.

'I'm okay there. Really. Please tell Mum that,' he had beseeched Patrick one night after dinner in Wellington Square. 'I'm not going to do anything stupid. I just feel better there. I can't explain it.'

'You don't have to,' Patrick said affectionately, 'I'm just doing my brotherly duty. How do you think your mum's doing – really?'

'Better. She's stopped hitting the bottle like a madwoman.' He paused. 'She seems stronger.'

Patrick studied his tall, clear-eyed nephew, his fresh-air face, his broad shoulders no longer hunched against the world, his London carapace shed. Maybe Iona had gifted him the possibility of a different life. Perhaps that's why he stayed at the loch. Patrick choked back tears with a cough as he stood up with his cup of coffee and disappeared into his study.

In the middle of autumn when the Galloway Hills were a tapestry of purple and ochre and evergreen, Walter suggested a visit to Tongland Power Station. 'A modern marvel,' he always called it, as fine a building, and just as grand as the stately home of Drumlanrig a few miles away. 'Not as old of course, but a lot more useful.'

As they drove south from Carsphairn on the Sunday morning, through the Land Rover's open window they heard the thin sound of the organ belting out a harvest hymn. 'They have to make do with a kirk, but we are going to a cathedral.'

Carson twisted round to Pete who was sprawled across the back seat with his long legs sticking out of the window. 'Do you know how many times I've heard that?'

'Try having breakfast with Granddad every morning.'

It was the nearest thing Walter had heard to a teenage conversation in a long time. 'That's enough mockery, thank you,' he said, chuckling.

Pete pulled his legs back in, sat up and spread Walter's Ordnance Survey map over the back seat and traced the ink line Walter had made along the route of the hydro project. Walter glanced over his shoulder. 'I tell you, Pete, this is green energy cascading all the way from Loch Doon to the Solway Firth before anyone had dreamed up the idea of being green.'

Walter pulled alongside the imposing rectangular building by the side of the road. In the centre of the gleaming white facade was an oak-panelled door and on each side a series of symmetrical double-height windows. On the lintel above the door was carved the date, 1934, and the inscription: 'Galloway Water Power Scheme, Tongland Power Station'. Attached to one end of the building was a huge round water tank painted pale blue and at the other a huge sluice. Walter took a key from his pocket and waved it at Pete. 'There are perks to being an occasional tour guide.' He ushered them into a cool oak-panelled hall, past a glass-paned wall behind which was huge machinery, its banks of levers and dials long since abandoned in favour of blinking computers, towards the vast turbine hall.

They stood on a high metal platform, looking out over three turbines below, lined up in harmony with each other like an art installation, a steady thrum filling the air. They could feel the power of it moving up from their feet, vibrating through their hands as they rested on the rail, all the way up their spines.

Walter closed his eyes. 'Isn't that just a wonderful sound? I heard it every day, no matter which power station I was working in. Drumjohn, Kendoon, Carsfad, Earlstoun, Glenlee, Tongland.' His voice danced as if he were reciting a spell.

Carson laughed. 'I used to know that better than nursery rhymes.' She closed her mouth tightly. There was a fizz in her stomach, a lightness about her and she realised that what she was feeling was a moment of happiness and nothing else.

Walter understood that something was amiss. 'A penny for them, Carson?'

'I'd forgotten about Iona,' she said in a shaky voice.

Walter shook his head. 'No, Carson. You haven't forgotten about Iona, you're just not thinking about her right now and that is fine. What would be the point of being sad all the time? Who would that help?'

Pete stood, pensive, his eyes downcast.

'Pete. You too. It's fine to enjoy life. Believe me.'

They walked back outside and stood on a high bank on the opposite side of the road the better to appreciate the power station in its setting. 'This is classical modernism at its best, no doubt about it. Six handsome buildings set in the landscape. The engineers who designed the power stations were celebrating the latest technology.' He nodded towards Tongland. 'How would you have liked to design that, Pete? You could do it. Engineers and architects are in your blood.'

Pete gazed at the building, recognising its soaring simplicity. 'It's wonderful but—'

'But what, Pete?' Walter broke in.

'Maths.' He looked crestfallen. 'I don't think I'll pass.'

Walter took him by the shoulders, a stern look on his face. 'Believe me, Pete, you will. Haven't I got my old brain back in gear?'

Pete nodded slowly, a smile fighting its way onto his mouth.

At that moment Carson knew that Pete would stay and would, for sure, study architecture in Glasgow, and it gave her a queer feeling when she too was starting to harbour thoughts about a future. When she looked furtively at black and white images of New York in the book that was positioned at the top of the bookcase she imagined being part of a bustling crowd, and not in a town where it seemed to her everyone knew everything. What she could not imagine was how Elinor and Patrick would be without her.

Since the accident Carson had spent more time in the kitchen with her mother. Patrick observed them from a distance, hastily wiping his eyes when he heard her trying to coax Elinor back to her old self.

'Don't you think these primulas would make a lovely greetings card, Mum?' Carson asked, as she put down a small pot she had bought on the way home from school.

'Mmm, they're pretty, darling, but I don't really feel like painting today.'

It was always the same. Other times Carson would suggest a variation to a recipe.

'What a girl you are!' Elinor exclaimed as she took her jacket from the hook on the door. 'You don't need me to help you. You're becoming a much better cook than I am.'

Then Patrick and Carson would hear the sound of Elinor running down the stairs and the bang of the front door as she headed for the beach. She never asked for company and the stormier the weather the more likely it was that she would take off. Sometimes Carson went to Patrick, hunched over his desk, essays piled high, or lying on the sofa, eyes glazed, football on the TV. He would recognise his daughter's agitation. 'Car, she'll be fine. She just needs to be on her own.'

But it was no use. She could find no substance in his reassurance. Often she would leave the house and follow her mother unseen as Elinor moved with her head low, hands thrust deep in her pockets, hurrying along the promenade onto the beach.

Carson felt like a spy when what she wanted to do was run at her mother full pelt and cleave to her, but there was a force field barring her way, and, more than that, she feared that if she did reach her, at that very instant, at the moment of impact, Elinor would be thinking about Iona, summoning her up out of the swirling wind, her smell, her skin, making her solid, the way she was, feet planted, arms folded, mischievous, beautiful. Carson could do nothing except stop at the wall where the promenade met the sand and watch her mother walking along the edge of the frothing waves until she was but a dot in the distance.

CHAPTER 21

Walter lay in bed staring out at the big winter moon that filled his window like a searchlight. Since the day on Craiglee Hill with Carson, he had turned her questions about Marie Doherty over and over in his mind on nights when the other side of the bed was cold and empty, and even more when he heard her soft breathing beside him.

He should have fought harder for her place. When he felt Marie's restraining hand on his arm, maybe he willed it there and the truth was he was just a coward. There was a time when Marie saved his family. She had gathered them up, had been their guardian angel, but she had never once judged him, or his wife. He thought back to a time when he should have been firmer, bolder, a few days before his and Jean's tenth wedding anniversary.

'My turn to surprise,' Jean said excitedly when he got home from Tongland. 'The children are staying at Stoneleigh on Saturday night. We're going to Turnberry with Joy and Tommy.'

Walter could not hide his consternation. He smiled feebly.

'What is it, Walter?' Jean's voice was suddenly razor sharp. 'Are you the only one allowed to spring surprises?'

He quickly calculated that Turnberry Hotel, on the coast south of Culzean Castle, was three times as expensive as

Peebles Hydro, the place to see and be seen, a favourite spot for what Edith derided as 'the fast set'.

'No, of course not. But Jean, it's so expensive and . . .' He trailed off.

Jean snapped open her lighter and lit a cigarette, firing out a jet of smoke. 'That's what my money's for, darling.' The endearment hit him like an attack. 'It's a treat for us both.'

Walter tried again. 'Couldn't we go somewhere quiet, just the two of us? After all, it's our tenth anniversary. It's a special one, isn't it?'

'Well, of course we could, Walter, but this will be fun. Don't you want to have fun? I'm thirty-two, for God's sake. You don't seem to realise how lonely it is with the children, and even when they're riding there's really hardly time for me to go anywhere.'

Walter was at a loss. The more he strived for promotion, the longer he was away from home each day, the more Jean was left to her own devices.

'I think I deserve some company, don't you?' she added as she poured herself a generous gin and tonic from the cocktail cabinet.

'Darling, it's only six o'clock,' he said, looking at her glass in dismay.

'So? Are you telling me I can't have a drink before dinner, the dinner that I prepared?'

Walter sighed. 'No, of course not.' He looked out of the window. 'Where are the children? They're very quiet.'

Jean came up behind him and nuzzled into the back of his neck and he smelled the strong perfume of gin. 'They're still at Craigenellen,' she murmured. 'When I dropped them off Marie asked if they'd like to stay for tea after their lesson.' She took his arms and gently pulled them behind her onto her buttocks, so that he suddenly felt the intense heat of her body. She pressed tiny kisses onto his neck. 'Be a dear and go back for them,' she whispered, pressing her hands on his, 'but maybe not quite yet.'

When eventually Walter drove back along the loch, a dread feeling spread through his chest. Was it something in Jean's behaviour that occasioned Marie's invitation, a stumbled word or too bright a laugh, a trace of alcohol on her breath? Did she fear for the children's safety? When he drew up at the stables and the children ran out to hug him, Marie at their heels, he searched her face for a clue, but she greeted him with an open, friendly smile.

'They were good as gold. They always are,' she said unprompted, her hands on her hips.

'Thank you, Marie. It was very kind of you to have them. Jean and I appreciate it very much.' It was then that he detected a questioning look in her eyes and sensed she was about to speak, but instead she raised her hand in farewell.

'Bye, you two. See you on Saturday. Remember a camera. You'll be helping with the new foal.'

Walter stopped as he was about to get into the Land Rover. 'Sorry, Marie, did Jean forget to say? They're going to their grandma's on Saturday.'

She shook her head slowly. 'No. She just dropped them and left.'

When Walter saw how much effort Edith had put into the children's stay he was ashamed of his churlishness. His own parents had died within months of each other not long after Walter and Jean were married, so if Patrick and Fiona were going to enjoy the influence of grandparents he wanted that to fall to Edith, and not her husband. Walter was silently thankful that Billy Thompson had already departed for a weekend at the British Grand Prix.

Edith had set up a card table in the middle of the drawing room. She'd had Jean's doll's house and Tommy's Hornby train set brought down from the attic, and in the dining room, on a red-checked tablecloth with napkins to match, was a tray of brown bread sandwiches filled with chocolate spread and a bowl of home-made trifle. First though, she told the children solemnly, they would have to play a game in the garden. They would have to hop, skip and jump ten laps of the perimeter and each time they passed her they would collect threepence.

'Well, you two,' Walter said as Patrick and Fiona ran over to the starting line, 'I think you are the ones who are going to have a ball!'

Jean walked ahead of Walter and Edith out of the garden door that led to the drive, eager to be away. When Walter turned to say goodbye to his mother-in-law, he kissed her on the cheek without thinking, in a gesture that surprised them both. 'Thank you very much, Mrs Thompson, the children are going to have a wonderful time.'

Edith's turquoise eyes sparkled with pleasure. 'It's Edith, please, you've been married to my daughter for ten years, long enough to dispense with the formalities.' She put her hand on his arm. 'And Walter, please try not to let her drink too much.' She held his eye and he felt as if an arrow had pierced his chest.

'She'll be fine, really. We'll have a great time I'm sure.' Even Walter heard the strain in his own voice.

But Jean was not fine, and after she had passed out at the dinner table and fallen off her chair, Walter left Tommy and Joy to deal with the sly stares and stifled laughs and carried her the length of the formal dining room, and up the grand staircase like comatose Scarlett O'Hara.

Walter sat up all night on a wicker chair on the balcony, draped in a blanket, smoking one cigarette after another,

looking out at the Firth of Clyde into the coal-black nothing-
ness, until the great granite cone of Ailsa Craig revealed itself
on the horizon, hazily at first, and then so sharp and clear he
could make out the long pointed wings of the gannets as they
rose from their craggy perches in search of fish. He stubbed
out the last Gold Flake in the packet and stood up stiffly. He
coughed to try to clear the grittiness in his throat and when he
put his hands to his face to rub away the night he felt his sand-
paper stubble. He shivered as he stepped into the bedroom
and sat down heavily on his side of the bed.

Jean snored and half opened her eyes to the ceiling. 'Mama,'
she asked drowsily, 'is that you? Are you here?'

Walter held his breath, hoping for something more, but
Jean turned her head away. He imagined Edith in the room,
looking down on her still drunk daughter. He had failed them
both. He had fooled himself into wishing away Jean's drinking. He had never found a way to face down her demons, he
was so afraid of multiplying them.

And what were those demons? He thought back to the
time when Jean was still working in the library. Books had
been ordered by a colleague for a Mrs Leithhead, but when
she arrived at the counter to collect them, Jean realised that
under the powdered face and sharply pencilled eyebrows
and bottle-red hair was the leader of the most vicious cabal
of girls in school, the one who, with perfected cruelty, always
asked Jean if her mother would be attending sports day, or a
parents' night or, worst of all, a school play. That day at the
library counter, Jean laid the three books out slowly and
deliberately, spacing each one of the trashy romances out
evenly, as if they were rare exhibits. Then she looked at the
former Nancy Lumsden in exaggerated puzzlement. 'Are
you sure these are what you ordered? I must say I'm surprised.

I never realised you were such a fan of the Modernists.' Nancy turned scarlet, grabbed the books and fled, Jean's laughter chasing her all the way out of the library and along the street.

'Was it hard for you?' Walter had asked, seizing the opportunity.

'What? The bullying?'

'Well that too, of course, but having a mother who could never see you in school plays or take you shopping, or to the theatre?'

Jean put on a bright smile and shook her head. 'I'd rather have my mother who is clever and witty and beautiful and trapped in her tower like Rapunzel, than some of the vapid social climbers that the others were saddled with.' She threw her head back, in her stride now. 'It never mattered to me that she couldn't see me play Titania or Blanche Dubois. I just put on a solo performance for her at home. I liked it better when it was just the two of us.'

He searched her face, trying to divine whether she thought she had delivered a convincing performance or whether she too had heard the hurt in every syllable.

The sounds of the hotel waking up and the noise of waiters trundling breakfast trolleys along the corridor brought him back to the moment, and he lay down beside his beautiful, damaged wife and felt a deep sadness wash through him.

Now more than forty years later, he remembered the loss he felt that morning, that he had allowed Jean to slip from their family life into a more furtive state, to the point that he was fearful of leaving her alone with her own children. Sometimes she would lacerate them with her tongue and then clutch them to her, telling them she loved them. When Walter attempted to engage her about her unpredictable behaviour she distracted him with passion. Guilt clung to him like skin. He loathed his own weakness.

He looked out at the unforgiving moon, trained on him like a searchlight. And he wondered which of his children had suffered more.

In the days after Iona's death, when the family had existed in the half-light, Fiona's self-loathing had terrified him. 'Look at me,' she had screamed at her father, her face mottled with drink, 'who do you see here, Dad?' She did not wait for his answer. 'You see Mum, don't you? Not the beautiful woman you married. No . . . no. You see the mother I remember best. Or should that be worst. Look at me, Dad, I am just the same, amn't I?'

Another memory sent Walter's head spinning as he stared at the moon. Not long after the Turnberry weekend he had come home from work and was immediately alarmed by a faint smell of burning. He raced into the living room and found Jean passed out on the sofa, six-year-old Fiona kneeling beside her, dabbing Pond's Cold Cream liberally over her face. 'I'm making Mummy's face better. See, Daddy, it's all puffy,' she had said, looking up at him anxiously. 'Patrick put out Mummy's cigarette. She dropped it on the rug.'

Walter was horrified. 'Where is Patrick, darling?' he had asked as gently as he could.

'Making a crane.'

When Walter put his head round Patrick's bedroom door, he stayed on the floor hunched over the beginnings of his hoist. Pieces of his precious Meccano set were lying all over the floor as if he had opened the box and strafed the room. Walter knelt down beside him and put his hand on his arm. 'Patrick, it's okay now. I'm home. You must have acted very quickly. You were very brave.' It was then that he saw the tears falling on the flimsy instruction pages, and saw that Patrick's hands were clenched by his sides.

Walter cooked dinner for the three of them. They sat together in the kitchen eating fish fingers and chips which he had found in the new freezer, while Jean slept off the contents of a bottle of gin that he had turned upside down and marked almost full, the day before. 'Mummy won't smoke in the house again. I promise,' he said.

In the middle of the night he had felt her crawl into bed beside him and he spoke into the dark of their bedroom. 'You have to see the doctor, Jean. I know you realise that too. I don't think you are well, in yourself. You have to get help. You could have burned the house down and the children in it.' He listened to her heavy laboured breathing, waiting for even a grunted acknowledgement. But there was nothing. His words fell on the floor, but he was sure that she had heard him.

There were many mornings when Fiona and Patrick sat with Walter at breakfast quietly eating their porridge and toast and marmalade, stealing solemn glances at him, after he had polished their shoes and checked their homework and made their play pieces. Too often he arranged for the stable-girl at Craigenellen to collect them from the school bus at the road-end and take them to Marie Doherty. They were there most days now, mucking out ponies and playing in the yard on the days they did not have riding lessons. More often than not she fed them too along with her own children, and when Walter arrived after work, a haunted look in his eyes, she watched him flounder, oscillating between love for his wife, and hate.

And late at night when the only sound on the loch was a blackbird on the branch outside the bedroom window practising sweet melodies, Walter would lie awake, his children's bewildered, fearful faces in front of his eyes. The edifice of his family was crumbling, but he was terrified that if doctors knew the extent of Jean's problem she might be sent away to a sanatorium. Then he would fear for her life. He was like a man trying to repair a breach in a concrete dam with the cork from a bottle.

PART FOUR

The Double String of Pearls

Carson sat curled up on the huge velvet sofa in the Stratton House reading *To Kill a Mocking Bird* for her English class, but it was hard to concentrate on Scout's story with her grandfather and Pete at the table discussing quadratic theory. 'You know, Fiona,' he said, looking over to his daughter who was quietly preparing dinner at the counter, 'I think I have jump-started part of my brain. Can you believe it? I actually know about the use of the double angle formulae and vectors.'

Fiona shuddered. 'It sounds like Double Dutch to me. How did I ever do that?'

In the year and a half since Iona's death Carson had noted Fiona's increasingly frequent visits to the lochside house, and with it the house's slow transformation. She softened it with bright fabrics, huge floor cushions and sheepskin rugs, and piles of magazines and design books. She cooked elaborate meals for Pete and Walter, and each glass of wine she drank lasted longer.

That Saturday in October she had arrived at the loch unexpectedly after a dawn departure from London. Just before noon Carson heard the unmistakable purr of the Range Rover as it wheeled into the compound. Pete and Walter had left early to go to the opening of the new red kite feeding station near Castle Douglas, but Carson ran out from the cabin to greet her, and as her aunt came towards her, her mane of caramel-coloured hair flying, and a bright silk scarf at her neck, Carson thought, yet again, that something was different about her.

'I didn't know you were coming. You look especially great, Aunt Fiona,' she added instinctively, echoing Elinor's encouragement, always.

Fiona hugged her. 'Well, there is something.' Just as she was about to go on, Elinor appeared from her vegetable garden in her old dungarees, her hair stuffed into one of Patrick's ancient beanies, and embraced her sister-in-law. 'Have you told Carson my news?' Fiona asked in a stage whisper.

Elinor shook her head. 'It's your surprise.'

'Mum and Dad seem to have forgotten me.' Carson frowned.

'Well, I've decided to move up here full time,' she said in an excited rush. 'I've been thinking about it for a while, and Pete's likely to do architecture in Glasgow so . . .'

'That's great, really, Aunt Fiona. Pete will be so happy,' said Carson, smiling quizzically, the question on her lips to which she was sure she knew the answer. 'Are you coming on your own?'

'You've guessed. That's no surprise, is it?' As she pushed her hair behind her ear, her silver bangles tinkled gently. 'Roland and I are separating. It's perfectly amicable. Actually, his relationship with Pete is better than it's ever been.' She smiled at her niece.

Carson looked a little crestfallen.

'Why so sad, darling? It's time. Believe me, and I've missed Pete so much. It all just came apart – noiselessly actually. No big showdown.' She squeezed Carson's shoulder. 'We're all fine about it.'

It quickly dawned on Carson that she might hardly ever see

Roland again. For all her parents' sneering, he inhabited a bigger, more exciting world, just like Meg. Maybe she should have confided in him about the thoughts she harboured of New York. She imagined him looking at her approvingly, admiring her guts for even considering it.

As Fiona and Elinor sat together on the sofa in the cabin drinking coffee, Carson surreptitiously studied her aunt as if she were studying a portrait, looking for clues; the choice of costume, the angle of the head, the expression on her lips, that might unlock the secrets of the sitter. Over the months Carson had witnessed a gradual change in her aunt. Her face was less pinched, and the grey pallor had given way to a sunnier complexion, her bones were less angular, and although her expression was often still one of the sadness imbued in each of them, she was more present now. It was as if someone had lifted her under her arms and straightened her out.

'Now, Carson,' she called over to where her niece was making some scones, 'put those in the oven and come and help me persuade your mother to join forces with me.'

Elinor shot her daughter a warning, pleading look.

'I'm going to start a small architecture practice in Ayr and I'm trying to convince your mum to come and join me.'

Carson hesitated, her brain fizzing at the idea, groping for the right words. 'Mum's her own person; it would be a big step, but you would be great together.'

Fiona smiled. 'You, my darling goddaughter, would make an excellent diplomat.'

'I said I would think about it,' Elinor said emphatically. 'It's just that I like to be free to come here; there's so much to do in the garden and up at the sheepfold, especially with the new planting. And I must be at home for Car. We'll leave it for now,' she said, in a tone that brooked no protest.

Ahead of Fiona's previous visit Elinor had been consumed for days with plans for a planting ceremony at Iona's grave. She had read about wood anemones and the way that the white wildflower spreads itself across the woodland floor at the start of spring. The petals open in the sunshine but close again at night so as not to drown in the morning dew. Folklore has it that fairies nestle among the petals and it is they who draw them shut like curtains for shelter. Each day she researched, Elinor seemed to uncover a new fact. She called Patrick at school to tell him excitedly that the wood anemone's name means 'daughter of the wind'. He listened patiently as she breathlessly relayed her new-found information. 'Listen to this, Patrick, according to the botanist Linnaeus, the wood anemone flowers as the first swallow returns. Isn't that lovely?'

'Why don't you do an illustration,' Patrick ventured finally, 'for the day we'll be together to plant the corms?'

'Don't be ridiculous,' Elinor snapped. 'You know I can only paint with the specimen in front of me. Or haven't you noticed anything in the last twenty years? But I suppose it isn't real work, not like being a teacher.'

'Whoa, Eli, where did that come from? You know I think your work is wonderful.'

He heard her start to sob quietly. 'I can't work. I can't lift a brush. I just want it to look beautiful for her. I want to surround her with flowers.'

'And you will. We all will.'

Long after Patrick put the phone down he was still lying face down on the old matted rug on the floor of the history department, bombarded with images of Iona, each one more vivid. She was so clear to him he felt he could touch her soft warm cheeks, and then he writhed with the shock of it. And he could not banish the image he dreaded most, the small girl on the mortuary table, her elfin face porcelain white and framed with dark curls, and over her, like a cruel joke, a pink sheet tucked tightly, just as if she were sound asleep in her bed. Patrick hoisted himself onto his knees and pressed his fingers into his eyes.

On the evening of the wood anemone ceremony, the air was soft and shimmering with insects and the sky was summer bright. Elinor ushered everyone to the sheepfold and set down a pail of corms that she had soaked all day. Then she handed out trowels and wooden sticks. Carson and Pete glanced at each other uncertainly but were brought to attention by Elinor's prepared words. 'Iona must always be surrounded by beauty so in springtime this will be a glorious white carpet, and when you are working I want you to think a beautiful thought about her.' Patrick glanced anxiously at Pete and Carson, registering their quiet distress, but Elinor was too caught up to notice. She took a piece of paper from her skirt. 'Just before we begin I'm going to read you Iona's first poem. She wrote it when she was six and it was printed in the *Ayr Advertiser*. We were all so proud.' Elinor's voice faltered and Carson's heart, already racing, tripped and, thinking she might faint, she steadied herself against the stone wall, desperate not to make a scene.

'I saw a little fairy tip toing a-bowt in and out of the dasisse and buttercups. She had a blue bell hat. It tingeld all the time she skipped a-bowt in and out.'

No one made a sound. Fiona put her hand in Pete's and squeezed it and then he gently pulled his away and put his arm around his mother's shoulders. Then Elinor directed each of them to an area of the copse while she commanded the ground nearest the grave. They worked silently, each bent over, pushing their pointed sticks into the mossy grass and then dropping in a corm. Next they sprinkled a little compost and tamped it down with their feet. To an onlooker it would have seemed as if they were engaged in a strange ritual or perhaps an avant-garde ballet. After a few minutes Walter stumbled when he straightened up to collect a trowelful of compost and Patrick rushed to his side. 'I'll put the bulbs in, Dad, and you stamp the compost in for me,' he said quietly. Elinor raised her eyebrows as if they were spoiling the rhythm of the performance but said nothing, and eventually, when the trees around them were a dark mass against the fading vermilion sky and the slate-grey hills, the sheepfold was filled with five hundred wood anemones safely buried and awaiting spring.

Carson looked around the cabin. Before, a profusion of drafts of Elinor's latest illustrations were stuck to the walls and the mirror and the windowpanes, but since Iona's death it looked as if the whole room had been drained of any colour. Even the picture that had launched a series of gift cards, and delivered her biggest cheque by far, was missing. Elinor had inked Julia Childs's saying, 'A party without a cake is just a meeting,' in delicate pink spirals around a coral-coloured cake, out of which exploded iridescent fireworks. It was Iona's favourite.

She looked across at the two women, deep in conversation. Despite it all, Iona's death and Pete's survival, there was no chasm between them, no animosity that could not heal. Carson marvelled at that and clung to the idea that now, perhaps, her mother might paint some colour back into her life again. 'I must be at home for Car.' The words rang round her head, and it came to her with a jolt that it might be better for her mother when she was no longer at home, when Elinor would not have that excuse.

CHAPTER 23

When Walter and Pete returned from Castle Douglas, Fiona sat with her father on the cedar wood armchairs in front of the Stratton House and when she told him she was staying for good he thought his heart might burst.

'You have a strength all of your own.' Walter's voice choked. 'God knows you didn't get it from me – or your mother. I'm proud of you.'

'Actually, I got some of it from some very expensive therapists. Roland paid, though, and it certainly wasn't all his fault. I wasn't happy for a long time and I got myself into a state.'

'Well, it was money well spent, m'girl, for both of you.'

'I've something else to say, Dad, and therapy certainly helped with this. I am sorry for all the years that I've been so childish about Marie. I've been thinking about it a lot. I think I was just angry at everything, and feeling powerless.'

Walter looked at his daughter's expressive eyes and the shape of her cheek, and saw Jean. 'Wheesht now, it wasn't your fault . . .' He put his face up to the unexpected warmth of the autumn sunshine, thinking to go on, but the words stopped in his throat, and he lowered his head again into the shade of his fore and aft, unable to exchange one confession for another when Patrick was too young to know.

He had been preoccupied for weeks at work, trying to design

a system to stop energy being wasted in the hydro system. When he was trying to figure it out he would take the children to watch the explosion of frothing white water pounding through the valves from one reservoir to the next. Patrick and Fiona screamed with excitement when the pressure forced the water high into the air and covered their faces with a fine cold mist. But then, just as his design was completed, and praised by his superiors, the government decided that nuclear technology was a better bet for the future. Walter's plans were shelved, his expertise diminished.

The day he was informed of the decision he drove home, reeling from the bitter blow, his eyes staring ahead blankly, but as he reached the Craigenellen road-end his eye was caught by an orange flag on a stick tied to the fence. He was due to collect the children that day, but something told him it was meant for him. A dread feeling coursed through him as sharply as adrenalin. As he arrived at the courtyard Marie walked briskly towards him from the stables. 'It's all right, Walter,' she said calmly, 'the children are here.' Marie explained that she had told the stable-girl to drive Jean home when she had arrived to collect the children.

Walter's mind was in disarray as he tried to absorb what she was saying. 'I don't understand it. She had a doctor's appointment.' He detected uncertainty in Marie's eyes and, alarmed now, spoke more persistently. 'Then she was having lunch with her great-aunt in Castle Douglas. She wasn't . . .' His voice fell away.

'She was acting a little erratically.' Walter heard the reluctance in Marie's voice. 'It was probably nothing, but it was easy for Shona to take her– just to be on the safe side. She just popped her bike in the back of Jean's car.'

Walter was struck by a terrible thought. 'Did she protest? She wasn't difficult, was she?'

'Not at all – she just seemed exhausted, relieved even.'

Walter's face grew darker. 'You're being too diplomatic,' he said sharply, 'she was drunk, wasn't she?'

Marie flinched a little. 'Walter, I don't know that for sure.'

As she turned to walk to the house, Walter put his hand on her arm. 'I am so sorry, Marie. Please forgive me. That was very rude of me. I can't thank you enough.' He looked directly into her eyes, a look of hopelessness on his face. 'The irony is, this was the day Jean was meant to start getting better. She had finally agreed to get some help.' He knew there was no need for any further explanation.

Marie smiled from her heart. 'Come and see the children. Perhaps it's best if you tell them they can stay the night as a treat and feed the horses in the morning. After all it's Saturday tomorrow.'

Walter felt a moment of pure relief. 'Is there no end to your kindness?'

He gunned the Land Rover down the loch, swerving to miss Shona pedalling the other way. He tooted the horn and waved his arm out of the window in apology, and then put his foot to the floor, his head a swirling mess of emotions, most of all rage and dread.

The house was silent, as if holding its breath waiting for Jean to be found. Downstairs doors stood open to empty rooms, taunting him. Walter bounded up the stairs and immediately saw his wife lying across their bed on her back, her eyes half-open, a glass spilled on the eiderdown. All the pent-up emotion of the day sprang out of Walter's mouth. 'For God's sake, Jean,' he roared at her, 'can't you stay sober for one day? And this of all days; or were you celebrating after seeing the doctor?' he hissed in her ear. 'You were with your great-aunt. What the hell were you drinking?'

Jean tried to focus. 'What do you mean?'

'I said, what were you drinking with your great-aunt?'

Her eyes blinked for a moment or two and she uttered a short dry laugh. 'Oh, you know, just a little dry sherry.'

'What if Marie hadn't been at the stables? You could have driven the children right into the loch.'

'Oh yes,' she slurred, 'Marie's a saint, isn't she? Saint Marie of the stables.'

'How dare you. You disgust me,' he flung out as he turned on his heel and slammed the bedroom door.

'If I didn't live in this godforsaken place I wouldn't have to drink!' she shrieked as he stamped downstairs and slumped in despair on the bottom step.

After that day Walter made a firm arrangement with Marie to have the children collected at the road-end after school by one of the stable-hands and remain with her until he collected them on his way home. Jean agreed quietly, without any protest, and she began a pattern of abstinence and then bouts of drinking, and whether drunk or sober she increasingly kept to the house. Walter calculated that supplying some alcohol at home was better than her seeking it elsewhere, and more often than not he drove her to Edith's, or to collect provisions, or to a doctor in Ayr that he had found after discreet enquiries.

It was two years later, when Patrick was twelve and Fiona nine, when the three of them arrived home one autumn evening, that Walter sensed something was amiss. The bedroom curtains were still shut, and the butcher's weekly order hung over the handle of the back door. A package of books he had ordered for her birthday lay on the garden seat.

He told the children to play in the garden and walked around downstairs calling her name, but his words echoed around in the silence and crashed back to him. A sudden image of Jean sleepwalking out into the loch assailed him and he shuddered, quickly took in a gulp of air and charged upstairs.

As he reached the landing he saw her. She was lying in bed in her silk nightdress, the eiderdown folded down at her waist, just as it was when he had left her that morning, when he kissed her goodbye and, as he did every day without fail, told her that he loved her. He called to her softly but he knew that there would be no reply. As he reached the door his legs gave way and he sank to the floor.

Eventually he crawled into the room and as he reached the bed he laid his hand on her ice-cold cheek and then he lay down beside her and put his arm across her. He thought how beautiful she looked, as if she had been freed of the poison that made her life so impossible. And then he wept, tears of fury and for their wasted life together, and for Patrick and Fiona; he wept because he had been too weak to save her from herself and now it was too late. When he stood up and looked down on her again he realised that around her neck lay the double string of pearls. He was sure she had not been wearing it when he kissed her goodbye.

Just then he heard Fiona yelling at Patrick to stop pushing her. He looked out of the window and saw Fiona upside down on the swing, her head barely missing the ground as she moved jerkily back and forth. He pulled up the window and called to Patrick to stop as if the commotion might disturb their mother.

He settled the children on the sofa and knelt in front of them. Patrick was studying him intently and before Walter could say anything, his eyes flickered and he started to cry. 'What's wrong, Patrick?' asked Fiona, as she looked from Walter to her brother with alarm.

'Mummy's dead,' he wailed, and Fiona started to scream.

The next day when Walter went to tell Edith, it was as though she were expecting him. She gave him a quiet sorrowful look and tucked her arm through his and leaned on him as she guided him through the garden, past the hydrangeas turning from blue to purple and the vivid red Japanese maple, to the garden seat. They sat there, unspeaking, her arm still in his, each lost in their own devastation.

'I didn't give Jean what she wanted or what she needed.' He turned to look at Edith. 'I think I knew that all along. I am so sorry.'

'But you did, Walter.' Edith clasped his hand in her small strong one, her turquoise eyes clear. 'And she loved you. She often told me that. You gave her as much as anyone could have given her.' Edith faltered and quickly put her hand to her mouth.

'The doctor said she had a seizure.' Walter's eyes filled with tears. 'But perhaps she just gave up. We should have left the loch, moved to Ayr. I see that now. Maybe I always saw it, but I was just too selfish.'

'No.' Edith shook her head slowly. 'It was better she got away from here. Ayr and the house. This was not a happy house.' She narrowed her eyes as if she were trying to see something in the far distance. 'I did not make it a happy house.' A weariness echoed in her voice.

'But you were . . . You are unwell. What could you do?' He felt a tightening in his throat. 'If we had lived in town maybe Jean would have been able to help you.'

Edith closed her eyes. 'It would have made no difference. Nothing would. And it was me who let my daughter down – no one else.' She smiled at him sadly, the creases at the corners of her eyes gathering like silken threads. 'You better get back to the children. They will be missing you.'

He helped her to her feet and they stood for a minute beside the apple trees heavy with their harvest.

'Perhaps if I had tended to my daughter as well as I tended

to my garden . . .' Edith's voice trailed away. She turned and put her hand up to her son-in-law's cheek and held it there.

'Goodbye, my dear Walter,' she said, her turquoise eyes so bright and intense he felt her looking into his soul. 'Give my grandchildren a kiss from me.'

He watched her walk slowly up the steps and through the French window into the dark room beyond. He knew that he would never see her again. A week later Edith Thompson was found dead in her garden, sitting on the wooden garden seat, leaning against the arm, wrapped up in her tweed coat against the autumn chill. She died of natural causes, Tommy said when he rang, and Walter thought that might be true, if someone could die of a broken heart.

The following spring Walter and Patrick and Fiona moved into the stone cottage in Carsphairn which had lain empty since Walter's parents had died. There was no alternative. It was just too hard to manage on the loch with a ten-year-old and a thirteen-year-old. Besides, Jean was everywhere in the house on the loch. When he opened the wardrobe her perfume spilled into the air. Even the sight of her sewing box wrenched his heart. It was as though the very house itself missed her and grieved for her.

Walter had decided to send the children to Ayr Academy. It was a way to keep a connection with the town. The Christmas of Fiona's first year there she asked Walter nervously if she could look through Jean's jewellery box for something to wear. The fine pieces were in a safe in the bank, along with the half of Edith's jewellery that had been assigned to Jean in her will, but Jean's cornucopia of costume jewellery, chunky enamel bracelets, semi-precious earrings and cocktail rings, were in a purple leather box under Walter's bed.

Fiona carried the box to her bedroom, laid it on the

candlewick bedspread and clicked open the top. She emptied the two compartments, carefully laying out the contents on the bed, and then folded the compartments back on their hinges and removed the jumble of silver pendants and beaded neck- laces and sorted them out, the better to choose her favourite. It was once the box was empty that she noticed what looked like a lid in the velvet base. She traced her finger around it and it sank slightly. She felt like a spy from *The Man from Uncle*. She pressed it harder to see if it would move a little more and as her finger reached the back of the rectangle, the front popped up revealing a hidden space. Inside was a folded piece of paper. Her heart pounded as she realised she might be about to find something secret, and not for her eyes, but despite that she did not call on her father or Patrick. Instead she inched the paper from its hiding place and carefully opened the folded page.

As she read it she became more distressed as she tried to fathom its contents. Finally, she ran to find Patrick, trying not to alert Walter who was reading by the fire in the living room. When Fiona burst into her brother's bedroom he whipped round from his desk, irritated at being disturbed from his history homework, but then he saw tears pouring down his sister's face and her finger shaking in front of her lips, shush- ing him as she handed him the page.

My darling Walter,

I have thought about this letter for a long time, more than a year now, and I have written it in my head more times than I can remember, but then my 'problem' means that I cannot compose the same letter twice. I am ashamed of myself, Walter. I truly am. Ironically that is the only phrase that I have no trouble remembering. I am truly ashamed.

I denied to myself, and to you, over and over again, what I knew to be true. I am a drunk. I am a drunk. The words look horrible on the page, but they are much, much worse in real life. I have failed to be a good wife. I have failed to be a good mother and that breaks my heart even more. Worse than anything, I have put all our lives at risk, and the lives of others.

You know I am not being melodramatic when I write these words. I don't want Patrick or Fiona to think that I am what a mother should be like, just as I do not believe it of my own mother, even though I love her so much. It is my great hope that they will have children of their own one day and I don't want them to think that it has to be like this.

Walter, my darling, I absolve you of all responsibility for me. I do not deserve you, or the children.

I saw you the other day when you did not see me looking. You were standing beside Marie. You were laughing, and you looked so handsome and gay. I don't make you laugh any more, do I? And that makes me so very sad. But I can't find any way out. Part of me is terrified that if I go, my hold on reality, such as it is, will be gone too. You and the children tether me to the world. So here is my choice, dear Walter. I go and perhaps I will not survive, or I stay and put you all in mortal danger. Either way will cause pain, I know, but I think I should go and give you and our precious children another shot at happiness.

All my love, always,

Jean

Patrick lowered the page, his hands shaking, his face ashen.

'Patrick . . . Patrick' – Fiona searched his face for a reaction – 'what does it mean?'

He said nothing but swallowed hard, trying to suppress the nausea welling up in his throat.

'Please, Patrick, tell me.'

'Mum had a drink problem,' he said finally.

'What do you mean, Patrick?' Fiona asked urgently, frightened by the disturbed look on her brother's face. 'Do you mean she was an alcoholic?'

Patrick nodded very slowly, as if it were a huge effort to move his head.

'That's bad, isn't it?' she asked in a scared voice. 'But what does she mean about Marie – is that Mrs Doherty?'

'That's not important, Fiona,' he said, trying to muster a grown-up voice.

But Fiona would not be deflected. 'Was Daddy . . . you know . . . with Mrs Doherty?'

'No, I don't think so. Anyway, Mum never left.' His voice wavered now as he tried to work out what could have happened to the letter. He felt as if the world had slipped sideways.

'But now is Daddy going out with Mrs Doherty?'

'I don't think so. But what if he is?'

Fiona let out a wail and ran out of the room only to collide with Walter in the hall. He caught her in his arms. 'Steady, m'girl.' He laughed. 'What's the rush?'

'Leave me alone!' She pushed Walter off and ran out of the house along the road to the kirkyard.

He frowned at Patrick. 'Have you two had a row?'

Patrick shook his head and, his colour rising, he folded up the letter.

Walter nodded towards it. 'What have you got there, son?'

Patrick handed the letter over, without looking at his father.

Walter started as he recognised Jean's handwriting and glanced at his son's stricken face. He began to read and his fingers tightened on the page as he tried to maintain his composure, aware of Patrick's lowered head.

'Where did you find this?' he asked gently.

Patrick did not look up. 'Fiona found it when she was looking for jewellery to wear at the school dance.'

It was then that it dawned on Walter that Jean must have hidden it in the jewellery box. Maybe she had forgotten she had written it. Maybe the writing of it was enough for her. As he imagined her desperation when she wrote such words he was almost knocked to the floor by a wave of grief.

Walter fought back tears to speak. 'I would never have been unfaithful to your mother, Patrick. I loved her very much. All I wanted to do was keep you safe.'

'I know that, Dad.' Patrick's eyes were swimming. 'Maybe there was something I should have done to help.'

Walter shook his head and put his hands on his son's shoulders. 'You did. You made her happy.'

He found Fiona crouched on her knees beside Jean's grave, pulling weeds away from the headstone. He saw her stiffen as he walked towards her. 'I'm sorry you found Mum's letter like that, sweetheart. Do you want to talk?'

He walked around to face her, but she would not look at him.

'If Mum was ill, why didn't you get help to make her better?' Fiona said flatly, staring at the grave.

Walter chose his words carefully. 'Alcoholism is a disease. It's an illness and there is no cure. Sometimes people can stop themselves from drinking, but sometimes it has too strong a grip on a person. That's what happened to Mum.'

'But maybe you didn't try hard enough to make her stop.'

At that moment Walter felt as if all the air had been sucked from his lungs.

CHAPTER 24

Carson was a good daughter. There was no teenage rebel-
lion, no pushing against boundaries. After Iona's death
it would have been unimaginable. It was as if she had forfeited
the right. Now Elinor and Patrick worried that she was too
subdued.

'Have you noticed, Eli,' Patrick said, one night in bed, 'that
she would rather spend time with Dad than her school friends?
Or just be with us at the cabin. It's not healthy.'

'Perhaps she's just trying to knit the family together again,'
Elinor replied eventually.

Patrick stroked Elinor's hair and looked at her with sad eyes.
'We can't leave it to her, Eli. That's not a good thing.'

At the beginning of Carson's fifth year at school and Pete's
second and last, a poster went up announcing that auditions
would be held in October for a senior school production of
The Crucible. It was to be staged in the New Year.

Over dinner, Carson told Elinor and Patrick that a particularly obnoxious classmate, Sophie Leithhead, who ran her own
clique, was already lobbying hard for the role of Abigail
Williams.

'She's more suited to playing Giles Corey I'd say,' Flora had
whispered in Carson's ear. 'You should be Abigail Williams,
Car.'

'Flora's right,' said Patrick, when she told them. 'You should audition. You're good, really good. Juliet . . . Malvolio . . .'

Carson groaned. 'What? And one of the witches in a second-year production of *Macbeth*?'

'A particularly striking witch,' Elinor chipped in.

Carson shook her head, her face clouded. 'That was all before . . .'

Patrick and Elinor exchanged glances. 'You would be a very beguiling Abigail – or any of those girls,' Elinor said in a rush. Then she pushed her chair back from the table abruptly and disappeared out of the kitchen. A minute later she returned with a paperback copy of Arthur Miller's play, its lime-green jacket tattered and torn, and put it down on the table at Carson's elbow. 'Please, Car. For me,' she said emphatically, and kissed her forehead.

Over the next few weeks nothing more was said about it, although Elinor was desperate to ask.

'Couldn't you check with her English teachers?' she wheedled Patrick.

'Not a chance,' he said with a laugh, waggling his finger in front of her face.

At the beginning of November Carson came home from school, clattering her keys into the dish on the hall table, and calling out to her mother. She found Elinor sitting at the kitchen table. Open in front of her was a book that Carson recognised, seventeenth-century botanical drawings by Elinor's favourite artist, Maria Sibylla Merian. She was taken aback. 'I haven't seen you with that book for so long, Mum.' She was about to add, 'not since Iona died', but stopped in time.

'I realised how much I missed it.' Elinor looked up at Carson. 'It's my bible.' She put her finger to the edge of her eye. 'I've decided to study a page again every day.' She sighed and then gave her daughter an appraising gaze. 'You look a little flushed. Is there something I should know?'

Carson put her hands flat on the table. 'Here's a puzzle for you. Why would I be excited and terrified at the same time?'

Elinor opened her eyes wide. 'You got a part!'

Carson smiled shyly. 'More than that.'

'You're Abigail!'

'Yes.' She flushed with pleasure. 'I just couldn't stand the idea of having to watch that cow Sophie Leithhead.'

Elinor clapped her hands. 'Good girl. Tell me more. What was your audition piece?'

'"Tam O'Shanter" – the whole of it. I acted it out.'

'Brava!' said Elinor.

Had Elinor been able to spy on the audition she would have witnessed, as did the two teachers, Mary Mulhearn and John Anderson, her daughter's emergence as if from a chrysalis as her body responded to the rhythm of the poem, her hips swaying, her limbs expressive, Burns' words rolling around in her mouth, her voice strong and confident.

'It felt great, Mum,' she said tremulously.

Elinor's eyes welled up. 'How thrilling. I can see you in Salem.' Elinor pointed her finger up to the pulley, laden with washing 'Why do you come, yellow bird?'

Carson seized the moment. 'We need lots of help: costumes for Abigail Williams, Betty Parris' – she reeled them off – 'Mercy Lewis, Elizabeth Proctor . . .'

'Whoa!' Elinor put up her hand.

'Really, Mum. The costumes are almost all the same. It will be a cinch.'

As Elinor started to shake her head, Carson put her hand firmly on her mother's. 'Sorry. I've already volunteered you.'

Elinor took in her daughter's direct gaze, her glowing skin, the strong arched eyebrows and the chiselled cheekbones, her willowy body. She had sloughed off childhood without Elinor noticing. She asked herself how that could have happened, but there was no mystery in the answer.

'I'll need to get my sewing machine from the cabin. It's as rusty as I am, but I'll give it a go.'

Carson broke into a wide smile, a smile that Elinor had rarely seen since Iona's death, and it made her heart ache for the daughter who was standing in front of her, the daughter she still had.

The following weekend Carson sat with her grandfather on the high deck of the Stratton House looking out over the winter loch. A few bright red berries clung on to the branches of the rowan tree at the gate to the compound, and the willow and juniper Walter had planted the previous year waved gently as if defying the November chill.

Walter was hunched over the table, his sleeves rolled up despite the cold and, in front of him, Elinor's old Singer sewing machine lay in bits on a sheet of newspaper. A tiny set of screwdrivers and a pair of pliers were at his elbow and his head was bent low; every so often he rubbed the nape of his neck and tried to pull his back up.

'I can help with that,' said Pete eagerly.

'Not at all. Just you get on with those equations. I've already done them all of course.' Walter winked at Carson and whispered behind his hand, 'It took me hours.'

Just then there was a faint droning sound in the distance. In seconds, the rumble became a full-throated roar until it cracked through the sky low above them like a thunderclap and set the plate glass shuddering in the huge windows. Carson screamed and Walter, ashen, gripped the side of the table.

Elinor and Fiona ran out onto the deck just as a seaplane appeared in front of them like a winged monster almost brushing the tops of the trees, and swooped down onto the loch, gliding along the water. The engine faded to a guttural thrum as the pilot idled on the waves. 'That was too damned close,' shouted Fiona angrily. She turned to her father. 'Dad? Are you okay?'

Pete looked perplexedly at his grandfather who was watching the plane bobbing up and down on the water, his eyes staring, unblinking, a boy again.

Suddenly the pilot cranked up the engine and powered the seaplane on down the loch until it rose from the water like a giant gannet. As the plane tilted its right wing, a flash of silver glinted in the low sun of the late afternoon before it disappeared northwards.

Walter shivered and pulled himself back to the present. 'Come on, lass,' he said to Carson finally, when the plane was long out of sight and there was an empty silence over the darkening hills, 'you and Pete help me inside with all this.'

Carson noticed how slowly he moved, as if his bones were out of kilter. 'Are you okay?' she said apprehensively.

'Of course I am. I just need to put this little tin of oil on my joints instead of the sewing machine, that's all.'

Once everything had been laid out on the big ash table he got to work again. He reattached the body of the machine to the wooden base, calibrated the tension on the wheel, positioned the needle holder precisely, adjusted the spindle for the thread and polished the enamel to a beautiful gloss. Then he dug into a pocket of his overalls and retrieved a tiny pot of gold paint and, with a brush as fine as many of Elinor's, he touched up the lettering and floral decoration that wound around the word 'Singer'.

Elinor appeared at his shoulder. 'Goodness, Walter,' she said warmly, 'it looks as good as new – and it must be eighty years old. You really are amazing.'

'It's a lovely piece of engineering. Nothing to do with me.' But he could not hide his pleasure.

That evening they gathered at the long table in the Stratton House, the room lit by two candelabras, only Patrick missing, leading a history teachers' symposium in Glasgow. Fiona put down a tagine of lamb and apricots and the room filled with its warming aroma. Elinor had made a couscous laced with sultanas and toasted almonds, and Walter poured everyone a glass of red wine.

Carson's eye was caught by an illustration of Elinor's on the wall that she had not seen before, five tear-drop horse chestnut leaves which, from a distance, looked like a delicate fan.

'Is that a new painting, Mum?' she said hopefully, pointing towards it.

'Isn't it lovely?' Fiona burst in. 'I actually bought that at your mum's degree show. I think I was nineteen. I brought it up from London. It belongs here, don't you think?'

Carson nodded and smiled at her mother. 'I just thought you might be painting again.'

'I'm thinking about it, darling.' Elinor nodded. 'But right now I'm still happy volunteering with the Primary Ones.'

'But thinking about coming in with me too?' Fiona leaned across the table towards her sister-in-law an eager look on her face.

'You seem to be doing just fine without me!'

'But you get on so well,' said Carson. She turned and looked pleadingly at her cousin. 'Don't they, Pete?'

Pete barely registered the signal. That his mother was there, a whole person, flesh and blood, was more than he had dared hope for, but it had come at a terrible, cruel price. Everyone knew it, and nobody said. His eyes strayed to the balsa wood model of the Stratton House on the floating shelf in the middle of the empty wall. It looked like a shrine. It occurred to him it was the symbol of their family, remade. He knew that Roland called Fiona almost daily, or she him. When they separated, they had stored away their affection for each other like fine china, and when they were all together as a family they displayed it beautifully for all to see. And Pete knew too that, however many young women came and went, he was the love of his father's life as well as the centre of Fiona's universe. It had not always felt like that.

'Of course we get on well,' he heard his aunt say with great certainty, 'but I've got costumes to make. That's plenty work for now.'

Late that night, at home in Carsphairn, Walter took the call he was waiting for from Sergeant Sturrock. 'I'm sorry, Walter, that seaplane had never been in the area before,' he said, 'but please assure the family we will keep looking.'

'I know you will. Thank you, Jock. Goodnight.' Walter replaced the receiver and stood leaning heavily against the hall table. He felt Marie's hand on his back and he let out a long sigh. 'There's nothing I can do, but I know they heard something. It was unlikely . . . but we had to check. They heard a roaring in their ears. They believe it and so I believe it.'

CHAPTER 25

Christmas in Ayr had been a quiet affair. The Strattons had gone to Mallorca to visit an old family friend, the son of the architect who had designed the Sydney Opera House. Pete had been bowled over by a quote he'd read about the opera house: 'The sun didn't know how beautiful its light was until it was reflected in this building,' and so when the invitation arrived to spend Christmas, Roland quickly accepted, not least because he wanted Pete to see the home the architect had built on the rugged coastline, and to touch the stark sandstone walls, walk through the light and shade of its columns and be enthralled by it all.

Walter joined the others at Wellington Square, as he always did, but since Iona's death his presence was a welcome bulwark against a day redolent of childhood rituals. He engineered a role for himself helping Carson with her lines during the too quiet hours between smoked salmon and champagne and presents in the morning, and the dinner at night. Patrick lay prostrate in front of the log fire, and snored gently, Elinor's present of an antiquarian book on Napoleon open on his chest.

Elinor had disappeared out into the icy afternoon without warning, calling over her shoulder as she ran down the stairs that she was off to the beach. Carson saw her in her mind's eye, hurrying to spend some of the day with Iona, tracing her usual route, and when she returned an hour later she looked more serene as if she had given up the sadness of the day to the wind and the pounding waves. She immersed herself in her carefully constructed cooking routine and the creation of the dining table as a work of art with pots of evergreens and home-made crackers and vintage glasses she had amassed from char-ity shops over the years. As she moved about, as silent as a Carmelite, she smiled inwardly as she listened to Walter and Carson.

'Oh, I marvel how such a strong man may let such a sickly wife be.'

'You'll speak nothing of Elizabeth!'

'She's blackening my name in the village! She's telling lies about me! She's a cold, snivelling woman, and you bend to her!'

As they went on Elinor had to stifle a laugh at Walter's absurd over-acting, but gradually all she could hear was Carson's voice infused with her character.

In a pause she walked over and caressed Carson's shoulder. 'It's sounding good, Car,' she said, her voice catching. 'I can hear Abigail.'

Walter looked at his daughter-in-law over the top of his reading glasses. 'She gets her talent from you, Elinor; and from Jean too,' he added wistfully.

Carson thought about Meg's Christmas card. 'Dear Car, great news about *The Crucible*. I can see your name in lights!'

Meg's Christmas box had arrived the day before, each of the packages within elegantly wrapped. For Patrick there was a limited edition of the *Last of the Mohicans* bound in umber-coloured leather and for Elinor an exquisite turquoise enamel bracelet. Walter opened his gift of a pair of deerskin gloves and glanced down at his calloused hands. 'Too late, I think, but she's a thoughtful girl.' Carson undid the rick-rack ribbon on her own small black box. Nestled in tissue was a cream-and-white checked voile shirt with flowers embroidered on the collar and cuffs. As she held it up in front of her she noticed a silver envelope at the bottom of the box marked with the letter C.

'What a lovely shirt,' said Elinor appreciatively. 'Try it on, Car.'

She shook her head. 'I'll do it after.' She folded the shirt and put it back inside. Later, in her bedroom, she opened the envelope and found four fifty-dollar bills sheathed inside a folded-up piece of writing paper on which were the words, 'For a New York visit. Come soon! Love, your (fairy) godmother, Meg.' She stared at the four crisp notes. It was a fortune. She would choose a time to tell her parents.

Rehearsals for *The Crucible* began at the start of term. Carson was immediately unnerved by the casting of John Proctor. Flora, who was to be Elizabeth Proctor, nudged her when Rory Strang came into the old gym. 'I can't believe it's him. He's such a loner. I'm surprised he wanted a part.' Flora giggled. 'But he'd be a shoo-in for Heathcliff though.'

Carson blushed, despite herself. Rory Strang, from the year above, was often in her peripheral vision, a figure in the distance, alone and seemingly preoccupied. They had never spoken. He had a strong angular face that was attractively off-kilter, his aquiline nose a little crooked, his dark hair unkempt, and when he loped through school, hands thrust into the pockets of his black duffle coat and a heavy rucksack slung over his shoulder, he always gave the impression that he was just passing through.

'Right, Carson and Rory,' said Mary Mulhearn, head of the English department, 'let's read through your scenes first.'

As they sat facing each other Carson was unsettled by the
intensity of his dark green eyes, but as she began to enjoy the
rhythm of the lines she relaxed and sensed the seeds of a shy
intimacy.

'Good,' said Mary Mulhearn. 'Now stand a little too close
to each other. Be in each other's space.'

Carson suddenly lost concentration and burst out laughing,
and Rory, turning scarlet, frowned at her in dismay.

'I'm sorry,' she said, looking up at him, embarrassed, 'it's
just that I read through this scene with my Granddad. I realise
now that that was a little weird.'

Rory relaxed. 'Yes. That must have been pretty strange all
right.' He grinned.

The night before the first performance Carson shouted
out and woke herself up. For a moment she listened in the
darkness as a cry barrelled towards her as if from the end of
a long corridor, but she could not identify who it came
from. Then a picture burst into her head and a wave of
nausea almost choked her. Iona was standing in front of the
fire in the cabin at Loch Doon staring ahead into the flames.
She was wearing a long black dress with a starched white
collar and her hair was scraped into a mutch. A length of
rope hung around her neck down to her waist, weighed
down at each end by a bag of stones, and the rope was so
heavy it cut through her neck and blood dripped through
the skeins. Then, as Carson stared at her sister, she realised
that in front of her was their old baby bath filled to the brim
with water.

Carson jerked upright on the bed and threw up over the
duvet. She was suddenly aware of the snap of the light and
Elinor rushing towards her. 'It's over. It's over, Car,' she said
as she gathered her daughter in her arms. 'Do you want to tell

me about it?' she asked as she stroked Carson's hair, but Carson shook her head.

'Just stay with me for a bit. Please.'

Elinor washed her daughter down gently with a flannel and changed her duvet. As she lay down beside her and wrapped her arms around her she wondered how she was ever going to let go of her. Who would be there to keep her safe?

When Patrick awoke the next morning he shivered and reached for his wife but instead his arm felt the shock of the icy sheet. He listened to the silence for a moment and then slowly tuned in to the early morning street, the hurrying footsteps, cars spluttering to a start, the rumble and whine of the diesel buses, a shouted 'Good morning. It's going to be a fine day.' He pulled the duvet round his shoulders and shuffled along the landing. Blinking away the grey gauze in front of his eyes, in shards of light that stole around the curtain edges he made out a mass of Medusa-like hair on the pillow, auburn and fair, and Elinor's arm in an arc around her daughter. The scene reminded him of a pre-Raphaelite painting. He wondered who had woken first and had sought the comfort of the other.

Early that evening Carson stood beside the row of starched black dresses, each hung on an identical black hanger to which was attached, on a piece of twine, a luggage label with both the name of the character and actor in vermilion ink in her mother's beautiful hand. She searched for Abigail's costume and there on the label was a tiny oil-painted illustration of a branch of bright yellow mimosa. Tears pricked her eyes as she imagined her mother dipping her tiny paintbrush into the pot of Windsor Lemon for the first time in almost two years.

She looked over at Elinor who was standing among the rails, like a seamstress in a couture house, ready to fix buttons, adjust buckles on shoes, pin on paper mutches. She had worked tirelessly for a month, engrossed in the task, often late into the night, and when she was almost finished Patrick watched her carefully edge a cuff with a perfect blanket stitch in black embroidery yarn. 'Eli. You've made the simple so beautiful,' he said admiringly.

She put down her needle and sighed. 'For so long now I've felt that my creativity had left me for good. I thought that I didn't deserve it – but maybe I was wrong.'

In the makeshift bar in the school cafeteria one of the sixth-year stage hands, dressed in black waistcoat and britches, moved among the theatregoers, ringing hand bells, calling them to Salem, Massachusetts. Walter immediately downed his shandy and, without a glance at his son or daughter, shot out of the bar to his seat, leaving Patrick and Fiona to follow in his slipstream, smiling wryly at each other. Carson had issued her grandfather with strict instructions not to say where either he, or her parents, were seated in the two-hundred-strong audience, sternly forbidding him to make any movement or, worse, an exclamation. He was to sit sphinx-like throughout the play.

At the very last moment, just as the theatre faded to black, Elinor slipped into the empty seat beside Patrick and squeezed his arm. 'I kept an eye on her. She's all set.'

'Just the twenty executions to go then,' he whispered back, but his heart was banging so hard against his ribcage he was sure Elinor could hear it.

As the light came up on the simple wooden set that Pete had designed, Abigail entered the room and saw the Reverend Parris bending over Betty as she lay in the low bed. She stood, poker straight, her presence at once ethereal and menacing, her solemn white face flickering in the light of Tituba's candle.

Elinor followed Carson's every line, her pulse racing so fast she was having trouble catching her breath. Out of the corner of her eye she saw Walter straining forward, his hands clasped tightly in front of him, his jaw clenched. At the climax of the play when dawn broke and the pale glow stole through the high windows of Salem's jailhouse, Elizabeth Proctor delivered her final words, her back to the audience, and John Proctor, unseen, met his death; as the thin sunlight slowly dulled to darkness, the audience held its breath, and then as if a dam had burst, it broke into thunderous applause. There was a piercing whistle and then a stamping of feet and cries of 'bravo'. When the stage lights went up again the cast was ranged across the stage, Carson in the centre, flushed and smiling shyly. The audience rose and Walter got stiffly to his feet, tears cascading down his cheeks unchecked by the rugged lines on his face.

At the party afterwards, even before she found the family, Carson and Rory quickly gravitated towards each other. 'You are a great Abigail,' he said effusively. 'I was pretty scared of you.'

She blushed. 'I know it's only a school play, but it didn't feel like that – to me anyway.'

'Me neither; but you should study drama, Car. Really you should.'

She liked that he had said that, but she stored the thought away and quickly turned the tables. 'What are you going to do?'

'English and American literature at Edinburgh.' He shrugged his shoulders. 'I wanted to study in New York, but it's way too much money. Hey,' he said suddenly, 'you should study there. There's a great drama school. One of the best in the world.'

Carson frowned. 'New York? I don't think so. If you can't afford it then neither can I.' Emboldened by the adrenalin still coursing through her, she was about to suggest they met for a coffee but at that moment Elinor, who had been hemmed in by effusive parents raving about her costumes until she was rescued by Patrick and Walter, squeezed through the mêlée to find her daughter.

'You were wonderful,' she whispered in her ear as she hugged her, 'just wonderful.'

Carson introduced Rory to her parents and Patrick slapped him on the back. 'You were a great John Proctor – and you're not a bad history student either.'

Carson rolled her eyes apologetically at Rory and then turned to find Archie Forrest, the avuncular head teacher, his hand outstretched. 'Congratulations, Carson. Your grandfather tells me you're very keen on pursuing acting.'

Carson cursed Walter silently. 'I didn't really know before *The Crucible*, but yes.' She spoke with a resolve that surprised even herself.

'Are you really, Car?' Patrick couldn't hide his enthusiasm.

'Well,' said Archie Forrest, 'I'm pretty sure you could ace Higher Drama in a year if you really put your mind to it.'

Carson's head was buzzing. 'I might like to study in New York,' she blurted out and stopped, all at once aware of everybody's eyes on her. Rory came into focus over Patrick's shoulder, Pete beside him, wide-eyed in admiration. But when she looked at Elinor she saw that she was thunderstruck, as she tried to fathom where such an extraordinary idea had come from.

Patrick put his arm around his daughter's shoulder. This was not the time, he reckoned, to say that New York would be an impossible stretch. 'Well, darling girl, there's nothing wrong with aiming for the stars. Nothing at all,' he said as he handed Carson a glass of prosecco.

As the adults started to make their farewells and leave the party to the cast and crew, Walter signalled to Patrick that he wanted to have a word.

'What's up, Dad?' Patrick asked as they walked out into the playground, wrapped up against the freezing night.

Walter pushed his hands deep into his pockets. 'I was going to sit down with you and Fiona soon, but maybe now is better.'

'What's wrong? Are you ill?' said Patrick, startled.

'No, no. I'm fit as a fiddle give or take my legs and a bit of lumbago.' He looked directly at his son. 'Maybe it's an odd time to tell you, but it was just the talk about New York.' He paused. 'I've got a fund for the children. It was for the three of them . . .' He faltered. 'It's quite a bit of money. Some land I sold and some of your mother's money. It was going to be a surprise.'

'Well, it's certainly that,' said Patrick, astonished, 'though of course I knew Mum had money—'

'What I mean,' Walter interrupted, 'is that there's more than enough, I imagine, if Carson did want to study in New York – maybe three hundred thousand now.'

Patrick reared back. 'Bloody hell, Dad. I had no idea.'

'How could you have? I didn't tell you.' He balled his hands in his pockets. 'I probably should have just given it to you and Fiona; there is more of course.'

Patrick put his hand on Walter's arm. 'Dad, we're fine – but this is amazing.'

Walter tipped back his tweed cap and scratched his head. 'I had the idea they'd get it when they were twenty-one, but I think Carson especially might need it sooner.'

Patrick put his hand across his brow as if he were trying to smooth out the creases in his thoughts. 'That was some secret, Dad. Do you have anything else to tell me?'

Walter looked at him thoughtfully and shook his head. 'I think this will do for now.'

Patrick laughed. 'You're a dark horse, right enough. Do you want to tell the children?'

Walter shook his head vehemently. 'I'll talk to Fiona. But Patrick, no fuss now.' He turned to go to his car and then stopped. 'Did you see Marie with her grandchildren? She thought Carson was terrific too.'

Patrick smiled warmly at his father. 'That's lovely to hear, Dad. I didn't see her but say hello, would you?'

The next morning, when Carson and Pete were still sleeping off the effects of the party, Elinor and Patrick sat at breakfast and relived their daughter's success. 'But where did the idea for New York come from?' asked Elinor, looking into her teacup as if trying to divine the answer. 'I wonder if Meg had anything to do with it?' She swirled her tea. 'Anyway, we could never afford it.'

Patrick poured himself a fresh coffee. 'Actually, we could or, more accurately, Carson could.'

Elinor looked at her husband, mystified. 'What on earth do you mean, Patrick?' she said testily.

'Last night Dad told me he's got a fund for each of the children.' A shadow crossed Patrick's eyes. 'It was for the three of them . . . It's a lot of money.'

He reached out and cupped Elinor's face in his hands. 'If she wanted to go we'd have to encourage her, Eli. We can't hold on to her for ever.'

CHAPTER 26

Walter had followed Carson's every movement on stage, the almost imperceptible inclination of her head, the stiffening of her arms. He held his breath when she was still and when she lashed out with her tongue, or when she writhed in agony, he went rigid in his seat and felt his blood beating in his temples. But no matter how much he concentrated on Carson's performance, it was as if Jean were standing in the glare of the stage lights. He imagined too the crushing sensation she must have endured knowing, when she looked out into the darkness, it was the wrong parent in the audience, the one for whom her attendance at Wellington School for Young Ladies was merely as a symbol of his status, not the mother who encouraged her, who imbued her with a love of books and plays and who believed in her intelligence. When Walter had carefully asked his wife if she missed the stage he remembered her bravado, the wave of her slender hand, trailing cigarette smoke through the air as she insisted to Walter that it mattered not one jot that it was over.

'I don't believe you,' Walter had said, 'you were too good.'

'No, really I wasn't, Walter. I was just an amateur.'

'You made it look effortless.' He searched for what he wanted to say. 'I believed you were Lady Windermere.'

Jean smiled faintly. 'Maybe I was happy to lose myself in her.'

When Carson was on stage Jean was so present, so real, it was as if she were there experiencing Carson's performance, and he wanted to keep her there; so during the interval he chose to stay in the almost empty auditorium and think of her.

It was a warm spring day and Jean was out of bed before him. As he lay luxuriating in their new bridal bed he heard a laverock on the wing, high in the sky, trying out a new song, trilling a few sweet notes over and over, but then he heard another sound, as if it had become a duet. It was Jean's voice high and clear in the distance. He threw back the covers and leapt over to the open window and he saw her at the far corner of the garden, looking even younger than her twenty-two years, a fresh sheet from the washing line tied around her like a long train and a circlet of flowers in her hair. She was talking into the air.

I pray thee, gentle mortal, sing again:
Mine ear is much enamour'd of thy note;
So is mine eye enthralled to thy shape;
And thy fair virtue's force perforce doth move me
On the first view to say, to swear, I love thee.

As she uttered the last line she knelt down on the grass and put her hands together in front of her. Walter started clapping out of the window and she looked back at the house, startled. 'Bravo!' he called to her. She laughed and headed for the house, holding her makeshift train out regally, pausing to curtsey towards him.

'What role are you playing?' he asked, leaning out of the window.

'Can't you guess?'

Walter shook his head.

'Titania, Queen of the Fairies. I'm speaking to my love.'

'I'm guessing that is the king?' he said, eager to appear in some way knowledgeable.

Jean shook her head. 'No, it's not.' She started to laugh. 'I'm in love with an ass,' and then she looked up at him coquettishly. 'And so art imitates life.'

He bounded downstairs, lifted her in his arms, the bed sheet trailing, and carried her back up to bed.

The audience made its way back into the theatre and settled down for the second act. Without Carson on stage he became completely preoccupied. He summoned up Jean as she was that day, her hair held by the band of flowers, her feet bare on the grass. Had he loved her more selflessly and not wished her torment away, perhaps she would have been sitting by his side, clutching his arm excitedly as she watched her granddaughter on stage. But another thought forced its way in, one that had persisted through the years, gnawing at his soul. How much of Jean's life with him had been the work of a talented actress? Had he been fooling himself?

He remembered the first day he learned the sound of fury, not long after Patrick was born. He returned home early from the power station, excited to surprise his wife. As he parked the Land Rover he heard a repeated loud crack from inside the house, as violent as a wrecking ball, and with each blow, a loud shout. He raced inside and as he entered the living room Jean was standing with her back to him raining down blows on the sideboard with an axe with such force it sent splinters in every direction.

'Jean!' he shouted. 'What are you doing? Stop it. You'll hurt yourself.'

Jean spun round to face him, wild-eyed, the axe above her head. Walter stepped back involuntarily. She stared at him as if he were a stranger, perspiration streaming down her face and onto her blouse, tiny pieces of wood trapped in her hair. Suddenly she narrowed her eyes at him and let out a howl. 'You ...' she snarled, 'you leave me here in this fusty old house. What am I to do? Who can I speak to?'

Walter tried not to fixate on the axe still poised above her head. 'Jean,' he said quietly, his heart louder in his head than his voice, 'where is Patrick?'

Jean blinked at the sound of her son's name and she stood still for a minute. Then she lowered the axe, breathing hard. 'Asleep in his cot,' she replied in a staccato, distracted voice.

He looked at the wreckage of the heavy old Victorian sideboard. 'What were you doing, darling?' Walter said, stunned, the sound of axe-blows still echoing in his head.

Jean uttered a strange light laugh. 'I just thought I'd chop it up for firewood before the new furniture arrives. You said you didn't much like it anyway.'

'I know, but I could have done it for you.' He stepped forward to take the axe from her hand, but he saw her resist, just for a moment. 'Is there something wrong, Jean, something troubling you?'

Jean shook her head dreamily. 'No, darling, not a thing. Patrick was a bit grousy today, that's all ... Let's have a gin and tonic to celebrate your being home early. In fact,' she said, unknotting Walter's tie, 'let's have it upstairs.'

After Jean's death, when he thought back to that day, it dawned on him with a terrible clarity that, if she could have, Jean would have smashed the house on Loch Doon to smithereens.

Walter took such a gulp of air that Patrick squeezed his arm in the dark. 'You okay, Dad?'

Walter shook himself and gave Carson's return to the stage for Act Three his full attention. He had read and rehearsed the play so often in the past few weeks that he found himself mouthing the lines until Patrick jabbed his arm. 'Shh, Dad, I can actually hear you!' Walter pressed his lips together waiting for Elizabeth Proctor's final words: 'He hath his goodness now. God forbid I take it from him.' And then he closed his eyes until a torrent of tears forced their way through his eyelids and spilled onto his hands.

He did not expect sleep when he arrived home to Carsphairn, and when the glittering coal-black night gave way to the lemon light of dawn he was still lying, staring at a tiny picture of Jean in a silver frame, gazing out at him, her lips parted, as if she were about to talk to him.

Only once during the night had he turned from her and closed his eyes in search of sleep, but then he saw another face, encased in a flying helmet, and as it came level with his, Frantisek Hekl looked at him for an infinitesimal moment, awareness dawning that he would drown in a Galloway loch, that he would never again rise up in the air, or see his loved ones again. And as his eyes locked with the eyes of the young boy teetering at the water's edge, the look the pilot gave him said, 'I am going to die trying to save my country but you, Walter, you, one day, will not even be able to save your wife.'

CHAPTER 27

The play had somehow changed the air around the MacMillans. The barometer had risen for the first time since Iona's death.

Carson and Rory met most days at Poosie Nancy's coffee shop at the back of the bookshop in the Sandgate. Walter always like to point out that the street was so called because centuries earlier there was a barrier that had been built to stop the sand dunes spilling onto the old cart track. Now the sea was half a mile back and the Sandgate was in the heart of the town. 'I didn't know that,' replied Rory graciously when Carson, on the first rendezvous, had regurgitated her grandfather's story by rote. Then it was Rory's turn. 'My grandfather always tells me that Robert Burns used to walk along the cobbles of the Sandgate as a poet – or an exciseman. He said Burns was either searching for fine words or fine smuggled wine and brandy.'

'Our grandfathers are indoctrinating us, just in case we leave.' Carson smiled.

'And I'm pretty sure we will,' said Rory, 'and you'll go furthest.'

'But you're going to Camp America.'

'Only for the summer.'

'New York?' asked Carson eagerly.

Rory burst out laughing. 'No, the wilds of Wyoming. I'll be bivouacking with the kids. We have to check for illegal trapping and logging sightings of muskrats and bobcats. Maybe I'll feel like a frontiersman.'

Carson laughed. 'You'll be "The Emperor of Wyoming".'

'Who's that?'

'It's the title track on Neil Young's first solo album.'

'Wow.' He looked at her appreciatively. 'Impressive.'

'We were made to listen to it a lot; and I mean a *lot*.'

'Your dad's a great teacher.'

'In what way?' Carson was taken aback. She smiled. 'I'm fishing for compliments.'

'Well, he doesn't patronise. He's a great communicator. He knows his stuff. There's just one small problem.'

Carson bristled. 'What's that?'

'His jokes are beyond bad.'

Carson laughed with relief. 'He gets that from Granddad.' She paused. 'Actually I think it helps them to cope with everything.'

Rory put his hand on her cheek. 'I'll miss you when I'm in the middle of nowhere.'

Patrick and Elinor kept their new anxieties about Carson's dream of America to themselves, their 'what if' conversations stored away for the times they were on their own.

'But how would she cope? It's so big. People get shot,' Elinor said fretfully, looking at Patrick across the pillow.

'Eli, she hasn't even applied yet – and it's not a huge place, by the way.'

'But you know she wants to go? And she can now, money-wise I mean. Wouldn't you be worried all the time?'

Patrick shook his head. 'No, she's got Meg. She'd make friends. It's not the other side of the world.'

'But how would we be?' Elinor searched Patrick's face.

Patrick thought how beautiful his wife looked; the few soft lines around her eyes were graceful, and there was a pretty freckle on her upper lip that he had never noticed before. 'We'd be different, that's all. We can't let her think we would fall apart.'

Rory came to Wellington Square in his drainpipe jeans and slogan T-shirts and tipped the plays of Caryl Churchill and Gregory Burke and Mark Ravenhill out of his rucksack. In return Carson had lent him her precious hardback copy of *The Secret History*, and she passed on *Brooklyn* too, the novel that Elinor had just given her.

'Does this mean you're warming to the idea? Now you're engaging in some kind of literary semaphore?' Patrick had joked as Elinor had laid Colm Tóibín's paperback at Carson's place at breakfast the week before, along with a postcard from Meg.

'Don't try to be so damned clever, Patrick MacMillan,' she chided lightly. 'It's a long way off – if it happens at all.'

He got up from the table and put his hands on his wife's shoulders. 'Eli, she's got the bit between her teeth now. And she could be good, really good.'

Carson devoured the set texts at school, *Men Should Weep, The Cheviot, the Stag and the Black Black Oil*, plays that wove together politics and tragedy, humour and song, and the thrilling *Mary Queen of Scots Got Her Head Chopped Off*. But sometimes reading the lines wasn't always enough, sometimes she wanted to hear the words out loud, out of her own mouth, and, standing on Walter's great slab of granite, all alone, she performed for the loch. She found the videos of the television adaptation of *The Slab Boys* in the school library and stopped and started them over and over again at her favourite bits. And then she went back to *Romeo and Juliet*, and watched Elinor's copy of the Zeffirelli film, staring at Olivia Hussey, and cried every time.

She logged on to the website of the Tisch School of the Arts at New York University and scrolled back and forth until she knew the pages by heart. And although she said little outside the family about the plan she was forming, except to Rory and Flora, news of Carson's application that autumn spread through the school faster than knotweed, and Patrick's colleagues offered to help in any way they could, relieved, finally, to have found a way to convey their sympathy.

Mary Mulhearn came to Wellington Square several evenings and over a cup of tea guided Carson through her audition pieces. Between them they had settled on a passage in *Sunset Song*.

Patrick dragged a long mirror through to the living room and left them to it. Mary asked Carson to stand in front of the mirror. 'When you are in the room, imagine the mirror is there. What does Chris Guthrie see? What does she want?'

'She wants to be a woman. She's ready. She sees herself as a young woman, not a girl. But it's her wedding day . . .' – Carson wavered for a moment – 'and she aches for her mother.'

'Good. Now control your voice. Drop your shoulders; imagine I am lifting your head with a string.'

Carson became aware of her spine, her elongated back, the line of her neck, a sensuous tingle on her skin. She felt stronger, calmer.

One evening, Elinor passed the open door to the living room slowly and caught sight of her daughter as she moved fluidly across the room, a lithe Chris Guthrie, and in that moment she saw more clearly the young woman Carson was becoming.

'It was as if the air moved as she walked. It was amazing,' Elinor whispered to her husband as they lay in bed in the bright moonlight. She stretched across and found his hand. 'I know we were all paralysed when Iona died . . . but when I saw Carson just now, I felt an immense relief. She's found a way to cope.' Elinor's eyes shone with tears. 'She's the light of our lives, Patrick.'

Just then Patrick pulled Elinor to him and they fell asleep entwined and, for the first time since Iona's death, they stayed that way until morning.

CHAPTER 28

Walter sat in his favourite chair waiting for Carson to arrive. It had belonged to his father before him, and as he ran his hand along the brown leather, mottled with the complexion of age, he felt the punctures made by the flaring embers of his father's pipe. He had calculated that it was more than one hundred and fifty years old and he joked with Carson and Pete that the chair and he would eventually become one.

When spring arrived he always turned it round from the fire and positioned it where he could see a mud cup stuck to the stone lintel at the top of the window frame, and he could sit, mending a fishing reel, or sewing on a button, watching for the return of the house martins. He liked to think that the same pair returned year after year and when they arrived safely he was always elated. He wedged open the window with a stone so that he could listen to their soft chirrups as they spruced up their summer home, looping up stray pieces of straw and strands of hair that had escaped on the winter winds. Often he sat for more than an hour, his field glasses trained on the nest, marvelling as they flittered back and forth, working against their yearly deadline.

He jumped when the doorbell rang, so absorbed he had forgotten to fret that Carson had passed her driving test just a week before.

'You're my first destination, Granddad,' she said eagerly when she called to tell him. 'The road from Ayr's quiet on a Saturday. I could drive it in my sleep.'

She sat on the stool opposite his leather chair and looked at him solemnly. 'I want to talk about the money,' she said, straight out of the traps. 'It's too much and it's far, far too generous.'

Walter put his hands out. 'What else am I going to do with it, Car? I want you to have it now. It would have come to you eventually.'

'Hey, stop. I don't want to think about that. Don't sound so morose.' She folded her arms. 'I want to make a deal.'

Walter raised his eyebrows. 'I don't know if I like the sound of this.'

'Well, too bad. If I get into Tisch, and that's a big if, I'll only go if you agree to come and see me.'

The thought had never crossed Walter's mind. 'Oh, I don't know about that,' he replied, searching for an excuse, 'my legs aren't what they were. It would be hard to get about.'

Carson rolled her eyes. 'Have you never heard of yellow cabs? Sorry, you have to promise.'

Walter had never imagined that he would leave Scotland, never mind cross the Atlantic for the first time. 'I tell you what,' he said eventually, 'I'll come to your graduation.'

Late that afternoon, once he had waved Carson off, telling her twenty times to check her mirrors, Walter and Marie walked Marie's Border Terrier through the forest at Eriff by Loch Doon. After he had recounted Carson's visit, and the bargain they had struck, Marie put her arm through his. 'You're a good man, Walter, and an especially good grandfather.'

Walter stopped and shook his head at her. 'You know that's not true, Marie. I'm just trying to make amends, that's all.' He looked into her pretty blue-grey eyes. 'And if I was a good man I would have asked you to marry me a long time ago.' Marie put up her hand to silence him but he ignored it. 'I was too concerned about Patrick and Fiona.'

'Stop it, Walter,' Marie said, irritation in her voice, 'I don't want to talk about this again. I'm happy the way things are.'

'I want to make an honest woman of you – even if that's an old-fashioned thing to say.'

'It's a ridiculous thing to say, and I don't want it.' She put her hand on his cheek and stood on her tiptoes to give him a tender kiss; they stood in the dark pines, arms around each other, holding on tightly, until the dog pushed its way in between them. 'See, Brutus doesn't want you to make an honest woman of me either.'

That night Walter lay awake imagining what his life would be like without Marie. He loved her in a way that was as deep as the loch. There was an ease to it, a steadiness. She had saved him, of that there was no doubt. He knew too that if anything were to happen to him, she would carry on, self-contained, composed. But if it happened the other way about, he would be lost. He almost cried out at the thought of it. He lay still, willing his heart to slow down. He took the glass of water from his bedside, steadying it with both hands, and slaked his thirst, swallowing hard. Finally, he turned into Marie's back and clung to her.

CHAPTER 29

The yellow cab turned into East 16th Street and sped along between the elegant brownstones until Elinor spotted number 125 and called out to the driver to stop. He stood on the brake and Carson and Elinor lurched forward. 'Sorry, ladies,' he cackled, 'I never seem to get these feet of mine to work properly.' He unfolded his tall frame out of the driver's seat and reset his baseball cap on his head. 'Too tall for this business, that's my problem. I always thought I'd get smaller over the years.' He chuckled in his rich Jamaican accent as he carried their bags up the steep front steps. 'Enjoy your stay. I always wanted to visit Scotland. My granddaddy was a ship's captain from Greenock. In this city of immigrants, it's nice to meet a fellow Scot.' Carson smiled at him in wonderment.

When the email arrived from the Tisch School of the Arts calling Carson for an audition, exactly a year after the performance of *The Crucible*, she had to read it several times over before she took her laptop to the kitchen to show Patrick and Elinor. 'Bloody hell, girl,' Patrick yelled as he lifted her clear off the ground and swung her round, and each time Carson spun past her mother she tried to read her expression, the stunned look in her eyes.

'The end of March,' Elinor said as brightly as a spoon hitting crystal, when Patrick set Carson down. 'School's in. I'm going to take you. It'll be an adventure and anyway I'm not letting you go alone.'

Patrick grinned with relief. 'Eli, that is a great idea.'

The brownstone was bathed in early spring sunshine. As they stood on the top step Elinor turned around to admire the street. She spotted dogwood buds and wild plum behind wrought-iron railings, and occasional pots of frilled parrot tulips, coaxed out by a burst of warmth in the city. 'This is a lovely neighbourhood!' she exclaimed as she surveyed the tall sash and case windows of the houses, some navy blue, others dark green, and their elegant maroon front doors.

Every so often a forlorn house, its shabby blinds like half-closed eyes, the stairs to the street strewn with old flyers and newspaper pages like dirty confetti, would interrupt the otherwise perfect facade that ran from First to Second Avenue. One even had most of its windows boarded up as if exhausted at not being able to keep up with its neighbours, four-storey town-houses owned by rich doctors and lawyers or people like Meg who had, before her job at the Morgan, paid more rent for a small apartment than she could properly afford just to live in Gramercy Park.

Elinor rooted around in her pocket for a piece of paper and entered the door code. Once in the hall she stooped down to retrieve Meg's apartment key from under a terra-cotta pot filled with a profusion of slender paperwhites. The door opened into a long living room. A pair of floor-to-ceiling windows looked over the street and at the rear of the room a little open-plan kitchen was filled with a colourful array of crockery on shelves backed by mismatched Moroccan tiles. On the top one sat a mixture of stemware, crystal and modern glass, including three orange-rimmed highballs from a glass-blower in the Borders. Elinor had sent them to Meg after she had scrimped and saved to rent the apartment five years before.

Carson picked up a note from the counter. 'Hi E&C, should be back from my meeting by 5. Mezze platter and wine in the fridge. You are in the back right-hand-side bedroom. I can't wait to see you both! M xx'

She pulled back the cream cotton curtains billowing like sails on their open bedroom window and looked at the tangle of fire escapes and blank windows, some with flaking window boxes whose dusty plants and desiccated herbs had long been abandoned. 'You can hardly believe it's the same place when you look out here.' She beckoned.

Elinor leaned over the bed and craned her neck. She shuddered. 'There are a lot of strangers in this city.'

'That's okay, Mum. It's kind of exciting, isn't it? Anyway, we're strangers too. Have you thought of that? You can't assume they're all scary.'

'True. Meg likes it. From the very beginning she liked to meet all sorts. She was always one for befriending waifs and strays. When we were children she once brought home an old man from the bus stop in the pouring rain and demanded Dad gave him a lift home.'

'And did he?'

'Yes.' Elinor laughed. 'But he lived in Girvan. It was a forty-mile round trip. Dad wasn't very pleased.'

Carson sank into the yellow velvet sofa to read over her audition pieces, but her eyes wandered to the photographs on top of a blue lacquered cabinet. There was a black and white picture in a tortoiseshell frame of the twins' parents, her grandparents whom she had never met, he in a dinner suit, a cigarette in one hand, the other in the trouser pocket, while her grandmother in a black sequined sleeveless dress, her arm looped through her husband's, smiled exactly like her daughters did, her head tilted to one side. Beside it, in a frame decorated with psychedelic swirls, was a photograph of her mother and Meg, their heads together, both sporting flower print, bandanas, porcelain-white make-up against their black eyeliner and scarlet lips. Then she spied a little photograph of Iona and her on the bench outside the cabin. She noticed how tightly she was gripping her sister's shoulder. Perhaps she was responding to a command from the photographer, or maybe she was squeezing her a little too hard. She felt the familiar pang of guilt and loss that accompanied her like a shadow.

She bit her lip and looked at the final photograph in a beautiful pale blue leather frame. Meg was sitting on the sand with a slender woman with jet-black hair wound casually on top of her head, a halter-neck swimsuit accentuating her toned arms. Behind them in the distance was a big wheel. Both women were wearing oversize sunglasses and holding sticks of candyfloss and looked as if they were laughing out loud. Maybe, Carson thought, this was Meg's girlfriend. On the plane from Scotland Elinor had told her that Meg had been on her own on and off for a long time, but when the twins spoke on the phone to make all the arrangements, Meg said that finally she had found someone who made her laugh.

Just then Carson heard the key turn in the lock and Meg rushed in, dropping a bag of groceries at her feet. She hugged Elinor tightly, spilling the tea in her hand, and then she plopped down on the sofa beside Carson and gave her a kiss. She turned over Carson's book. 'Ah . . . Chris Guthrie. We thought she was wonderful, didn't we, Eli?'

Elinor nodded wistfully, the memory threading them together.

Meg had taken the next day off so that she could go to the audition with Carson and Elinor. As the three walked down Broadway Carson saw the purple flags of NYU billowing high above the street and she stopped, rooted to the ground, a sick feeling welling up in her throat. 'C'mon, Car,' said Elinor as she found her daughter's hand and held it tightly. 'You're ready.' Carson looked into her mother's shining eyes, 'I know you are.' Elinor propelled her through the door and let go and Meg blew her a kiss.

She found herself in the middle of a melee of teenagers, a kaleidoscope of baseball hats and braids, tattoos, Day-Glo Doc Martens, ripped jeans, floaty dresses, scribbled-on Converse shoes. She heard smatterings of shy conversations, a shout of laughter, an exuberant greeting. Others were sitting clutching their audition pieces looking around nervously, overwhelmed.

'Carson MacMillan,' called out a tall African-American woman holding a clipboard.

Carson walked towards her, her heart thumping.

'Ruth Anne Hudson,' she said as she approached, hand outstretched. 'Lovely to have you here.' Carson relaxed a little at the professor's beautiful smile and her easy elegance, her gold hoop earrings and her mustard silk wrap dress. 'You're definitely the only candidate who's crossed the Atlantic for this year's auditions. Come and join the others.'

For the next hour Carson felt as if she had been sucked down a rabbit hole into another world. She improvised with three others whose names and faces she hardly registered except for one, a gregarious tousle-haired Colombian girl, Camila, who partnered her during the instruction 'to be the shadow of each other in three exercises'.

Then she rested for a few minutes in the corridor before a Tisch student showed her to a cavernous black rehearsal space where Ruth Anne and two others were seated, ready for Carson to perform her audition pieces. First, she settled down and stilled herself to become Chris Guthrie in a monologue which, she had explained in her application, she devised from the novel, and then turned her back, paused and turned again, and mustered all the fever, cunning and sadness that she had found in the character of Abigail Williams.

'Thank you,' said Ruth Anne, once Carson had finished. 'It was clever to choose two such different women, but both trapped in their own way by the restrictions of their society, both missing their mothers too and both near your age. Smart.'

Carson blushed, unsure how to respond. 'Thank you,' she said shyly.

'As you know we welcome students from all over the world. Do you know many people in the city?'

Carson looked straight at her. 'No, but my aunt lives here. She's my godmother too. And I hope I'll make friends,' she said, before she quickly corrected herself. 'I hope I would make friends.'

'I am sure you will,' replied Professor Hudson with a twinkle. 'That was good, Carson. Thank you.'

That evening, when she woke from a short sleep, so deep it obliterated all dreaming, Carson found her mother waiting at the end of the bed holding a box from Rag and Bone. 'Something from Dad and me to complete your big day,' she said eagerly.

Carson carefully unwrapped the parcel and held up a silk leopard-print minidress with a row of diamanté studs at the neck. 'Oh my God, it's amazing, Mum,' she exclaimed. 'It must have cost a fortune.' Then she looked back into the box and found a pair of gold Converse trainers. 'Mum!' admonished Carson.

Elinor held out her hands. 'What's money?' she said, laughing. 'Besides, you need a bit of sparkle in New York.'

Carson looked at her mother steadily. 'And you look sparkling too, Mum.'

'Try it on,' said Elinor quickly and turned away before her daughter could see her face quivering.

As soon as Carson pulled on the dress and tied the gold laces of her shoes, Meg dragged her to the long mirror in the hall. 'Well, look at you,' she said admiringly. 'Stay there,' she ordered and a moment later she returned with a vintage Chanel bag which she slung over Carson's shoulder. Then she applied a bright lipstick to her niece's lips. 'Ta-da!' she sang. 'Quite the New Yorker.'

Carson stared, self-conscious and bemused by her unfamiliar reflection as Meg handed her a glass of champagne.

Then Elinor emerged from the bedroom in a linen shift, patterned with bright paint-box squares and black patent leather ankle boots, stylishly complementing her twin who was dressed in a cream silk shirt and wide black trousers cinched with a green leather belt.

'You both look amazing,' said Carson, astounded by the transformation in her mother.

As they walked along the street arm in arm, Carson in the middle, she regaled them with her grandfather's reaction when she called home after the audition. 'You'll be just like Deborah Kerr, a Hollywood star born in Scotland. But you do know she loved the theatre more than anything.'

'How does he know all that stuff?' asked Meg.

'He carries the strangest facts around in his head,' said Elinor with a laugh. 'His brain is uncatalogued. What he needs is a librarian of the mind.'

'Wasn't Granny Jean an actual librarian?' asked Meg.

'She stopped before Patrick was born. Maybe things would have gone better for her if she'd kept on working, but that was the way then.'

'Why did Granny Jean drink so much?' ventured Carson.

'Oh, I think there were probably a lot of reasons. It's not something Walter talks about. Or Patrick for that matter.' Elinor flicked her head up. 'We're about to have some rather good wine, I imagine, so can we have a cheerier conversation please?'

Carson wondered about all the times when she had watched Walter, unawares, lost in thought, and it struck her that she had seen the same expression hundreds of times, as if he were with someone else, and it occurred to her now that he was. He was with his wife.

The bistro sat on the corner of Bowery and Houston Street behind a simple red-brick facade. The heavy wooden door lent the restaurant the air of a speakeasy, and it was only when Meg pushed back the inner glass one that they were assailed by the general commotion of tinkling glasses, raucous laughter and the scrape of chairs on the tiled floor. Bottles of wine were lined up on shelves on mirrored walls, and scrubbed tables were set with red and white napkins and etched stemware.

Meg had originally planned two surprises for the evening, imagining the excited scene as first Michelle and then Roland appeared at the candlelit table, but at the last minute her nerve had failed. It did not seem fair on her girlfriend, on what would be their first and only meeting of Elinor and Carson's trip. On the way to the restaurant she had told Elinor and Carson that Michelle was working flat out over the weekend to close a corporate deal, but she was determined to slip out to join them for dinner. Carson saw the delight on her face as she said to her twin, 'I hope you like her. I feel like I've finally found my soulmate.'

So Roland was to be the big surprise. Meg loved his company, not just because of his entertaining knowledge of some of the more obscure architectural treasures in New York, but also because he was so deliciously caustic about the behaviour of some of his wealthiest clients, names now familiar to her from the roll-call of Morgan Library benefactors, whom she had no option but to court for sponsorship for this exhibition or that.

'You could not begin to fathom their demands, Meg,' he would say conspiratorially. 'I just about understand a kitchen on every floor. We're talking five floors. That's just what you do, but seriously? A dog grooming room *and* a playroom for them, a flower-arranging cool room, a humidor. A coat of arms etched into the facade? The upside is the blank cheque. The downside is that my reputation as a serious architect might teeter on this one.' He sat back expansively in his seat in the cocktail bar of the Carlyle. 'Luckily my avaricious nature won, so the drinks are on me.' They laughed as they clinked glasses.

A waitress in a floor-length white apron monogrammed with the restaurant name led Meg, Elinor and Carson to the horseshoe-shaped banquette where Michelle was already seated, reading some papers and sipping a glass of wine. Carson watched as Elinor greeted her effusively and then Michelle turned to Carson, her fine-featured face open and friendly. 'It's lovely to meet the two people Meg talks about the most,' she said, her brown almond-shaped eyes creasing up as she smiled.

Meg leaned down and kissed her. 'Hellish day?'

'Oh, just the usual, pretty crazy. Dealing with testosterone-fuelled lawyers who think I'm just some timid little Asian woman. My absolute favourite.' She leaned towards Carson. 'But much more importantly, how did your big day go?' She pushed her glossy black hair behind one ear to reveal a diamond stud as big as a button.

Carson blushed. 'I don't know, but' – she glanced at her mother who smiled encouragingly – 'I do know I really, really want it now.'

'Well then, may your dreams come true. It would be lovely for us to have you here, wouldn't it, Meg?'

No sooner had the waiter poured wine for the new arrivals, studiously avoiding eye contact with Carson, lest he was obliged to ask her age, than she was aware of a tall figure looming over her, blotting out the light. She raised her eyes and let out a spontaneous cry of delight when she saw Roland grinning down at her. He bent over and kissed her on both cheeks, leaving behind the scent of something very expensive, and proceeded to answer a question no one had asked. He was in the city to see clients, he said, and when Pete told him who was going to be in town, he called Meg straight away. 'I couldn't pass up the chance for dinner with three of my favourite women, could I now.' He blew a kiss across the banquette. 'Michelle darling. You look fabulous tonight. Make that four.'

Meg and Elinor shook their heads at each other and snorted with laughter.

As they ate lobster ravioli and kale salad and berated a defiant Roland for ordering pan-fried foie gras, Carson stared in the mirror on the wall hanging slightly at an angle, watching the conversations dance around the table. Elinor inclined her head towards Michelle affectionately , while Roland flourished his napkin at Meg to emphasise some point or other, and every so often someone would exclaim that Roland was being

outrageous again, and he would smile contentedly in the
intimacy of a group he had no need to impress. Carson's eyes
settled on Elinor and as her mother threw back her head with
a laugh, she realised she'd never seen her look quite like this
before. She wished she could capture the moment in a photograph, because it was the first time since Iona's death that
Elinor seemed wholly alive.

'Pete says he misses her now that he's staying in halls of
residence in Glasgow, but he still gets down some weekends.'
Carson tuned in to the conversation and realised Roland was
talking about her. He gave his niece a gentle nudge. 'He's
always saying how talented you are, Car.'

Carson grimaced, embarrassed by the compliment.

'But I know that already. Look at your mother, after all.' He
smiled ingratiatingly at Elinor, and waited just a moment. 'So,
Eli,' he finally went on, 'what about working with Fiona? She's
longing to have you on board.'

Suddenly it seemed as if the room had hushed, other diners
had stopped their conversations and refrained from clinking
glasses as they waited for Elinor's reply. She put her arms on
the table and narrowed her eyes at her brother-in-law. 'Oh,
Roland, I see your game. Get me tipsy and take advantage!'
She frowned, gazing beyond the table, and took a long sip of
wine. 'Maybe if Car does come to New York I might . . . well,
at least it would be time to consider it . . . maybe.' No one
spoke, for fear a word out of place would smash the idea to
smithereens. 'I know that Fiona has got the contract for the
refurbishment of the Bernat Klein house near Selkirk in the
Borders. I've always loved that house.'

'Yes.' Roland nodded. 'Just being in it makes one feel better
about life. I think it's the finest modernist house in Scotland
– apart from the Stratton House, that is.'

A groan went around the table and Roland put up his hands. 'Kidding, only kidding. Fiona often tells me I'm just a tad pompous.' He waited, but no one demurred and when he looked crestfallen they all dissolved into gales of laughter, Roland loudest of all.

That night Carson and Elinor lay in bed together, moonlight washing through gossamer-thin curtains. Carson studied her mother's face as she lay on her back, her hair loose around her shoulders. She reached over and lifted a strand of hair from Elinor's cheek. 'You looked lovely tonight at dinner, Mum. Why didn't you tell me you've changed your mind about working with Aunt Fiona?'

Elinor turned her head. 'I only decided there and then, that's why.' She stroked Carson's face. 'You'll be gone. Here, I don't doubt. Dad's doing such good work he deserves to get the head of department – at last. I need to make myself useful. I have to do something.'

The image of Elinor at her work table, paintbrushes and paints beside her, came to Carson vividly. 'Can't you work with Aunt Fiona and go back to illustrating too?' Carson whispered. 'Remember how much I loved to watch you.'

Elinor smiled sadly and shook her head. 'I just can't seem to do it yet, darling, but sometime, maybe.' She leaned over and planted a kiss on Carson's forehead, like a seal. 'Now goodnight,' she said with a gentle finality, and turned to stare ahead again.

Carson dutifully burrowed into the duvet and closed her eyes, but when she opened them again a moment later to study her mother, she saw a silver tear fall from the corner of Elinor's eye onto her pillow.

CHAPTER 30

Walter stood as close to the International Arrivals sign as was humanly possible, straining to see Carson and Elinor, ready to greet them from the overnight flight as if they were long-lost relatives. When Marie spotted him setting two alarms she had disappeared to the spare room and as he lay awake watching the hands tick around he realised how rarely he slept alone now, and how much he missed the comfort of her.

When he spotted them both he swept his rolled-up umbrella into the air, narrowly missing the man beside him, and rushed forward to hug them both. 'Welcome home. I've missed you. Patrick's missed you.'

Elinor laughed. 'Walter, it's been five days, not five years.'

'Well, it felt like that, I can tell you.'

'You're going to have to get used to it, won't he, Car?'

'I don't know. Mum doesn't know, Granddad. Really they all looked so . . . well, dramatic and talented.'

Walter waved his umbrella again. 'And so are you, my chickadee.'

'That's called blind faith' – Carson smiled indulgently – 'and at school we're taught that's never a good idea.'

As they headed to Ayr, rain assaulting the windscreen, Walter looked in his rear-view mirror to see Elinor sleeping, resting against the window as Carson stretched back and gently put her scarf between her mother's head and the glass without disturbing her.

'How did Mum enjoy herself?' asked Walter quietly.

Carson glanced back again at Elinor. 'It was good for her to spend time with Aunt Meg. They feel like a pair to me when they're together. *And* she made a big decision. She'll tell you about it herself, but she's going to work with Aunt Fiona.'

Walter broke into a wide smile. 'Now that is wonderful news.' He leaned over towards the passenger seat and whispered, 'Dad's got a surprise for her too.'

That Saturday, Walter and Patrick had lugged a broken-down iron bench from Walter's back garden in Carsphairn to the MacMillan cabin, strapping it onto the roof of the Volvo. The car spluttered in protest, belching fumes of diesel so dense and acrid that Walter, travelling behind, made a mental note to write his son a cheque.

Patrick set about the restoration of the gothic bench with great gusto, carefully brushing off every last piece of flaking paint and soldering a loose arm, before carefully applying several coats of dark green gloss. Then he and Walter balanced it across a wheelbarrow and the two men processed carefully up the moor to the sheepfold.

'I remember when it last looked as good as that,' said Walter admiringly, once they had manoeuvred it into place. 'Your mother loved that seat. She used to sit on it under her parasol with Fiona beside her. I remember Fiona had an identical wee parasol, and Jean would read to her. She said it made her feel like a member of the Bloomsbury Set. I had to look up what she meant.' Walter stopped, suddenly back more than forty years.

'Are you okay, Dad?' Patrick said, clasping his shoulder.

His father nodded and inhaled deeply. 'You won't remember, but when we moved to Carsphairn I couldn't bear to leave it behind.'

Patrick ran his hand over the seat. 'And now it's back on the loch.' He looked at Iona's grave dappled by the trees. 'We could never have imagined why it would be here, could we, Dad? It still seems so unreal to me.'

'I know, Patrick. I know . . .'

They sat together on the bench looking down over the stone dyke all the way to the loch. Neither spoke; there was solace in the view, some comfort in the sunlit pillow-soft hills. They listened to the goldfinches twittering among the new leaves of the yellow rowan and watched them sent up in a frenzy now and then by a passing red kite.

When Walter drove into Ayr, Elinor was still asleep. Carson was silently acting as a second pair of eyes for her grandfather in the sheeting rain which rendered the road ahead a cloudy grey. They passed the Carnegie Library, over the Brig, and into the Sandgate and pulled up at the pedestrian crossing. A man stood waiting for the lights to change and, as the Land Rover passed slowly by, he gave Walter a wave. Walter lifted his hand from the wheel and put it against the windscreen in reply.

'Who's that?' asked Carson.

'It's Graeme MacMillan, my cousin's son,' Walter said, clearing his throat. 'I haven't seen him since he and his brother came to Iona's funeral.'

'Isn't he young to have a walking stick?'

'His leg was injured in an accident when he was a boy.'

'That's sad,' said Carson. 'What happened?'

'He was cycling near Dalmellington and a car hit him.' Walter hesitated for a moment. 'And it didn't stop.'

'But did the police catch the person who did it?'

Walter shook his head slowly. 'They never did.'

'That's awful, Granddad.'

'Yes,' Walter agreed with a deep sigh, 'it was a terrible time.'

When they pulled up at Wellington Square and Walter turned off the engine, Carson saw her grandfather sink down into his seat. 'Come in and have a rest before you drive home.'

Walter shook his head wearily. 'I've got things to do. I'll be fine. Don't you worry about me.'

He took the road to Carsphairn slowly, the image of Graeme MacMillan's greeting repeating before his eyes.

That afternoon Patrick hurried home after school and swept Elinor up in his arms, kissing her as he lowered her back down. Then he leaned over Carson who was sitting sipping a home-made iced coffee, her carefully observed New York discovery, and enveloped her in a bear hug. 'I've missed you both, my beauties,' he said, 'but I've been busy. Into the car. We're off to the loch before it gets dark. I've got a surprise for you.'

'So has Mum – got a surprise, I mean.'

Patrick stood back, his face expectant. 'Tell all!'

Elinor gave him a flicker of a smile. 'I've decided to work with Fiona on the Bernat Klein house.'

Patrick let out a whoop and did a quick jig, clapping his hands above his head ridiculously. 'That's what I've longed to hear. Good for you, Eli!'

The three walked up to the sheepfold, Patrick's arm loosely around Elinor's shoulders. Ahead of them new leaves fluttered in the trees, as if drying themselves in the spring sunshine now that the rain had cleared. As they approached the gate in the stone wall, Elinor let out a gasp. All around Iona's grave was a dazzling carpet of wood anemones with splashes of yellow in their centres. Sitting in the middle of it all, as if waiting for them, was a mountain hare, front legs rigid, soft ears high, nose twitching for an instant before it leapt the dyke. Carson started in amazement, first at the strange presence of the beautiful animal looking directly at her, and then as it bounded off into the perfect sea of white.

'Isn't it wonderful, Eli? There must be five times as many flowers as last year. It was your brilliant idea.'

Elinor leaned against the gatepost, overcome by the glorious scene in front of her. Patrick took her hand. 'Come on. There's something else.' They picked their way through the flowers and Elinor spotted the dark green seat standing out against the stone wall behind it. 'Patrick, where did it come from?' She ran her hand over the seat made up of intertwined flowers. 'It's perfect.'

'It's been lying rusting in Dad's garden for years.' He gestured to her to sit and then he joined her. 'We'll sit here together as we grow old' – his voice faltered – 'watching over Iona.'

She put her hand up to his face. 'Yes, we will. We will. Thank you.'

Carson watched her parents from the other side of Iona's grave. If she went to New York, this would be the picture she would keep in her mind, and when she looked at it she would know that all four of them were there together.

CHAPTER 31

When the email arrived a fortnight later offering Carson a place at Tisch she was alone in Wellington Square. She stared at the screen, her hand pressed firmly against her mouth until her face hurt. She kept the page open for more than an hour. She made herself an iced coffee and looked at it. She emptied the washing machine and hung the clothes on the pulley and stared at it again. She wanted to tell her parents in person, to see in their faces if they were going to be all right. Finally she sent a text.

'Hey Rory. You started this so now you have to come to see me in NYC. I got into Tisch!!! C xxx'

His reply pinged straight back. 'Fucking hell! I knew you would. Come to Edinburgh. We'll celebrate. We'll go to the Traverse!'

She called Walter next. 'Well, well,' he said, his voice suddenly hoarse, 'that's the best news I've had since I heard someone took a six pounder out of Loch Kendoon.'

'You promised to come.'

'Did I really? Well, I'm like fine wine, I don't travel well.' Carson heard a tremor and imagined her grandfather clutching the receiver and sitting down heavily.

'Granddad. We made a deal,' she coaxed. 'Marie will get you there safely.'

That evening Carson sat at the kitchen table with Elinor and Patrick, a bottle of champagne almost drained. Elinor had been rehearsing for this moment. 'I'm happy about all this, Car, I really am. I wouldn't want you to stay, for us' – she took Carson's hand – 'or for Iona. You know she'll be with you wherever you are.' The air relaxed as if the threat of thunder had passed and a cool breeze moved through the room. 'I don't think I'd be able to cope if Meg wasn't there though. She'll be able to do her godmotherly duties.' She stroked Carson's face. 'I want you to get to know her properly, and I want her to know you too.'

'Our almost eighteen-year-old daughter is going to New York. Wouldn't we have loved to do that, Eli?' Patrick swung his chair back on two legs and winked at Carson. 'I mean, we are the Woodstock generation.'

Carson thought for a moment, and quickly worked away at her mobile phone. 'It's not too late. The Greyhound bus from Manhattan to Woodstock is only twenty-five dollars. I'll get tickets for you as a present for when you come over.'

Elinor laughed. 'I think the Woodstock bus has long gone.'

When Rory met Carson on the concourse at Waverley station he lifted her up and whirled her around, much to her amazement and embarrassment. It was almost two months since he had gone back to Edinburgh and as he set her down she took in his appearance. His shoulder blades protruded though his grey sweatshirt and his jeans hung a little looser. His sea-green eyes were framed by his dark lashes under his long hair, and his smile was as wide and inviting as ever. Then she noticed his teeth were strangely white.

'You stopped smoking?'

'Yeah. It's too expensive. How did you guess?'

'Your teeth. They're dazzling.'

He grinned at her and a small electric charge ran up from her feet to the top of her head.

'No, you're the dazzling one. I'm so proud of you.'

They headed along Princes Street Gardens to the Traverse, to a new production of *The Girls of Slender Means*. Carson had read the novel at school and had tried to imagine its house of young women all trying to find their way in life after the war. They took their seats to the sound of Vera Lynn singing about a nightingale singing in Berkeley Square.

'This will be you some day,' Rory whispered, 'ready to come on stage.'

As the song faded away, the insistent, murderous drone of a flying bomb in the sky above London filled the black space as the actors walked silently around the stage. Each young woman spoke directly to the audience: 'seventy a day . . . out of the blue'; 'bombs with no dashing evil men in Jerry planes to drop them'; 'death was just a tick away'.

It was thrilling to watch the way the words came alive on stage, but Carson was more aware of Rory's shoulder pressed against hers, and the warmth of his breath when he put his face close to hers and asked if she was enjoying the play. She glanced down at his hand resting on his knee and put hers on top, pressing down hard, threading her fingers through his long slender ones. She saw the corner of his mouth turn up as he kept his eyes on the play, but he raised her entwined hand to his lips and kissed each of her fingers one by one. Before she knew it, wild applause broke out in the Traverse and as the actors took their bow Rory stroked her arm. 'Shall we?'

When they stepped inside Sandy Bell's bar on Forrest Road Carson looked round at the warm wood interior, the gleaming rows of whisky and the array of fiddles and mandolins along the top shelf.

'This feels familiar,' Carson mused. 'I think my dad used to drink in here.' She smiled. 'I think I've been here on a previous cultural tour – when I was about fourteen. I'm sure we were in Edinburgh for the Festival.'

'He probably knew Hamish Henderson. He drank here. He's a legend.'

'How strange you say that. Dad's got a book of his poems beside his bed.'

'Awesome. That's the problem with having philistine parents,' he added despondently.

'Feel free to borrow mine. Seriously. I'm a bit worried how they'll be. You can keep them amused.'

He emptied his glass and stared at the dregs. 'And how do you think I'll be?'

'Aren't there all sorts of Pippas and Arabellas hooraying after you?'

'Fuck off,' he replied affectionately as he swung her small rucksack over his shoulder. 'Right, last stop. I'm taking you for the best curry in Edinburgh.'

Half an hour later, after a stroll through The Meadows and a stop at the off licence, they were shown to a candlelit window table Rory had reserved at the restaurant whose walls were decorated with designs of flowers and animals made from thousands of pieces of mirrored glass. Rory handed over a bottle of wine and the waiter poured them both a large glass as they studied the menu: dishes with marinated aubergines and north Indian spices, and pooris of chickpeas and tamarind date sauce.

Carson looked around. 'Mum would love it here. I'll ask Dad to bring her. Maybe they could have a weekend in Edinburgh after I go.'

Rory folded his arms on the table and bent his head towards her. 'Car. Your mum and dad are going to be fine. Really they are.'

Anyone walking past and glancing through the window would have seen their two heads almost touching, faces a little flushed. They would have seen Rory wipe away a crumb from the side of Carson's mouth.

'Will you visit me?'

'I'm there.' He smiled and gave her a lingering kiss.

They walked unsteadily to the halls of residence that sat squat and drab beneath the brooding escarpment of Salisbury Crags. 'Sometimes I look out of my window late at night and I think I see Hyde dragging his prey along the top of the Crags,' Rory hissed in Carson's ear.

'Whaaat!'

'Shh . . .' said Rory. 'You're not meant to be sleeping in my room. Remember?'

She giggled as they stumbled through the door. The shabby room was tiny, and crammed with built-in seventies furniture decorated with graffiti. Carson peered at the desk top. 'They fuck you up your mum and dad but at least they're five hundred miles away.' She looked askance at Rory. 'Is that the best they could do?'

Rory laughed and pointed at the bedhead. 'It starts when you sink in his arms and ends with your arms in the sink.'

Carson grimaced. 'Very retro.' She giggled again. 'Actually I've seen that on a postcard in Mum's bedroom.'

She looked down at the cigarette burns on the nylon carpet. Rory followed her gaze. 'I know. It's a complete shithole. You take the bed. I'll use your sleeping bag on the floor.'

She pulled her clothes off in the adjoining bathroom, steadying herself against the wall as the room tilted a little, and raked around her rucksack for her nightshirt. Then she quickly squeezed some toothpaste on her finger and rubbed it on her teeth, licking her slightly numb lips.

When she returned to the bedroom Rory had switched off the strip light and draped the Anglepoise with a blue T-shirt, lending the room a dark glow. He looked up at her from her sleeping bag. 'Are you channelling Wee Willie Winkie by any chance?'

'Funny, funny,' she said as she lay down on the bed and simultaneously leaned down to try to mess up his hair, banging him on the nose instead. She erupted in gales of laughter and eventually Rory stretched up and put his hand across her mouth.

'Come in beside me, please,' she mumbled into his palm.

She saw the uncertainty flash across his eyes. 'Car. Do you think it's a good idea? Is it because you're a wee bit drunk?'

Carson shook her head, her brain lurching from side to side.

Rory looked baffled. 'Which do you mean?'

'It's a good idea. I've wanted to for ages.' A look of consternation crossed her face. 'Haven't you?'

'Since I kissed you on stage,' Rory murmured as he manoeuvred himself into the single bed. He kissed her on the lips and then her nose and eyes and she did the same back, and she laughed and put her hand into her bag which was hanging on the bedpost and fished out a small packet and put it under the pillow.

Then she put her mouth to his ear. 'I wanted it to be with you.'

CHAPTER 32

As soon as the summer holidays began Patrick roped Walter into a project at the cabin. In the weeks since Carson's news he had watched as his father's air of ebullience had ebbed away, as if he were pining for her already.

The cabin was as it had always been, its shabbiness its charm, its comfortable threadbare furnishings equal to muddy feet and the mess of life. Patrick used to joke it was Elinor's 'hippy heaven'. Besides, there had been no money to do anything other than to enjoy it, wind, rain or shine, and it had held, perfectly, the shape of their family life. But since Iona's death the cabin had felt, if not unloved, then treated carelessly, no longer adorned with still wet watercolours or festooned with brightly coloured paper chains and scattered toys, and vases of cherry blossom or wild flowers.

After Elinor had started work with Fiona, all manner of interiors magazines had started to appear at Wellington Square, and Patrick's eye was caught by one cover, a cabin, not unlike theirs but painted navy blue, with cream window frames, a neat porch, and on the side a sunroom with windows on three sides and skylights in the roof. The interior was washed in cream and pale grey, with splashes of brightly coloured sofas and hand-painted lampshades. A month before the end of the summer term, as Elinor was preparing breakfast, Patrick slipped up behind her and put his arms around her waist. 'I need your professional opinion,' he murmured in her ear. She turned around, her gaze sceptical. 'Take a look at this.' He handed her a large piece of paper on which he had sketched the cabin with a summer room looking out to the mountain of Cairnsmore of Fleet. Stapled to the page was the magazine article and even a selection of dark paint colours. 'I know my drawing skills are woeful, but what do you think?'

Elinor looked at him, perplexed. 'What is it?'

'Ouch! It's our cabin.'

She studied it carefully now. 'But why have you done this?'

'It's my unpaid holiday job. Dad's too. And Car. What do you think?'

'Are you serious?' She half smiled.

'Completely – if you agree.'

She nodded slowly, her eyes still quizzical. 'But why now?'

'Well, a few reasons. We three can be together while you're hard at work; but I want you to be involved too,' he added quickly. Then he paused and took her hands in his. 'It's time to spruce the place up. Change it a little.'

'Maybe it is,' she said pensively and smiled. 'Not sure that's the right shade of blue though.'

Patrick and Walter worked together companionably while Carson acted as their apprentice. Pete, on a summer internship with a famous Catalan architect, bemoaned his absence and demanded daily photographic updates. 'I'm jealous,' he said in a dejected phone call to Carson. 'All I'm doing here is cataloguing architectural plans. I could have done that with Dad. *And* Flora's in London.'

Walter directed the construction of the kit frame for the summer room, checking the cut timber was seasoned sufficiently, inspecting the bales of roof insulation, ordering around the local electrician, and insisting that Patrick triple-check the spirit level.

'It's a spirit level, Dad. That's what it does.' Patrick tried to keep his voice on an even keel.

Walter thrust his hands deeper into his blue overalls. 'I know, Patrick, but that run looks a little bit off. If something is worth doing, it's worth doing well. And that floorboard has to lie on perfect plywood on a perfect joist.'

Patrick bit down hard on his tongue to keep an injudicious remark from escaping. Carson and her father always deferred to Walter, sometimes wisely, other times humouring him, both keen to give him his place. Once he and Carson had sanded and primed the pine exterior of the cabin Carson set to work painting the wood a beautiful dark blue.

'There's too much paint on your brush, Car,' Walter chided her anxiously. 'Don't rush at it. You would never see your mother rushing, would you?' Walter stopped, his own brush dripping in mid-air. 'I'm sorry, Car. I shouldn't have said that.'

'It's okay, Granddad. Maybe this will make a difference. I can see her sitting at her work table in the summer room. It's going to be lovely.'

One evening towards the end of July, the smell of fresh paint wafted through the air and at the end of a long and fruitful day Patrick and Walter sat in the Adirondack chairs in front of the Stratton House sipping cold beer.

'Do you know what day this is?' asked Walter, looking out over the loch, flies hovering over the surface, tantalising the fish below, the Galloway Hills an almost technicolour pink and green in the warm evening sunshine.

'No, Dad,' Patrick replied, trying to disguise his alarm that he had forgotten an important moment. 'I'm sorry.'

'It's the day you helped to raise the Spitfire.'

'How could I have forgotten,' said Patrick, shaking his head.

That day, twenty-six years before, Patrick had taken the boat down the loch to where the divers were getting ready to make the lift. Walter watched through his binoculars from the shore as his son cut the outboard engine near the crash site and rowed towards the group of boats. There was a tremendous feeling of excitement in the air as the helpers waited patiently for the divers to bring the plane up to the surface. As it broke the water Patrick helped manoeuvre it within the buoys. It looked like the skeleton of a giant dragonfly cocooned in the Day-Glo orange airbags, rescued from the deep, its wings shredded but the fuselage and the tail intact.

'I remember that the Merlin engine was bound up in weeds, as if the Spitfire's heart had been clogged up,' said Patrick.

'Aye,' replied Walter, 'and somehow I had hoped that there might have been something left of the pilot. But there was nothing, not even a scrap of uniform. Yet he would have been strapped in. It was as though he had been sacrificed to the loch.'

They both sat, memories of that day forming and sharpening.

Walter clasped his hands together, kneading his calloused knuckles, working the ache out. 'I was always glad that you helped with the recovery. I felt it was only right.'

PART FIVE

Love is not love
Which alters when it alteration finds

CHAPTER 33

Meg helped Carson drag her bags through dorm security, past chattering students and clucking parents, all encumbered by suitcases, trunks and boxes of all shapes and sizes, and bin bags overflowing with pillows and towels and soft toys and fairy lights. Meg could not resist a smug smile that she had insisted on buying Carson's bedding and having it delivered ahead. They took the lift to the second floor and as they approached the room that Carson had been assigned they heard voices remonstrating.

'Don't you leave your door unlocked – ever, Camila. Do you hear? There are all sorts here.'

'Mom, we're from Colombia. We *are* the all sorts.' The voice lowered. 'Anyway, why are you speaking English?'

As Carson appeared at the door Camila's eyes popped. 'The Scottish chica from the audition!' She leapt forward and pumped Carson's hand. 'How cool is this? Mom, this is the girl I told you about. It's Carrie, isn't it?'

Carson smiled and corrected her gently.

'Oooh, Car-son,' said Camila's mother, separating the two syllables. 'Like Johnnie. I am Daniella.' She put her arms out as if expecting a hug. 'We live in California; almost as far away as Scotland, no?' She looked at Meg. 'Are you the mom?'

'No, I'm Meg Campbell, Carson's aunt. I live in New York. Pleased to meet you.'

Daniella's eyes lit up. 'You live here? It's good that Car-son has you here; maybe you could keep an eye on Camila too?'

'Mom! *Deja de avergonzarme!*'

Daniella pointed her perfectly manicured diamanté-studded nails in front of her daughter's nose. 'You can never be too careful in this city, *carina*. Take all the help you can get.' She turned and beamed at Meg. 'I'm right. No?'

That night Carson and Camila found their way to a spit-and-sawdust bar behind Tisch, its neon sign flashing 'Brad's' in green and red by turn. They looked inside at the walls decorated with theatre and film posters, above the noisy throng of students. As they were about to open the door, Camila stopped dead. 'Oh *mierda*. You can't get drink. We need to get you fake ID.'

Carson smiled conspiratorially. 'Sorted. Someone I know at Edinburgh University got it for me. The drinks are on me.'

Camila looked at her with deep respect, her strong cheekbones rounded as she broke into a lovely smile and she put her hand through her short black bob making it stand on end. 'Well, girlfriend. That is sweet.'

The sat drinking neat whisky at a scrubbed table under a poster of Brad Pitt. Across his face was scrawled, 'Brad got shitfaced at Brad's'. Soon a rag-tag group congregated around them and by the end of the evening Carson started to feel, not *the* outsider but just one of many, from Turkey, Canada, Syria, Japan and more who were all, once upon a time, from somewhere else.

When Carson and Camila wandered back to their dorm, arm in arm, Camila wet one of her socks and then stood on a chair and pulled it over the smoke alarm. Then she stood back to admire her handiwork. 'Ah *esta!*' She slid open the window and Union

Square exploded into their bedroom: a cab driver cursing someone who'd had the temerity to step into his path, a street vendor
trying to shift the last shrivelled hotdogs in his oven, an exhausted
mother screaming at her child. Camila retrieved a soft turquoise
pack of cigarettes from her denim jacket and offered one to
Carson. She shook her head vigorously. 'No thanks. I smoked
like a lum with Aunt Meg on her stoop last night. It must have
been nerves. My throat's as rough as a cheese grater.'

'What's a "lum"?'

'It's a Scottish word for a chimney.'

'Cute. I like it.' Camila smiled, then took a long drag and
sent a series of smoke rings out of the window. 'See, *carina*, I'm
blowing them out of my lum.'

A fortnight later as Carson careered out of the dorms she
noticed a letter sticking out of the box marked for their room,
her address written in the teal-blue ink that was Elinor's
favourite. She ripped it open excitedly as she raced to class.

Darling Car,

It was so lovely to hear your voice last night. I hope you
have settled into your dorm now. I like the sound of
Camila but I'm a bit worried about the smoke alarm –
apart from the fact that it's dangerous I don't want you to
get chucked out of your dorm. Likewise, the ID I won't
mention. So glad you're going to Meg's for a night soon.
She and Michelle are dying to spoil you.

Fiona and I are getting on so well together. She's missing Pete at the loch, but second year is tough. (I think he
might be dating Flora properly now, so he stays in
Glasgow at the weekend – but you'll know about that
anyway!!)

Did I mention on the phone that we're starting work on a house on the coast at Auchencairn for a rich Edinburgh lawyer? (Is there any other kind?) It's a wreck but it could be wonderful.

I bought a book of Elizabeth Bishop poems in that lovely bookshop in the Sandgate and it fell open at one called 'Letter to NY' – I think it was for her lover – but it felt right for me and you. It begins:

> In your next letter I wish you'd say
> Where you are going and what you are doing;
> How are the plays and after the plays
> What other pleasures you're pursuing:

EB talks about imagining her lover coming out of a brownstone house and the side of the building rising with the sun. It somehow comforted me and made me feel I was there with you. I remember the walk from Gramercy to Tisch, the three of us, arm in arm, and I marvel at how well you will know your way, how quickly you will recognise a window on this corner, a shop sign on that. How assured you will be. It makes me happy, Car.

Anyway I better get this off to the post office. I'll email most of the time but I wanted to put ink to paper.

Granddad and Marie are off to Edinburgh to the Tattoo. Dad and I are going to the Citz tonight to see *The Rivals*. I've popped in some dollars – spend unwisely!

Love you, sweetpea,
Mum xxx

Carson put the letter away to savour after class and pushed open the door of the rehearsal space, walking straight into the glare of the hot morning sunshine that shot through the four tall windows overlooking Broadway, illuminating the metal chairs scattered around the otherwise bare room. Students trailed in slowly, greeting each other and discarding backpacks and layers of exercise clothes and began a series of stretches and bends alone and with partners.

'Okay,' said Ruth Anne, clapping her hands, 'I want you to partner up and imagine you are water, a fountain, a tiny river, an ocean ... Whatever comes to you. Intuit each other's moves. I want to see you twisting and turning, flowing and crashing, using every part of your body.'

Carson stood stock still, her mind in freefall. She could never do it. Before she could draw a breath Devante, a tall striking boy from Boston who played basketball, took her hand and immediately played with her resistance. Tears came to her eyes as he lifted her and turned her and then pulled them both low. 'Hey, Carson, go with me, it's okay,' he whispered.

Blindly she twisted her body and then she felt his hands in hers pulling her taut. She tried to think of the falling water of the dams but all she could see was Iona's face and she suddenly went limp in Devante's arms.

The teacher clapped her hands to end the exercise. 'Good work, but some of you need to immerse yourselves in the idea. It's important to allow yourselves to be fully present in what you are doing.'

Carson kept her eyes on the floor.

As the class ended Camila appeared from the other side of the room. '*Carina*, are you in a trance? We got to get going.' She propelled her friend along the corridor, up the stairs and into a black box space.

Stephen Sheen was a compact, charismatic man in his early forties with an easy smile and intelligent eyes. He moved

among the acting class quietly, speaking to each student indi-
vidually, resting a palm on the base of a spine, or gently
straightening a neck. As he stood behind Carson and pressed
down her hips, anchoring her, she pushed away thoughts of
the movement class, knowing that if she did not she would
never be able to do this class. Slowly she felt a calmness enter
her body.

'Today we are going to work on the exercise that I set from
the Scottish Play. Act one, scene five. Lady Macbeth's soliloquy. Let's hear it. All of you now.'

'The raven himself is hoarse . . .' began twelve voices in different accents and registers, and at different speeds, creating a strange
incantation that filled the room. As the last student finished the
final line the professor put his hands up to still them all.

'Remember what I said about character. What is Lady
Macbeth's weakness?'

'Her desperation for Macbeth to be king,' Carson said
calmly, 'her passion for power, and the fact that she finds
power an aphrodisiac.' Stephen nodded encouragingly. 'If
Macbeth won't kill for the crown, she won't find him sexually
attractive.'

'So,' he said, looking around at the other students, 'how are
we going to use that information?'

Later, as the class ended, Stephen Sheen walked over to
where Carson was packing up her notes and gave her a playful
knock on the arm. 'Good job.'

Carson blushed with pleasure as she left to reread Elinor's
letter.

That night Carson and Camila hosted an impromptu party in
their room. Students whom they had passed in the corridor
day after day with no more than a desultory nod came and

drifted about, beer in hand, trawling through Carson's biscuit tin, and helping themselves to the cigarettes that Camila thought she had stashed safely under her pillow. Some brought six-packs of ale, others vodka premixed in bottles of Seven Up, and a Swedish white-blonde girl, dressed in a multicoloured home-knitted minidress and pink lace-up boots, handed round hash brownies.

Eventually, at two in the morning Carson politely, and Camila not so politely, asked the South Korean twin brothers, both astrophysics majors, who had settled in with their bong, to leave. Camila snapped off the Killers CD mid-song and pushed the others out of the door, pulled the sock from the smoke alarm, and dowsed a huge bowl of cigarette butts.

Carson made hot chocolate and they sat in their beds in the near dark, the windows strafed now and then with flashing red lights which contrasted with the orange and lemon fairy lights stuck to the wall in a huge citrus swirl.

'There's something I want to tell you, Camila,' said Carson, warming her hands around her mug. 'Is that okay?'

'You can tell me anything, *carina*.' She smiled drowsily.

'My little sister drowned.'

'Whaaat?' Camila started forward. 'Oh Jesus. I am so sorry. When, Carson? When did it happen?'

'Three years ago, in early summer.'

As Carson talked on, the sounds from Union Square faded until only the occasional warning 'beep-beep' from a reversing delivery truck punctured the night. It was as if the whole city were listening in. Camila hardly spoke, careful not to press for any detail as Carson described what happened that day, and in the aftermath, and as Camila's eyes strayed to the photographs almost hidden in the dark on Carson's shelf, the smiles that she had studied took on a much sadder expression.

'Have I ever cried out in my sleep?' Carson asked hesitantly.
Camila shook her head.

'It's just that I have nightmares and sometimes it is so real
all over again I think I scream out loud.'

'No, *carina*, but if you do I will be here to comfort you.'

Then they both fell asleep as the dawn light stole into the
city between the tall buildings that seemed to lean towards
each other in the vista that stretched all the way up to Central
Park.

One Saturday morning two months later Carson woke up in
a quite different room. She lay in Meg's apartment in Gramercy,
curled up like a dormouse in the sumptuous spare-room bed,
listening to the now familiar exchanges between her aunt and
Michelle as they prepared the weekend meal they had planned
together, a fusion of Scottish cooking and Asian dishes, a menu
that Meg had written out in beautiful copperplate the night
before while Carson composed her weekly postcard to Walter.

She had promised him that, each week, she would tell him
something about New York that he did not already know. This
time it was the fact that Andrew Carnegie and Mark Twain
were lifelong friends. She knew that Walter would write back
topping that fact with something or other he had found out at
the Carnegie Library in the intervening week. She wanted to
think of Walter delighting in his fact-finding, and not as he
was when she left him, his broad smile belied by a tremulous
hug.

As Carson inhaled the infusion of smells wafting from the
kitchen she burrowed deeper under the duvet again, and only
surfaced from a dreamless sleep at noon. By the time she
appeared, dressed in an embroidered corduroy dress, a present
from Meg, the table was set for three with decorated crockery,
scented candles and crystal glasses, and beside them Elinor's

highball glasses from the Borders. She couldn't believe it was all for her.

'This will keep you going,' said Michelle as she handed her some French toast and maple syrup.

'I want to pick up some flowers. Mum is always sending me dollars. Where should I go?' Carson asked through a mouthful of toast.

'Try the shop on the corner of Second Av. The display is so beautiful, sometimes I photograph it,' said Meg.

Carson stood admiring the profusion of roses, wondering where to begin. She bent over some huge peach-coloured blooms, their musky perfume so strong she let out an involuntary sigh.

'You like these ones, young lady?' She turned and saw a portly South American man smiling at her from under his straw hat. 'They're beautiful, no?'

She asked the price. 'For you, one bunch for ten dollars, but two for fifteen.'

He squinted at her as she handed over the money. 'You don't sound American,' he said in a strong Spanish accent. 'Are you on holiday from someplace?'

'I'm Scottish. I'm studying here.'

'Ah, my grandson is at Edinburgh University. My daughter married an oilman from Aberdeen' – he frowned at her – 'but he sounds nothing like you. He sounds nothing like anything I have ever heard.'

He plucked a third bunch of the peach roses from the pail and wrapped them together into a huge bouquet. 'For you. Come again – and we can speak Scottish, no?'

That night Carson confided to Meg and Michelle that sometimes she found the dorms and the campus and the personalities there a little crazy, and that much as she really did love Camila she craved peace to think and work. 'It sounds so ungrateful and bratty,' she said, and then her eyes searched out the photograph of her sister, 'and sometimes I just need to think about Iona when it's not too painful to remember. I mean I don't want to forget anything about her. Sometimes I like to write things down.'

'Of course you need peace sometimes, Car,' Meg replied as she pushed her chair back from the table. 'Michelle darling, could you put out the cheese, I just need to make a call,' she threw over her shoulder as she disappeared into her bedroom.

The next day Carson walked the twenty blocks to the Morgan Library on Madison Avenue, in her rucksack a new writing pad, box of pencils and her laptop. She stood outside, survey-ing the marble facade and the slender columns of the Palladian arch. Meg said it was the epitome of America's Age of Elegance. 'Sometimes I have to pinch myself that I work here,' she had said. Carson walked in through the glass box atrium that served as the new entrance and stopped at the front desk.

A receptionist in uniform sat behind a long wooden counter studying the papers in front of her, her glitter-edged half-moon glasses perched on her nose and her perfectly applied lilac eyeshadow swept across her eyelids contrasting with her flawless black complexion. 'Welcome to the Morgan,' she drawled slowly as she looked up. 'How can I help you?'

'I've come to pay my student membership. I'm Meg Campbell's niece.'

'Of course you are! Another of my long-lost relatives!'

Carson looked mystified. Then she glanced at Precious Campbell's name badge.

'Some of us are more Scottish than others, I guess,' Precious said sardonically. Then she broke into a lovely smile. 'Just teasing. Meg telephoned me last night at home to say to expect you. I've put a reserved sign on the little corner table in the library. It's quiet in there. It's quiet altogether on a Sunday.'

Carson had never been in a room so grand. She looked at the three storeys of walnut bookcases and then her eyes travelled on upwards to the signs of the zodiac painted on the vast ceiling. In front of her was an intricately carved stone fireplace, so cavernous she could have walked right inside without ducking her head. A tapestry hung above it, and beneath her feet a sumptuous Turkish rug stretched almost the length and breadth of the parquet floor. She laid out all her materials, closed her eyes, and thought of the black and white photograph beside Walter's bed. As her pencil hovered over the page, she began to imagine a dialogue between the two on their wedding day.

CHAPTER 34

Two weeks before Walter was at home wandering from one task to the next. He filled the birdseed hoppers and then he fiddled with the dripping kitchen tap. 'You don't know what to be doing with yourself,' said Marie. To Walter the time that Carson had been in New York was an eternity; only the weekly postcard and the odd phone call made her absence bearable.

'Come with me to Castle Douglas. The Farmers' Market's on.'

Walter shook his head. 'Not for me, thanks. I don't need a fancy striped awning and heritage straw bales to get me to buy expensive eggs and butter. The village shop manages that just fine.'

'You're becoming a curmudgeon, Walter MacMillan.' Marie put on her jacket and picked up her basket. 'You've got a face on. You're right to stay. I wouldn't be seen dead walking down the main street beside that face. I wonder what I should say when people ask after you?' She did not wait for an answer. 'I know, I'll say, oh Walter's fine – but he's busy knitting his brows just to keep his frown in place.'

Walter looked downcast. 'Am I really that bad? I'm sorry. I'll be better when you get back.'

'If you want something useful to do, you promised to look out stuff for the Lifeboat bric-a-brac sale.'

'I'll have a coffee first.'

'Have one as you go. It'll be like attaching jump leads,' she called over her shoulder as she headed out.

He felt he owed it to her to make a start. After all, she'd done nothing to deserve this morose companion. He poured a cup from the flask she'd made first thing and, bending lower than was comfortable, delved into the far end of the cupboard under the stairs and felt for some old cardboard boxes.

He set them on the kitchen table and opened the first one. It was full of old Kodak packets of photographs and, resting on top, a photo frame, face down. He turned it over and looked at the picture of Jean, Patrick on her knee, the ripples of Loch Kendoon behind them. He gripped the table to fight a dizzy turn and blew his cheeks in and out, his mouth open.

Patrick could have been no more than two years old. Jean must have been pregnant with Fiona, he calculated. It was a day as fresh as clean linen. Jean was wearing a navy Guernsey and khaki trousers and her hair was tied up in a scarf like a land girl. Pearl studs gleamed in her ears and, even in black and white, he could see the colour in her cheeks.

They had been away from home all day, first at the sheep-dog trials at Moniaive where Patrick, high on his father's shoulders, had banged his hands on Walter's head, squealing with excitement as the sheepdogs moved their flocks this way and that as if by magic, chasing down escapees, menacing their heels and sending them into a frenzy of baaing.

Jean had packed a picnic and he distinctly remembered that when they arrived at Loch Kendoon she put her flask to his nose. 'Look, Walter, I've brought tea – that's all.' And he had reached out to her and kissed her hard as if she had given him a priceless gift. He had rowed them all the way from the

boathouse to the iron bridge, a quarter of a mile away and
back again, while Jean held their son on her lap and sang to
him.

My Patrick lies over the ocean, my Patrick lies over the sea.
My Patrick lies over the ocean, Oh, bring back my Patrick
to me.

Patrick swayed along with her, clapping his chubby hands and
giggling at Walter. It was as idyllic a day as it could be. When
they had arrived home and Patrick still lay on the back seat,
asleep, his arms open above his head, his face warmed by the
sun, Walter had stopped the car and leaned over and kissed
Jean, and her mouth tasted fresh and cool. In that moment his
heart soared and everything seemed possible, but then, as he
tucked Patrick up in bed, still in his romper suit, he heard the
familiar sharp sound of ice being dropped in a glass.

Walter rubbed his eyes as if trying to rub away the memory.
He closed the box and set it to one side and opened the next
one gingerly. On top was a fine baby blanket folded neatly,
with a little boat embroidered on the silk edge, the letter P in
its sail. He folded it back to find an identical one below on
which there was an F and beside it a delicate rose made up of
tiny stitches. At that moment the silence was shattered by the
insistent ring of the telephone, and Walter heaved himself up
from the table, glad of the interruption.

'Hello, Walter here.'

'Hi, Dad. Lovely day. How are you?'

There was something strained about Patrick's voice.

'Fine, son. Just sorting through some old things.'

'Are you going to be home later this afternoon?'

'Yes. Why?'

'Pete and I are going to be down at the loch. We'll come and see you after.'

'Something wrong?'

'No, no, see you then.'

Walter listened as Patrick put down the receiver. He stood for a moment, trying to fathom what could be wrong. He put the lid back on the box. He had no heart for it, and he wandered out to the garden to do battle with the weeds.

It was early evening before Patrick and Pete pulled up in Patrick's new SUV. Marie was already at the door to greet them. 'Walter's been a bit agitated, just to warn you. Is everything okay?'

'We've found something – or at least Pete has. About Iona.' Patrick took her hand. 'I'm glad you're home. So glad, Marie.'

Walter appeared behind her.

'Hello, Granddad,' Pete said, his voice taut.

'Not out with your girlfriend tonight, Pete?' he said, searching his grandson's face.

Pete shook his head and glanced at Patrick. 'No, but I was with her this morning.'

'Let's sit down,' Patrick interjected.

Marie made a pot of tea as Patrick settled himself beside Walter at the kitchen table.

'Dad, I think we've found the speedboat that Pete and Carson heard on the loch.'

Walter felt his chest tightening as if someone had compressed his ribs against his spine. 'Where? Where did you find it?' he wheezed.

'Pete, you tell Granddad.'

Pete took a gulp of his tea.

'Come on Petey,' said Walter, impatient now.

'I took Flora to see a second-hand car this morning. It was listed for sale in the *Ayr Advertiser*. She had made an appointment for nine at an address just outside Dailly, and when we arrived at an old stone cottage a tall man in overalls came out of the house. He didn't introduce himself, he just took us to the barn.'

Something nagged at Walter. He tried to pinpoint the cottage in his mind, but he could not get a fix on it.

'Granddad, are you okay?'

Walter realised he had closed his eyes. 'Yes, yes. Go on, Pete.'

Pete explained that when the man pulled back the sliding door, the Ford Fiesta they had come to see was parked at the front. On the walls were rows of tools fixed neatly to the wall, and beside them orange overalls with the insignia of the RNLI hung on a peg. There was an old broken-down Massey Ferguson tractor as well as a dusty motorbike and two or three wheelbarrows. While the man showed Flora over the car, Pete's gaze was drawn towards the back of the garage and as he adjusted his eyes to the gloom, first he saw an outboard on a wooden stand and then he noticed a fibreglass hull poking out from under a huge black tarpaulin. It was decorated with three undulating lines, silver, blue and white.

'I froze. I couldn't believe it. I quickly said that we had to be somewhere else and said I was sure Flora would be in touch. Flora looked at me like I was mad. It was then that he said he was at the Lifeboat station at Girvan most days. He told her the mobile signal wasn't so good in Dailly so she could get him there. He said, "Just ask for Robert MacMillan."'

Walter was stupefied. 'My cousin Kenneth's son.' He stared at Pete. 'Was his brother Graeme there too?'

Pete shook his head. 'We only saw Robert.'

Walter turned to Patrick, his head swimming, a buzzing in his ears like radio static. 'What does this mean?'

'Well, at first when Pete called me I thought it might not mean anything. As the police keep telling us there was no trace of anyone else on the loch. But then I remembered Robert grew up at the farm on the moor. He knows the loch.' Patrick paused. 'And then I remembered that there had been rumours of smuggling along the coast near Girvan and talk of all sorts of people being involved.'

'Smuggling what?' asked Walter.

'Drugs, drink, cigarettes.'

'But he has always been a stalwart of the Lifeboat. It's in his blood,' said Walter faintly, a sick feeling spreading across his stomach. Then he suddenly grabbed Patrick's arm. 'Did you call the police?' he asked urgently.

Patrick shook his head. 'Not yet. But Pete and I went to the loch today.'

Walter was finding it hard to keep up. He put his head in his hands. 'What for? Why?'

It was Patrick's turn to explain. 'Do you remember the well hole, the place we used to call the Murder Hole, beside the Head of the Loch sheep pen? No one ever goes there. It's all broken down.'

Walter concentrated hard, trying to visualise the place. 'I remember it. It was covered with a stone slab – for safety.'

Patrick picked up a bag from his feet. Walter had not even noticed it.

'Oh no!' said Marie softly, and put her hand over her mouth.

Patrick turned the plastic bag upside down. A large oilskin package, attached to a long thin chain wreathed in green slime, slid onto the table, a fresh piece of masking tape down one side.

'We found this in the well hole. Pete and I pulled back the slab and I put my arm down until I felt a rock. The rope was attached to a metal ring drilled into it, but it didn't come up easily. I'm sure it's been down there for a long time. Do you know what it is?' Patrick laughed mirthlessly. 'It's rolling tobacco, about five hundred packets. I looked it up. They're worth about two thousand pounds on the black market.' Patrick banged his fists on the table. 'Two thousand pounds for Iona's life.'

Walter felt the room spinning and put his head in his hands.

Patrick's voice sounded muffled. 'We have to go to the police.'

'No,' Walter heard himself say. 'I want to talk to him.'

'No, Dad. Not in any circumstances. Absolutely not.'

He looked up at his son. 'But there's no evidence to link him to this,' Walter persisted. 'I need to talk to him. He might tell me the truth. We're family.'

'Dad! What the hell has that got to do with it?' Patrick tried to keep his voice in check. 'We're not close, remember? I'm going to call Sergeant Sturrock first thing.'

He got up from the table and threw Marie a pleading look. 'Dad. Get some rest. And we're not going to tell Carson yet. We can decide when to tell her. She's home in six weeks.' Patrick turned to Pete. 'She'll be amazed you found the boat.'

'It doesn't make it any better.' Pete broke down now with the weight of everything, tears spilling onto his cheeks.

Patrick put his arm round his nephew's shoulder and guided him out to the car.

After she saw Patrick and Pete away, Marie found Walter in his leather chair, staring at the embers of the fire. 'I think you should lie down for a while, Walter, you're white as a sheet.' She felt his hand. 'And frozen.'

'In a minute, please. I just want to think.'

She dug at the fire and threw on a log. 'Only a few minutes then, you have to get some rest.' She put her hand on his arm.

'I can't imagine how awful this is for you, Walter. I'm so sorry. But you can't blame yourself.'

He stared at her, a wretched look on his face. 'Can I not?'

He looked into the fire as Marie left the room, as if he wanted the flames to burn out his eyes. The image of the newly painted cabin and the glass box beside it came to him clearly. It was all for him. Had he not been so desperate to keep his children close, and his grandchildren, Iona would still be alive. All the time teaching Carson about the hills, instructing Pete on fishing flies, reciting Iona poems, laying out Elinor's garden, keeping the builders on track for Fiona: all that was for him, not them. He suddenly felt his skin clammy beneath his clothes and wiped away perspiration from his brow. If he had not been so thirled to the loch, Jean might be alive still, and no one else would have suffered.

He gripped hold of the arms of the chair and tried to push himself up. Suddenly a sharp pain shot through his chest and spread out like forked lightning, travelling down his arm to the tips of his fingers. He tried to take a deep breath but only managed a few short gasps and he slumped forward, knocking his teacup off the table onto the hearth, shattering it into little pieces.

'Walter?' Marie was beside him in seconds. She ran to the kitchen and grabbed an aspirin and then forced it into his mouth. 'Chew, Walter,' she ordered, trying not to shout, and then she dialled 999.

In the ambulance Walter lay strapped on the gurney, his head propped up on pillows. The paramedic applied a spray under his tongue and then gently put an oxygen mask over his face. Marie sat at the side of the ambulance, her hands tightly clasped in front of her. He turned to her and saw the wet creases around her eyes, her mouth pressed shut. She started suddenly as Walter pulled his arm from the binding and lifted his mask. 'Are you all right, Marie?'

'Don't speak. Please, Walter.'

He looked into her frightened cornflower-blue eyes. 'I'm fine. Patrick and Fiona will make a fuss. I don't want a fuss, Marie,' he rasped. He put his hand over hers. 'Two things. Carson mustn't know about me, and I don't want the police involved. Tell them, please.'

She leaned in to him and put his mask back onto his face. 'Walter, there are things I can do for you, but I can't do either of those. I'm sorry.'

He lifted the mask again. 'You do more for me than you will ever know.'

'Stop talking,' commanded Marie as she shook her head wearily and put the mask back over his face again and held it there.

CHAPTER 35

Carson walked back through the airy garden court of the Morgan Library, her exercise book full of ideas for her dialogue, her step light, musing who in the class she might ask to play Walter and Jean for her first share day, when she heard a voice echoing around the hall. 'Bye-bye, young lady.' Precious Campbell popped her head up from behind her desk. 'And don't be a stranger.'

Carson gave her new friend a bright smile. 'I won't be. This is going to be my Sunday afternoon place.'

'Well, I'll be here waiting for you.'

As she stepped out onto Madison Avenue she was dazzled by a glint of late autumn sunshine that had squeezed low along West 37th Street and walked straight into the path of a tall man striding uptown.

'I'm so sorry!' she said as she bounced off his shoulder.

'Carson? Whoah. Carson? I don't believe it!' boomed the unmistakable voice of Roland. 'What are the chances?' he said, breaking into a wide grin. 'Were you visiting Meg?'

Carson shook her head. 'Just doing some work in the library. What are you doing—'

'Wonderful place, isn't it?' Walter broke in. 'I have to take my hat off to Renzo Piano. He managed to improve on the original. Not easy I can tell you.'

Carson had no idea what he was talking about. She squinted up at him. 'Are you here for business? Aunt Meg didn't say.'

'No time. I arrived at lunchtime and I'm going back tomorrow overnight. It's my needy, but very rich, Kazakh client. She sent her plane for me because she can't even choose a light bulb without my holding her hand. Anyway how are you, Carson?'

'I'm good. I'm looking forward to going home next month and seeing everyone.'

'I'm glad Walter seems to be on the mend,' Roland said, smiling at her.

'What did you say?' Carson froze. 'What do you mean, "on the mend"?'

'He's fine now. He's fine,' Roland said quickly, realising his error. 'He's home now – he just had an episode.'

'What do you mean, "an episode"?' Carson's voice rose hysterically.

'Well, the doctors aren't sure. They think it could just be angina.' Roland tried to rearrange his face into a semblance of reassurance. 'I'm sorry, I shouldn't have said. It was stupid of me.'

Carson would not be deflected. 'Or? What else could it be? Please tell me, Uncle Roland.'

'Or, it could have been a mild heart attack.'

Carson felt her legs give way and Roland reached out to steady her. 'Why didn't I know?' She clutched his arms.

'I think that might have been Walter's doing,' Roland said gently, quickly calculating what else Carson did not know.

She fought back tears and then tensed and stared into the middle distance, a thought taking hold. Eventually she looked back at her uncle and he twigged. 'You want to hitch a ride, don't you?'

She nodded, marshalling her argument. 'I'll only miss a month or so of class and then it's Christmas break. It'll be fine, and it's too bad if it's not. Can I come with you?' she blurted in a way that brooked no opposition.

'Of course you can. Can you be at the Carlyle at seven tomorrow night?'

'I'll be there,' she replied with a small smile, and he watched as she relaxed as if her whole body had sighed with relief.

Roland gave her arm a squeeze. 'It'll be good to have your company.'

At seven o'clock the next morning Meg brought a cup of tea to Carson's bed and got in beside her. She sat quietly with her arm around her niece, her head on her shoulder. 'I'm going to miss you, Car,' Meg said finally, 'but you're right to go. You should always go back when you need to and when you think you may be needed. Nothing's more important than being with Walter. I know that.' She kissed the top of her head. 'I'll see you after Christmas,' she added emphatically.

At eight forty-five sharp, fifteen minutes before class, Carson stood at Ruth Anne Hudson's desk, the autumn sun lighting them both.

'Lovely to see you so bright and early, Carson. What can I help you with this glorious Monday morning?'

Carson started to tell her professor about the uncertainty of her grandfather's condition in a calm and measured way, until her composure suddenly left her and her face crumpled.

'Sit down, Carson, please.' Ruth Anne came around to join her and leaned back against the desk beside her. 'Tell me.'

'I have to go. I have to. I don't know how ill he is and . . .' Carson put her head in her hands. 'My little sister drowned three years ago and I can't lose him too.'

A flicker of a memory crossed the professor's face as she recalled the early class exercise where she had watched Carson struggle imagining herself to be in water. 'I'm so sorry to hear that, Carson. How terrible for you; of course you must go. Do you need any help to get ready? Do you want to talk some more now? I'm here as long as you want me to be.'

Carson looked up and shook her head. 'I'm fine really. Maybe when I get back after Christmas.'

Ruth Anne smiled. 'You will come back, Carson, won't you? You're making your way so well.'

Carson nodded. 'Yes I will.' She hesitated. 'I love being here and I think I'm growing into it.' She shook her head slowly. 'I don't want to let go of that.'

CHAPTER 36

Walter heard a car pull up on the gravel. He straightened himself in his chair, rubbed his face vigorously, brushed some hairs from his sweater, put on his glasses and picked up a crossword and a pencil. Carson pushed open the door to the sitting room and sped towards him. As she bent down to hug him she stifled a sob.

'Come on, Car,' he said, stroking her back, his voice trembling. 'Enough of this, you'll drench my new sweater.'

She stood up and drew her hand across her eyes. 'Why didn't anyone tell me?'

'There was nothing to tell. Seriously. Look at me. I'm right as rain.'

She took in his smart checked shirt and tie, his new spectacles, his tidy hair, his familiar smile, but there was something wrong. It came to her. He was acting.

'Don't I look well?' he went on. I have a *very* good nurse. She's waiting on me hand and foot,' he said too brightly.

When Carson had stepped off the train from London in Glasgow early that afternoon she felt a wave of relief when she saw Elinor and Patrick scanning the passengers swarming along the platform. She stopped, just for a moment, obscuring herself behind a group of Chinese tourists and studied her mother. She was wearing an electric-blue mohair coat and was swathed in a plaid scarf against the chill of the day and her wide eyes darted anxiously around the platform. Just as Carson switched her gaze to Patrick he spotted her and instantly altered his strained face into a cheerful smile.

'I am so happy to see you both, even if I am mad at you,' she said as they walked out of the station, arm in arm.

'What brought on the heart attack?' Carson asked, once they were settled in the car. Patrick gripped the wheel. 'A lot has happened, something else we couldn't tell you on the phone. We are pretty sure we've found the speedboat.'

Carson felt tiny electric shocks exploding all over her body. 'What? Where?'

Patrick explained Pete and Flora's visit to Robert MacMillan, and the discovery of the package and Carson, astonished, tried to take it all in. She felt no satisfaction, no feeling of vindication, instead she closed her eyes and saw Iona's face in the whirling water, terrified, pleading, and the open life jacket floating on the water like the wings of a red bird.

'What have the police done about it? You always said the police had to look harder, Mum.' Her voice was agitated now.

Patrick flexed his hands and gripped the wheel even more tightly. 'Granddad didn't want us to go to the police. For some strange reason he thought he had to deal with it. But then he had his heart attack.' Patrick paused. 'And, of course, we went to the police. Sergeant Sturrock has told us there is no proof it was Robert MacMillan's boat on the loch; and he has denied he was anywhere near Loch Doon that day.'

'What about the tobacco?'

'Still no proof.'

'Have you asked him yourself? I bet he couldn't lie to you?'

Patrick shook his head. 'Sergeant Sturrock said that would be a bad idea.'

'But what did Granddad say?'

'Sergeant Sturrock spoke to Dad in the hospital. I don't know what was said, but he told us it was best not to discuss it with him just now.'

'So we're going to do nothing?'

'Let's talk about it after you've seen Granddad.'

No sooner had Walter praised his nurse than Marie appeared with tea and banana bread.

'Speak of the angel,' he said.

Marie looked baffled and turned to Carson. 'Your granddad has been counting the minutes since you called,' she said fondly.

'I would have been fine until Christmas. I don't like to think of you missing university.'

Carson shook her head. 'It's just a month.' She looked at him expectantly. 'And I'm *very* glad to be home.'

'You know about Robert MacMillan?' Walter took a couple of quick breaths and shifted in his chair.

Carson nodded, but just then she caught Marie's warning look as she handed her a cup of tea. 'Dad says you're not to get agitated. We'll talk about it tomorrow. I've got to get the car back for Mum.'

'Tsk,' he said, his face weary. He looked round at the table. 'Why don't you take that cardboard box home? There are some baby things of your dad's and Aunt Fiona in it.' He looked at Marie. 'I don't think that's one for the Lifeboat sale.'

By the time Carson got back to Ayr the stars had studded the sky with pieces of silver and her limbs felt leaden as jet lag kicked in. She could not even stay awake for dinner. The last thing she remembered before morning was sinking into her bed and reaching onto the chair for Iona's patchwork baby quilt before burrowing beneath the duvet, holding the quilt to her face.

When she surfaced the house was still and there was a note on the kitchen table. 'Back from Selkirk in time for dinner – your favourite, LASAGNE (Joke!) Mum xx. PS Dad's car keys on the hook.'

Carson made herself some scrambled eggs and toast and a cafetière of coffee and put Walter's cardboard box in front of her on the table.

She took out the baby blankets and studied the embroidery at the edges. She put her father's one to her nose and felt the softness of the wool still infused with the scent of lavender. Beneath the blankets was a clear plastic bag full of skeins of embroidery threads of all colours and rolls of velvet, peacock blue, black and emerald green, tied together neatly with a cord.

Next, she opened a metal biscuit tin full of an assortment of beads: glass and seed pearls and jet, and packets of sequins. Buried among it all were two rattles, one a little plastic clown, the other a wooden doll. Lastly, Carson took out a large cotton drawstring bag and pulled it open. Inside was a variety of exquisite velvet evening bags, each one decorated painstakingly with different embroidered motifs. One was a bright blue square fastened with mother-of-pearl buttons, another was a crimson-red pouch dotted with purple sequins in the shape of a sailing boat. She put her hand to the bottom of the bag and pulled out the final one, a black rectangular clutch, covered with silver beads shaped into stars. It was the most beautiful bag she had ever seen. As she admired it, turning it round in her hands, she heard a crackling sound and felt something more solid than the soft fabric. She unhooked the jet bead fastening and inside found three pieces of folded cream-coloured writing paper. She took the pages out carefully, and unfolded the first one, her fingers tingling and aware that, no matter what the papers contained, she was prying, and that it was most likely her grandfather had had no idea they were there when he gave her the box.

Dear Mama,

I watched you today as you stood, head bent forward a little, edging the grass as slowly and carefully as if you were trimming precious velvet. I was standing in the shadows, in the drawing room, watching you from the tall window as I have so many times before, I confess. I wonder what you were thinking. Were you thinking about me, Mama? Were you thinking – is Walter right for Jean? Will she be happy? Will it be a good marriage? It makes my heart sing when I see you with him. I can tell that you like him by the way you look at him and pay attention to his conversation.

I set my cap at him, Mama. Before I met Walter, I had had a few flirtations, but I had never met anyone like him, so I have no one to compare him to. I long to ask you if you think I am making the right decision, but what would you say? I would rather die than hurt you so how can I say to you that I do not want to make the same mistake that you made. How can I ask when did you stop being happy? Or, worse, if you knew when you met Daddy that it was all wrong from the start? Was that what led to your withdrawal from the world like a nun inside the walls of a nunnery? I know that Daddy brought the best doctors to Stoneleigh to talk to you but what happened? Why is the world outside so bad? Daddy once told me that you just woke up one morning after we had moved to Ayr and said you would never leave the house again. Is that true? Is that it?

You have an air of serenity, but is that just an act for my benefit? I'm too scared even to ask if you are taking any medication. I have never seen any evidence. Sometimes I want to scream at you to tell me what is really going on in your head, but I am so afraid that you might collapse and disappear before my eyes. I could not bear life without you, Mama. Sometimes I am happiest when we are sitting together quietly sewing, like two women from a bygone age, or reading all the books that you collect, but then I literally snap. I need to live life and be gay and drink cocktails and feel young and alive. I love Walter. I know I do. He is strong and handsome and clever and a straight arrow, and I know he adores me, but am I simply travelling from one safe house to another? Is that what you thought you were doing when you married Daddy?

I started this letter, Mama, thinking I would post it to you or slip it into your sewing box, but the act of writing it has calmed me down a little. You taught me that I should follow my instincts and do what will make me happy. I think Walter will make me happy, and I hope and pray that I will make him happy too.

Your daughter who adores you.

Carson put the letter down and exhaled loudly. She felt she had scarcely breathed since she read the first line, as though Jean were standing beside her, speaking the words, pouring out her heart. Carson carefully opened the next page, the fear of what it might contain outweighed by her curiosity and the chance to meet her grandmother again.

My darling Mama,

You looked so beautiful at our wedding party. I'd never seen you smile so much, and I would not have had our marriage day anywhere other than with you, in your sanctuary. When we repeated our vows again for you, it was as if the flowers themselves stood a little taller, their petals more vivid, their leaves greener. In my imagination you had been preparing the garden for the occasion since you created it.

And I remember when I was little you gave me and Tommy each our own patch at Dunure and handed us a packet of seeds. Tommy was too impatient for results and lost interest, but I copied you diligently, marking little sticks with the names of the flowers, watering the rich earth, and you were as excited as I was when the first tiny shoots appeared. You never stopped teaching me.

Oh my Mama, I am bereft without you. I want to see you every day. I fantasise that I could drug you and kidnap you so that you could wake up in our house, and you being there would make me feel better. I know that I am drinking too much, but when the first sip reaches my throat I feel stronger and more alive. When I was at the library I felt I was more in the world. I know the work was sometimes dull but I created something new there, with your help, and I had the company of lovely, bright women. Now I look in the mirror and I don't know what I see. I don't know who I am, and that terrifies me. But Walter loves it here and I yearn for him when he is at Tongland. He has worked so very hard for promotion. We're sprucing this old place up and it looks quite swish and modern.

If I were going to send you this letter I would tell you simply that we have a Frigidaire now, and a new chequered rosewood cocktail cabinet and that we replaced the ugly Victorian furniture with the latest designs in elm wood from Ercol, but the truth is I took an axe to an old mahogany cupboard.

It sat like a brooding evil monster in the corner, the two drawers its evil eyes, mocking me and challenging me. I had to kill it, to smash it up. I was fighting it, fighting everything. I felt invincible as I sent chips of wood flying and I must have been shouting and grunting because when Walter arrived I could see the shock and fear in his eyes. He couldn't understand my behaviour and I realised that if I tried to talk to him about it I would hurt him dreadfully and try his endless sweet patience. But the house around me, no matter how much I try to make it mine, means nothing to me if you will never see where I live and where Patrick and maybe other grandchildren will grow up.

I might as well tell you that sometimes I open that damned cocktail cabinet at lunchtime and feel a stab of excitement when I look at the crystal glasses lined up neatly and the silver engraved cocktail shaker Daddy gave me and the preserved lemons and maraschino cherries and the array of enticing bottles, all colours and sizes. Sometimes Joy comes over for the afternoon because it is too quiet and the walls are closing in, and I think I am going mad.

When Walter comes home I talk incessantly and cling to him. I am like Zelda, or maybe Mrs Rochester. I am frightened of myself and what frightens me more is that maybe it would just be the same no matter where I was. I know Walter is my anchor, and I love him more and more but what if I start to show it less and less and he starts to despise me and hate me? I will be completely alone.

PLEASE, MAMA. PLEASE COME TO ME. I NEED YOU.

Your ever loving daughter

Carson's heart was thudding as she read the capital letters, written so hard that the tip of the fountain pen had dug into the paper. As she unfolded the final sheet her hands shook as she realised that she already knew more about her grandmother's turmoil than her own husband.

Dearest Mama,

It's two o'clock and I have just put Patrick down for his nap and I am resting on the sofa. I keep a picture in my mind of the first time you held him when he was a baby, your darling grandson. I wish I had had a camera that day. And now he has grown so much!

But I also remember how frightened I was the day he was born. It was the worst day of my life. I actually hated you that day, Mama. You broke my heart. You could not take your daughter to hospital even though I begged you, and I will always know, and so will you, that another hour and Patrick would have been dead.

Sometimes I wonder if you rejected the help that the doctors offered, preferring to hide from the world. Maybe life is easier if all you have to do is tend a beautiful garden.

I can only write this down knowing that you will never read it but, sometimes, I stand at the edge of the loch and scream so loudly it echoes for miles and sends up every bird in Galloway, just to let out all the awful poisonous words that I want to shout at you.

But when I see you and Patrick together I see how happy you make each other. I see the way he holds on to your cheeks and calls you Gan-Gan. Who is he like? Of course he is a MacMillan but do you think he is a Kennedy or a Thompson? I want him to be sensitive and creative, not coarse and acquisitive. What did you wish for me when I was born? Did you want me to be like you? I hope so, with all my heart, but I am so scared that I am becoming someone I do not want to be.

On Saturday Walter and Patrick and I had a wonderful day. I wish you could have seen how excited Patrick was watching the sheepdogs round up their flocks at the trials in Moniaive. It is just as well that Walter is so strong because Patrick wanted to be on his shoulders all day, even when he was eating his ice-cream cone, and of course Walter would never complain, even when ice cream dripped down his neck! Patrick shouted at the sheep as if he were trying to round them up too. He has so many words and sentences now. I think of all the time you two spend on the swinging seat in the garden and he loves it when you read to him so patiently, repeating pages over and over again. After the sheepdog trials we had a picnic and Walter rowed us all the way to the iron bridge and back. The sun seemed to dance on the water and I felt we had been transported to a magical world. Mama, it was glorious, the three of us together, laughing and singing, without a care in the world, and I could see Walter looking at me, hoping, and I wanted to make him right, with all my heart.

But when we returned home, I felt a desperate longing. I tried closing my eyes and conjuring up Patrick's sweet hot face as Walter put him up to bed. I thought of Walter's disappointment, his sad eyes, his hurt incomprehension, but when I tumbled the ice into my glass a warm fire spread through my body.

I feel as if I am drowning, Mama, and there is nothing you can do to help me.

Your daughter who loves you so much, Jean

Carson searched out the picture of Walter and Jean on their wedding day that had sat in the same place on the shelf for as long as she could remember. She studied Jean's eyes for any trace of doubt, for something in her body language to suggest a sadness, but all she saw was a wide smile, her head inclined a little, just as Fiona's head inclined sometimes, as if waiting for something to happen, and Walter, so fresh-faced and boyish, nothing but elation in a smile that said he was the luckiest man in the world that day. Then Carson picked up the three letters. They were not hers to keep, nor to share. They belonged to only one person.

Soon Carson was on the road to Carsphairn in Patrick's new SUV, travelling too fast, her apprehension rising with every mile. When she arrived in the village she realised with a start that she remembered nothing of the journey.

'Well, hello, Carson,' said Walter when he opened the door, surprised and strangely dismayed to see her. He scratched his head. 'I'm going out for a while. As of today I'm a free man again, but come in, come in.'

Carson gave him a kiss on the cheek as she walked into the hall and asked casually if Marie was home. 'No, her nursing abilities are needed elsewhere today. A grandchild with a broken arm. Coffee? I'm allowed one a day.'

Carson nodded, a cannonball banging against her ribcage. 'Are you better? Really?'

'Like I was sprightly and sixty again.' He set the coffee down on the kitchen table and she took the letters out of her shoulder bag.

'What have you got there?'

'Letters that I found in one of Granny Jean's bags that were at the bottom of the box you gave me.'

Walter heard her worried tone. Suddenly the room was alive with the loud tick-tock of the wooden clock on the mantelpiece. He stared at her hand, in two minds about taking the pages she was holding towards him.

'Are you okay, Granddad?' Carson asked urgently.

'Yes, Car, I'm all right,' he said, but still he did not take the letters from her. 'You've read them?' he asked gently, searching his granddaughter's face for clues.

She nodded and stammered an apology.

'No need to apologise.'

'They're from Granny Jean to her mother, but she never sent them. They were in a black velvet clutch,' she whispered.

A look of recognition crossed Walter's face, and he put his hand to his forehead to shield his eyes.

Carson laid the letters on the table and stood back. 'Can I cut a little holly for home?'

'No need to leave, Car.'

'I'd like to go outside for a bit – really.'

Carson stood outside and filled her lungs with cold autumn air until she thought they might burst. She looked beyond the garden to the purple and lilac rise of Cairnsmore of Carsphairn. Overhead a huge flock of black and white barnacle geese flew in a perfect V, honking insistently. She tried to concentrate on cutting the holly, making sure not to choose all the branches that were heavy with red berries, and as she was wrapping them in newspaper Walter appeared at the back door.

'Come on, Carson, let's walk together down to the church.'

They set off, Walter's hand resting on his granddaughter's shoulder, his other tapping his shepherd's crook on the road, neither wanting to speak. Walter was thankful that the main street was deserted. He had no desultory words for anyone. It was only when they reached the iron gates of Carsphairn kirk that he stopped and turned to his granddaughter. 'I'm glad of these letters, Car. Sometimes you see things more clearly, even with the long distance of years. I want to be near Jean for a while, and I think she would like you to be near her too.' Walter smiled sadly at his granddaughter.

'You must miss her so much.' Overwhelmed, her words tumbled out. 'She tried her best, didn't she?' She searched Walter's face.

Walter sighed as they walked towards the graveyard. 'Drink had an iron grip that neither she nor I could break. Perhaps she didn't want to, or maybe I refused to see it for what it was. The truth is I let her destroy herself, and she very nearly destroyed the lives of others.' They looked down at a handsome red sandstone gravestone. Walter took a little brush from his pocket and began to scrub away some moss and lichen that had worked its way into the chiselled letters. Slowly the inscription emerged.

In Memory of Jean Kennedy MacMillan
Beloved wife of Walter
Mother of Patrick and Fiona
Died 24 June 1968, aged 37 years.
'Love is not love
Which alters when it alteration finds'

Suddenly something dawned on Carson. 'Her own mother never saw where her daughter was buried?'

Walter shook his head. 'You read in Jean's letter that Edith couldn't leave the house to get her to hospital when she went into labour early with your dad. If there was a time, that would have been it.'

'What was she like – Edith, I mean?'

'She was very refined, gentle, but steely in a way. I liked her very much. She was kind to me.' An image of Edith came to him, the first time he saw her in the shadows in Stoneleigh, wraithlike. 'But deep down she was very unhappy, I think.'

'And she made Jean unhappy.'

'Not intentionally. I'm sure of that . . .'

He looked down at the headstone, the shadow of long-lost and long-remembered years on his face. 'I loved your grand-mother with all my heart, but that was not enough, not nearly enough. I should have done much more.'

CHAPTER 37

Walter watched Carson's car disappear from view and, dizzy now, lurching to one side, he steadied himself against the front door, the past now before his eyes, inescapable. He remembered the writing paper beside Jean's armchair, he realised now, kept for the purpose, there in plain sight. The letters, suffused with her scent, still, the expansive cursive hand, even the manner in which the paper was folded, perfectly, edge to edge, broke him in two. The three letters looked exactly the same as the one Fiona had found, all those years ago, the one he hid in a tin box at the bottom of his fishing bag, unopened since that day thirty-six years ago.

He telephoned Patrick and left a message, asking him to bring Elinor and Carson to the loch that evening. He knew Fiona and Pete would be there because Roland was coming for the weekend. Then he left a note for Marie. He picked up his Land Rover keys for the first time in a fortnight. The doctor had said that he could leave the house now, not that he could not drive, and where he was going he needed a car.

When Walter finally arrived at Loch Doon several hours later the night was a dense cerulean velvet. He drove on, past the entrance to the compound, another mile along the water, towards the old red sandstone house, back to his childhood and his marriage. He pulled the car off the track near the stone slab he had returned to often over the years, so often that he used to wonder if it bore the imprint of him just as he had once said to Carson, and he plunged the shepherd's crook into the soft peat until he found enough purchase to help him heave himself up.

Up on the rock, he looked out to where the inky glimmer of the loch met the edge of the shore and then he traced the familiar line of the hills, every fold and gully, to where the peaks and crags touched the huge dome of stars. Sometimes when he sat on the smooth slab in the endlessness of night, it seemed impossible to him that such a peaceful place had witnessed such torment. Then, as he traced Orion's Belt, it misted over without warning as a squall arrived over the Merrick, sending him hastily to the car, and back towards the Stratton House.

Patrick had listened in dismay to Walter's peremptory answerphone message. Then, when he tried to reach him the telephone at Carsphairn rang out. To make matters worse his mobile, which he never used anyway, was switched off. Even Marie was at a loss, and so the family had no choice but to gather at the loch and wait for his arrival.

'Dad! You're not meant to be driving!' hollered Patrick as he marched towards the Land Rover, unfurling an umbrella. 'What's going on? Why the skulduggery? You know it's a hard time for us all,' he added more gently.

'There's no skulduggery, I promise.' Walter leaned on his son as he stepped from the running board onto the gravel.

'But where have you been?'

Walter hesitated for a moment. 'To see Robert and Graeme MacMillan. But let me tell—'

'What?' Patrick interrupted. 'For God's sake, Dad.'

'Is everyone here?' Walter went on, intent now.

Patrick nodded, bewilderment in his questioning eyes. 'Yes, Roland arrived not long ago, Marie too.'

As Walter reached the top of the stairs everyone looked at him with a mixture of anticipation and consternation. He shook Roland's hand and inclined his head to the others and walked to the table slowly, stiff from the hour outside in the chill night. He lowered himself gingerly into the empty chair at the top of the table and Carson and Pete exchanged anxious looks.

Then he cleared his throat and took a small sip of the malt whisky Roland had put down before him.

'What I am about to say, I should have said a long time ago. I can never say how sorry I am.' Walter put his hand into the wallet pocket of his jacket and took out a folded piece of paper. He looked at Fiona. 'When you were thirteen you found this letter. Jean had written it, but she had never given it to me. It upset you for many reasons and I never talked to you about it then, not properly. I couldn't.' He looked around the family. 'But it's important I talk about it now.' He laid the page on the table. 'First, though, please read it.'

He looked reassuringly at Carson. 'There are others I want you to read, but they can wait.'

As they huddled together to read the letter and then pass it on in silence, Walter looked at the reflection of the family scene through the rain-patterned window and thought how easily a picture can lie. He watched as one by one the shape of their bodies changed and stiffened a little as they recoiled at Jean's words.

'Your mother wrote that she was putting our lives, and other people's lives, at risk.' He stopped, steeling himself for a moment, anxiously clearing his throat again. 'But she was writing about something that had already happened, a terrible thing that she had done – but the greater fault was mine.'

Patrick, aghast, looked at his sister who had buried her head in her hands. No one spoke. Elinor searched for Carson's hand beneath the table. At that moment Roland leaned over towards his father-in-law. 'Walter, I beseech you, maybe it's not the best time . . .'

'Please,' Walter pleaded and put his hands flat on the table in front of him, 'I am going to speak.'

He glanced round at Marie beside him as she sat twisting her hankie in her lap, and then he pushed himself up in his chair and looked at Patrick and Fiona, his rheumy eyes semaphoring his love.

'It began with a lie. There were many lies but on this day, the 23rd of August 1966, Jean told me she was going to Castle Douglas to have lunch with her spinster great-aunt, after a doctor's appointment. She arranged that Marie would collect you both from the school bus and keep you at the stables until she picked you up on the way home. But that day your mother did not drive south to Castle Douglas. Instead she headed in the opposite direction, to Joy's house in Alloway.' Walter's face twitched a little and he put his hand to his mouth for a moment. 'And there they drank together all day. Her sister-in-law. When she arrived back at the stables Marie thought she was too drunk to drive you home along the loch, so she asked the stable-girl to put her bike in the back of Jean's Morris Traveller and drive her home. Then Marie put an orange flag at the turn-off to the stables, in the hope that I would realise it was meant for me.'

Walter looked at Marie. 'I had a gut feeling it was a signal for me. You were very discreet. I remember you didn't say much, just that Jean didn't seem well. When I got home with you both, I found Jean passed out on our bed. I got no sense from her. The next morning when I asked her where she had been she insisted over and over that she was with her great-aunt, but, finally, she gave in. There had been no doctor's appointment of course. She had been in Alloway, drinking vodka tonics all day with her sister-in-law. And, of course, she told me it would never happen again – over and over – as she had many times before. But this time it was too late for promises.

'When I got to work at Tongland that next morning, I heard an apprentice lad from Dalmellington telling the others about a terrible accident on the road, just south of the town, the afternoon before. A vehicle of some sort had glanced a child on his bicycle and had driven straight on. The boy was left on the verge pinned under his twisted bike.'

Walter's throat was too dry to go on. He took another sip of whisky and everyone looked at the glass shaking in his hand. 'His leg was mangled below the knee.'

There was a gasp in the room. 'Oh my God, oh my God, Dad,' Fiona called out. Carson looked at Patrick as he gripped his head in his hands, his knuckles white.

Walter went on, more agitated now. 'The boy was my cousin Kenneth's younger son, as I think you realise now. Graeme was Fiona's age at the time. He didn't see what hit him and no one had come forward. And there were, apparently, no witnesses. When I heard the name I remember I went to the lavatory and threw up. There was no doubt in my mind. I knew that Jean had hit him.'

Carson thought about the greeting Graeme MacMillan had given her grandfather at the pedestrian crossing the day she and Elinor returned from New York. All along he had known what had happened, but he had told her only a half-truth. She stared at Walter as it sank in. She could not bear to think of him carrying around such an enormous lie for all those years.

'When I got home that evening I went straight to check the

car before I even spoke to Jean. Sure enough, there was the
tiniest paint scrape on the nearside wing. It was the end of
everything. My own wife had driven into a child and hadn't
stopped. She had maimed a child; she could have killed him.'
Walter shook his head. Everyone could understand now that
he had spent his life reliving that day. Elinor stifled a sob, and
Carson put her arm around her shoulder.

'I sent you both out to play and I found your mother darn-
ing socks in the sitting room. It was as if she were doing
penance for her drunken day with Joy. I tried to speak calmly
but I wanted to shout and scream till the roof came off. I
confronted her with what she had done – and I remember she
started to shake uncontrollably and she couldn't form any
words. I shouted at her then, to tell me what had happened. I
almost broke when I saw the sheer terror in her eyes; but the
fact was she had no recollection of the drive home, much less
hitting Graeme MacMillan. For once, she was telling the
truth, of that I have no doubt. She went into the bathroom and
I remember I could not bear the sound of her retching, but I
couldn't go to her either.' Walter stopped and clenched his
hands together, trying to hold on to his composure. 'I felt a
cold fury. At her, but at that disease too. But I also had to work
out what to do. I had to think quickly. What happened to
Graeme was terrible; but I was frightened of what would
happen to Jean. I knew that she would go to prison. Then what
would happen to her? I didn't think she would survive jail. And
what would happen to you two?'

Walter stared down at Patrick at the other end of the table,
Pete next to him, beside his mother. 'Then I realised – I saw
very clearly that it was my fault. I should have known how
much danger you, and others, were in because of Jean's drinking. We should have left the loch and moved to Ayr. I should

have taken the job Jean's father offered me in the car business.
I was so stubborn. I was stupid and selfish; just as I was selfish
giving you those cabins. I did it for me, to keep you close.' He
shook his head and sighed deeply.

'That night I made a decision. I put Jean's car in the
garage and used the small pot of trim colour and I made it
perfect again.' He looked around the table. 'I covered it up.
I covered up a crime. All I could think was that I had to
protect her.'

'Oh, Dad, I can't believe this . . .' Patrick's voice trailed
away as soon as he spoke.

'I told Jean that she must never, ever, say a word about it. If
she did she would go to jail. And now, I would too.'

Walter faltered. 'She was broken then. I remember she sat
at the kitchen table that night, smoking mechanically, unable
to meet my eyes. She was terrified. I think she was desperately
trying to work out how she had got to this point and what had
gone so wrong. She was in the depths of a sadness from which
there was no escape. I could not get her to respond. And our
hearts were breaking. Eventually I went to bed and in the
morning she was still there, the place shrouded in stale cigarette smoke. I made breakfast for you both and your little faces
were so scared and when you asked me what was wrong with
Mummy and why was she so quiet I remember I said to you
that she had such a bad headache she couldn't even speak.' He
looked at Patrick and Fiona. 'You were used to Mummy's
headaches.

'I had to make sure that Joy would never say anything, and I
couldn't risk a telephone call in case someone listened in at the
exchange. After work I drove to Alloway and warned her never
to talk about that day to anyone. I watched as it dawned on her
that not only had she helped Jean to her own destruction, a

child could have died too. I remember that she began to cry hysterically. It was sickening. I made her promise not to tell Tommy when he got back from whatever godforsaken race-track he was at. And then I made her swear that she would never give Jean another drink.'

Walter put his hand over Marie's tightly clasped ones. 'I stopped at the stables on the way back. I thanked you for taking such good care of the children and I was desperately trying to work out what you knew, and what to say. I remember as I was walking back to the car you called after me. You said that if I wanted to thank the stable-girl it wouldn't be possible because she had left that morning for a job in a stud on the Kent coast. That is all you said. But you knew, and I knew that you knew.'

Marie bowed her head.

'I tried to carry on as normal. Then one day, about six months after the accident, after I'd dropped you both at the stables, I went to fish for an hour or so at Loch Kendoon. When I got to the boathouse there was a young man there. His name was Jock Sturrock, the same Jock Sturrock who is the sergeant now. He was a constable then, and he'd come back to Dalmellington from Glasgow. I knew his late father who had been a member of the angling club at Kendoon. When I introduced myself, he asked if I was any relation to the young boy who had been injured in the hit and run. It knocked me for six. I was sure I had blanched, but Jock just kept on talking. He said that no one had come forward, and what sort of a person would do such a dreadful thing?'

Walter stared around the table. 'I am so sorry. I know this is hard for you all to hear,' he said in a weary, defeated voice, and then stopped as if he had run out of words. No one spoke and Walter looked around the table. 'I had to protect her. I couldn't do anything else, but part of me hated myself for it. That poor boy . . .'

Fiona stared out at the misty blackness beyond the window, the rain a soft smirr now, clinging to the glass like a pall. She held on to Roland and Pete on either side of her, tears streaming down her face.

'Dad, why did you go to see Graeme and Robert MacMillan today?' Patrick asked gently. 'Robert told Sergeant Sturrock he wasn't anywhere near the loch. You knew that.'

There was a stunned silence. Patrick had not told anyone that.

'I went to confess. I told Graeme how sorry I was for what Jean had done to him. I told him that I had covered it up, that I was to blame.'

'Granddad!' Carson cried out, and shock vibrated through each of them and oscillated all around the room. Pete put his head down on his arms, moaning.

Walter's eyes started to fill. 'Graeme looked at me so strangely. He didn't seem surprised. He smiled at me with such compassion; then he just shook my hand and thanked me. It knocked me for six.' Marie passed Walter her handkerchief and he wiped his tears. 'I should have done it many years ago and when Pete found the speedboat it seemed to me that what had happened on the loch was a terrible reckoning. I know that is absurd, but I couldn't get it out of my head. And when Jock Sturrock told me Robert had denied it, I had to have it out.'

Elinor started to weep quietly, and Patrick gently took her head on his shoulder. 'Dad, what did you do?'

'I asked Robert if he was on the loch that morning.'

Walter faltered and bowed his head, and as they all waited, the wind rose and hurtled around the house, knocking against the plate-glass window, as if it too was impatient for the answer.

'I didn't know what I expected him to say. But I knew he was there. It had to be him, but he just kept staring at me.' Walter paused, his mouth dry. 'It was as if he were trying to work out what kind of man he was; and what kind of man I was. Then he started to shake his head, but at last he said it. He said, "Yes, I was on the water, but I was travelling so fast that I passed them and had no idea what had happened." Then his brother slumped forward at the table. Graeme knew nothing – nothing at all, I'm sure of it.'

Walter looked over at Elinor, her head buried in Patrick's neck. 'Robert said that had he known that Iona had fallen into the water, he would have gone back, no matter what he was doing there. He swore it.'

'No matter what he was doing there?' Elinor's voice crashed in, her pent-up despair and fury spilling everywhere as she broke free of Patrick. 'No matter what he was doing there? We know what he was doing there! Smuggling cheap tobacco. He wouldn't have gone back, but he can say that he would have now. Of course he can. That's easy.'

Patrick tried to gather her back in, cradling her tightly in his arms. 'Shh, Eli, shh, it's over now.'

'He let Iona drown . . .' She leaned in to her husband and her heart broke again.

'No, Eli, he's telling the truth. I believe him. I do.' Patrick closed his eyes. 'And what good would it do to believe anything else?'

Carson looked at Walter anxiously. He seemed a smaller, frailer version of himself, sunken, so lost and diminished she thought he might disappear altogether. 'Granddad,' she said in a thin voice. 'Are you going to be okay?'

He started, lost in another world, as though surprised anyone was in the room.

'Granddad,' Carson persisted.

Marie patted his arm gently and finally he nodded towards his granddaughter. 'I think I've done all the damage I'll ever do; but it was more than enough, wasn't it?'

He looked at Elinor. 'I am so sorry, so deeply sorry. To you and Patrick and Carson.' Then he turned to his daughter. 'I'm so sorry, Fiona, you didn't have the mother, or the father, you really deserved.'

'Dad, please,' Fiona said, looking steadily at Walter, shaking a little, 'you have been everything to me, everything.' Roland and Pete, on each side of her, leaned in to her as if to staunch her sorrow, and Roland reached for her hand and intertwined his fingers gently with hers.

Carson got up and walked to the end of the table and knelt down beside Walter and pressed her cheek against the jagged tweed of his jacket as she had done a thousand times before.

They sat in silence for a while, each immersed in the enormity of what Walter had told them.

Finally, Elinor spoke, her voice even. 'Tomorrow I'm going to spend some time with Iona. The yellow rowan is doing well. Perhaps we could all go up?' She put her hand on Patrick's and looked at Walter. 'Then we should go to the kirkyard so that we can be close to Jean for a while. I don't like to think of her alone, especially now. Maybe we could plant some forget-me-nots. It's a little late in the year but I'm sure there will be flowers in the spring.'

CHAPTER 38

December arrived sharp and clear. Carson sat on the stone jetty on the shore of Loch Kendoon, her eyes trained on the shallows, which sparkled until a milky-white cloud tamped down the winter sun. She pulled her jacket around her. After the noise and chaos of New York she had almost forgotten the world could be so quiet.

As she concentrated her gaze on the long finger of the loch, towards the sharp geometry of the metal footbridge, she saw, in the distance, the low prow of a wooden boat and the dark outline of a seated figure and, behind, the glimpse of another. As the boat carved through the water towards her the figure in front raised a hand in greeting while the other slowed the outboard motor before he finally cut it and let the boat drift to the jetty.

Carson stood up, irritated to be interrupted but also embarrassed to be on angling club property, and surveyed the two elderly men, almost identically dressed in old tweed jackets with leather elbow patches and canvas life vests strapped at the front. One was wearing a flat cap, the other a fore and aft stuck with such a profusion of fishing flies it was hard to see the tweed beneath. They had the same weather-beaten look as Walter. She smiled to herself. Perhaps they were all part of a prehistoric tribe.

'Catch the rope please, lass,' the one in front called out, and flung it towards her without waiting for a reply.

Carson caught the line and tied it expertly to the iron ring sunk into the jetty.

'There it is after all, Johnny,' exclaimed his friend from the stern. 'I was sure I'd left it there.' Carson turned around and saw the small aluminium tin lying on the concrete slipway. 'My best flies,' he said, grinning at her as he stepped stiffly out of the boat up onto the jetty. 'Can't catch a trout on a morning like this without my Red Tail Sedge.' He put his hand to the side of his mouth conspiratorially. 'Not that we should be fishing at all now. The season's closed. It's more of a skiddle about on the water.'

'Don't listen to Davey. It's just a lame excuse. I've caught a couple of brownies today. And they're beauties.' He stood with his hands on his hips and gave Carson a friendly, quizzical look. 'Now who are you, young lady?'

She raised her chin a little. 'I'm Carson MacMillan. I sometimes come here with my grandfather, Walter.'

'Well, well. Pleased to meet you.' He put out his hand, and Davie followed. 'Johnnie Bourne and Davie Carswell. How is Walter? We heard he'd had a bad turn?'

'He's much better,' she said, 'but I don't think he'd be strong enough yet to be fishing.'

A flicker of recognition crossed Davie's face. 'Am I right in thinking you're Patrick's daughter?' he said in a kindly voice. 'Your little sister was the one that drowned?'

Johnny gave him a sharp look.

Carson, taken aback, stammered her reply. 'Yes . . . Her name was Iona.'

Johnny cleared his throat and put his hands in his plus-fours pockets. 'Well, Carson, would you like to come out with us on the water, instead of your granddad?. We could do with some help with the rowing. Davie's not as young as he once was, are you, Davie?'

Carson felt everything around her stop. She pressed her feet down on the concrete as she fought to keep her balance.

'There's no pressure – none at all,' said Johnny quickly.

Carson took a deep breath and felt the blood coursing back through her veins. 'I would like that,' she said quietly.

The angler rummaged in the pocket of his life vest and pulled out a leather-covered hip flask. 'Would you like a little nip,' he asked as he poured some whisky into the metal cup, 'just to warm you up?'

Carson put her hand out in protest, smiling at him. 'Granddad has one just like that; but no, thank you.'

'Here, have some coffee instead.' He handed her a cup from his thermos. They all sat in amiable silence for a minute or two when they heard a plop on the loch and caught sight of rings of water eddying prettily just feet from the shore.

'Right, Johnnie, they're taunting us now.'

Davie brought a life vest from the boathouse and handed it to Carson. It had a fusty smell and the canvas was stiff. 'It's an old one but it will do the trick,' he said. He saw her hands trembling as she fastened it tightly. As he watched her the details of Iona's drowning came back to him. He shot Johnnie a look. 'That's perfect, m'girl,' he said.

He stepped onto the boat first and offered her his hand. It felt firm and safe, like a promise.

As Carson sat down on the bench the boat rocked and the water lapped against the side, sending her pulse racing. She stopped a cry in her throat and gripped the plank with both hands. Johnny, who was standing in the water ready to push off, smiled reassuringly. 'Right we are, lass. You're in safe hands.'

'I'm not much good at rowing,' she said nervously.

'Not at all. It's not hard when you get the feel for it,' said Davie gently. He helped her manoeuvre the oars into the rowlocks. They felt unwieldy in her slender hands. 'Now find their balance. Put them into the water carefully, so they don't make a fuss, and pull them towards you. Don't grip them too tightly or your hands will ache, and you won't get a smooth motion.'

Carson concentrated on Davie's instructions and moved the oars slowly, setting them in the loch and feeling the heaviness of the water as she drew them back and raised them again, almost silently.

'Right,' he said encouragingly, 'now head straight to that shady piece of water.'

Carson began to row with an easy rhythm, countering the water's resistance. She folded her elbows outwards, her shoulder blades tightening together, and then, as she straightened her arms out in front of her, she brought the handles of the oars together. She slowed her breathing to time with her strokes, exhilarated by the effort.

She felt the sun flit across her face as she held the oars down in the water and watched as Johnny raised his right arm at an angle and, with an elegant flick of his wrist, sent the line quivering through the air. He laid it on the water as lightly as if it were gossamer. She heard a swishing sound behind her as Johnnie cast next and landed his line parallel to the first one.

'Come on, my darlings,' he whispered, 'come and get this tasty fly.'

Carson rested the oars while the two men fished, casting over rises in the quiet of the Galloway day.

'Ah-ha,' said Johnnie suddenly, startling her, 'I've got one on!' He raised his line into a beautiful arc. 'She's a big one, and she's putting up a fight.' He played the fish beneath the surface, reeling in the line stealthily, the rod handle against his stomach.

Davie lifted the net from the floor of the boat and extended the pole. 'Just tell me when you're ready for it,' he said calmly.

Suddenly a flash of coppery brown and silver caught Carson's eye and the trout flew out of the water, its scales shimmering as it arched from side to side like a dancer.

'What a beauty! Must be a pound and a half, Davie,' Johnnie exclaimed as his friend positioned the net under the writhing fish, and together they brought it in.

Davie put his arm into the net and grabbed hold of the trout, quickly removing the hook from its lip. He laid it on the bench, and, with a swift tap, knocked it dead.

'Well, well, Carson,' Davie said, 'it was a good job we went back for my tin. You can tell Walter you're an angler now. I think you've brought me luck.'

At that moment everything around Carson dissolved and the world receded to a vanishing point. She gripped the oars as her tears flowed. All the nightmares, the flashes of Iona's eyes, the thrashing waves, Pete's anguished shouts, the roaring speedboat, all of it washed down her face.

The two men sat mute, listening as Carson's weeping rippled over the loch. Davie reached out and put his hand on her arm and kept it there, holding it firmly. Slowly her sobs subsided like the passing of a thunderstorm, and there was silence, broken only by the trilling of skylarks on the grassland just beyond the shore. A breeze lifted the water into soft swells and Davie, his eyes glistening, smiled at Carson. He released his grip on her arm and held out his hand.

'Change places with me, lass. The wind is getting up. I'll row us back to the boathouse.'

That afternoon at the cabin, Carson and Elinor sat together on the bench outside, wrapped up against the cold. Elinor stroked her daughter's hair. Carson was aware of a new quietude about her mother. It unnerved her at first but then she realised that Elinor was beginning to reconcile her inner and her outer world, and Iona was by her side in both, all the time. That way she could look forward.

She went inside to the shelf at the back of the living room and pulled out her old pink paisley-patterned box. She carefully removed the botanical sketch of the sundew Elinor had made the day before the drowning. 'Do you remember this, Mum?' she said as she handed it to her. 'It's wonderful, isn't it?'

Elinor studied the page, the spiky red tentacles round the base of the bog plant and, in its centre, atop a long red stem, velvety white petals. At the corner of the page were an exquisitely painted flower head and a brown seed pod. Elinor looked at her daughter, as if seeing something different, recognising her for the wise mature woman that she was becoming.

'Perhaps in the spring I'll bring my portfolio to New York and seek my fortune.'

Just as she spoke they heard the sound of a distant jet. Carson squinted up into the cloudless sky and high above the Galloway Hills she saw pure white vapour trail of a plane that had passed overhead before arcing west, out over the Atlantic, bound for America.

THOSE WHO LEFT

The stone is a potent symbol of the Scots who went abroad, of the tremendous upheaval they made, or were forced to make, when they left Scotland . . . these arches are a celebration and monument to the Scottish people and the travels they have made, and they will act as a connection between those who have left and those who have stayed here.

Andy Goldsworthy on the Striding Arches

ACKNOWLEDGMENTS

My love and appreciation to Alan, Caitlin and James – and to my patient friends, all of whom lived this book with me. Thank you to the Reverend Dr David Bartholomew and the congregation of Carsphairn Parish Church who welcomed me in, and to Peter Galloway who took me out fishing on Loch Kendoon – the first time I had been on the loch for thirty years. Charlie Ewing and David Reid, tireless volunteers at the Scottish Aviation Museum in Dumfries, where the remains of Frantisek Hekl's Spitfire rests. Stuart Ferns of Scottish Power guided me around the soaring Tongland Power Station, and retired engineer Gordon Ross lent me a hard-to-source book *Tunnel and Dam: the Story of the Galloway Hydros* (Scottish Power, 1984).

I would also like to thank my literary agent Felicity Bryan whose encouraging smile I could always see in my mind's eye, and, of course, to my wonderful editor, publisher, and friend, Lisa Highton, who coaxed *The House by the Loch* out of me, gently nudging me in the direction she knew I wanted to go, but for which she set the right co-ordinates. Special thanks also to the book's early readers and to Morag Lyall, whose copy-editing magnifying glass saved me from errors. And lastly, to the Two Roads team who work so hard, and to Rosie Gailer, publicity wonderwoman.

This novel means a great deal to me. It expresses my love of Scotland and the power it holds over me, and it also expresses the complexity of what family is and the way that it remakes itself endlessly.

ABOUT THE AUTHOR

Kirsty Wark is a journalist, broadcaster and writer who has presented a wide range of BBC programmes over the past thirty years, from the ground breaking *Late Show* to the nightly current affairs show *Newsnight* and the weekly arts and cultural review and comment show, *The Review Show*. She has conducted longform interviews with everyone from Margaret Thatcher to Madonna, Harold Pinter, Elton John, the musician Pete Doherty, Damien Hirst, George Clooney and the likes of Toni Morrison, Donna Tartt and Philip Roth.

Kirsty has won several major awards for her work, including BAFTA Awards for Outstanding Contribution to Broadcasting, Journalist of the Year and Best Television Presenter. Her debut novel, *The Legacy of Elizabeth Pringle*, was published in March 2014 by Two Roads and was shortlisted for the Saltire First Book of the Year Award, as well as nominated for the 2016 International DUBLIN Literary Award. *The House by the Loch* has been inspired by her childhood memories and family, particularly her father.

Born in Ayr, Scotland, Kirsty lives in Glasgow.

THE LEGACY OF ELIZABETH PRINGLE

Elizabeth Pringle lived all her long life on the Scottish island of Arran. But did anyone really know her? In her will, she leaves her beloved house, Holmlea, to a stranger – a young mother she'd seen pushing a pram down the road over thirty years ago.

It now falls to Martha, once the baby in that pram, to answer the question: why?

A captivating story of the richness behind so-called ordinary lives and the secrets and threads that hold women together.

An extract follows

Holmlea
20, Shore Road
Lamlash
Isle of Arran

1 January 2006

Dear Mrs Morrison,

A long time ago, almost thirty-four years past, you wrote to me requesting that I contact you should I ever wish to leave my home. I knew then that I would never live anywhere else, and so there was no point in my replying to you. I have lived in this house since I was eight years old but I am what people these days describe as 'ancient' and somewhat frail, and though I have managed perfectly well on my own until now, I know I am not long for this world. I have told my doctor I will move to a small nursing home as I realise it will be less trouble for him, and I have finally locked up the house.

My family such as it was, is long dead. There is no one alive but me.

I recall very clearly the summer that you put the letter through my door. I was sewing in the cool shade of the dining room when I heard the letter box clatter. I was so startled I put my needle into my finger and dropped a spot of blood onto my canvas.

I saw you almost every day, pushing your carriage pram along Shore Road, your long hair flying, and your bright skirt billowing about your ankles. You looked very young. The sound of your voice carried up my garden as you sang to your daughter, or perhaps it was just the lilt of your voice as you talked to her, and she made a soft mewling sound back. I remember that on one occasion you waved to me, and I think I tilted my head towards you. Perhaps you did not see. There have been times when that scene has come to me vividly, and I have wondered what has become of you both. My life has been spent here on this island.

I am instructing my solicitor to write to you at the address on your letter. Holmlea is yours if you still wish it. If he does not hear from you within three months, or if you write to say you no longer have any interest in living here, he will follow alternative instructions.

This may of course now seem a fanciful idea to you, but if you do still think my house is 'the loveliest in Lamlash', and you come to live here, I ask only that you keep my garden well. It has been a source of peace and joy to me.

Yours sincerely,
Elizabeth Pringle